BADGE OF HONOR

*W.E.B. Griffin's electrifying epic series of a
big-city police force . . .*

"DAMN EFFECTIVE . . . He captivates you with characters
the way few authors can."

—Tom Clancy

"TOUGH, AUTHENTIC . . . POLICE DRAMA AT ITS
BEST . . . Readers will feel as if they're part of the investigation, and the true-to-life characters will soon feel like old
friends. Excellent reading."

—Dale Brown, bestselling author of
Day of the Cheetah and *Hammerheads*

"COLORFUL . . . GRITTY . . . TENSE."

—*The Philadelphia Inquirer*

"A REAL WINNER."

—*New York Daily News*

"NOT SINCE JOSEPH WAMBAUGH have we been treated
to a police story of the caliber that Griffin gives us. He creates
a story about real people in a real world doing things that are
AS REAL AS TODAY'S HEADLINES."

—Harold Coyle, bestselling author of
Team Yankee and *Sword Point*

"FANS OF ED MCBAIN'S 87TH PRECINCT NOVELS
BETTER MAKE ROOM ON THEIR SHELVES . . . *Badge of
Honor* is first and foremost the story of the people who solve
the crimes. The characters come alive."

—*Gainesville Times* (GA)

"GRITTY, FAST-PACED . . . AUTHENTIC."

—Richard Herman, Jr.,
author of *The Warbirds*

W.E.B. GRIFFIN

THE LAST HEROES

Volume One of MEN AT WAR

Originally published under the pseudonym
Alex Baldwin

JOVE BOOKS, NEW YORK

This novel is a work of fiction. Names, characters, places, and incidents
are either the product of the author's imagination or are used
fictitiously. Any resemblance to actual events or locales or persons,
living or dead, is entirely coincidental.

THE LAST HEROES

A Jove Book / published by arrangement with
the author

PRINTING HISTORY
G. P. Putnam's Sons edition published June 1997
Jove edition / September 1998

The Penguin Putnam Inc. World Wide Web site address is
http://www.penguinputnam.com

ISBN: 0-515-12329-3

A JOVE BOOK®
Jove Books are published by The Berkley Publishing Group,
a member of Penguin Putnam Inc.,
200 Madison Avenue, New York, New York 10016.
JOVE and the "J" design are trademarks belonging to
Jove Publications, Inc.

PRINTED IN THE UNITED STATES OF AMERICA

10 9 8 7 6 5 4 3 2

*For Lieutenant Aaron Bank, Infantry, AUS, detailed OSS
(later, Colonel, Special Forces),
and
Lieutenant William E. Colby, Infantry, AUS, detailed OSS
(later, Ambassador, and Director, CIA).
They set the standards, as Jedburgh Team Leaders operating
in German-occupied France and Norway, for valor, wisdom,
patriotism, and personal integrity, which thousands who
followed in their steps in the OSS and CIA tried to emulate.*

AUTHOR'S NOTE

Nothing ever written
about Washington
is true.

THE LAST HEROES

Volume One of MEN AT WAR

PROLOGUE

In January 1939, Professor Niels Bohr, a German physicist who had fled Germany and was then living in Copenhagen, traveled to the United States and visited with Professor Albert Einstein, a German mathematician who had also fled Germany and was then living in Princeton, New Jersey.

Among other things, they discussed an interesting phenomenon observed when uranium, a natural element, was bombarded with neutrons: barium and krypton were formed, indicating that the uranium atom had been split into two nearly equal fragments.

Professor Bohr further discussed this phenomenon, which he called fission, with a number of other eminent scientists. Among these was Professor Enrico Fermi (then of the University of Chicago). At a conference in Washington, D.C., on January 26, 1939, Fermi suggested that neutrons might be released during fission, and if this were the case, a continuous disintegration—a "chain reaction"—might be possible. Fermi believed that such a chain reaction might release energy of a rather stunning magnitude.

The first contact between the scientific community and the government concerning nuclear fission took place in March 1939, when Professor George B. Pegram of Columbia University arranged for Fermi to discuss the matter with certain officers of the U.S. Navy.

Energy yields were of considerable importance to the U.S. Navy, whose engineers were constantly striving to extract a few more British thermal units from each gallon of bunker fuel oil and aviation gasoline. An increase of fifty percent in energy yield would give whoever owned the secret a tremendous advantage over his enemy, and these respectable scientists were talking of greater than tenfold or even hundredfold energy increases.

And even if there were technical drawbacks that would keep the Navy's fuel tanks from getting a sudden miracle energy boost, perhaps there was something in this mysterious process that would work for ammunition. Increasing the power of a cannon shell was always a welcome possibility.

Professor Fermi told the naval officers that though he didn't have any precise figures, still, as an educated guess, fission of one hundred pounds of uranium 235 would probably release as much energy as twenty thousand tons of an explosive like, say, trinitrotoluene, *commonly called TNT.*

The Navy found that fascinating and asked if there was much interest in this sort of thing in Europe. Professor Fermi said there was. The Germans seemed curious about the subject. And there were uraninite mines in Germany.

The Navy inquired if mining and refining this new explosive was difficult.

Professor Fermi sadly indicated that it was, since not just any uranium would do. The kind of uranium required for a chain reaction, uranium 235, was an isotope, one part in 140. The current total world's supply of pure uranium 235, he told them, was 0.000001 pound.

In the summer of 1939, Alexander Sachs presented the views of Einstein and others to President Franklin Delano Roosevelt.

Approximately six months later, Roosevelt made funds available to look further into the matter. The scientists thought they could do everything that had to be done for six thousand dollars, and that is how much the President gave them.

How much money naval intelligence spent looking for a source of uraninite ore somewhere outside the borders of Nazi Germany has never been revealed, but it is known that by December 6, 1941, when the atomic fission project was put under the direction of the U.S. Office of Scientific Research and Development, the Navy knew there were several hundred tons of uraninite ore in Kolwezi, a small mining town in Katanga Province of the Belgian Congo.

ONE

The United States Naval Academy class of 1941, having more or less patiently endured the more or less predictably inspiring remarks of the secretary of the Navy, formed a line according to academic rank and moved across the platform to receive their diplomas and handshakes. As they walked back to their seats, they glanced toward the sky. The next item on the program was a flyover of Navy fighter aircraft.

The commandant of the Naval Academy had not been enthusiastic about the flyover when it had been proposed to him. So far as he was concerned, the graduation exercises should not be turned into an air show. Indeed he privately believed that the Navy did not need combat aircraft at all, that the battleship remained the ultimate weapon of naval power, and that the Navy needed airplanes only in order to locate the enemy fleet. The notion of bright young ensigns applying for flight training offended him. They should be learning their profession aboard battleships and cruisers.

An assistant secretary of the Navy, however, "asked" the commandant to change his mind. Fox Movietone News, as well as the press, would be attending; and it was entirely possible, the assistant secretary added, that if there were to be a flyover, The March of Time would also send a motion-picture newsreel crew. Between Fox Movietone News and The March of Time, a newsreel sequence of the graduation ceremonies would be in every movie theater in the country. It was a public-relations opportunity that should not be ignored.

Thus the commandant "decided" that a squadron of Grumman F3F-1 fighters would be permitted to fly over the Academy immediately before the brand-new ensigns, in keeping with long tradition, threw their hats in the air.

The Grumman F3F-1, a biplane, was then the standard Navy fighter aircraft. It was powered by a 950-horsepower Wright Cyclone engine, which gave it a maximum speed of just about 230 miles per hour. And it was armed with one .50-caliber and one .30-caliber machine gun.

On schedule, the first V of three F3F-1s passed over the campus. They were flying at their maximum speed at an altitude of fifteen hundred feet, the minimum altitude permitted over populated areas by naval and Federal Aviation Administration regulations.

Even at that altitude, the roar of their engines was impressive, and it seemed to last much longer than was actually the case, for six more Vs of three F3F-1s followed the first at thirty-second intervals. Even the commandant somewhat reluctantly admitted it was an impressive exhibition of naval might.

As the last three-plane V of F3F-1s passed over and began to gain altitude, and just as the commandant was about to step to the microphone again, there came the sound of another—and much noisier—aircraft engine. It was louder both because the airplane was flying only at about five hundred feet and because the Wright supercharged 1200-hp engine, which powered the Grumman F4F-3 Wildcat fighter, gave off a mighty roar as it propelled the stubby silver-bodied monoplane. The aircraft approached more quickly than had the F3F-1s a moment before. The Wildcat, with its throttle pushed to full military power, had a maximum speed of 330 miles per hour, 100 miles faster than the F3F-1.

The not yet wholly accepted F4F-3 would eventually replace the F3F-1 as the standard Navy fighter. It was so new that none of the people participating in the graduating exercise had yet seen one.

With one notable exception. On the reviewing stand was a vice admiral, whose uniform bore the golden wings of a naval aviator. The second, unscheduled flyby had been his idea. He had reasoned that if getting F3F-1 Navy fighters into the newsreels was good, getting the new, greatly superior F4F-3 was better. He had also reasoned that if he suggested this, he would be turned down. Only a few Wildcats had come off the production line, and these were occupied with testing. They could not be spared for a showy display like this one, it would have been argued.

The admiral beamed as the first F4F-3 did a barrel roll at 330 knots and then climbed out. Instantly another Wildcat came, also made a barrel roll at 330 knots, and then disappeared. Then came a third and final one. By the time it had passed over, the audience, including the secretary of the Navy, had broken into applause.

The band began to play "Anchors Aweigh!"

The commandant was smiling. He had no other choice. The battleship bastard could hardly scream about broken regulations and unauthorized flybys to a secretary of the Navy who was smiling like a proud father.

2
Anacostia Naval Air Station
Washington, D.C.
1355 Hours 4 June 1941

Anacostia Tower cleared Navy zero zero three—a flight of three F4F-3 aircraft—to land singly, at sixty-second intervals, on runway two zero. Commander J. K. Hawes, USN, flying the first F4F-3, broke off from the formation over the District of Columbia jail and General Hospital, and made a steep descending turn to the left. He passed over the Sousa Bridge, at the Washington Navy Yard, came in low over the Anacostia River, and touched down. A Follow Me truck waited for him.

Sixty seconds later, Lieutenant (j.g.) Edwin H. Bitter, USN, landed the second F4F-3, and sixty seconds after that, Lieutenant (j.g.) Richard L. Canidy, USNR, landed the third.

Commander Hawes was forty-three, a veteran naval aviator, and an Academy graduate. He was the F4F-3 project officer stationed at the Grumman factory at Bethpage, Long Island.

Lieutenants Bitter and Canidy, each twenty-four years old, had been selected from the large pool of naval aviators at Naval Air Station, Pensacola, where they were both instructor pilots. The requirement had been for two pilots who had more than the usual capacity to guide the aircraft. These two had to have something extra—the talent really to fly. They also had to be bright enough to understand both the real purpose behind the flyover and the damage they could do to naval aviation if they screwed something up.

Lieutenant Edwin H. Bitter fit the requirement perfectly. He was an earnest, intense-looking young man who had graduated from the Naval Academy with the class of 1938. Though on the small side, he had earned his letter on the football field; and he still exercised regularly—and looked as if he did. In spite of their unorthodox nature, which at other times would have bothered him, Bitter had taken particular pleasure in today's maneuvers over Annapolis. He considered, correctly, that his selection for the job was an honor.

Lieutenant Bitter was, in other words, the straightest of straight shooters. Lieutenant Richard L. Canidy was another thing entirely. Though if anything he was a better pilot than Bitter, he was not an Academy man, and—more damaging still—his attitude disturbed more than a few people who counted. All too often, when his name came up, one would hear words like cocky, blasé, arrogant, or defiant. Canidy was thought to cut too many corners. He was even thought by some not to be "serious." The trouble with Canidy, it was generally agreed, was that he was too smart for his own good. Not smart-ass smart, really smart. He had received (cum laude) a Bachelor of Science, Aeronautical Engineering, from the Massachusetts Institute of Technology in 1938.

Canidy was dark-eyed, dark-haired, and quick to smile. He was tall—nearly a head taller than Bitter—and moved with fluid grace, but he was not really good-looking. This deficiency, however, in no way hindered the frequency or the (mutual) pleasure of his encounters with more than usually beautiful and attractive members of the opposite sex. In fact, he was often said to have the same talent for women that Alexander the Great had for territory.

And Canidy was also a magnificent pilot. When he had entered the Navy, he was already a skilled airman with a commercial pilot's license, an instrument ticket, and 350 hours of solo time. And his skills had steadily improved. An easy way up the Navy ladder was open to him, if he wanted to go that way. He didn't. He had lost no time letting it be known that while he would, to the best of his ability, do whatever the Navy asked of him, he was not planning to become an admiral.

A Navy scholarship, in exchange for four years of post-graduation service, had gotten him through MIT. That four years would be up in June of 1942. At the moment Canidy intended to swap his gold stripe-and-a-half for an engineer's slipstick. The Boeing Aircraft Company of Seattle, Washington, had made him a very good offer of employment, based just about equally on his B.S., A.E., cum laude; on the opinion held of him by several of his professors; and on his thesis, "An Hypothesis of Airfoil Tip Vibrations at Speeds in Excess of 400 MPH."

In the end, it had been decided that Bitter and Canidy were the best choices to be sent to Bethpage because of their flying skill, and that Canidy's attitude, though leaving a good deal to be desired, was more than compensated for by his other qualifications.

With secrecy Canidy thought it would have been appropriate had a surprise attack on Toronto or Montreal been in the works. He and Bitter (who, because rooms had been assigned alphabetically, was his Bachelor Officers' Quarters roommate) had been summoned to the office of the deputy commandant at Pensacola, introduced to Commander Hawes, and informed that they had been selected from their peers for an important mission that involved flying the F4F-3.

They had gone to Bethpage, been checked out in F4F-3s fresh from the assembly line, and then practiced low-level aerobatics just out of sight of land over the Atlantic.

Canidy, as an engineer, was very impressed with the Wildcat. As a pilot, he had been very impressed with the airplane as an airplane. Privately, Dick Canidy thought the last three weeks had been enough proof, if one was needed, that insan-

ity and childishness were no bar to promotion in the United
States Navy.

He was not sorry he had volunteered for the hush-hush
childishness. For one thing, it had taken him out of the backseat of a Kaydet, the 90-mph biplane in which he taught
basic flying techniques to fledgling naval birdmen. For another, it had given him the chance to fly the F4F-3. This
would add to his general fund of knowledge, and when he
took off the sailor suit, it just might result in a larger pay-
check. He had taken pains at Bethpage to subtly let Grumman officials know that while he was looking forward to
working for Boeing, he had not actually committed himself
to going to Seattle.

When Canidy touched down at Anacostia he felt a mild
tinge of regret that this was the last chance he would have
to fly the F4F-3 for a while. Finishing the landing roll, he
taxied to the end of the runway where Hawes and Bitter
were lined up behind a Follow Me, a Ford pickup truck
painted in a black-and-white checkerboard pattern.

The aerodrome officer was waiting for them, smiling
broadly, and handed Commander Hawes a telephone message form. Hawes read it, smiled happily, and showed it to
Lieutenants Bitter and Canidy.

```
Pass to Commander Hawes
Well Done. Derr, Vice Admiral
```

"Well, gentlemen," Commander Hawes said, "we pulled
it off."

"Yes, sir," Lieutenant Bitter said.

"There's going to be a little dinner tonight at the Army-Navy Club," Commander Hawes said. "You're of course invited."

"Sir?" Canidy said.

"Yes?"

"Is it a command performance, sir? The reason I ask is that I have a friend in Washington I'd hoped to see."

"A friend?"

"Yes, sir."

"No," Commander Hawes said, somewhat taken aback but making an effort to be pleasant. "Of course it's not a command performance. Go see your friend."

When he had been a young lieutenant, it would not have entered his mind to turn down an invitation to dinner from a superior, particularly when he would have an opportunity to bask in Vice Admiral Derr's approval. Although his performance of duty could not be faulted, Canidy did not have quite the proper attitude for a junior officer.

"If my absence would in some way be awkward, sir . . ."

"Not at all. Go see your friend."

"Thank you, sir."

Bitter waited until they were alone in the BOQ before he told him he thought he had made a mistake to decline the invitation.

"Eddie, you want to be an admiral. You go to the dinner. My sole ambition at the moment is to get laid, and I don't think I'd have much chance to do that at the Army-Navy Club."

"You are coming back here tonight?"

"I devoutly hope not," Canidy said.

"In case I have to get in touch with you, where will you be?"

"At the house of a friend of mine on Q Street, NW. It's in the book under Whittaker."

Eddie Bitter wrote the name down in a notebook.

Thirty minutes later, a taxi left Dick Canidy standing on the sidewalk in the Embassy District of Washington near Rock Creek, outside a ten-foot brick wall. He had changed into a jacket and slacks and was carrying only a small overnight bag with a change of linen. He didn't think he would need other clothing, since what he looked forward to was a couple of sets of tennis, and then some girl chasing.

A bell button was mounted in the brick wall. Canidy pushed it and waited for the buzz that would open the lock. Then he pushed the door and went through it. There were trees and paths, and even Central Park–type benches between the wall and the house itself.

The house was a turn-of-the-century mansion, stately in its ugliness. The building was faced with sandstone. Gargoyles at the roofline spouted rain from the slate roof. A widow's watch crowned the peak of the building and two snarling stone lions guarded the massive double front door. There was a marble veranda twenty feet wide across the entire front of the house, and four sets of cast-iron tables, each with four cast-iron chairs. Canidy had been coming to the house on Q Street since he was a fifteen-year-old, gangly second former at St. Mark's School, and he had never seen anyone sit on one of the cast-iron chairs.

It was the tradition at St. Mark's School to assign first formers (freshmen) to share rooms with upperclassmen, the notion apparently being that the older boys could look out for, and set an example for, younger ones. An exception was made for fourth formers (seniors), who could, if they wished, room with other fourth formers. But first formers, without exception, were assigned to second formers. The new students were called hacks, and Jim Whittaker had been his.

St. Mark's semisacred customs had made little impression

on Dick Canidy, who had been born and raised in a mid-western copy of St. Mark's, St. Paul's, of which his father, the Reverend George Crater Canidy, D.D., Ph.D., was head-master. Though second formers were supposed to hold themselves aloof from first formers, he had liked Jim Whit-taker more than he liked the other two boys who shared their two-bedroom, one-bath apartment. And they had be-come friends.

Jim had asked him to visit that year for the Thanksgiving holiday—holding out the bait that his uncle Chesty had tick-ets for the Army–Navy game—and he had accepted.

On his arrival Canidy paid the ritual compliment to Jim's uncle and aunt, "Lovely home you have," but their aston-ishing reply was that the compliment properly belonged to Jim.

"The house is his," Chesley Haywood "Chesty" Whit-taker, Jim's childless uncle, said. "It was his father's."

Seeing the confusion on Canidy's face, Chesty Whittaker had explained: "After Jim's father died, the idea was that once the house was known to be available, an embassy or an ambassador would snatch it up at an outrageous price. In the meantime, just for a couple of months, of course, Barbara and I would use it when we were in Washington. That was ten years ago, and we've yet to get that first out-rageous offer."

Canidy had liked Uncle Chesty from the first. For one thing, Chesty Whittaker had not concluded that because Dick was a priest's son, he was therefore a good moral influence on Jim, and neither did he spare him dirty jokes or keep him from anything smacking of sin. And later Jim's uncle had been responsible, Canidy was sure, both for his acceptance at MIT and for the Navy scholarship without which MIT would have been out of the question. Jim had shown him copies of the letters his uncle had written to the secretary of the Navy on Canidy's behalf. The first, ad-dressed "Dear Mr. Secretary," had painted Canidy out to be a paragon of virtue and academic prowess whose services the Navy could ill afford to pass up. The second, addressed "Dear Slats," said: "I mean everything I said in the at-tached letter, and if the Navy doesn't see fit to give Dick a scholarship, you had better be prepared to explain to me why not."

Over the years, Canidy had come to think of the house on Q Street as almost a second home and of the Whittakers as a second family. And Canidy had spent happy summer weeks at Whittaker's home on the New Jersey coast, where Jim's aunt had been as kind to him as her husband was.

A silver-haired black man in a gray cotton jacket, whom Canidy had never seen before, opened the door.

"Yes, sir?"

"Mr. Whittaker, please," Canidy said. "Either, but pref-erably both."

"Neither Mr. Whittaker is at home, sir."

"My name is Canidy," Dick said.

"Oh yes, sir, we've been expecting you," the butler said. "Won't you come in?"

"Is Mr. Whittaker here? Jim?"

"Lieutenant Whittaker called, sir," the butler said. "He asked me to tell you that he can't get away from the Air Corps. And he told me, sir, to make you as comfortable as I possibly can."

Damn, Canidy thought. When he'd called Jim, who was an Air Corps reserve second lieutenant at Randolph Field in Texas, Jim had thought he'd be able to make it up for a night on the town. With Jim around, the house on Q Street was a great place to be. Without him, it was about as ex-citing as a library. There was still plenty of time to return to Anacostia and the dinner at the Army-Navy Club.

"What I think I'll do," Canidy said, "is say hello to Mrs. Harris, and then call a cab." Mrs. Harris was the housekeeper.

"Mrs. Harris has retired, sir. I have, in a sense, taken her place," the butler said as he opened the door wider. "There is a telephone in the sitting room, sir."

Canidy was looking in the telephone book for a cab company number when he heard a female voice asking about him.

"It's Mr. Canidy, miss," the butler said. "He asked to use the telephone."

When he heard footsteps behind him, Canidy turned around. It was Cynthia Chenowith. She was a few years older than he was, a disadvantage he was perfectly willing to ignore; for she was well set up, with nice breasts and rich dark brown hair. But she also had a distant, off-putting look that left you not knowing where you stood with her or if indeed you had anywhere to stand. Canidy had a hunch that there was heat and passion beneath all that. But very deep down. Very. She was "a friend of the family," and he had known her, not well, for a long time.

"Hello, Canidy," she said. "What brings you here?"

"Hello, Cynthia," he said. "You make a lovely consolation prize."

"In lieu of what?" she asked, her voice level.

"I was supposed to meet Jim here."

"Then he didn't get in touch with you? He said he would try."

"No," Canidy said.

"Is there something I can do for you?" she asked, clearly hoping there wasn't.

"I was about to call a cab," he said.

"You're perfectly welcome to stay here, of course," she said.

"That's very kind of you, Cynthia," he said, slightly sarcastic.

She caught his tone. "I'm living here now. In the garage apartment. I sort of keep an eye on things. Mrs. Harris has retired, you know."

"Oh," he said.

Canidy knew from Jimmy that Cynthia's father, who had dropped dead on the twelfth-hole fairway of Winged Foot, the New York Athletic Club's golf course, had not left his widow and only child enough money to pay for his funeral. Chesty Whittaker, who had been Thomas Chenowith's Harvard classmate and an usher at his wedding, had consequently fulfilled his obligation as a gentleman and a friend. He had "found" some interest-bearing municipal bonds, which had escaped the Chenowith financial debacle, enough of them to ensure Tom Chenowith's widow and child a comfortable existence. He had further "arranged" for scholarships to be provided for Cynthia from the Emma Willard School and later Vassar and still later Harvard Law. It was thus not surprising that the garage apartment had suddenly become available—rent-free—to Cynthia.

"Where are you going—in the cab, I mean?"

"Back to Anacostia," Canidy said.

There was the muted ring of a telephone somewhere else in the house. Cynthia Chenowith, smelling of something interesting and expensive, stepped past Canidy and picked up the telephone he had been about to use. She listened a moment.

"Mr. Whittaker, I'm on the extension," she said. "Dick Canidy is here." Then, a moment later, she handed him the telephone.

"Dick? Jim couldn't get away. He tried to call you."

"Yes, sir. So I have just found out."

"You do plan to spend the night?"

"I was about to go back to Anacostia."

"Could I talk you into filling in at dinner? Or is whoever is waiting for you at Anacostia a goddess defying description?"

"He could hardly be called a goddess," Canidy said.

Chesty Whittaker laughed. "Have Cynthia make you a drink. You're going to take her and another young lovely to dinner tonight."

"Splendid," Canidy said. "If you're not just being kind. I don't want to intrude."

"Don't be an ass," Chesty Whittaker said. "Actually, I consider you a gift from heaven. I'll be there in an hour or so."

He hung up.

Canidy put the phone into its cradle.

"We are going to be dinner partners tonight," he said.

"Paul?" she called, raising her voice.

The butler appeared.

"Yes, miss?"

"Mr. Canidy will be staying. Would you put his bag in Jimmy's room, please, and then see what he will have to drink?"

Not quite understanding why, Canidy was suddenly annoyed. Cynthia's housemotherish "I'm in charge of the young people" attitude irritated him.

"Put my bag in the room across from Jimmy's," he ordered. "That's my room. And I know where to find the whiskey."

He got an annoyed, angry look from Cynthia Chenowith, but she didn't countermand his order. She nodded her head at him and walked out of the sitting room.

She had a very nice walk, he thought.

3
The Willard Hotel
Washington, D.C.
7:40 P.M., June 4, 1941

Richard Canidy got out of the limousine and walked up the
stairs to the lobby of the Willard. He was wearing one of
Jim Whittaker's dinner jackets and one of Jim's stiff shirts;
because it was about a size too small at the neck, he was
sure it would leave his skin irritated and sore by the time
he could get rid of it.

He went to a bank of house phones and asked to be connected with Mrs. Mark Chambers. The phone rang four
times before a soft Southern voice answered it.

"Yes?"

"Mrs. Chambers, I'm Dick Canidy. Anytime you're
ready, I'm in the lobby."

"I'll be down in just a minute," she said. "How will I
recognize you?"

"I look like a waiter," he quipped, and immediately regretted it. "I'll recognize you. Mr. Whittaker said you were
a tall and lovely blonde."

"Oh my," she said, and hung up. Canidy thought he
shouldn't have said that either.

Chesty Whittaker had in fact not described her as a "tall
and lovely blonde" but somewhat less kindly as "your typical Southern magnolia blossom, Dick. I'm sure you know
the type. Blond and helpless. 'Po' l'il ol' me.' Too afraid
of the big city to get in a cab and come out here by herself.
Hence the limousine. But I promised her husband that I
would watch over her, so you're elected to fetch her and
take her home."

"My pleasure," Dick had said.

"No, not your pleasure, I'm afraid. But I will owe you."

"My pleasure to be of service, then," Canidy said.

Chesty Whittaker had squeezed his arm then in gratitude and friendship.

Three minutes later, Mrs. Mark Chambers got off the elevator. She *did* look Southern. He was sure it was her even before he walked up and asked, "Mrs. Chambers?"

"Sue-Ellen," she said, giving him her hand. She looked right into his eyes, and he found that disconcerting. "Mr. Canidy?"

"Dick," he said.

"It was so nice of you to come all the way here and get me."

"My pleasure."

And she *was* tall and lovely, he thought. Probably thirty or so.

"I hate to be a burden on Mr. Whittaker," she said, taking his arm. Innocently, he believed, she pressed her breast against his arm as they made their way across the lobby and down the stairs.

"Mr. Whittaker is looking forward to having you in the house," Canidy said, and thought: *You have all the makings of a gigolo, Canidy. Charm oozes from your every pore.*

"My husband was delayed on business in New York," she said.

"So Mr. Whittaker told me."

He got into the old Rolls beside her. In the closed car, her rich perfume became powerfully evident. It was surprisingly wicked perfume for "your typical Southern 'po' l'il ol' me' " magnolia to wear.

At the house there were cocktails, and then dinner was announced. Chesley Haywood Whittaker sat at one end of the table, and at the other was a New York lawyer named Donovan. Sue-Ellen Chambers as guest of honor sat beside

Whittaker, and Canidy sat beside Sue-Ellen. Cynthia Chenowith sat on the other side between the other guests, who
were British and Canadian. One of the Englishmen, on hearing that Canidy was in the Navy, introduced himself as a
sailor himself, Commander, Royal Navy Reserve, Ian Fleming.

Canidy liked Donovan, a fascinating man, full of sparkle
and energy and a longtime Whittaker buddy. He had met
Donovan a dozen times before in New Jersey. Donovan was
called Colonel Donovan, even though he had long ago taken
off his colonel's uniform, which was adorned with the blue,
silver-starred ribbon of the Medal of Honor, won while he
was commanding the "Fighting 69th" Infantry Regiment in
the American Expeditionary Force in France.

He was a stocky, white-haired, charming, yet intense man,
the only man Canidy knew who had won the Medal of
Honor. As a result of his Navy experience Canidy had come
to understand something of what command was all about.
Canidy could see instantly that this man Donovan was one
hell of a commanding officer. He possessed that rare talent
that caused other men to eagerly carry out orders they would
not accept from someone else. It wasn't just that he was
persuasive. It was a much, much rarer talent than that (FDR
had it): Donovan was a man you just couldn't say no to.

Canidy could also tell—from some of the amused but
admiring glances he from time to time shot at the colonel—
that Commander Fleming held opinions about Donovan
similar to his own. When Canidy made a comment to that
effect to the commander, Fleming laughed. "Oh yes, Lieutenant," he said, pronouncing it *Leftenant,* "I know exactly
what you mean. I've had considerable dealings of late with
Colonel Wild Bill Donovan."

"I'd like to hear about those," Canidy said.

"I'm afraid I can't tell you very much, Leftenant," he

said mysteriously. "It's all rather behind closed shutters."

Canidy shrugged acceptance. He was not surprised that Donovan was up to something secret.

Before long, the reason for the dinner came out. Whittaker Construction was building maritime fuel transfer facilities in Nova Scotia. Canidy knew a little about this. And what he did not know, Colonel Donovan quickly made clear.

American petroleum products were to be shipped in American bottoms from the Gulf Coast. So long as they were in American waters, they would be safe from attack from German submarines. The British and Canadian navies would then provide protection for the tankers during the short voyage from the Canadian–American border to a port in Nova Scotia, where the petroleum would be pumped into English ships for the trip across the Atlantic. If the petroleum had been loaded into the English ships on the Gulf Coast, the ships would have been fair game for German submarines the moment they were fourteen miles at sea. Since the British had neither enough tankers to ship their fuel directly from Texas and Louisiana, nor enough naval vessels to protect them, other arrangements had to be made.

Sue-Ellen Chambers's husband owned a shipyard in Mobile to which Whittaker Construction had subcontracted the manufacture of the fuel-handling barges and other equipment that would be used in Canada. This yard was not only building tankers, but was about to hand over fuel-handling equipment to the Canadians. Ol' Magnolia Blossom's husband was a subcontractor, making the equipment for Whittaker Construction, who had the prime contract.

From what Canidy had been taught about the rules of warfare, what the Americans were doing was undeniably a violation of the laws governing neutral countries during a war; but he was a lieutenant junior grade, Reserve, and no one had asked for his opinion.

Cynthia Chenowith, however, did not share Canidy's reluctance to speak out. "What all this amounts to," she said to Donovan, "is that America is going to be in the war on Britain's side, only not officially. Neutrality doesn't count anymore, then, does it?"

"I think, Miss Chenowith, that you've made a more or less reasonable interpretation," Donovan said.

"I don't like it," Cynthia said. "I don't like going into war through the back door."

"You realize, miss," said Commander Fleming, "that America will be in this war *officially*—and sooner rather than later."

Cynthia paused a moment in order to take hold of that. Then, with a not quite nice smile, she said to Fleming, "Is this why you've come to Washington, Commander, to help make that happen sooner rather than later?"

"Something like that," Fleming agreed, grinning, liking her directness.

"Ian is *very* good at doing things through the back door," Donovan said in a loud, stagy whisper.

"What kind of things?" Canidy asked innocently.

Donovan took a long, thoughtful sip from his goblet, weighing what he could reveal. "Wars were fought, once upon a time," he said after draining the goblet, "by tribes who came at one another with clubs and stones. Each tribe beat on the other until only one tribe was left standing. All wars, until recently, have been conducted pretty much the same way. . . . Oh, there've been a few changes. We have airplanes now, which, in effect, let us throw stones farther than our grandparents could. But otherwise, one side continues to bash at the other until only one is left standing. What has changed from what our grandfathers did is that much of the battle now is fought—long before the armies, navies, and air fleets clash—in the minds of the opposing forces. That may even be the decisive part of the battle. . . . Which means that we need to know the mind of an enemy before he commits his forces—what he *can* do to us and what he *intends* to do to us—so that we can prevent the moves that could harm us or at least counter them. And we need to conceal from our enemy what we can do to him and what we intend to do to him. Of course, we want him to believe that we are extremely powerful. That, too, is part of the war of the mind.''

He took another sip of water from his goblet, which a servant had refilled. Then he went on. ''Unhappily, our nation has been woefully unprepared to wage this kind of warfare. Happily, Commander Fleming and some of his colleagues in England are very skilled at it, indeed, and have graciously agreed to help us put matters right.''

Meanwhile, as this talk of spying was going on about the table, a truly clandestine action was starting to happen beneath it.

During the crab cocktail, Sue-Ellen Chambers, apparently mistaking Candy's foot for the table leg, stepped heavily on his instep. He waited until the opportunity presented itself, then moved his feet far out of her way.

During the entrée, leg of lamb with oven-roasted potatoes, her shoe again found his, and again he moved it. He looked up in some surprise, for his foot was some distance from where hers should have been. When his glance reached her face, she looked directly into his eyes again.

It was, he told himself, his overactive imagination that suggested she was anything different from what she claimed she was: a mother of two, who had come to Washington only because ''the way things are'' it was the only time she got to see her husband.

There was Brie and toasted crackers for dessert, along

with a very nice burgundy. While Canidy was spreading a cracker, he felt a tug at his pants leg, and a moment later there was the unmistakable pressure of the ball of Sue-Ellen Chambers's stockinged foot against his calf.

When he looked at her this time, she was smiling at him, and the tip of her tongue was peeping out from between her lips.

Jesus Christ! Was she drunk, or what?

There was to be bridge after dinner, but Mrs. Chambers asked to be excused. She had things to do in the morning, she said, and she really wasn't used to the late hours everybody up north seemed to keep.

"Dick will take you to your hotel, Sue-Ellen," Chesty Whittaker said.

"Oh, he can just see me to the car," Sue-Ellen said.

A goddamned tease is what she is. She had no intention of delivering what she seemed to be offering. If I made a pass at her, she would act like a goosed nun.

"I had to send the car to New Jersey," Chesty said. "Dick will take you in the station wagon."

"If you'll just call me a cab," she said.

Fuck you, lady. Now it's my turn to tease.

"I wouldn't think of it, Mrs. Chambers," Canidy said. "I'll drive you home."

And I won't go within three feet of you. But I'll give you a chance to worry a lot about whether or not you're going to have to fight me off.

"Would you get Dick the keys to the station wagon, Cynthia?" Chesty said.

She sat as far away from him as she could, against the door of the three-year-old but immaculate Ford station wagon. He drove down New Hampshire Avenue to Washington Circle, and then down Pennsylvania Avenue.

As they passed between Lafayette Square and the White House, she laughed.

"You're not going to make a pass at me, are you?" she asked.

"No, ma'am," he said.

"Because you're afraid Mr. Whittaker or Colonel Donovan might find out? Or because you're afraid of me?"

He didn't reply.

"I knew," she said, "Chesty Whittaker being what he is, that he would not send me home alone."

He looked at her as he turned down Fifteenth Street. She was fishing for something in her purse. She threw something in his lap. He felt for it. It was a hotel key.

"When you come up for a nightcap," she said, "try to make sure no one sees you." When he didn't respond, she added, "If I don't appeal to you, or if you can't work up the courage, drop it in any mailbox. They guarantee postage."

He let her out in front of the Willard and started back across Washington to the house on Q Street.

He got as far as Washington Circle before he changed his mind. There he made a complete circle and went back to the Willard. He put the station wagon in a parking garage and entered the hotel.

When he put the key to the door, she pulled it open.

She was wearing a negligee and a garter belt.

"I probably shouldn't admit this," she said. "But I was afraid you weren't coming."

4
The Monroe Suite
The Willard Hotel
Washington, D.C.
5:15 A.M., June 5, 1941

When Canidy came out of the bathroom, Sue-Ellen was sitting up in the bed. She was even at first light a fine-looking female. Ladylike. To look at her, the fact that she was a married woman; that she had gone after him, rather than the other way around; and that she had been both so passionate and so delightfully, so wickedly inventive in the bed seemed hardly credible.

"Sorry I have to run," he said. "When am I going to see you again?"

"You're not," Sue-Ellen Chambers said, pleasantly but firmly.

He found his trousers and put them on. He looked across the room at her.

"Was I that much of a disappointment?"

"Not at all," she said, and chuckled. "You were all I thought you would be, and more."

"But?" he said.

"I like to quit when I'm ahead," she said, matter-of-factly.

There was nothing of the magnolia blossom about her now, he thought. She was, under the drawl, about as soft as stainless steel. She had seen what she wanted, and taken it, and now it was time to make an end to the scene. Sue-Ellen was a tough cookie. Still, though she might want to stop him right here, he wasn't willing to quit so easily.

He turned away from her to zip his fly. "Because you're married?" he asked, without turning around. "Is that it?"

"Obviously," she said.

"That didn't seem to be a consideration last night."

"Don't be nasty," she said.

"I'm crushed," he said wryly. "And a little curious."

"I can't take the chance of getting involved," she said. "I could easily get involved with you."

"Guilty," he said. He slipped his feet into his shoes.

"Every once in a while," she said, "I do this. The conditions have to be right. I have to be alone, in circumstances that are in no way suspicious. And there has to be a suitable man."

"I'm pleased that you found me suitable," he said, hoping that the sudden anger he felt didn't show in his voice.

"Very suitable," she said. "You struck me as someone who wouldn't make trouble for either of us when I explained the circumstances. Someone who wouldn't, for example, try to telephone me."

"I really would like to see you again."

"Don't ruin everything now," she said, and there was steel in her voice.

"OK," he said. He looked around for his cummerbund, and couldn't find it.

She read his mind. "You left it in the other room," she said. "When you first got here."

He remembered. She had been so anxious to get at him that she had dropped to her knees the moment she had closed the door. The cummerbund had been in the way.

"Oh," he said. "Thank you."

"Good-bye, Dick Canidy," she said.

He inclined his head toward her, sort of a bow, but said nothing. He went out of the bedroom, closing the door after him.

The driveway gate in the wall of the house on Q Street was closed, and the key for it was not on the key ring Cynthia Chenowith had given him. But there was a key to the walk gate, so he got out of the station wagon and entered the property that way.

He was almost through Whittaker's private park and at the driveway gate when a motion caught his eye.

Chesley Haywood Whittaker, in a silk dressing gown, was walking quickly across the cobblestones between the garage and the kitchen.

Canidy ducked behind a tree so that he wouldn't be seen.

Sonofabitch, Chesty is screwing Cynthia Chenowith. Why else could he have been in the garage . . . at five-thirty in the morning . . . where she had an apartment?

He thought that over a moment. The first thing that came to his mind was that Chesty Whittaker was a dirty old man, demanding sexual services in repayment for the bills he was paying. But he knew Chesty Whittaker better than that. Chesty wasn't the one who'd started whatever was going on.

Was there a phrase to describe a Yankee version of a Southern magnolia blossom?

Canidy stayed behind the tree until he was sure Chesty was inside the house, and then he opened the driveway gate and drove the Ford station wagon in, purposefully making a lot of noise opening and closing the doors.

He went to his room, removed his clothes, and took a shower. When he came out, Chesty Whittaker was in the room.

"I heard you come in," he said. "I thought you might want some breakfast."

"I'm sorry I woke you," Canidy said.

"Don't worry about it. Apparently the hunting was good after you took Miss Magnolia Blossom home?"

"Can't complain."

"Are you hungry?"

"I stopped for scrambled eggs on the way home," Canidy said.

"And you can't stay?"

"No, I wish I could."

"It was good to see you, Dick, and thanks for filling in."

"Thank you again, for having me."

"Don't be silly, anytime," Chesty said. He put out his hand, patted Canidy on the back, and left him.

I don't think he thinks I know. I hope not.

5
Transient Officers' Quarters
Anacostia Naval Air Station
Washington, D.C.
0630 Hours 5 June 1941

When Lieutenant (junior grade) Edwin Howell Bitter, USN, woke he saw that the bed of Lieutenant (j.g.) Richard Canidy, USNR, had not been slept in.

This bothered Ed Bitter, as did many other Canidy escapades in and out of bed. Dick Canidy did not, in Bitter's opinion, conduct himself as a commissioned officer and gentleman was expected to. He was less interested in discharging his duties to the best of his ability than he was in chasing skirts. If Dick Canidy was aware of the hoary naval adage that officers were supposed to keep their indiscretions a hundred miles from the flagpole, he paid no attention to it.

It wasn't that Ed Bitter didn't like Dick Canidy. He did. Canidy was not only an amusing companion, but he had, in a number of ways, made it clear that he liked Bitter, which was of course flattering, and that he considered him to be highly intelligent, which was even more flattering. But Can-

idy seldom bothered to conceal his disdain for the limited
brainpower of their peers.

Nor did Bitter believe chasing skirts was dishonorable.
What it was was that he was a professional naval officer—
with corresponding standards—and Dick was not. Dick was
a civilian in uniform.

Bitter got out of bed, stripped off his pajamas, and
marched naked to the shower. Naked, he looked even more
muscular than he did dressed. While Dick Canidy was
spending weekends lifting the skirts of Smith coeds, Ed Bitter was lifting weights in the Naval Academy gym. It
showed. He was in splendid physical shape, firm-muscled,
capable of great physical exertion. But to Bitter's annoyance, so was Dick Canidy. Half-jokingly, half-pridefully,
Canidy had announced that the only college athletic program
he had joined was performed in the horizontal attitude.

He had just finished returning his safety razor to its
stainless-steel snap-shut case when Dick Canidy came
home.

"Home is the sailor, home from the sea, and the lover,
home from God only knows where," Bitter greeted him.

"From a very nice house in Georgetown, actually," Canidy said, smiling as he started to take off his uniform. "The
smell of spring in the air. The gentle murmur of Rock Creek
wending its way inexorably toward the Potomac. Very ro-
mantic."

"And what about her parents? Were they conveniently
away?"

"I don't know about her parents," Canidy said. "Her
husband was away."

"She was married? You can get your oversexed ass court-
martialed for that, you know. They call it conduct unbecom-
ing," Bitter said as he buttoned the cuffs of a heavily
starched gray khaki shirt. Canidy stuffed his civilian cloth-

ing in his bag, took a gray khaki shirt from his chest of drawers, and started to put it on.

After that he took a twill aviator-green uniform from the closet. He pulled the trousers on, and as he tucked the tail of the shirt in, he looked at Ed and asked: "How was the dinner party? Did you learn anything useful?"

"I did, but I'm not sure I should tell you."

"Come on, you're dying to!"

"Did you know that we're shipping petroleum products from the Gulf Coast to Nova Scotia?"

"Yeah," Canidy said, straight-faced. "Where they are transferred to British ships for the Atlantic crossing. Who told you? That's supposed to be classified."

"Who told you?" Bitter asked, disappointed that his secret was known.

"I couldn't tell you that, Eddie, you understand," Canidy said. "Suffice it to say that I broke bread with Colonel William 'Wild Bill' Medal of Honor Donovan last night."

"Really?" Bitter wasn't sure if his leg was being pulled or not.

"Really," Canidy said. "I learned a lot more than I really cared to learn about the strategic implications of economic warfare."

Still not sure whether he was being teased or not, Bitter challenged, "Did you also know that we are going to start Catalina flights to keep an eye on our shipping?"

"As a matter of fact, I did," Canidy lied easily. He loved to keep Eddie Bitter off balance. "Who's been telling you all this stuff?"

"Admiral Derr mentioned it last night. I didn't say anything to him, of course, but I wondered if it might not be a good idea to apply for that duty. It's obviously important, and you could pick up a lot of hours."

"Eddie, if there's any job worse than sitting in a Kaydet

teaching dummies to fly, it's in a Catalina, flying endless circles over the ocean.''

"It's something to think about," Bitter said.

"I don't suppose there's any chance the weather is going to keep us on the deck?" Canidy asked. "I could use another day in Washington."

"Not a chance. I checked before I went to bed. Cloudless skies for the foreseeable future."

"Shit," Canidy said.

Officers might swear, Bitter thought, but they should abstain from vulgarity.

When they were dressed, they left the BOQ and walked across the base to the officers' mess, where they had breakfast. Then they returned to the BOQ, picked up their luggage, and went to Base Operations.

The glory of their selection to buzz the Naval Academy graduation was over. As soon as they could hitch a ride, which might take all day, they had to go back to Pensacola, where they could count on spending many long hours in the backseat of a Kaydet, the slowest airplane in the Navy.

TWO

Pensacola Naval Air Station
Pensacola, Florida
0615 Hours 8 June 1941

Bitter and Canidy, in Bitter's month-old 1940 dark green Buick Roadmaster convertible, drove across the pleasant, almost luxurious tropical base to the Mediterranean-style officers' club. There they had breakfast.

They had been back a day and a half, doing hardly anything but waiting to see the deputy commander so he could vicariously experience their triumph in buzzing Annapolis. But today it was back to work, and with a vengeance, Canidy thought: a long cross-country training flight.

Canidy ate an enormous breakfast, and then, in the men's room, read the *Pensacola Journal* cover to cover, while he got rid of as much liquid and bulk as he could. There were no toilets in Kaydets; and despite the many hours he had in them, he had not yet mastered the relief tube.

Finally, they drove to the airfield, where two ensigns, already in gray flight suits, were waiting for them at Student Operations. The students followed them into the locker room, and reported on the flight plan they had laid out as Bitter and Canidy changed into their flight suits. The two instructor pilots carefully folded their green uniforms and put them into canvas flight bags. While the odds against something going wrong on their cross-country training flight were remote, if they did have to spend the night someplace they would need uniforms. Naval officers could not go into public wearing gray cotton overalls.

They picked up their parachutes, then were driven out onto the flight line in a Ford panel truck. Dick and Ed jammed into the front seat with the sailor driver. The student pilots and the parachutes rode in the back.

The cross-country flight (Pensacola–Valdosta–Montgomery–Mobile–Pensacola) they were about to make was the last training flight of the primary flight training program. Their students already knew how to fly, and when this flight was completed would be awarded naval aviator's wings and sent to advanced flight training. Ed Bitter and Dick Canidy would then start the whole process all over again, with four new officer students.

Teaching fledglings how to fly was hard work and not very much fun. They both would have preferred other duty. But—for different personal reasons—both were aware that instructor pilot duty was better for them than an assignment to a fighter squadron or to an attack torpedo squadron aboard a carrier or to observation planes catapulted from a battleship would have been.

Ed Bitter believed that duty as an IP meant several things. First, that the Navy recognized he was a better pilot than most pilots. Second, that demonstrating the leadership characteristics IPs had to have to be successful would enhance his career (a tour as an IP was considered a prerequisite to command of a squadron). He also believed that the primary duty of a commanding officer was not so much to command, to issue orders, but to teach.

The main things that instructors did was fly. Aviators assigned to regular squadrons were lucky if they got forty hours in the air in a month. That was two hours a day, five days a week. Instructor pilots often flew three hours in the morning and three in the afternoon. In a two-year tour as an IP, Dick Canidy expected to acquire very likely more than three times the hours he would have had he been sent to an operational squadron. Aeronautical engineers with a lot of flight time were paid more money than those who had less, or who couldn't fly at all.

The world looked a lot different today than it had in 1938 when he'd graduated from MIT. The only worry he had had then was putting in his four years' service. The world had been at peace then, but now that world had changed. France had fallen. Japan was fighting China. Young men his age were flying Spitfires against Messerschmitts over England. Still he refused to think about what he would do if, in June 1942, the Navy would not discharge him.

Advanced flight training was conducted in North American SNJ-2 Texans, single-wing, all-metal, closed-cockpit six-hundred-horsepower retractable-landing-gear aircraft that cruised at about two hundred knots. Primary training was conducted using open-cockpit, fixed-landing-gear Stearman Kaydet biplanes. They weren't really Stearmans, Boeing having some time before taken over that company, and while they were splendid basic training aircraft, stressed for acrobatics and sturdy enough to survive the inevitable hard landings, they were not really suitable for cross-country flight. The planes they would fly today, officially N2Ss, had Continental R670 engines producing a little over two hundred horsepower and a cruising speed of just over one hundred miles per hour.

When he had been a student pilot, Ed Bitter had thought (as had just about every other student pilot passing through Pensacola) that it would have made a lot more sense to wait until the students were advanced and let them make their cross-country flights in the faster Texans. It was only after he had gone through the rest of the flight training program— including carrier qualification—and been made an instructor that he understood the Navy's reasoning.

A six- or seven-hundred-mile dead-reckoning flight, in an open-cockpit airplane making a hundred knots, while check-ing his position by looking for landmarks on the deck, was an experience the student pilot never forgot. It took him back to Eddie Rickenbacker and the Lafayette Escadrille, whose planes came with no more sophisticated navigation equipment and about the same performance as the Stearman. It was something they might need to remember when they were flying fighters capable of more than three hundred knots off the decks of aircraft carriers.

Bitter and Canidy each watched their students perform the preflight check, and then watched them climb into the for-ward cockpits. They took a last look themselves, and then climbed into the aft cockpits and put on leather helmets. The plane captains and the ground handlers pulled the props through a rotation, the engines were started, and the chocks were pulled.

Ed Bitter's ensign turned around and looked at him. Bitter nodded and pulled his goggles down over his eyes.

"Pensacola Tower, Navy One-oh-one," Bitter's student called over his radio.

"One-oh-one, Pensacola."

"Pensacola, Navy One-oh-one, a flight of two N2S air-craft, destination Valdosta, Georgia, requests taxi and take-off."

Pensacola Tower gave them the time, the altimeter, and the barometer, then taxi clearance to the threshold of runway 28. When the student pilot reported them in position, the tower gave permission to take off at one-minute intervals.

They climbed to five thousand feet, and took up a course that was almost due east. Canidy's student took up a position two hundred yards above Bitter's Stearman. Canidy's student would fly Bitter's student's wing for half the trip, and then their positions would be reversed.

Two aircraft were sent on each cross-country flight, alternating as leader, so there would always be one aircraft checking on the other. Now that he had come to understand the reasoning behind the flight program, Ed Bitter had concluded that, like many other odd-on-the-surface facets of Navy policy, there was sound reasoning behind it.

One part of the program was even an officially sanctioned "confuse your students" portion of the cross-country flight, designed to ensure that simply because they were about to be awarded the gold wings of a naval aviator, it would never enter their minds that they were anything but rank amateurs:

13. DISORIENTATION.
    (a) Purpose: to give student pilots the experience of suffering location disorientation, and the techniques of recovery therefrom.
    (b) Method: At some point during the Montgomery–Mobile leg of Flight #48, while flying over the area marked on Aerial Navigation Chart (Instructors Only) NAS Pensacola 239, instructor pilots will, without previous warning to the student, take over the controls of the aircraft, and attempt to disorient the student pilot by such maneuvers as aerobatics, stalls, and low-altitude flight. The controls will then be returned to the student and he will be ordered to resume his original course and altitude.
    (c) Evaluation: Instructor pilots will grade the student on his ability to reorient himself, taking into consideration the time and degree of assurance with which he is able to do so.

The area marked on Aerial Navigation Chart (Instructors Only) NAS Pensacola 239 was a 25,000-acre property owned by the Carlson Publishing Company. It was in the pines, the management of Carlson Publishing Company being strongly convinced that it was just a matter of time before chemists came up with a means of using fast-growing loblolly pine for newsprint. Carlson Publishing Company published eleven medium-sized newspapers throughout the South, and these consumed a good deal of paper, all of which had to be purchased from mills using New England and Canadian pulpwood.

While they were waiting for the chemists to find a solution to this expensive and galling problem, the property was used by the chairman of the board of the Carlson Publishing Company primarily as a hunting preserve in the fall, and a vacation site in the spring and summer.

The chairman of the board, on behalf of his company, had been more than happy to grant the U.S. Navy permission to conduct low-level aerial flights, to include landing privileges, on the area now marked on the map. He understood the necessity to train pilots as realistically as possible, he and the admiral and the others having been sent off to fight the Hun with less than twenty-five hours' total time in the air. Brandon Chambers had never forgotten that literally nauseating feeling of terror. He saw giving the Navy permission to use the land as his patriotic duty. And if some young pilot did dump his plane in the forests, the Navy would pay for the damages.

Lieutenant Ed Bitter had heard the story about the admiral who had flown with the Lafayette Escadrille getting permission from another Escadrille pilot to use the land long before it was told to him while he was receiving training to become an instructor pilot. He had heard it from Brandon Chambers himself. Ed Bitter's mother and Genevieve (Mrs. Brandon) Chambers were sisters.

So far as he knew, no one at NAS Pensacola knew of his

personal connection with The Plantation. Neither did anyone know that his father and his brother were respectively chairman of the board and president of Bitter Commodity Brokerage, Inc., of Chicago.

Edwin Howell Bitter was an officer of the Regular Naval Establishment. It was neither seemly nor wise for a Regular naval officer to let it be known that he had an outside income from a trust fund that was approximately four times his Navy pay.

2

At 10:20, almost exactly two hours after they had taken off from Pensacola, they landed at Valdosta, Georgia, where the airport had a Navy fueling contract. They topped off the tanks, checked the weather again, and were airborne at 11:05. This time, Ed's student flew Dick's student's wing.

They made Maxwell Field, the Army Air Corps base in Montgomery, Alabama, at ten minutes to one. The officers' mess there closed at one, and they just made it in time to eat. It was five minutes to three before they got off the ground again, with Ed's student again assuming the role of flight leader.

An hour out of Montgomery, when they were just about halfway between Maxwell Field and Brookley Field, the Army Air Corps base in Mobile, Alabama, Lieutenant (j.g.) Ed Bitter clapped the speaking tube over his mouth and shouted to his student that he had it.

The student pilot signified his understanding of and compliance with the order by holding both his hands above his head. Bitter pushed the stick forward, and the Stearman, the wind screaming in the guy wires of the wing, dove for the ground.

Behind him, Dick Canidy took the controls from his student and dove in pursuit. For fifteen minutes, sometimes right on the deck, sometimes climbing to eight or nine thousand, they engaged in a mock dogfight, always moving south, paralleling their original course, toward The Lodge on The Plantation.

By prearrangement, once they spotted The Lodge, Dick Canidy would break off the dogfight and fly out of sight of Bitter's aircraft. He would swoop down the Alabama River with his wheels ten feet off the water. That always served to disorient student pilots. Bitter, meanwhile, would go down on the deck, fifty feet above the pine treetops, and buzz The Lodge. He would then roll the Stearman, while flashing over The Lodge at no more than a hundred feet, straighten it out, and then shout over the speaking tube to his student: "You've got it. Take us to Mobile."

Out of sight of them Canidy would do much the same thing to his student, and they would each complete the fifty-mile flight to Mobile alone. Over coffee in the snack bar at Mobile, the students would be told the reasons for this exercise; then they would make the final, fifty-mile leg home to Pensacola.

Ed Bitter's student was usually the most disoriented. Not only were mock dogfights proscribed, but buzzing houses was NAS Pensacola's version of a mortal sin. Buzzing a three-story antebellum mansion sitting alone in the middle of twenty-five thousand uninhabited acres (with apparent disregard not only for life and limb, but for what would happen to him when the occupants—obviously rich and important—complained to the Navy) usually upset the student pilot to the point where he could be sarcastically reminded that when one is lost, and all else fails, one might consider having a look at the compass.

Everything went according to plan until it was time to buzz The Lodge.

Ed almost had the Stearman on its back when the engine quit.

In the time it took the sweep second hand on his aviator's chronometer to move two clicks, two seconds, his emotions shifted from near rapture to abject terror. It was one thing to have an engine quit in the middle of a roll when you had a couple of thousand feet under you to recover. You just fell through—and recovered.

He had no more than one hundred feet of air beneath him.

A body in motion tends to remain in motion. So there was sufficient momentum to just barely complete the roll. Now nearly disoriented himself, he looked hastily for someplace to put the Stearman on the deck. There was nothing in sight. He was, he realized, surprisingly calm, about to crash his airplane. There was nothing he could do but put it into the trees, and hope that the nose would not go into a tree trunk.

And then the engine spluttered and caught.

Sonofabitch was fuel-starved.

But there was full power again. He inched back on the stick and picked up a little altitude. He looked frantically around for The Plantation's airstrip, and saw it behind him. Fighting down the urge to make a steep banking turn toward it, he made a safer, slower, nearly level turn to line up with the runway. He had no idea of the wind. He was going in right now, no matter what it was.

When he got the wheels on the ground, he heard himself expel the air in his lungs.

Did I really hold my breath from the moment the god-damned engine quit until now?

He braked the Stearman, turned off the dirt runway, and stopped.

"Get out of there, Mr. Ford," he said to his student. He waited until Ensign Ford clambered out of the forward cockpit and onto the wing. Then he climbed out of the aft cockpit onto the ground, walked fifteen yards from the aircraft, unaware of the chilling effect the wind was having on his sweat-soaked flight suit. Without warning, he was sick to his stomach.

For a moment, he thought he was actually going to faint, but that passed, and he was then faced with shame and humiliation. Not only had he almost killed his student, but Mr. Ford was now standing there, looking at his IP's instantaneous change from near God to literally scared sick, nauseated, and nauseating human being.

Ed became aware of the peculiar roar a Continental R670 engine makes when it is throttled back. He looked up and saw Dick Canidy's plane about to land.

"What happened, sir?" Mr. Ford asked, having found his courage.

"The engine stopped, Mr. Ford," Ed Bitter said. "I would have thought you would have noticed."

He had put his student into his place with the sarcastic superiority expected of instructor pilots. Doing so shamed him.

Canidy landed, taxied up beside him, and shut down his engine.

"What happened?" he asked, and then he saw the sweat-soaked flight suit and repeated the question, this time with concern in his voice.

"The engine quit," Bitter said. "Just as I started the roll."

"Jesus!" Canidy said.

"I thought I was going into the trees," Bitter confessed. "But when I got it right side up, it cut in again."

"Fuel starvation," Canidy diagnosed confidently. He

walked to Bitter's Stearman and climbed on the wing. The main fuel tank of the Stearman was located in the center of the upper wing, with the fuel line running down the wing strut to the engine.

"Christ," Canidy called from the wing. "Fuel's pouring out of here. I'm surprised you didn't catch on fire."

Bitter forced himself to climb up on the wing. He saw for himself what had happened. The brass fitting attaching the fuel line to the fuel tank had either been improperly tightened or had vibrated loose since the last time someone had looked at it. In level flight, the suction of the manifold had been sufficient, aided by gravity, to provide fuel to the engine. And spillage had been instantly vaporized by the slipstream.

Inverted, however, that hadn't worked. Not enough gas had reached the engine to keep it running. And now, as Dick Canidy said, the fuel was really pouring out of the fuel tank.

"I don't suppose you have a wrench, do you?" Canidy asked. Bitter shook his head no.

"I can't tighten it very much with my fingers," Canidy said. "It'll really soak the fuselage."

"I'll walk up to The Lodge," Bitter said. "They're certain to have tools there."

"That *Gone With the Wind* mansion?" Canidy asked.

"Yeah," Bitter said. "And I'll call in and tell them what's happened."

Canidy jumped off the wing and called to the two student pilots. "Either of you guys got a wrench?" he asked. "We've got a loose fuel line connector. Or a pair of pliers?"

They shook their heads, and then remembered to reply militarily. "No, sir. Sorry, sir," they said, almost in unison.

"Stay away from the airplanes," Canidy ordered. "And no smoking. Mr. Bitter and I are going to find a wrench and a telephone. I can't imagine it happening out here in the boondocks, but keep anybody who shows up away from the airplanes.''

"I think it would be better if you stayed here, Dick," Bitter said.

Canidy looked at him a moment, then raised his eyebrows and smiled.

" 'Reserve officers,' " he began to quote, " 'serving on active duty, will exercise all the—' "

"Suit yourself," Bitter cut him off. "It's about a mile from here to The Lodge, if you insist on going."

"I wouldn't miss Tara for the world," Canidy said.

What he had begun to quote was the navy regulation that stated that reserve officers on active duty had equal rank with regular officers. He had graduated from MIT and been commissioned an ensign two days before Bitter had graduated from the Naval Academy. His automatic promotion to lieutenant, junior grade, after two years of satisfactory commissioned service had consequently come two days before Bitter's automatic promotion. Lieutenant (j.g.) Canidy outranked Lieutenant (j.g.) Bitter, and it was sometimes necessary to remind him of this, for Bitter had a tendency to give orders.

They had walked about half a mile when a Ford station wagon came down the road toward them. When it reached them, it stopped and a trim, attractive woman got out.

"Well, I'll be damned," she said. "Look who just dropped in out of the sky." She advanced on Ed Bitter, grabbed his arms, and gave him her cheek to kiss.

"Aunt Genevieve," he said. "May I introduce my roommate, Lieutenant Richard Canidy? Dick, this is my aunt, Mrs. Brandon Chambers."

"How do you do, Mrs. Chambers?" Canidy replied formally.

"Oh, call me Jenny," she said. "Eddie, and maybe his

father, are the only stuffed shirts in the family.''

"He would make me call him sir," Canidy replied. "But I outrank him."

"Oh, I'd like to be in a position to order him around," Genevieve Chambers said, laughing. "Now, what's this all about? I don't think it's a social call, dressed the way you are in those overlarge boys' rompers."

Canidy laughed. He liked this woman.

"I had a little engine trouble," Ed said. "I'm going to need some tools, and then the telephone."

"Hop in," Jenny Chambers said. "That's no problem. I've got Robert with me. Robert can fix anything with a coat hanger and a pair of pliers."

The house was even larger than it looked from the air.

"Is this where they made *Gone With the Wind?*" Canidy asked innocently.

"Of course," she said. "Clark Gable made us a deal on the house when they were finished with it. It comes apart for shipment."

Canidy was aware that he was getting another of Ed Bitter's looks of shocked disapproval. He smiled at Jenny Chambers.

"Actually, it's quite old," she said. "Antebellum. My husband's father restored it."

"It's gorgeous," Canidy said.

"It's a shame that no one lives in it," she said. "It's just a vacation place. My husband hunts from it, and the wives and children get to use it when there's no hunting."

Robert turned out to be a very large black man in a pin-stripe suit.

"Hello, sir," he said. "Was that you scaring hell out of the chickens?"

"How are you, Robert?" Ed Bitter replied.

"Robert," Jenny Chambers said, "this is Lieutenant Canidy. He's Eddie's friend, and his commanding officer. He can actually tell him what to do."

"Oh, I'd like to be you," Robert said. He shook Canidy's hand.

"Robert's been taking care of me, keeping me out of the clutches of evil, since I was a baby," Jenny Chambers said. Robert beamed with affection at her.

"I understand you might be able to come up with a wrench for us," Canidy said. "I'll settle for a pair of good pliers."

"They'll probably send a maintenance crew from Mobile," Bitter said.

"We should stop that gas from dripping all over the plane," Canidy replied. "I think it'll be all right to fly out of here."

"I got some tools in the car," Robert said.

"Why don't you get on the horn, Eddie, and call in and tell them what's happened. Don't tell them to send anybody till we have a chance to take a good look at it."

"Yes, sir, Mr. Canidy, sir," Bitter said. He gave Canidy a mock salute. But there was something not entirely joking about the exchange.

"And I'll see, in the meantime, what I can fix for you to eat. A sandwich, at least. Robert and I just came down this morning. I don't know what's here, but there should be enough for a sandwich," Jenny Chambers said.

The car was a 1939 Lincoln coupe with Alabama license plates. A very expensive car, in keeping, Canidy decided, with Tara. And Eddie was a member of the family. That was very interesting. It also explained a number of things about him, not only his Buick Roadmaster convertible.

The trunk of the Lincoln held a toolkit, with a set of open-end wrenches in individual compartments. Tightening the fuel line connection—even taking great care to make sure the wrench didn't slip and spark—took no more than a minute. Robert handed Canidy a rag, and he wiped the line down. There was no drip, and therefore no reason Eddie couldn't fly the Stearman.

Canidy was aware that he was disappointed. It might have been interesting to have been forced to spend the night here. There was a moment's rebirth of hope when he thought that the gasoline might have dripped into the fuselage, where it would have formed dangerously explosive vapors. But when he looked, he saw that it had fallen onto a solid piece of the aluminum, and from there down the solid aluminum wing root to the ground. Once an hour had passed to allow any chance vapors to disperse, the plane would be safe to fly.

Canidy ordered the student pilots into the Lincoln's backseat, and rode with Robert back to the mansion. Jenny Chambers had opened a tinned ham, and made sandwiches and tea.

"I'd love to offer you something stronger than tea," Jenny Chambers said, "but Eddie has told me that you can't drink and fly."

"Not very far, anyway," Canidy replied. "But I appreciate the spirit of your offer."

She laughed. "I like you, Lieutenant Canidy," she said. "And is it really true you can order Eddie around?"

"Yes, ma'am," Canidy said. "Is there anything you would like me to have him do for you?"

"Order him here for the weekend," she said. "All of you, of course."

"I don't . . .," Eddie began.

"Tell him to let me finish," Jenny Chambers said.

"Let the lady finish, Lieutenant," Canidy said.

"Or he'll clap you in irons," she said, and then she went on. "My daughter, who is in college, up north, Bryn Mawr, is coming here with two friends," she said. "So there would be people about your own age. And my husband used to be a pilot, and loves to talk flying. And then your cousin Mark is coming up from Mobile, Eddie, with his wife. You haven't seen them in years, either."

·"The girls are a little young for Dick, Aunt Genevieve," Ed Bitter said.

"Just the right age," she argued. "I'm five years younger than your uncle."

"And you're putting Dick on a spot, you realize."

"Not at all," Canidy said.

Dick Canidy suddenly got out of his chair and walked to a photograph sitting on a table just outside the dining room.

"Can I get you something, Dick?" Jenny Chambers asked.

"I thought this photograph looked familiar," he said. It was a picture of Sue-Ellen Chambers and her husband.

"And is it?"

"No," he said.

"That's my son, Mark," Jenny Chambers said. "And his wife, Sue-Ellen."

"You'll meet them this weekend," Ed Bitter said. "Since it has been decided we're going to come up here."

If he were a gentleman, Dick Canidy thought, he would say sorry, he'd already made plans for the weekend. But he said nothing. He wanted to see Sue-Ellen again.

Did this reveal, he wondered, yet another previously undetected dark and unpleasant facet of his character?

He took another look at Sue-Ellen Chambers's deceptively innocent face, and turned around.

"We'd better be going," he said.

3

On the half-hour flight from Mobile back to NAS Pensacola, Ed Bitter was unhappily aware that the engine trouble he had had at The Plantation by now had come to the attention of the brass, who were likely to find out that he had violated regulations by doing acrobatics under five thousand feet.

But it had not been a crash landing, so he felt sure he could get away with having the incident officially determined to be an "unscheduled, precautionary landing," rather than an "emergency landing." Unscheduled, precautionary landings occurred all the time, the precaution generally having to do with an airsick student, or a piss call for an instructor who had forgotten to take a leak before taking off.

So he would probably be officially off the hook. *Where* they landed was then going to be the real problem, since the students, Ford and Czernik, were likely to rush back to the student BOQ to regale their fellows with the fascinating tale of landing at a private airstrip, near a mansion that, no shit, belongs to Mr. Bitter's family.

So he would have to explain the situation to them, and ask them as a personal courtesy not to tell the story. He probably still couldn't keep it all completely quiet, but he probably could keep it from being a sensation. *If* he could talk to them about it the right way.

Fortunately, there was a ritual after this particular exercise, which would give him the opportunity to talk to the students. On the satisfactory completion of their last training flight in primary training, Ensign Paul Ford and Ensign Thomas Czernik had stopped being "Mr. Ford" and "Mr. Czernik" to their instructors and became fellow officers, who could be addressed by their first names and permitted to drink with the instructor pilots as social equals.

It was in a sense more of a rite of passage than either their first solo flight had been (about a fifth of all students who made their solo flight were subsequently busted out of primary for inaptitude) or the official awarding of wings in the parade on Friday would be.

"Dick," Ed Bitter suggested as the two instructors and the two students turned in their parachutes to Flight Equipment, "why don't you take Paul and Tom over to the club and buy them a couple of beers, until I can fill out my reports and get there?"

"I think you'd better lie about your altitude when the engine quit," Dick Canidy said. "We'll back you up, if they ask."

Czernik and Ford nodded willingness.

That was embarrassing. Officers were expected to be wholly truthful. But Canidy was right. Unless he lied, he was going to be in trouble.

"Thank you," he said barely audibly, and then forced himself to smile.

The officers' mess served a two-quart pitcher of draft beer for thirty-five cents. Canidy and the two students had just started on their second pitcher—enough beer to give Paul Ford courage to raise the question of what had happened to the Kaydet—when a Marine orderly appeared in the room. Canidy glanced up and then ignored him. He could think of no possible reason that a Marine orderly who ran errands for admirals would be interested in him.

But the orderly, after the bartender identified him, headed directly for Canidy's table.

"Mr. Canidy?" the orderly asked crisply.

"Yes," Canidy said.

"The admiral's compliments, sir," the orderly snapped. "The admiral regrets the intrusion. The admiral will be pleased to receive Mr. Canidy at Mr. Canidy's convenience.''

"You sure you have the right Canidy, son?" Canidy asked.

"The admiral's car and driver are outside, if Mr. Canidy would care to make use of them to make his call upon the admiral, sir."

Canidy was wholly confused. He had seen the admiral (there were several flag officers at Pensacola, but only one "the admiral," the base commander) only twice in his life, once when his aviator's wings were pinned on him, and once again when the admiral had given the new draft of instructor pilots a five-minute ritual pep talk before they had begun their training.

He could think of nothing he had done, good or bad, to merit the admiral's attention. Lieutenant junior grade instructor pilots in primary training came to the admiral's attention only when they killed a student, or vice versa.

He stood up and looked down at Ford and Czernik.

"Gentlemen," he said, mockingly solemn, "you will have to excuse me. The admiral requests my professional judgment on a subject of vital importance to the Navy, and, indeed, the nation!"

Ford and Czernik smiled. Bitter looked at the Marine orderly. The Marine orderly was not amused. He marched out of the beer bar, and Canidy followed him out to the admiral's car, a two-year-old Chrysler driven by a natty young sailor who held the door open for Canidy and then closed it after him.

Canidy decided the whole thing was going to turn out to be a hilarious case of mistaken identity. There was probably a *Commander* Canidy on the base somewhere, or maybe even a *Captain* Canidy (who probably spelled his name Kennedy), and the admiral had asked for him with his false teeth out, and the aide had misunderstood him.

The car drove under the portico of the admiral's residence and stopped. The Marine orderly leaped out of the front seat and raced around the front of the car to open the door for Canidy.

I wonder, Canidy thought, *if after they find out they have the wrong guy, I'll have to walk back to the O Club.*

The admiral's aide-de-camp, a full lieutenant, opened a side door to the residence.

"Canidy?" he asked.

"Yes, sir," Dick replied.

"You would have been here somewhat sooner, Mr. Canidy," the aide said, "if I thought to tell the orderly to try the beer hall first." He waved Canidy ahead of him into the kitchen, where a white-jacketed Filipino steward was tending an array of bottles.

The admiral's aide stepped around Canidy and pushed open a swinging door to the dining room.

"Mr. Canidy, Admiral," he announced.

"Come on in, Canidy," a gruff voice ordered.

There were two ruddy-skinned, gray-haired men sitting at a long, brightly polished dining-room table. A large candelabrum had been pushed aside to make room for some manila folders (obviously service records), lined pads, a telephone, and two ashtrays. There was a cigar box and coaster, on which sat glasses dark with whiskey.

Both the middle-aged men were wearing insignialess khaki shirts and trousers, and it was a moment before Canidy was sure which of them was the admiral.

"Lieutenant Canidy reports to the admiral as directed, sir," Canidy said.

"I have one official thing to say to you, Mr. Canidy," the admiral said, looking at him with unabashed curiosity. "What you see in this room, what you hear in this room, you will not relate to anyone, in or out of the service, without my express permission. You got that?''

''Yes, sir.''

So it wasn't a case of mistaken identity. He was expected and something very unusual was about to happen. This was, obviously, one of the wild days Canidy had infrequently experienced in his life. For months, or sometimes years, everything went according to some dull plan, and then, all of a sudden, strange, unexpected, and exciting things happened, one after the other.

This insane day had begun with Eddie goddamned near killing himself; and then he had learned, in a Southern plantation mansion, that Sue-Ellen Chambers was Eddie's cousin's wife; and now he was in the admiral's dining room.

The admiral looked at him from rather cold gray eyes for a long moment, and then he raised his voice.

''Pedro!''

The Filipino steward pushed open the swinging door.

''Tell Pedro what you'll have to drink, Canidy,'' the admiral said. ''And then sit down. Close. This old birdman is as deaf as a post.''

''Fuck you, Charley,'' the other gray-haired man said, smiling, and without rancor.

''Sair?'' the steward asked, wanting Canidy's drink order.

''Bourbon, please,'' Canidy said. ''Over ice.''

''Yes, sair,'' the steward said. The admiral held up his glass and looked at the other man, who nodded.

The steward ducked back into the kitchen.

''Canidy, this is General Chennault,'' the admiral said. ''Of the Chinese Air Force.''

That didn't surprise Canidy either. Then he remembered who Chennault was. He was a former Army Air Corps pursuit pilot, one of the old-timers, who had gone to China to help the Chinese in their war with the Japanese.

"For the way you emphasized 'Chinese,' " General Chennault said, "fuck you again, Charley."

"As you may have guessed, Canidy," the admiral said, "General Chennault and I go back a long way together. But this isn't a social call. General Chennault is here with the express permission of the Commander in Chief."

"Yes, sir," Canidy said, because he could think of nothing else to say. It took him a moment to realize that the admiral was speaking of *the* Commander in Chief, not the commander in chief of naval aviation training, or even the chief of naval aviation training, or even the chief of naval operations. He was speaking of the President of the United States.

"Aren't you just a little curious, Lieutenant?" General Chennault asked.

"Yes, sir, I'm curious," Canidy said. "But I'm also a junior grade lieutenant."

Chennault chuckled. "Before they retired me from the Air Corps," he said, "I was a captain. Before I was a captain, I was a first lieutenant. I was a first lieutenant, your grade, for fourteen *long* years."

The steward delivered three glasses, just about full of bourbon over ice.

"Don't you think we're about to get in a war, Canidy?" the admiral asked suddenly.

"I hope not, sir," he said. The question made him uncomfortable.

"Yes or no?" the admiral asked impatiently.

"I don't see how we can avoid it, sir," Canidy said. The admiral snorted.

"How would you like to get into it early, Canidy?" General Chennault asked.

"I'd rather not get into it at all, sir," Canidy replied, after a moment's hesitation. He had decided that this was one of those occasions when he would say what he was thinking, rather than what he was expected to say.

"I'm surprised," Chennault said. "The admiral told me you've been flying the new Grumman."

"Yes, sir."

"All that power scare you?" Chennault asked.

"No, sir," Canidy replied. "The airplane's first-rate. But nobody was shooting at me."

The two leathery-faced old pilots looked at each other, and then General Chennault looked into Canidy's eyes. "What do you want out of the service, Canidy?" he asked softly.

"I'm afraid my answer would sound flippant, sir," Canidy said.

"Out, you mean? What you want out of the service is yourself?"

"Yes, sir."

"And then what?"

"I'm an aeronautical engineer, sir. I've been offered a job by Boeing."

"They'll have you designing ashtrays for transports," the admiral said, smiling, but meaning it. "You won't be flying."

"They've offered me a job in high-speed airfoil design, sir," Canidy said, unable to let it pass.

"What do you know about high-speed airfoil design?" the admiral asked disparagingly.

"That's my specialty, sir," Canidy said.

"You're one hell of a fighter pilot, according to your records," Chennault said, ending the sparring. "They didn't let you fly the F4F-3 because they liked you or because they thought you were a wing expert."

"General Chennault is a highly qualified judge of fighter

pilots, Canidy," the admiral said, offering an olive branch. "That's a hell of a compliment from him."

"I've read the general's book, sir," Canidy said.

"On your own? Or because it was suggested to you?" Chennault asked.

"I was ordered to read it, sir," Canidy said.

"I want your honest opinion of *The Role of Pursuit Aviation*," the admiral said.

"Theoretically, it sounds fine," Canidy said.

"Just 'theoretically'?" the admiral asked.

"It's never been put to the test of actual combat, sir," Canidy said.

"And if it was?" Chennault asked.

"I'm not in a position to judge, sir," Canidy said.

"But you have, haven't you?" Chennault said. "Speak up, Canidy. Where did I go wrong?"

Chennault's book was a treatise on the interception and pursuit of enemy bombardment aircraft. Canidy had given it a lot of thought.

"I wondered about armament and armor, sir," he said.

Chennault made a "come on" signal with his hand.

"The larger bombers get, the greater their weight-carrying capacity," Canidy said. "Which means they can armor their engines and fuel tanks, and carry more and larger-caliber weaponry, and some armor. And that obviously means a decrease in their speed and maneuverability and range. So long as the enemy doesn't have really large airplanes . . . like the Boeing B-17 . . . it won't be a problem. But if they do . . ."

Chennault was impressed with Canidy's analysis of his theory. He had himself seen the problems Canidy had spotted. But he did not like to hear them from a young man still damp behind the ears.

"How would you like to go into combat as a pursuit pilot,

in, say, sixty days?'' Chennault asked abruptly.

Canidy felt the skin at the base of his neck curl. The question was asked in dead seriousness.

''I don't think I'd like that at all, sir,'' he said.

''Christ, when I was your age . . .'' the admiral said.

''Within a year, give or take a couple of months, we're going to be at war,'' General Chennault said. ''If you believe that we're not, you believe in the tooth fairy. You also believe in the tooth fairy if you think the Navy is going to release a healthy, highly skilled pursuit pilot with demonstrated qualities of leadership just before the war starts.''

Well, Canidy thought, *there it is, right out in the open. Two unpleasant facts that I have been unwilling to face.*

''I'm very much afraid that you're right, sir,'' Canidy said.

''Of course I'm right,'' Chennault snorted.

''What is the general proposing, sir?'' Canidy asked.

''I'm offering you a one-year contract, Canidy, on behalf of the Central Aircraft Manufacturing Company, Federal, Inc., to go to China and participate in the construction, maintenance, and development of civilian aircraft for the Chinese Air Transport Ministry.''

''I'm in the Navy, General.''

Ignoring him, Chennault went on. ''What you'll be doing is flying Curtiss P40-Bs against the Japanese. The pay— your pay, I'm offering you a job as a wingman—is six hundred dollars a month, plus rations and quarters and a bonus of five hundred dollars for every aircraft you down.''

That was nearly twice what he was paid by the Navy. And, of course, there were no five-hundred-dollar bonuses for primary flight instructor pilots.

''At the conclusion of your contract year,'' Chennault went on, ''you will be taken back into the Navy with no loss of time in grade. If you get promoted flying for us, you will receive a similar promotion in the Navy."

"I would be discharged from the Navy?" Canidy asked. "Not just released from active duty, subject to recall?"

"Discharged," Chennault said. "You would leave the United States as a civilian."

"And if I didn't come back in the Navy?"

"You are a gutsy bastard, aren't you?" Chennault asked admiringly. "Saying that in front of the admiral." He paused. "You do your year, and if I'm wrong, and there is no war, I'll guarantee you can come home and go to work for Boeing. You could probably get more money as an engineer in China, come to think of it. But if the United States gets in the war, and I think it will, you'll have to make your own arrangements with the draft board."

"And if I don't want to go to China?"

"Then you go back to your BOQ and forget you ever met me," Chennault said. "You won't be able to do that, of course. You'll remember this little encounter, no matter what you decide, for the rest of your life."

"When would I have to go?"

"Sometime in the next thirty days," Chennault said.

"How many others are being asked?"

"In the first group, a hundred pilots. We have a hundred P40-Bs en route to China."

"Why P40-Bs?"

Chennault paused before replying. "Because our noble English cousins don't want them. They consider them obsolete," he said. "OK?"

"I've never flown a P40," Canidy said.

"No one has, the first time," Chennault said dryly.

"May I ask why I'm being asked? I don't have all that much experience."

"All we have to go on is records, Mr. Canidy," the admiral said. "Yours are outstanding."

"One year. And when that's over, I'm out. Is that the proposition?"

"That's the deal," Chennault said. "I won't muddy the waters with any talk of duty, honor, country."

"And how much time do I have to make up my mind?"

"Take whatever it takes," Chennault said. "Two, three minutes."

Canidy had a sense of being caught in something he had no control over. He thought of the cliché "swimming against the stream," and he thought that he really was being recruited for this because of the performance he'd turned in in advanced training. He held the training command record for most holes in a towed target, and he had shot down (according to the motion-picture cameras mounted on the Grumman F3F-1 where the .30-caliber Browning machine gun was normally mounted) all four of the advanced fighter training instructors they'd matched him against, one after the other.

It was also, he thought, equally possible that he was being asked to go to China because he had been judged expendable by his Navy superiors. If that was true, that the Navy felt they could do without him, that could really be dangerous when the war started. Fliers the Navy felt it could do without would be the ones sent on missions where severe losses were to be expected.

"Shit," Canidy said, the word coming without his intending it to. He was aware that both the admiral and General Chennault were looking at him with distaste.

"I'll go," he hastily added.

"OK," Chennault said. He stood up and offered Canidy his hand.

4

When the admiral's Buick took Dick Canidy back to the officers' club, Ford and Czernik were gone. He thought that he hadn't been gone all that long, despite all that had happened, and that Bitter might still be trying to explain why he had made the unscheduled landing. He went to the bar and ordered a pitcher of beer. He would wait for him.

Bitter didn't show up for two hours. By then, Canidy had decided that "Salty Sam, the Perfect Sailor" had come back to the beer bar while he had been with the admiral, bought the two students the ritual pitcher of beer, and then gone to the BOQ. Salty Sam really hated to drink even a glass of beer during the week, even if he was not scheduled to fly the next day.

He was genuinely surprised when Ed Bitter, in a dress white uniform, slipped onto the bar stool beside him.

"I'd given you up for lost," Canidy said. Something was bothering Bitter. He wondered if Bitter had been struck with a sudden case of officer's honor and confessed his sins to the squadron commander.

"I wasn't sure you would still be here," Bitter said.

"I said I would be," Canidy said.

The bartender, a moonlighting whitecap, came up. "What can I get you, Mr. Bitter?"

The question, Canidy thought, was one Bitter was not prepared to immediately answer. The skipper had obviously chewed his ass.

Indicating Canidy's glass, Bitter asked, "What's that?"

"Bourbon," Canidy said.

"Give us two of the same," Bitter said to the bartender.

"Hard likker? The next thing you know, you'll be out wenching!"

Bitter looked at him uncomfortably for a moment, and

then opened the catch of the high-collared blouse before replying. "I suppose it's a delayed reaction to what happened this afternoon."

"I suppose," Canidy said. "Well, hell, it's over. Or did something happen when you reported to the skipper? That is why you're all dressed up?"

That innocent question produced another strange look.

"No. I mean to say, he accepted my explanation that it was nothing more than an unscheduled, precautionary landing."

"Lying is like fucking, Eddie," Canidy said. "The first time is sometimes difficult, but after a while you get used to it."

The drinks were served. Canidy downed his and reached for the fresh one.

"Have you ever thought of selling your Ford?" Bitter asked.

"What brought that up?" Canidy asked.

"Well," Bitter said, uncomfortable, "when I saw the skipper, he told me I'm being considered for a temporary duty assignment at NAS Anacostia."

"And?"

"I thought I'd sell my car before I went," Bitter said. "And if you sold your Ford, and needed a car, I could make you a good price."

"What are you going to do at NAS Anacostia?" Canidy asked innocently.

"I . . . uh . . . really haven't been told," Bitter said.

"Christ, I hope you were more convincing, not that it really matters, when you lied to the skipper about your altitude when your engine quit," Canidy said.

"What do you mean?" Bitter demanded sharply.

Canidy put his fingers to his temples. "Confucius say," he said, " 'Every man fly P40-B once for first time.' "

Bitter was genuinely surprised that Canidy knew.

"Keep your voice down. Someone is liable to hear you."

"I've got bad news for you, Eddie," Canidy said.

"What's that?"

"That since I signed on about an hour before you did, I'm going to outrank you in the Chinese Air and Rickshaw Service, too."

THREE

There was a little slop time written into the primary training program, slack time between the cross-country flight and the graduation ceremony on the last Friday of the training period when the students would get their wings. Things went wrong. Bad weather could delay training flights; students or instructors could become ill. But if everything went according to schedule, there were anywhere from three to four days with nothing for instructor pilots to do.

IPs would check in at 0730 with the primary flight skipper, and he would then tell them to take off. That meant spending the day playing golf, or lying on the incredibly white beaches of the Gulf of Mexico, or just hanging around the BOQ.

Ed Bitter and Dick Canidy reported for duty the day after their meeting with General Chennault fully expecting to be told by the skipper to take off. But that didn't happen.

"Don't ask me what it's all about," the skipper told them, "because I don't know. All I know is that your services are required by the admiral for the rest of the week. You're to call his aide.''

He handed them a name and a telephone number scrawled on a sheet of notepaper.

They called the aide, and he told them to meet him at hangar six, across the field from primary training. When they got there, he was standing outside the hangar office. He walked them away from the hangar, onto the line of aircraft parked off the taxiway, until he stopped in the shadow of a transient aircraft, a Douglas TBD-1. It carried the numbers VT-8, the only shore-based squadron of the six TBD-1–equipped torpedo bomber squadrons in the Navy.

"Either one of you got any time in one of these?'' he asked, seemingly idly.

Both shook their heads. The aide shrugged and handed Canidy a thin sheaf of mimeographed orders. Bitter read over Canidy's shoulder: Lieutenants (j.g.) Bitter and Canidy were ordered by NAS Pensacola to make training flights in TBD-1 aircraft between points within the continental limits of the United States during the fourteen-day period commencing 8 June 1941.

"I don't know how to fly one of these,'' Canidy said.

"I'll walk you through it,'' the aide said, "and take you around the pattern once or twice.'' He had planned to tell them nothing more, but when he saw their confusion, he felt sorry for them.

"You didn't get this from me, understand?'' he said, and when they nodded their agreement, he went on. "General Chennault is trying to get fifty, or maybe the entire hundred of them in the Navy, for his Chinese. For your volunteer group. The admiral doesn't think the Navy will turn them loose. But it might, and if it happens, there should be somebody over where you two are going who knows how to fly them. Understand? Once an IP, always an IP.''

"What are we supposed to do, shoot touch-and-goes?" Canidy asked. "So people can see us, and ask what are two primary IPs doing shooting touch-and-goes with a torpedo bomber?"

"Do whatever you want with it," the aide said. "As long as you don't do it here. With the orders I just gave you, you can get fuel and whatever else you need at any military air base in the country. What you're supposed to do is get time in the airplane. How you do that—as long as you do it away from here, and are back for the graduation parade—is up to you."

The TBD-1, called the Devastator, was an old-timer, first flown in 1935. It had a nine-hundred-horsepower Twin Wasp radial engine and was primarily designed to launch torpedoes at enemy shipping. It carried a crew of three: a pilot; a torpedo officer/bomb aimer, usually an aviator; and an enlisted man, a tail gunner, who was known as an airdale. The torpedo officer/bomb aimer performed his function on his stomach under the pilot's seat, looking out through two windows in the bottom of the fuselage. The aircraft could carry one torpedo in a rack under the fuselage, or twelve one-hundred-pound bombs, six under each wing.

Normally, when pilots transitioned into a new aircraft, there was at least a week's ground-school training. This was then followed by an orientation flight, during which an IP gradually and carefully permitted the student to take over the airplane.

Two hours after Canidy and Bitter met the admiral's aide at hangar six, he certified them as qualified to fly the Devastator.

"Sir," Canidy asked, "please correct me if I'm wrong, but the way I read our orders, we are permitted to go any-place we want to. We could head for San Diego if we wanted to, is that right?"

"That's right," the admiral's aide said. "I thought I made that clear."

"Yes, sir," Canidy said. "Thank you, sir."

2
Cedar Rapids, Iowa
June 10, 1941

Canidy drove his Ford convertible straight through from Florida, stopping only to catnap by the side of the road. Ed Bitter was somewhat reluctantly flying the Devastator to Cedar Rapids himself. He wanted to see his father and had to get rid of his car, Canidy had argued, so driving his car home and selling it there seemed like a good idea. So far as their getting time in the Devastator was concerned, he would fly it back from Iowa.

"And what am I supposed to do with my car?" Bitter had protested.

"You really want a suggestion, Eddie?"

"Why don't I drive my car to Chicago, and you pick me up there?"

"We can make another trip if you like," Canidy said. "But it would make more sense to leave your car here and then turn it over to The Plantation."

"Why do I feel I am somehow being screwed?"

"After you really screw somebody one day, you'll be able to tell the difference," Canidy said. "In the meantime, don't rock the boat."

Canidy arrived in Cedar Rapids just after five in the morning and was afraid that he would disturb his father. But when he got to the campus, there was a light on in the apartment's tiny kitchen. His father was awake, shaved, and dressed, except for the tweed jacket he wore over his clerical dickey.

They shook hands. His father's hand felt soft and gentle in his. Gentle and old.

The Reverend George Crater Canidy, D.D., Ph.D., headmaster of St. Paul's School, long widowed, lived in a small apartment in the dormitory between the chapel and the Language Building, where he had his office. It was inconceivable that he would live off campus. For in a very real sense, the Rev. Dr. Canidy and St. Paul's School were one and indivisible.

Canidy told his father that he was being released from the Navy to go to China and work in the fledgling Chinese aircraft industry. With his engineering degree, that was credible. He did not want to tell his father that he had been given a job where bonuses were paid for the number of people killed.

The Reverend Dr. Canidy was pleased. He quickly concluded that his son was going to China as a practical missionary, to bring to its downtrodden masses the God-given miracles of Western technology. It wasn't quite the same thing as his son going to spread the gospel of the Lord Jesus Christ, but it was far better than his being a sailor in the Navy.

It would do no harm to let his father believe that, Canidy decided.

As always, as the morning wore on, the feeling came to Canidy that rather than coming "home," he was visiting a school he had long ago attended. Though there was a photograph of his mother on the table beside his father's chair in the living room, it produced no emotional response. He didn't really remember her. But of course, he corrected himself, he did. What he remembered was the horrible smell in the hospital room where she had taken so long to die.

His mind had mostly shut that out, he thought, and in doing so had erased everything, including the good memories. There must have been good times. It was just that he couldn't remember her. It wasn't until he saw him—touched his hands—that he remembered what a good man, what a good friend, his father was, and again became aware of the depth of his feeling for him.

He was also aware that he had to be sort of a disappointment to his father, although his father of course didn't show it. His father would have been most happy had his son followed in his footsteps, if not as a priest, then as an academic.

But Canidy's scholastic prowess was not the result of a love for scholarly things. He wanted to fly, and the price of that was academic success. He could not hang around Cedar Rapids airport, his father told him, while his grades were bad. The payment for his Saturday flying lessons was staying on the headmaster's list. He had simply raised his grades and kept them at a commendable level by paying attention to what was asked of him. His father's proud belief to the contrary, he had never really had to "put his nose to the grindstone and keep it there" nor had he ever demonstrated "remarkable self-discipline."

Canidy often wondered if a son's duty to his father included doing what the father, who was presumably the wiser, wanted him to do with his life. If that was the case, he was the undutiful son. He wanted neither to mold the characters of young men, which his father had once told him he considered the highest of privileges, nor to care for other people's souls.

The Reverend Dr. Canidy did not press the point when his son declined the opportunity to go to morning prayer. Canidy was almost immediately sorry, but by then his father had gone, and the smart thing to do was take a nap. His old room smelled musty.

He woke at lunchtime, nervous and hungry. He didn't want to go to the dining room and have the boys gape at him, so he drove the Ford into Cedar Rapids and had lunch in a restaurant, then drove around town until it was time to go to the airport and wait for Bitter and the Devastator to appear.

Eddie Bitter was very respectful of the Reverend Dr. Canidy when they met, and perfectly willing to put on his white uniform and give a little talk about the Naval Academy and naval aviation to the boys of St. Paul's at the evening meal.

After the evening meal, a dozen boys came to his father's apartment to hear more about the life of a midshipman at Annapolis and of a naval aviator. While Ed entertained the boys, Canidy and his father retired to the comfortable leather chairs of the library.

"Eric Fulmar sent me a lovely New Testament in Aramaic the other day," Dr. Canidy said.

"Eric Fulmar? My God! Where—and how—is he these days?"

"He's in Morocco," Dr. Canidy said.

"Morocco? What's he doing in Morocco?"

"Staying out of the war, or so he says. He tells me he's living with friends there. And his father's German, you know. They consider Eric a German, too. So he could be drafted."

"If I know Eric, he's up to more than hanging around with friends," Canidy said, laughing softly.

Eric Fulmar was always up to something. Fulmar had gotten the two of them into trouble more times than he'd care to remember. When Canidy had moved into the lower school at St. Paul's after his mother's death, he and Eric had become fast friends. Like gasoline and a match, his father said—obviously useful, but explosive when put together without adequate supervision.

Eric's mother was Monica Carlisle, the movie star who—happily for her career and income—looked considerably younger than her actual years. Her studio didn't want it known that Monica, instead of the virginal coed she regularly portrayed on the screen, was the mother of a son to whom (if her studio biography was to be believed) she had given birth at age seven.

The only time Monica Carlisle had made her presence felt in her son's life was to get him out of trouble. Canidy grinned to himself, remembering, while his father expounded on the finer points of the Aramaic Bible. One incident in particular stood out among all the scrapes he and Eric had gotten into.

Toy pistols were forbidden on campus, but they were readily available from Woolworth's five-and-ten for twenty-nine cents. And wooden matches were easily obtained from the school's kitchen. The matches, when shot from the pistols, ignited upon contact.

This was a great discovery, but what was more exciting was the potential of the white powder on the head of the match—removed from the wooden stick and piled in quantities, this stuff did great things. And later, even under the most severe of interrogations, Canidy and Fulmar steadfastly denied any knowledge of the rash of small, foul-smelling explosions that ruined the locks of the dormitory doors and terrorized the school for a week.

Then they were caught, literally with smoking guns, for a number of crimes all at once.

The day of the annual fall nature walk for the lower school, led by the biology instructor, seemed like the perfect time to test out some hypotheses concerning their tin guns and match heads. There were lots of tempting leaf piles along the street that led to the woods. First Canidy spoke earnestly with the teacher about chlorophyll while Eric, at the rear of the procession, gleefully let fly both guns. Canidy grinned as he remembered the small tussle they'd had when Eric hadn't shown up at the appointed time to take his turn discussing things with the teacher. So Eric got all the leaf piles on the street, and Canidy didn't get his turn until they reached the woods.

His first four were sadly disappointing. But the fifth was a beauty. There was a sharp crack, followed a moment later by a vulgar obscenity from the biology teacher.

"Shit!" he howled. "Jesus Christ, I've been shot!"

He dropped to the ground, pulling up his trouser legs. Blood oozed from a dime-size wound in his calf.

"Fulmar did it!" one of the boys announced righteously. "He's got the gun!"

A nearby teacher instinctively scooped up Fulmar by the collar of his jacket, considered for a moment what to do about Canidy, then grabbed him by the collar and marched the both of them back to the stricken biology instructor. Just then a deep, low, roaring boom reverberated from the street. Fulmar's work in the fall leaves had reached the gas tank of a Studebaker President four-door sedan.

The fire department, three police cars, and an ambulance rushed to the scene. In addition to the Studebaker, leaf piles for three blocks were on fire. The police knew a bullet wound when they saw one, and since the kid obviously hadn't done it with his toy pistol, that meant there was some kind of nut out there with a .22 shooting at people. Hands on their revolvers, they fanned out looking for him.

The Reverend Dr. Canidy's high reputation and considerable influence within Cedar Rapids did not keep Eric and Dick out of the Cedar Rapids Children's Home, at least not for two days. The picture in the paper showed the two boys being collared by the police.

This picture, more than anything else, brought in Monica

Carlisle's young lawyer, Stanley Fine. Fine bought a new Studebaker President in exchange for an agreement not to press charges. In court, he argued for the Reverend Dr. Canidy's exemplary reputation for dealing with boys, and the presiding judge of the juvenile court turned the malefactors over to the Reverend for rehabilitation. The real rehabilitation was administered by the physical-education instructor, who used a wide leather belt, which stung like hell and left red welts, but which did no real damage. Fine returned to Hollywood, leaving behind him two shiny silver dollars that were immediately traded in at Woolworth's for two more tin guns.

The question of expelling Eric came up, but it was dismissed. The two kids were in their last year at St. Paul's Lower School. In the fall, Canidy would be sent to St. Mark's School in Southboro, Mass., and Dr. Canidy recommended to Monica Carlisle that a military school might be perfect for her son's high-school education. The two friends believed they would never see each other again after they graduated from St. Paul's.

But when Canidy arrived in Southboro, Fulmar was waiting for him. And grinning.

"It took two full weeks of tantrums," he announced, doing a little joyful jig. His just-a-little-too-long blond hair kept flopping over his eyes, but he was too happy to notice. "But they finally caved in. What is this place, anyway? You know how hard it was to get me in here?"

They had not quite two years together at St. Mark's; then Fulmar was sent to stay with his father in Europe, where he was to continue his education.

They exchanged the usual letters for a while, but eventually stopped. Still, in Canidy's mind, Eric Fulmar was one hell of a guy.

Canidy focused his attention back on his father in time to

catch the tail end of his discourse on the Bible.

"It is a lovely book, Dad. When you write to Eric again, make sure you tell him I said hello."

"I've kept him abreast of your activities," his father said. "He's asked about you."

"Well, tell him I said hello," Canidy repeated. He was not actually surprised that Fulmar had succeeded in ducking the German draft. If nothing else, Fulmar was resourceful. Even as a little boy, he had had to learn to take care of himself, for with the exceptions of the Reverend Dr. Canidy and the lawyer, Stanley Fine, who had gotten them out of the arson episode, no adult had ever really given a damn about him.

In the morning, the Reverend Dr. Canidy drove them to the airfield in Dick's car.

He insisted on offering a prayer for their safe journey, and they stood for a moment with their heads bowed beside the Devastator.

As he looked up at his father after the prayer, Canidy was surprised that his eyes were watering and his throat was constricted.

3

The parade for the graduating pilots was held at 0930 Friday morning. The prescribed uniform for the staff (the IPs) was dress whites, with swords and medals. Neither Canidy nor Bitter had any medals yet, but the brass, particularly the older brass, had rows of them. From the World War, Canidy thought. The *last* World War.

The swords were absurd. No naval officer had ever used a sword in the last war, and now they were getting ready for another war, and they still wore them. He was amused that he would be taking the sword (because he had forgotten to pack it with the things he had taken to Cedar Rapids and didn't know what else to do with it) to China.

The parade was over at 1100 hours. They put their swords in the trunk of Bitter's Buick, where they had previously packed overnight bags, and left the base in their dress whites. They took off their uniform caps as soon as they were out of Pensacola, put the roof down, and headed toward Mobile.

They crossed the causeway at the upper end of Mobile Bay, and as they approached Mobile, they came to the Mobile Shipbuilding and Drydock Company. A dozen ships—cargo ships, tankers, and what looked like the hull of a light cruiser—were on the ways in various stages of construction.

"My cousin Mark works there," Bitter said. "He'll be at The Plantation. He's the assistant superintendent of construction."

That was not how Chesty Whittaker had described Mark Chambers's role at the shipyard. Chesty said he owned it.

"I'm impressed," Canidy replied.

He feared again that he was opening some Pandora's box by going where Sue-Ellen was.

But then he decided to hell with it. What he would do would be the perfect gentleman, faithfully pretending that he had never seen her before. If that made her a little uncomfortable, that was probably an appropriate punishment for a married woman who went around screwing strange sailors.

4

The deeper the Crescent moved into the Deep South, the more convinced Sarah Child felt that the trip was a mistake.

Sarah was slight, with dark eyes, light complexion, and black hair; she was nineteen years old, a Bryn Mawr sophomore, and a New Yorker. Her father, a banker, was the grandson of a banker who had been sent from Frankfurt am Main to open a New York branch. The grandfather and his son, and Sarah's father, had been more successful in the New World than anyone in Frankfurt had dreamed. Frankfurt was thus now considered one of several overseas branches of the New York bank.

Her best friends at Bryn Mawr, Ann Chambers and Charity Hoche, were what Sarah thought of as "healthy" (that is, taller, heavier, and larger-bosomed), blond, fair-skinned, Southerners and Protestant Christian.

Bryn Mawr was one thing, and entertaining the girls at the Child apartment on East Sixty-fourth Street and Park Avenue in Manhattan was one thing, but coming south with them to a "plantation" was another.

Sarah could not put her finger on precisely why she was scared and uncomfortable, but that didn't change anything. Partly, she knew, it was because her mother (a woman with what was called—to be nice—a nervous condition) was opposed to her coming down here, and partly it was because Sarah hadn't really had much experience with these kinds of people. Her first night at Bryn Mawr had been the first time she had been separated from her parents overnight. And then later Ann and Charity had become the first friends she'd ever made who weren't Jews.

They got off the Crescent in Montgomery, Alabama ("Heart of Dixie," a sign proclaimed. "See the first capital of the Confederate States of America"), at 5:20 P.M. on Thursday. An enormous, very black man named Robert met them with Ann Chambers's mother's Lincoln. Ten minutes later, they were driving out of town down a narrow, winding macadam road at seventy-five miles an hour into a seemingly endless forest of pine trees. An hour and a half later, the Lincoln stopped before the white columns of a huge house.

The Chamberses had held dinner for them, and they'd eaten—off fine china, with ancient silver, served by servants in aprons—in a huge dining room under the portrait of a man in a Confederate colonel's uniform.

Afterward, they sat on rocking chairs on the veranda of the mansion while hordes of noisy insects battered themselves against a hanging light.

Ann's mother announced there were some boys coming down from the university with Ann's brother Charley tomorrow afternoon.

"And your cousin Eddie, Ann," Jenny Chambers told her daughter. "He and his friend from the Navy will be here for the weekend."

She went on to say that Ann's older brother and his wife would also be coming up from Mobile. Sarah knew perfectly well what that meant. There would be two simultaneous parties at The Plantation. One for "the young people," she, Charity, Ann, and the young men being imported for them by Charley Chambers, who was twenty-one and an Alabama senior. And a second party for everybody else—everybody who'd be older and more interesting.

At half past ten, Sarah went to her room. It was furnished with antiques, another oil portrait of a Confederate officer, and a bed with a canopy.

It was so quiet that Sarah took a long time to go to sleep.

The next morning, an enormous breakfast was served in what they called the morning room. There were three kinds of eggs, and biscuits, and ham, and bacon, and sausage.

Afterward, the girls put on bathing suits. Ann and Charity wanted to take advantage of what they called *real* sun.

By noon, Sarah knew that she had had enough sun. She

tanned too easily, even under the shade of an umbrella. So after lunch, when the girls went back to poolside, she went instead into the library and looked around until she found something with pictures: Hincker's *Illustrated Chronicle of the Army of Northern Virginia,* an old, huge volume of etchings of the Civil War. She fell asleep with it on her lap.

She woke to the sound of an automobile horn tooting "Shave and a Haircut, Two Bits" and looked out the French windows to the drive in front of the house.

A shiny Buick convertible, with roof down and red leather upholstery, was pulling up. Two good-looking men were in it, wearing white uniforms that seemed very bright in the sunlight. And, she noticed, gold aviator's wings were pinned to their breasts. The driver got out, reached into the backseat, and picked up a white uniform cap. Sun glinted off the insignia and gold strap. Then he walked around the front of the Buick and came up onto the veranda, moving with muscular grace. She was disappointed when he disappeared.

He was the best-looking young man she had ever seen. He must be Ann's cousin, she thought, or Ann's cousin's friend.

Then the door to the library opened, and there he was.

"Hello," he said. He smiled. He had beautiful teeth. "I'm Ed Bitter. Where is everybody?"

Sarah felt naked in her bathing suit. Naked, she thought, but not ashamed, even when she saw him looking at her legs and chest.

Ann's mother appeared, then Robert and one of the maids.

"We were all upstairs, trying to bed down the army . . . or should I say, the Navy . . . we're going to have," Jenny Chambers said, giving Ed Bitter her cheek to kiss. She saw Sarah. "I see you've met Sarah. Sarah, this is Edwin Bitter, my sister's son."

"How do you do?" Ed Bitter said. The flicker of interest in his eyes died . . . she'd become only a friend of Ann's—which is to say, a kid.

"Go out by the pool," Jenny Chambers said, "and I'll send some beer out, and I'll sort out who's going to sleep where. Sarah, take him out and introduce him to Charity, will you?"

"Yes, ma'am," Sarah said, furious with herself for her polite, little girl's response. She should have said something adult: "I'll be happy to," or "Certainly," or something like that.

The other man in the car came in. He was taller, but not nearly so good-looking as Ann's cousin.

"Welcome back, Dick," Jenny Chambers said. "Follow Sarah to the pool. There's beer."

"Yes, ma'am," the other one said. "Hello, Sarah. I'm Dick Canidy."

She smiled, but she didn't say anything. She walked past the good-looking one into the foyer and led them through the house to the pool.

Bitter went to a galvanized washtub full of ice and beer and took out two bottles. He tossed one to Canidy, who snatched it out of the air. They sat down on folding canvas lounge chairs. Bitter unfastened the snaps of the high collar of his white uniform tunic. The way he was sitting on the lounge chair, with his legs extended and crossed, his white trousers were drawn taut at his crotch.

"So tell me, Ann," Bitter said, "how's Bryn Mawr? You catch a man?"

"Drop dead, Eddie," Ann said.

"Isn't that the whole idea of going to college? To catch a man?"

There was a timbre in his voice that Sarah felt in her belly.

Thirty minutes later, Charley Chambers arrived with his friends from the University of Alabama.

They were boys, Sarah thought, even though they were only a couple of years younger than Ed Bitter and his friend. Immature boys. Ed Bitter and his friend thought so, too, for just about as soon as the introductions had been made, he made a signal to his friend, and they left "to get out of the uniforms." Sarah really hated to see them go.

One of the boys who had come with Ann's brother said something to her.

"I'm sorry," Sarah said. "I was woolgathering."

"I said I'm David Bershin," he said.

Sarah smiled at him.

"Sarah Child," she said, giving him her hand. "I guess that you're at the University of Alabama, too, David?"

"Yes, but call me Davey," he said.

"That sounds Irish, not Jewish." She laughed. And so did he. He had a sweet, open laugh.

He was a nice boy, she thought. She knew she should try to like him and not Ed Bitter the sailor. But . . .

"Can I get you a beer?" Davey Bershin asked.

"When in Rome," Sarah said. He smiled his sweet, open smile at her and went quickly to the galvanized tub full of ice and beer.

Forty-five minutes later, a single-engine biplane flew over The Lodge at about five hundred feet.

"That's Daddy," Ann said. "Let's go get him."

When they went through the house and onto the veranda, Ed Bitter and his friend were about to get into Ed's Buick. Both were dressed for tennis. Sarah saw that Ed Bitter's muscular legs were lightly covered with pale hair.

"Where are you going?" Ann called to him.

"To get your father," Ed replied.

"*We* were going to do that," Ann complained.

"This car is here, dummy," Ed said. "Come along if you want to."

"All right," Sarah heard herself say, and started down the veranda steps. Ann and Charity did not follow her.

"That's all right, you go get him," Ann said. Sarah felt like a fool. She started to turn around, then decided she would look like more of a fool if she stayed.

"I'm interested in airplanes," she said to Dick Canidy.

"Me, too," he said. "This one is supposed to be special." He opened the passenger door for her and motioned her inside.

"What's special about this one?"

"It's a stagger-wing Beech with a big, fat Wasp engine," he said. "Makes it go like the hammers of hell."

She had no idea what that meant. Ed Bitter was now beside her on the hot leather seats, his hairy leg beside her smooth one, his knee brushing gently against hers as he pushed on the starter mounted on the accelerator pedal and turned the engine over.

When they reached the airplane three people were standing beside it, two men and a woman. Sarah recognized one of the men as Ann's father. And besides, Brandon Chambers was very hard to forget, for he was *very* large—280 pounds—and *very* present wherever he was, with a bellowing, almost always laughing voice that dominated his hearers more powerfully—though usually more cheerfully—than a great preacher's. He sailed up to the car and gave his enormous hand to Ed Bitter.

"We have," Ann's father said significantly, "just been talking about you, Ed."

"Have you?" Ed replied.

"Hello, Sarah," Brandon Chambers said. "It's nice to see you, honey." And then he looked at Ed's friend. "You must be Lieutenant Canidy," he said.

"Yes, sir." Canidy reached across Sarah to shake his hand. "How do you do, sir?"

"I was doing a lot better, frankly, Lieutenant," Brandon Chambers said, "before I found out about this China insanity. I'm glad you're here."

Sarah wondered what the "China insanity" could mean.

Ann's brother Mark walked up to the car and shook Ed's hand.

"You're out of your mind, you know, Ed," he said. "I thought you'd be smarter than that."

"And it's nice to see you, too," Ed replied. "Dick, this is my cousin Mark. Mark, Dick Canidy."

"The other crusader," Mark Chambers said dryly. "How do you do, Lieutenant?"

"And the lady, Dick," Ed Bitter said, "is Mark's wife, Sue-Ellen."

"How do you do, Mrs. Chambers?" Dick Canidy said.

She walked to him and gave him her hand.

"Please call me Sue-Ellen," she said. "Any friend of Eddie's, et cetera."

"That's very kind of you," Dick Canidy said.

"I'm Sue-Ellen," the woman said to Sarah, giving her her hand. "Why don't I get in the back with you and Lieutenant Canidy and leave the front seat to the broad-bottomed lairds of the manor?"

Sarah slid across the seat and got out the driver's side, and then climbed in the back. Sue-Ellen Chambers got in the middle, and Canidy got in beside her, while the other three men took suitcases from the plane and put them in the trunk.

"Is my leg bothering you, Lieutenant?" Sue-Ellen asked. "I'm sorry. I didn't get the first name."

"Dick," he said. "No. I was afraid my leg was in your way."

"There's never enough room in the backseats of convertibles," Sue-Ellen asked, "is there?"

"Nice flight?" Ed asked as they drove off.

"While we waited for you," Brandon Chambers said, "I figured it out. I made two hundred thirty-five miles an hour from Nashville to Mobile and then two hundred thirty from Mobile here."

"That's faster than an F3F-1," Ed replied.

Sarah noticed the hairs on Ed Bitter's neck, and wondered what they'd be like to touch.

Sue-Ellen Chambers pushed herself off the backseat with a hand on Dick Canidy's leg.

"Sorry," she said to him, and then to Ed, "I don't remember this car, Eddie. Is it new?"

"I've had it just over a month," he said.

"It's very nice," she said, then slid back, wiggling her hips.

At the house, they all went back to the pool, where they sat around a large, umbrellaed, round cast-iron table.

Robert appeared with what looked like a pitcher of tomato juice and glasses for all of them.

Sarah took a sip of the tomato juice. There was a bite to it. There was something alcoholic in it, gin or vodka, and Worcestershire, too, and some other flavors.

"Sarah, honey," Mr. Chambers said. "Would you excuse us? We've got a little private family business to discuss with these two innocents."

"Oh, certainly," Sarah said, flushing. "Excuse me."

"Excuse *us*," Mr. Chambers said, "but this just won't wait."

She went to the far end of the other side of the pool and sat down in an unusual wicker chair. It had a funny little parasol to shade whoever was sitting in it from the sun. She pushed herself all the way into it.

She could hear Mr. Chambers's voice, of course; but she was surprised that she could hear Ed's too, faintly but clearly, like at Carnegie Hall. She had once gone to Carnegie Hall when there was nothing going on, and her father had demonstrated that it was possible to stand on the stage and whisper, and the whisper was audible in the very last row of seats. Something like that was happening now.

"If you don't mind my asking, Lieutenant," Mr. Chambers said, and was interrupted by Ed Bitter.

"You're making him uncomfortable, Uncle Brandon," he said.

"My question, if you don't mind my asking," Brandon Chambers went on, ignoring him, "is how your parents reacted when they learned you were going to China."

"We're not supposed to discuss any of this," Ed Bitter said.

They were going to China!

"I'm not a goddamned Japanese spy, Eddie," Brandon Chambers said impatiently. "And it wasn't really that hard for me to find out more about this operation than you in all likelihood know."

"My father is a clergyman, Mr. Chambers," Canidy said. "I didn't think I had to tell him any more than what we are supposed to say, that we've been hired by the Central Aircraft Manufacturing Company, Federal."

"What kind of clergyman?" Sue-Ellen asked.

"Episcopal," Canidy said. "He's headmaster of a boys' school."

"Legend has it," she said, "that ministers' kids are really hell-raisers. You don't *look* like a naughty boy, Mr. Canidy."

"Sue-Ellen!" Mr. Chambers said impatiently.

"Sorry," she said.

"Well, I'll tell you this, when Eddie's parents heard about it, they had a fit," Brandon Chambers said.

"They should not have called you," Ed Bitter said. "I told them not to say anything about it to anybody."

"They wisely decided that they should call me because I was likely to know somebody, or Mark would, who could find out what is really going on. And I have. Mark and I have."

"Well, it's done," Ed said. "There is really no point to this conversation."

"It's not done," Brandon Chambers said. "You can still change your mind. You're still in the Navy. All you have to tell them is that you've changed your mind. Minds," he corrected himself. "Everything I'm saying applies to you, too, Dick."

"You went off as a volunteer pilot before the World War," Ed Bitter said. "And we're going off now. Why was it right for you and wrong for us?"

"I didn't have anybody, like me," Brandon Chambers said, "who had been there and who could tell me it was a damned-fool thing to do."

"It didn't seem to hurt you any," Ed said.

"I was lucky," Brandon Chambers said. "There were thirty-six people in my draft when we went to France. Eleven came back. Two out of three of us were killed."

Oh my God! Sarah thought. *He's going off to war!*

"You weren't a trained pilot," Ed protested. "We are."

"Just because you've got a few hours in the F4F-3 doesn't make you Eddie Rickenbacker, Ed."

"I didn't know you knew about that," Bitter said.

"Buzzing the Naval Academy," Brandon Chambers said, "is not the same thing as going to war, Eddie. Do you really think the Japs aren't well trained? Well equipped?"

"I didn't say that."

"For your information, Mr. Expert Aviator," Brandon Chambers went on angrily, "the Japanese have equipped their Air Corps with Howard Hughes's fighter plane."

"What?" Canidy asked.

"The Mitsubishi A6M," Brandon Chambers said. "It's a carbon copy of the low-winged monoplane Howard Hughes designed. I saw it being tested. He offered it to the Army and Navy, who were too dumb to take it. I don't know how the Japs got their hands on it . . . I heard through the Swedes, but that could be just a story . . . but they've got it, and they're mass-producing it."

"Is it any good?" Canidy asked.

"It's better than anything we have, including the F4F-3," Chambers said flatly. He turned to face Ed Bitter and went on. "If you have some schoolboy notion that you'll be able to sweep the Japanese from the skies like Superman, and come home a hero in a couple of months, covered with glory, forget it."

"I'm a naval aviator," Ed Bitter said levelly. "I'm going to go over there and be very careful and learn the practice of my profession. And then come back to the Navy and teach others what I have learned. That is not a schoolboy notion."

"You're a goddamned fool!" Brandon Chambers exploded. "The first thing a pilot who has been there learns is that only goddamned fools volunteer for anything."

Ed Bitter stood up, white-faced. That somehow interfered with the acoustics, and Sarah Child had to strain to hear him.

"Thank you for your concern and your hospitality, Uncle Brandon," he said stiffly, artificially. "Dick and I will be going now."

"Let me put one more question to your friend," Brandon Chambers said. "Is Eddie doing this because he is still young and stupid enough not to want to look like a coward in front of you? He can't quit now, in other words, now that you've led him into this?''

''I didn't lead him into anything, Mr. Chambers,'' Canidy said coldly. ''Nor he me. We were asked, separately, and we accepted separately. The fact that we're friends hasn't entered into it.''

''Then answer me this: Why are you doing it? Why are you going to go halfway around the world to fight a well-equipped, well-trained enemy in obsolete fighter planes?''

''Two reasons,'' Canidy said after a moment. ''For one thing, it's going to get me out of the Navy. With a little bit of luck, in a year I can be out of uniform once and for all, and finally working as an aeronautical engineer, which is what I am, and what I want to do. I've got an offer from Boeing.''

''And the other?''

''For the money. Six hundred dollars a month, and rations and quarters, is twice what I am making now. And there's five hundred dollars for every confirmed kill.''

''At least,'' Brandon Chambers said, *''he* has reasons.''

''So do I,'' Ed Bitter said.

Brandon Chambers said nothing else for a minute, and Sarah saw Ed Bitter staring off into the pine forest. After a moment, Dick Canidy got to his feet.

Ed Bitter's leaving, Sarah Child thought. *He's had a fight with his uncle, and he's leaving, and he's going to get killed in the war and I'll never see him again.*

But then Brandon Chambers got to his feet and waved at Ed's chair.

''Oh, sit down, Eddie,'' he boomed. ''I promised your mother I'd give it my best shot to talk you out of it, and I have. I also told her that I thought it would be a waste of time.'' He looked at Dick Canidy. ''I'm sorry I had to put you through this, Dick. I hope you understand.''

''Yes, sir,'' Canidy said. ''No problem.''

''Robert!'' Mr. Chambers called out.

''Yes, sir?''

''Enough of this stuff,'' Mr. Chambers said. ''Bring us some whiskey.''

5

The servants set up a supper buffet by the pool, but the bugs came out; so before they could start to eat, Jenny Chambers ordered the whole thing carried back inside the house.

The separation by generation went into effect. The girls and Charley Chambers and his friends were drafted into helping the servants move the dishes and the tables. Ed Bitter and Dick Canidy went into the bar with the ''adults.''

Charity saw her watching them go in, and whispered in Sarah's ear: ''I like the tall one.''

''All you think about is boys,'' Sarah replied cattily.

''And you don't?'' Charity laughed.

Not normally, Sarah thought.

The ''adults'' took their supper alone, too. Servants went down the buffet and filled plates for them. The ''kids'' went through a line. But then the meal was over, and everybody went to the playroom—a screened-in porch on the right side of the house. More ice was added to the galvanized tub, and more beer.

''What can I get you, Miss Sarah?'' Robert asked.

''I get blown up when I drink beer,'' she said.

''Fix her a weak Scotch,'' Ann Chambers ordered.

Sarah's drink tasted like medicine, but she sipped on it anyway, so as not to look like a child.

She was more than a little unnerved when a warm hand

tapped her bare shoulder (she had changed into a peasant blouse and skirt) and Ed Bitter's voice said, "Dance, Sarah?"

There was a phonograph playing, but no one was dancing, and Sarah blurted out this comforting truth.

"I know," Ed Bitter said. "I have been dispatched by my aunt because of that. She hopes you and I will inspire people."

"Us?" she said. "Oh my." But she had to giggle. She raised her arm so that he could take it.

They danced for a moment, and then he said, "Hey, you're good!"

She quickly changed the subject. "I understand you're going to China?"

"Christ, who told you that?"

"Is it supposed to be a secret?" she asked. "I'm sorry."

"Nothing to be sorry about," he said, and he gave her a little hug. That pressed her breasts against his chest; but he sensed that made her uncomfortable, and quickly released her. A moment later, she felt her breasts against his chest again, and she knew that she had moved against him.

She felt strange, dizzy, confused, out of control, as though she were trying to run on sheet ice.

"Dick and I have joined something called the American Volunteer Group," he said.

"Excuse me?"

"I said that Canidy and I are going over there with the American Volunteer Group, and fly for the Chinese. Against the Japs."

"But we're not at war with the Japanese," she said.

"That's why we had to volunteer," he said.

"When are you going?" she asked. "How long will you be gone?"

"In the next couple of weeks," he said. "We should be

back in a year. I mean, the contract is for a year.''

A year didn't seem like all that much time. It was sort of like going away to college.

She felt his fingers graze and then flutter away from her brassiere.

And then she felt him, in front. It made her feel even funnier, all flushed and dizzy.

"I need something to drink," he said, breaking away from her, and she saw that his face was flushed, too.

"A little touch of Scotch, please, Robert," he said, and then he seemed to remember that he was still holding her hand, and let go of it as if it burned him.

"And you, miss?" Robert asked.

"Nothing for me, thank you," she said.

"Want to try it with me, Sarah?" Davey Bershin asked.

She turned and smiled at him. "Thank you," she said.

It wasn't the same, dancing with Davey. His hand felt like any other boy's hand on her shoulder felt, and she didn't get dizzy or feel funny down there.

She desperately wanted Ed Bitter to dance with her again, but he didn't. He spent the rest of the evening sitting around a table with his friend and Mr. Chambers. From the way they were moving their hands around in the air, making believe they were airplanes, she knew what they were talking about.

6

Carrying drinks, Mark and Sue-Ellen Chambers walked to where Ed Bitter, Dick Canidy, and Brandon Chambers were sitting and dragged up chairs.

"If you come down on a guy," Brandon Chambers was saying, using his hands to illustrate his point, "and he tries to evade you by pulling up into a climb, then it's a test of engine power. You either keep up with him, climbing after him, which means overcoming the inertia of the dive, and you get your fire into him; or your engine won't do it, and he gets away from you, and then he's on top."

"Can two civilians join this ghastly conversation?" Mark Chambers said.

"Certainly," Brandon Chambers replied, a little embarrassed.

"I have a small announcement to make," Mark Chambers said. "I just called Mobile, and in the morning Stuart's going to bring the boat up."

"That's a good idea," Brandon Chambers said.

"It's near a hundred miles against the current, which means it'll be nearly noon before it gets here," Mark Chambers went on. "Would that be too late for you to fly Stuart and me back to Mobile?"

"I thought you and Sue-Ellen were going back tomorrow night?" Brandon Chambers asked.

"No. What Sue-Ellen did was call her mother, and the kids will be gotten out of bed at four, then Stuart will pick them up, and they'll come up and they'll stay with Sue-Ellen. I have to get back, but there's no reason the kids can't have some fun. They love the boat, and Charley's friends, and Ann and her friends. . . ." He left the rest unsaid.

"But who's going to operate the boat?" Brandon Chambers asked.

"You've just insulted an officer—*two* officers—of the United States Navy. You can run it, can't you, Eddie?" Mark asked.

"Why not?" Ed Bitter replied a little thickly.

"And if he's still drunk," Sue-Ellen Chambers said bitchily, "I'm sure Lieutenant Canidy can."

"Not drunk," Ed corrected. "Tiddly. There is an enormous difference."

"I'll take you to Mobile whenever you have to go," Brandon Chambers said. "I'm just sorry you have to go."

"You know what things are like at the yard," Mark Chambers said. "We're running three shifts, seven days a week. And you'd be surprised what comes up when I'm away just a couple of hours."

"Well," Brandon Chambers said. "It's very nice of you to think of the boat, Mark."

"Don't be silly," Mark said. "Anyway, it was Sue-Ellen's idea."

"It's clearly my patriotic duty," Sue-Ellen Chambers said, thickly sarcastic, looking directly into Dick Canidy's eyes, "to do whatever I can to bring a little joy into the lives of lonely sailors."

"What you're really doing," Dick Canidy said, "is drafting two sailors to amuse a bunch of college kids."

"That was uncalled for, Dick," Brandon Chambers said.

"Sorry about that, Sue-Ellen," Canidy apologized.

He looked across the room and found Sarah Child looking at him. Without thinking what he was doing, he winked at her. She looked quickly away, but then she looked back. He shrugged his shoulders. She smiled at him.

7

The boat, a fifty-two-foot ChrisCraft, appeared around a bend in the Alabama River just before noon the next day. It blew its horn as it passed The Plantation wharf, went several hundred yards upstream, turned, and then came into the wharf and tied up.

Dick Canidy thought that there was a good chance, if he

wasn't careful, that the five-year-old boy standing forward
with a rope in his hands would wind up in the river. But he
threw the rope as if he knew what he was doing, and then
the girl in the back of the boat threw one from there, and
Ed Bitter and Brandon Chambers caught them and tied it
up.

The children jumped ashore and were embraced by their
grandparents, and then introduced, rather formally, to Dick
Canidy. They were nice, polite kids, and when they had
started up the wide lawn to The Lodge, Canidy said so.

"Nice kids, Mrs. Chambers," he said.

"Thank you, Lieutenant Canidy," she replied.

"Unless you want me to come to the airstrip," she said
to her husband, "maybe I'd better stay here and help the
Navy fuel her."

"Right," Mark Chambers said. He was dressed in a suit,
ready to go to work as soon as he returned to Mobile. He
walked up to Eddie and somewhat awkwardly put his arm
around his shoulders.

"You be careful when you get over there, hear?" he said,
not comfortable with the emotion.

"Thank you, Mark," Eddie said, just as embarrassed.

Mark Chambers turned to Dick Canidy. "You, too,
Dick," he said. "We're counting on you two fellas to take
care of each other."

"Thank you," Canidy said.

"Good luck," Mark Chambers said, and shook his hand.

Then he kissed his wife perfunctorily on the cheek and
started up the stairwell from the wharf to the lawn.

"So much for the husband," Sue-Ellen said softly.

"I'm flattered," Canidy said.

"I thought that if you had the balls to show up here,"
she said, "it was up to me to give you an answer."

She stepped up behind him and slid her hand up the leg

of his shorts, her hand moving surely past his underwear to grab him gently but firmly.

"I'm a pushover for men with balls," she said, laughing deep in her throat.

She squeezed him and let him go. She stepped to the side of the cockpit and called to Ed Bitter: "It's run about seven hours," she said matter-of-factly. "And it burns about twenty-five gallons an hour against the current, so it'll take about two hundred gallons. Tell Charley to watch the dial."

She turned back to Canidy.

"Everything all right with you?" she asked.

8

The coolness of Charley Chambers and his friends toward him was understandable, Ed Bitter thought. They didn't mind competing among themselves for the virgins of the tribe, and they understood that there were not enough virgins to go around. But what they had not counted on was visiting warriors from a distant tribe, whom their own virgins found fascinating.

Ann Chambers had told him she thought Dick Canidy was a "doll." Dick Canidy showed absolutely no interest in any of the girls. Dick, Ed thought, was an accomplished *woman* chaser, and not interested in *girls* who had just completed their freshman year of college. Dick was interested in women whom he could lure into his bed with only perfunctory attention to the ritual of courtship. He barely concealed his lack of interest, which of course made him more attractive to them.

What really surprised Ed Bitter was how much Sarah Child excited him. When Jenny Chambers had sent him over the night before to make him dance with her, the moment he'd touched her warm back there had been a stirring in his groin.

There was no way in the world that he would so much as pat the delightful little rear end of a nineteen-year-old college girl . . . but the thought was not uninteresting.

His profound philosophical reverie at the wheel of the *Time Out* was interrupted by the appearance of Sarah Child herself. She was wearing white shorts and a sheer white blouse.

She handed him a bottle of beer.

"Thank you," he said.

"Why don't you make Mr. Canidy take his turn?" she asked.

" 'Mr. Canidy'?" he answered, gently mocking, aware that she thought of him and Canidy as adults and not boys. "Why, Miss Child, I will tell you the shameful truth. 'Mr. Canidy' confessed to me just as soon as we had let loose the lines that he had never piloted a boat like this before. Can you believe that? A naval pilot who can't steer a boat?"

She chuckled "I like him," she said. "Are you sure he's telling you the truth?"

"I hadn't thought about that," he said. Now that he did he realized it was entirely possible that Canidy had told him that because he didn't want to spend the afternoon at the wheel of a cabin cruiser moving slowly up a river.

He looked at her and met her eyes, and she looked away and flushed.

"I've been thinking about the riverboats," she said.

"You almost expect to see something out of Mark Twain coming around the next bend, with tall smokestacks and a paddlewheel."

"All there is on the river these days," he said, "are diesel tugboats. They push barges of coal downstream, and gasoline up."

"Pity," she said. She had an adorable expression as she said that.

"Yes, it is," he agreed.

Davey Bershin came up the ladder to the flying bridge a moment later, to ask Sarah Child if she wanted to play cards, and she went with him.

Ed Bitter was sorry to see her go, but realized it was probably a good thing. He had been unable to keep his eyes off her, and sooner or later she would have caught him at it.

When they returned to The Plantation at sunset, Dick Canidy spent the evening talking flying with Brandon Chambers, while the others played noisily at Monopoly in the game room. Ed Bitter sat quietly with them, not playing, drinking more than he knew he should, unable to keep his eyes off Sarah Child at the Monopoly board.

When the game was finally over, Ann Chambers got the phonograph going again and walked over to them. She stood there until her father noticed her.

"You need something, honey?" he asked.

"No, I'm just standing here with a sad look on my face, waiting to be asked to dance."

"You dance with her, Dick," Mr. Chambers said. "I'm old, fat, and tired, and I'm about to go to bed."

Canidy got up. "I'll dance with her," he said. "And then because I'm young and tired, I'm going to bed."

What the hell, Ed Bitter thought and went over to Sarah. She stood up and walked to him, as if she had known he would come to her. Her eyes met his, and then she averted them, flushed, and then looked at him again. There was something electric about the look, he thought.

When he put his hands on hers, it was warm, and thirty seconds after he had her in his arms, he actually started to tremble. He could feel the warmth of her belly against him.

When the record was over, he turned her over to Davey Bershin and went to the bar and drank a straight shot of Scotch to see if that wouldn't calm him down—knowing that drinking was the worst thing he could be doing. The next-worst thing was staying in the room with Sarah, especially since Canidy had made good on his promise to go to bed. Sue-Ellen was gone now too. He had no business here with these kids.

There was a flash of lightning and a moment later a clap of thunder, and he remembered that the convertible was sitting in front of the house with the roof down. After he put the top up, he would go to bed.

He went out the screen door behind the bar to avoid walking through the playroom, then went around the side of the house to the car. He got the boot off and into the trunk and got in the car and started the engine. He had just leaned across the seat to latch the fastener when Sarah Child appeared at the window.

Their eyes met, and this time, although she flushed, she didn't look away.

"Going for a ride?" she asked. Her voice was artificial, as if she were having difficulty controlling it.

"I was just putting the top up," he replied, in a tone as artificial as hers. He could feel his heart beating. "Would you like to go for a ride?"

She got in the car and closed the door.

He drove down the dirt road to the airstrip. Neither of them said a word until he had stopped beside the stagger-wing Beech.

He looked at her, and saw that she was looking at him. He reached his hand out and ran the knuckles against her cheek.

"Jesus!" he said.

She smiled and caught his hand in hers. He had never seen eyes brighter than hers were now.

"Jesus," she said, mocking him.

"I'm trembling," he said.

"Me, too," she said. She reached up and turned the ignition key off, and then pushed the armrest between the seats up out of the way and slid over to him.

He held her tightly against him, his face in her hair, aware of her breasts against his chest. It seemed to be a very long time before he kissed her, first on the hair, and then on the forehead, and only at long last on her mouth. When he kissed her on the mouth, her mouth was open under his, and he found her tongue, which was at the same time gently moving against his. Then she unbuttoned her blouse and slipped it off, and then her bra. And in a few seconds more, she was naked. In a few more seconds, so was Ed Bitter.

Later he drove her back to The Lodge. When they were almost to the road at the front of the house, she said: "Let me out here, and I'll walk. Then nobody will know we've been off together."

He stopped the car and she got out. He watched her as she walked toward the house, staying in the shadows of the trees. When she finally appeared on the veranda, he put the Buick in gear and drove to the barn and parked the car. He turned the engine off and sat there for a couple of minutes, trying to put together what was happening; and then he got out of the car and walked out of the barn toward the river. It was pleasant to sit there at night in the dark and the quiet and watch the river flow by, as it had for—what, a million years, two million?

He sat down on the bank and glanced at the boat. Some damned fool had left a light on in one of the cabins. The master cabin. He forgot whether or not he had plugged in the shore power line when they'd tied up that afternoon. If the shore power line was not connected, the lights would drain the battery.

The *Time Out* was docked with her bow downstream. The shore power connection was aft, just inside the cockpit. The stairs to the wharf put him on the wharf by the *Time Out*'s bow. As he walked past the ports of the master cabin, he thought he saw movement inside. The first thing he thought was that a thief had boarded her. He moved as quickly and quietly as he could to the porthole. The curtain had been drawn, but not completely. There was enough of a crack for him to see inside.

He didn't believe what he saw at first. It was the most shocking thing he had ever seen in his life.

Dick Canidy and Sue-Ellen Chambers were in the master bed, naked as jaybirds, Sue-Ellen on top, straddling Canidy, playing with her breasts as she moved up and down on him. The look on her face was absolutely wanton.

In turmoil—angry and confused—he went back up the stairs onto the lawn, and then up the lawn to the house. There were lights over the veranda, and the foyer lights were on, but the playroom was dark. Everybody else had apparently gone to bed.

He looked at his watch. It was quarter past twelve. Had he been gone that long with Sarah? Time seemed to have simply vanished.

He entered the playroom the way he had left it, by the screen door to its rear. There was a light switch by the door, but he remembered another light switch under the bar. Ed went over and turned it on, picked up a bottle of whiskey and a few ice cubes, and made himself a stiff drink. He took a large swallow and put the glass down. Supporting himself with both hands on the bar, he bent his head over between them.

What to do about Sue-Ellen and that goddamned Canidy?

His cousin's wife was a whore and an unfaithful wife and a sexual degenerate, and his "friend" was faithless. A gentleman would not dishonor . . .

"Is it that much of a problem for you?" Sarah Child asked.

"What are you doing here?"

"I watched out the window," Sarah said. "Until I saw you come back from the river."

"Oh," he said. Sarah was wearing a bathrobe. He sensed from her movement that she wasn't wearing much under it.

"If you're worrying about me, don't," Sarah said. "You're not obligated to me."

"To tell the truth," he said, "I was thinking about something else."

"China?" she asked.

"Yes," he replied. That should close that subject. He thought of what Canidy had told him about lying. Like screwing, it got easier with practice.

"Come on," he said to Sarah. "Let's get out of here before we wake everybody up."

She smiled and nodded. He turned out the light under the bar and then guided her through the darkened playroom, through the dining room into the foyer, and then up the stairs.

He had no idea where her room was, of course, but he was surprised when she followed him down the west wing corridor. He would have thought that Aunt Jenny would have put the girls in the east wing and the boys in the west wing. He came to his door. Jesus, it would be nice to get her in there!

An insane idea!

"Good night, Sarah," he said, and leaned over to kiss her.

She avoided his mouth, but wrapped her arms around

him. He was confused. And then, after a moment, she said:

"Hung for a wolf as a sheep."

"Jesus!"

She just smiled—a sweet, trusting smile.

He opened the door and she followed him through it. He turned around and fastened the latch. He turned to face her.

"Jesus Christ, you're beautiful!"

"I'm glad you think so," Sarah Child said. She met his eyes and then she pulled the cord of her bathrobe open and let it fall off her shoulders.

That, she thought, *was easier to do than I thought it would be.*

I was right, he thought, *when I thought she wasn't wearing much under the bathrobe.* She had worn nothing under it.

"Sarah, I . . ." he began. She shut him off.

"Let's not either of us say anything we might not feel like repeating in the morning," Sarah said. She turned around and walked to the bed and slid under the sheets.

FOUR

Transient Officers' Quarters
Anacostia Naval Air Station
Washington, D.C.
1645 Hours 16 June 1941

At 0815 that morning the admiral's aide had handed Lieutenants (j.g.) Edwin Bitter and Richard Canidy an envelope containing tickets on the Pennsylvania Railroad from Washington, D.C., to New York, and a slip of paper on which two addresses were typed:

> Commander G. H. Porter
> Special Actions Section
> BuPers Room 213 Temp. Building G-34
>
> CAMCO
> Suite 1745
> Rockefeller Center
> 1230 Sixth Avenue
> New York, New York

Then he drove them, in the admiral's car, to Base Operations, where he waited to make sure nothing unforeseen would keep them from getting seats on the courier plane, an

R4-D, the Navy version of the new Douglas DC-3 twin-engine airliner, which made an every-other-day round-robin flight from Washington to Key West, with stops at points of naval interest, including Pensacola, in between.

They landed at Anacostia a little after two, checked into the transient quarters, and then took a taxi to Temporary Building G-34, one of the buildings on the mall that had been built to provide temporary office space for the Navy during World War I.

It soon became apparent that Commander Porter knew only that higher authority had decided that Lieutenants Bitter and Canidy were to be honorably discharged for the convenience of the naval service—and as quickly as possible. Commander Porter was not aware, Canidy thought cynically, that the two of them had volunteered to sweep the Japanese from the skies over China in defense of Mom's Apple Pie and the American Way of Life, and thus he had reasonably concluded that the reason they were being discharged—and as quickly as possible—was to spare the naval service the inconvenience of court-martialing them for having been caught with their hands in the till of the officers' club, or in the pants of some brother officer's wife.

Commander Porter therefore treated them with icy courtesy, according to the book, and informed them that while the paperwork was being prepared to effect their separation, they would undergo a complete physical examination at the naval hospital. It did not matter, Commander Porter told them, that they had six weeks before been certified as physically fit for aviation duty. That was an aviation physical; this was a separation physical.

When they went to the naval hospital, they were told that separation physicals were given at 0800 in the morning, and they should return then.

"Look at the bright side, Eddie," Canidy said as they

came out of the naval hospital. "With a little bit of luck, we can get laid."

"Christ, is that all you ever think about?" Bitter snapped.

Something was bothering Bitter, Canidy knew. It was probably that Naval Academy graduates who wished to become admirals did not leave the Navy. Commander Porter's icy disdain had given weight to his fears.

"Let's go get out of our uniforms," Canidy said, "and then treat ourselves to a good dinner. And maybe a movie."

Bitter gave him a weak smile.

When they returned to the Transient Officers' Quarters at Anacostia, a tall, handsome Army Air Corps second lieutenant was waiting for them. He was wearing a green blouse, to which were pinned silver pilot's wings. There was a glossy Sam Browne belt. He wore pink riding breeches, and rested his glistening riding boots on the low table in front of him. His uniform cap, perched on the rear of his head, exposed light blond hair. The stiffener had been removed from the crown of the cap, and the cap itself looked as if it had been driven over by a coal truck. The crushed hat was the mark of the fighter pilot.

The handsome young officer was Jim Whittaker, who displayed a lot of white teeth and a warm smile when he saw Canidy, but he did not get up.

"What the hell are you doing here, Jim?" Canidy asked, smiling broadly. He went to him and shook his hand.

"I came to save you from this nautical squalor," the young aviator said, gesturing around the almost elegantly furnished foyer. "But the question is, what the hell are *you* doing here? And I don't mean 'why aren't you at the house?' "

"Eddie," Canidy said, "this is Jim Whittaker. Jim, Ed Bitter."

Bitter smiled, but not warmly. He had, he was sure, just

come across yet another Canidy, that is, someone who would embarrass him somehow within the hour.

They shook hands.

"Are you involved in what he's done?" Whittaker asked. "Or are you his guard?"

"We're together." Bitter smiled uneasily.

"How the hell did you find me here?" Canidy asked.

"When I called Pensacola," Whittaker said, "and got a mysterious runaround about you, I called back and led them to believe I was an aide-de-camp to an unspecified general officer who absolutely had to get in touch with you. After some hesitation, they said you could be found here. I came straight from the airport. What the hell is going on?"

"We're going to China," Canidy said.

"Dick," Bitter protested.

"China?" Whittaker said thoughtfully. "I don't think you can get to China from here. I think you have to go to San Francisco and take the Southern Pacific and Yangtze River."

Canidy laughed. "What are you doing here? Better late than never?"

"I'm sorry about that," Whittaker said. "The Air Corps was being beastly to me. Does the Navy use the phrase 'exigencies of the service'?"

"All the time," Canidy said.

"In the Air Corps, it means, 'Fuck you, you're Reserve second lieutenant, you don't get no leave,' " Whittaker said.

Canidy laughed.

Ed Bitter cringed as three officers, the most senior of them a full commander, sitting at a table across the foyer glanced their way in disapproval.

"Tell me about China," Whittaker said.

"I probably know less about China than you do," Canidy

said. "But I'll have a go at it. What exactly would you like to know?"

"Why are you going there, wiseass?"

"For a discharge from the Navy, and six hundred bucks a month," Canidy said.

"The American Volunteer Group," Whittaker said. "They were recruiting at Randolph Field, too."

"Regular little Charley Chan, aren't you?" Canidy said.

"Chesty and Bill Donovan were in Texas, is how I found out," Whittaker said. "The firm's got the contract for expanding the place, and for satellite airfields. Anyway, they had me to dinner at the Main Club. Chesty, Donovan, the base commander, and me. My squadron now treats me with a lot more respect."

Bitter laughed.

"So I asked what the volunteering was all about, and Donovan told me."

"What did he tell you?"

"That patriotic, courageous, highly skilled, and ergo not too bright pilots were being recruited to go to China and pretend they're the Chinese Air Corps until Roosevelt can get us in the war. He didn't put it in quite those words, but stripped of the bullshit, that was what he meant."

Canidy chuckled.

"Not that I was asked," Whittaker went on, "but I wouldn't touch the AVG with a ten-foot pole. What did you do, go crazy?"

"I told you, it got me out of the Navy," Canidy said. "I figured if I stayed until my four years was up, there'd be a war on and I'd never get out."

"From what Donovan told me," Whittaker said, "the American Volunteer Group is a euphemism for 'throw some Christians to the Japanese lions.' "

"We should not be having this conversation in a public

place," Bitter said. "If we should be having it at all. I don't want to sound stuffy, but that's—"

"I always try to be kind to naval aviators," Whittaker said. "But this ring-knocker sidekick of yours is trying my patience. Does he always interrupt serious conversations this way?"

"He means well," Canidy said. "And he's probably right. Let's go to our room, so we can get out of these uniforms."

"So you can pack," Whittaker said. "You're not going to spend the night here. Either of you." He saw the look of confusion on Bitter's face, and explained. "I've got a house here. Plenty of room for everybody. It will be easier all around."

"Not only that, it's free," Canidy said. "Say 'Thank you, Jim,' Eddie."

"Thank you," Bitter said.

He had decided that prudence dictated he join them. For he did not wish to have to tell Commander Porter, at 0800 the next morning, that he had no idea where Lieutenant Canidy was. Since Whittaker and Canidy were two of a kind, together they were liable to do anything.

As they walked up the wide stairway, Whittaker touched Bitter's arm. "No offense about the ring-knocker remark?"

"Not at all," Bitter said. "We ring-knockers always make an allowance for civilians in uniform."

"It does have a sense of humor," Whittaker said. "I think I like it."

"Screw you," Bitter said. He had to laugh. The word to describe Whittaker, he thought, was "effervescent." It was impossible to take offense at anything he said.

"And you have my sympathy, Sour," Whittaker said. "I have trod where you are treading."

"Bitter," Bitter corrected him, before he realized his leg

was being pulled. "Trod where, Whitefish?"

"Sleeping with Canidy," Whittaker said. "It isn't so much the snores as it is the smell."

"Well, we do have something in common, then, don't we?" Bitter said.

"Dick and I go back a long way," Whittaker said. "I was his hack at school."

"I was at Phillips Exeter," Bitter said.

"Small world, ain't it?" Canidy said dryly. Then he thought of something. "Jim, do you remember Fulmar?"

"Monica Carlisle's shameful secret? Yeah, sure. How could I forget the charming prick?"

"I was just out to see my father," Canidy said. "He told me Fulmar's in Morocco."

"What the hell is he doing in Morocco?"

"Don't know," Canidy said, "but I can imagine. . . ."

"You bet!" Whittaker said with a knowing look.

Curiosity got the better of Ed Bitter. Monica Carlisle was a movie star, possessed of spectacular breasts, blond hair worn hanging over one eye, who always portrayed the innocent about to be violated.

"What about Monica Carlisle's shameful secret?"

"He's an old pal of ours, and he was at St. Mark's with us for a while," Whittaker explained. "He's as old as we are. That's the shameful secret. America's innocent sweetheart either bred at eight or nine, or she's a lot older than her public believes. And considerably less virginal."

"No fooling?" Bitter said, genuinely surprised.

"His father is German," Canidy added, "and he went to college there. Since I imagine they'd want to draft him if he stayed there, or else we'd draft him if he came here, it's likely he's come up with the not unreasonable notion to sit the war out with some Arab friend in Morocco."

"Good for Eric," Whittaker said. "That's what we

should be doing, instead of going off to the mysterious Orient.''

"We should be doing? What's with the 'we'?" Canidy asked.

"I'm on my way to the Philippine Islands," Whittaker said

"You're not kidding, are you?" Canidy asked seriously after a moment. Whittaker shook his head no.

"Is that what you're doing in Washington?"

"More or less," Whittaker said.

They went into the rooms. Whittaker immediately lay on the bed, his battered cap now pushed down over his nose, his hands under his head, and his riding boots resting on the footboard, as Canidy and Bitter packed.

"Actually, Richard," Whittaker said, "I'm in Washington to have dinner with our Commander in Chief. He may well be, as Chesty says, a traitor to his class, and there is no question that he did me dirt, but I didn't have the heart to turn my back on the sweet old guy."

"How fine of you!" Canidy said. "St. Mark's would be proud of you. 'Greater love hath no man than that he dines with the Roosevelts.' ''

"I didn't think of it that way," Whittaker said modestly.

"Big affair?" Canidy asked. "Or just you and Uncle Franklin?"

"Uncle Franklin and Aunt Eleanor, actually," Whittaker said.

"And Aunt Eleanor will do the cooking herself, no doubt?" Bitter asked, going along with the joke.

"God, I hope not," Whittaker said. "She's a lousy cook."

"How did our Commander in Chief do you dirt?" Bitter asked.

"I joined up with the solemn promise from the Air Corps

that after I trained, I'd go immediately into the Reserve.
Two weeks before I graduated—by presidential order, or
executive order, or whatever the hell they call it when he
speaks *ex cathedra*—the rules were changed. All Reserve
officers on active duty have to do another year, and resignations will also not be accepted from Regulars for a year.''

''I hadn't heard about that,'' Bitter said.

''Me either,'' Canidy said. ''But it probably explains
Commander Whatsisname's icy attitude. I thought that sonofabitch was treating us as if we had been caught pissing
on the flag.''

''Who?'' Whittaker asked.

''The guy who's processing our discharges,'' Canidy explained. ''I'm sorry you got caught, Jim.''

''*You're* sorry?'' Whittaker snorted.

''Well, when you see your uncle Franklin,'' Bitter said,
''you can tell him what a stinking thing that was for him to
do.''

''I'm tempted, I'll tell you that,'' Whittaker said seriously.

Bitter looked at him in surprise, and then decided his leg
was being pulled again.

''Have you got the Rolls, or are we going to have to call
a cab?'' Canidy asked, moving his suitcases to the door.

''I told you, I came here from the airport,'' Whittaker
said. ''And anyway, the Rolls is in Jersey.''

Bitter decided that settled it. His leg was being pulled.

''We can call for a cab downstairs,'' he said.

2

''Why the wall?'' Ed Bitter asked when the cab dropped
them in front of the house on Q Street.

"My uncle Chesty built it when Roosevelt got elected," Whittaker said, "to preserve civilization as we know it from the barbarian Democrats."

Ed Bitter laughed. "That wall's at least fifty years old." And then he made the connection. "Chesty? Chesty Whittaker? Chesley Haywood Whittaker?"

"One and the same," Whittaker said. "You know the name?"

"He and my uncle Brandon are friends," Bitter said. "My father, too, I think."

"Brandon what?"

"Brandon Chambers," Bitter said.

"Newspapers, right?" Whittaker asked, and waited for Bitter to acknowledge the association. When Bitter nodded, Whittaker unlocked the heavy wooden door in the wall, pushed it open, and waved Canidy and Bitter through.

Paul, the butler, opened the door as they approached. "Good afternoon, sir," he said to Whittaker, and then looked at Canidy. "Nice to see you again, Mr. Canidy. Just set those bags down. I'll take care of them."

"How are you, Paul?" Whittaker said. "Is my uncle here?"

"I just sent the car to fetch Mr. Whittaker, sir," Paul said. "Miss Chenowith is in the library."

"Then that's where we'll go," Whittaker said. "Would you please bring some beer to the library, Paul? Unless you'd rather have something stronger, Ed?"

"Beer is fine," Bitter said.

"Yes, sir," Paul said.

Canidy and Bitter followed Whittaker across the wide foyer, where he slid open the double doors. Cynthia Chenowith, her shoulder-length brown hair parted simply in the middle, was sitting sidewards on a couch, with a newspaper laid open next to her. She looked up when the door slid open.

"I'm glad you're here," she said. "Your uncle was worried."

"Edwin Bitter, officer and gentleman, USN, say hello to Miss Cynthia Chenowith," Whittaker said. "But don't get your hopes up. Not only is Canidy smitten with her, but I have been in love with her since she was eight and I was four."

Cynthia smiled at Bitter.

"Didn't your mother ever tell you you are judged by the company you keep?" she asked. "Hello, Canidy."

"Miss Cynthia, ma'am," Canidy said, in a mock Southern accent, and bowed deeply.

"You could have called," Cynthia said to Whittaker. "We weren't even sure you were on the train. It was damned inconsiderate of you. Aren't you ever going to grow up?"

"That time of the month again, is it?" Whittaker asked, without thinking.

"You can go to hell, Jim," she said. With her face flushing with embarrassment and anger, she stormed out of the room.

"Why the hell did you say that?" Canidy asked Whittaker as soon as she was gone.

"Who the hell does she think she is, talking to me that way, my mother?" Whittaker replied. "And since when do you take her side? What happened between you when you were here before?"

"I didn't make a pass at her, Jimmy," Canidy said, "if that's what you are asking, though I confess the possibility entered my mind."

"Then what?"

"Could it be a case of mutual loathing, Jimmy?" Canidy

said, with an angelically innocent smile. "In my experience, that's the reason a man and a woman are at each other's throats every time they see one another."

"I think Dick is right," Ed Bitter said, trying to keep a straight face. "It couldn't be that you two actually *like* each other, could it?"

"Oh, fuck it," Whittaker said, wanting to stop the conversation before he was really stuck on the hook.

A few moments later a young black woman in a maid's apron and cap came into the room and set a tray with three bottles of beer and three glasses on the coffee table before the couch.

As she left, Cynthia Chenowith returned.

"Can I get you something, Miss Chenowith?" the maid asked.

"Nothing, thank you," Cynthia Chenowith said, and then looked at Canidy.

"Jim is sorry," Canidy said. "Tell her you're sorry, jackass!"

"To the extent an apology is required, I apologize," Whittaker said.

"Accepted," she said. "I don't know why I thought I had a right to give you hell, and I'm sorry."

"Truce?" Canidy said.

"Truce," she said.

"That's better," Canidy said. He made the sign of the cross. "Bless you, my children. Go and sin no more!"

Cynthia Chenowith smiled and shook her head.

"Why do I suspect that isn't your first of the day?" she asked Jim.

Canidy was afraid that would start it all over again, but Whittaker just grinned.

"To counterbalance your breathtaking beauty and overwhelming desirability," he said, "God has given you a nasty, suspicious nature. And it isn't. I had a couple of beers at Anacostia waiting for Dick.''

"What brings you back to Washington, Dick?" Cynthia asked.

"We're on our way to New York," Canidy said. "Tomorrow."

"They're on their way to *China*," Whittaker said. "The damned fools joined that American Volunteer Group."

"Have you really?" she asked.

Bitter was surprised to see that Cynthia Chenowith seemed to know about the American Volunteer Group.

"So," Whittaker said lightly, "it seems to me the least you can do before these brave boys go off to China is feed them, and otherwise let them know how much the home front appreciates their sacrifice."

Before she could reply, the door from the foyer slid open again, and Chesty Whittaker came into the room.

"Dick!" Chesty Whittaker said. "You're back. How nice!"

"You won't think so when you hear why," Jim said.

"My name is Chesty Whittaker," he said, putting out his hand to Bitter.

"Ed Bitter," Bitter said.

"He's Brandon Chambers's nephew," Jim said.

"Then you're twice welcome," Chesty said.

"My father is Chandler Bitter, Mr. Whittaker," Bitter said. "Aren't you acquainted?"

"What is Chan Bitter's son doing with these thugs?" Whittaker asked.

"Being embarrassed by this one," Jim said. "And going to China with the other one."

Chesty Whittaker looked quickly at Canidy.

"You went to the AVG, Dick?"

Canidy nodded.

"I hope you know what you're doing," Whittaker said.

"It has something to do with saving the world for democracy, and a lot more to do with six hundred a month," Canidy said.

"You heard Jim's going to the Philippines?" Chesty Whittaker asked.

Canidy nodded.

Chesty Whittaker gave his hand to Cynthia Chenowith.

"It's good to see you, my dear," he said. "And thank you."

"I'm happy to be asked," she said.

"Could I impose even further and ask you to amuse these two while Jim and I are off to see the king?"

"I'd be happy to," she said. "We were just talking about it."

No one who hadn't seen Chesty Whittaker sneaking out of her apartment in the wee hours would ever suspect they were lovers, Canidy thought.

Another man entered. Chesty turned and greeted him, and then he introduced the newcomer to the others.

"I want you to meet my lawyer friend, Mr. Stanley Fine."

Fine shook hands with Cynthia, Canidy, and Bitter.

As their eyes met, Canidy knew who Fine was.

"We've met," he said. "Professionally."

There was no recognition in Fine's eyes.

"The charge was arson," Canidy said.

"My God," Fine said after a moment. "Reverend Canidy's son, right?"

"Right," Canidy said.

"Arson?" Jim said, absolutely fascinated.

"Arson and inflicting grievous bodily harm with an explosive device," Canidy, smiling broadly, explained. "A kid named Fulmar and I stood accused of trying to burn

down Cedar Rapids, and of trying to blow up a teacher. We
were in jail about to undergo 'rehabilitation' for what a fat
lady in charge called our 'societal problem,' when out of
the west, on his white horse, comes Mr. Fine, who got us
out. I stand forever in your debt, sir.''

"My pleasure, Mr. Canidy," Fine said, smiling at the
memory.

"How did he get you out?" Jim asked. "How come I
don't know this story?"

"It was a painful memory," Canidy said. "You should
have seen the fat lady. It wasn't the sort of thing one talked
about.''

"It wasn't all that difficult," Fine said, laughing. "All it
took was a new Studebaker.''

He and Canidy laughed aloud.

"A new Studebaker?" Chesty asked, confused.

"To replace the one he and Fulmar blew up," Fine said.

"I want to hear about this in some detail, of course,"
Chesty Whittaker said, chuckling. "But right now there's
not the time. Save it for later.''

"How is Dr. Canidy?" Fine asked.

"Very well, thank you," Canidy said.

"Everybody's staying here tonight, right?" Chesty said.
"So we won't have the problem of moving people around?"

Everybody nodded.

"Then all Jim and I have to do is get dressed," Whittaker
said.

3
The Mayflower Club
Washington, D.C.
10:20 P.M., June 16, 1941

Stanley S. Fine, vice president, legal, Continental Studios,
Inc., swung his gaze in some surprise around the dining
room of the Mayflower Club. The club was not nearly as
elegant as Fine would have imagined. Tables had uneven
legs, and the wallpaper was peeling in spots. There were
indeed far more elegant places in California, with food at
least as good. But there was an ambience here that the more
elegant places he knew simply did not have—an ambience
born of white Anglo-Saxon money and power, an ambience
that practically screamed at Stanley Fine: *"You* have no
right to be here. *You* are to us an outsider forever." But
Stanley was equally aware that *here* he damned well was,
and he was also certain that he was absolutely right about
doing it.

When he returned to Los Angeles, he knew, he might
have some explaining to do. He might even have some problems with some other people's overly tender—but no less
important—feelings. He would have to tell his wife, for
instance, that he had managed to invade WASP heaven. And
through his wife, news would reach his employer's wife and
in due course the ears of Max Lieberman.

"Max," his aunt Sophie would say to Max Lieberman,
founder and chairman of the board of Continental Studios,
Inc., "you wouldn't believe what Shirley told me. When
Stanley was in Washington, Mr. Chesley not only had him
in his own house, but—would you believe it!—he took him
to the Mayflower Club!"

Not long ago (until the federal government broke its system up) Continental Studios had owned substantially all of

its motion-picture theaters. And Whittaker Construction had
designed and built virtually all of them.

In New York and in other large cities, these theaters were
usually housed within office buildings. And these buildings
were usually owned by corporations in which Continental
Studios, Whittaker Properties, and other interested parties
held a controlling interest. The government's successful an-
titrust suit against the studios had affected the ownership of
the theaters, but not the control of the real estate they were
part of. Colonel William B. Donovan's law firm had worked
out an agreement with the Justice Department, which had
softened somewhat the governmental edict that flatly for-
bade motion-picture studios to own or control motion-
picture theaters. Thus, so long as real estate owned by
Continental was managed by a third party (in this case,
Whittaker Properties) which had no interests in motion-
picture production, the studio would not have to sell its
stock in corporations (in a Depression-lowered real estate
market) which happened to own buildings which happened
to house movie theaters.

It was an unlikely alliance, but Continental Studios and
Whittaker Properties—and therefore Max Lieberman and
Chesley Haywood Whittaker—were in business together.

Max Lieberman had met Chesley Whittaker a dozen times
in Washington, D.C., but he had neither been in the house
on Q Street nor a guest at the Mayflower Club. Money
wouldn't get you in the door. A German-Jewish accent
would certainly keep you out.

Would Uncle Max be hurt that Stanley had made it where
he himself could not go? Or would he conclude with his
customary immodesty that it was one more proof that he'd
been right to spend whatever it had cost to get Stanley into
Harvard Law?

One of Uncle Max's dozens of profound philosophical

observations—"It's really a small world, isn't it?"—
seemed to be proved again tonight. Stanley S. Fine was in
Washington to deal with a problem involving Eric Fulmar.

As vice president, legal, of Continental Studios, Inc.,
Stanley Fine's duties were rather simple. He actually practiced very little law himself. It was another tenet of Max
Lieberman's philosophy that "it was cheaper in the long
run to go first class." As applied to matters legal, this meant
the retention of the best law firms available to deal with
specific problems.

Donovan's firm, for example, was retained by Continental
to deal primarily with the federal government. Other firms
handled labor relations, finance, artists' contracts, libel and
slander, copyright, and the myriad other specialized fields
of law with which the production of motion pictures was
involved.

Stanley Fine had two functions, and for these he was paid
very generously: to have at his fingertips the status of whatever of Continental's legal affairs Uncle Max had that moment wondered about; and, more important, to have a fast
answer when Uncle Max looked over a document and demanded, "Stanley, what the *hell* does this mean?"

It wasn't as simple as it sounded. Max Lieberman was by
no means the fool he often seemed to be. The questions he
asked were often penetrating, and almost always demonstrated his uncanny ability to "look for the dry rot under
the varnish."

The question Uncle Max had asked that had brought Stanley to Washington, at the moment, had no answer: "What
about Monica Carlisle's kid? He's in Morocco for some
goddamned half-assed reason. Find out. Also find out what
he's a citizen of," Uncle Max had said. "We'd look like
shit if he joined the Nazis."

Uncle Max had thought that over a minute and then

added, "Do it yourself, Stanley, and do it next."

Stanley had taken the first plane he could get, a Trans-continental and Western Airlines Douglas Skyliner to Chicago, and when his connecting flight to New York had been delayed, the train. The man to ask about this was obviously Colonel William B. Donovan, a man who was not only a good friend of Max Lieberman and Continental Studios but who also was the man Franklin Roosevelt most depended on for foreign intelligence.

Donovan was glad to hear he was in New York, he said. He had a few things to bring up involving the Whitworth Building—one of the buildings Continental owned a piece of—and if Fine was free, why didn't they have lunch downtown? Chesty Whittaker belonged to a luncheon club at 33 Wall Street, twenty-first floor, and he should be there, too.

After they had finished the Whitworth Building business, Fine brought up the question of Monica Carlisle's son. He asked Donovan if he happened to know anyone at the Department of State with whom he could discuss a confidential matter. Donovan not surprisingly did. Chesley Haywood Whittaker then insisted—not invited, insisted—that Fine come to Washington with him on the Congressional Limited and spend the night with him at his house on Q Street.

"I hate that damned train, alone, and there's no sense in you going to a hotel. I won't be able to have dinner with you tonight, but I'll see that you're entertained, and meet you afterward."

"Why don't I just go to the Hotel Washington? It's right around the corner from the State Department, and the studio keeps a suite there. . . ."

"Don't be silly," Whittaker said. "What I have to do is have dinner with Roosevelt. My nephew, Jim, is being sent to the Philippines, and Roosevelt wants to see him before he goes. He was close to Jimmy's father. I don't see how I can get out of it. But it'll be just that, dinner. It starts at eight-fifteen, and it'll be over by ten or ten-fifteen. What I've done, and I hope this is all right with you, is arrange for a very pretty woman, a lawyer by the way and the daughter of an old friend, to take you to dinner at the May-flower, and we'll meet you there afterward.''

"Aren't I putting you out?"

"Not at all. I'm just sorry about the damned dinner.''

There were few people in the United States, Fine thought, who could be sincerely annoyed by the necessity of taking dinner with the President of the United States.

The young woman had turned out not only to be as promised, young, attractive, and a lawyer, but also the daughter of the late Thomas Chenowith, another pillar of the New York legal establishment. And he was dining with the son of Chandler Bitter and nephew of Brandon Chambers.

The odd thing, Stanley S. Fine decided, was that he liked these people and was comfortable in their presence. He felt a little jealous of Canidy and Bitter—younger men about to embark on a great adventure. It was certainly illogical that he should be jealous of young men going off to war, but he had learned at Cornell something that had stuck in his mind: War was as much a part of the human condition as love and birth.

And there was a secret side to Stanley S. Fine that not even his wife understood. If he had had his way, he would have been an aviator, not a lawyer. His heroes were Lind-bergh, Doolittle, and Howard Hughes, not the august members of the Supreme Court. And while of course it could be the wine that let him think this, he sort of had the feeling that after he told Canidy and Bitter that he'd earned his commercial ticket and that he was trying to come up with the money to buy a Beechcraft, they seemed to hold him in a different light, maybe even consider him sort of an associate member of their fraternity. So far as Stanley S. Fine was concerned, being a fighter pilot was the realization of the ultimate dream.

About 10:30, Chesty and Jim Whittaker came into the dining room, followed by the headwaiter and a busboy carrying two chairs.

Jim Whittaker quickly ducked his head and gave an unsuspecting, and immediately annoyed, Cynthia Chenowith a quick, wet kiss.

"Jim!" she cried out, blushing. "Would you stop acting like a child and behave yourself?"

"I have been behaving myself," he said. "Isn't that right, Chesty?"

"With one or two minor little lapses, he was on his very best behavior," Chesty said, and turned to order brandy from the headwaiter.

"And did you tell Uncle Franklin how miffed you were that he's kept you in uniform?" Canidy asked.

"Oh yes," Chesty Whittaker replied, laughing. "He told him."

"And what did he say?" Canidy asked.

"He told me how proud the nation is of all of us who stand at the gates, defending freedom," Jim said dryly. He turned to Cynthia. "Has Canidy been making passes at you, my love?"

"Oh, for God's sake, Jimmy!"

"Bitter has," Canidy said. "Bitter's been feeling *my* knee and simultaneously making eyes at her. He's not very good in the dark. I would have said something, but he looked so happy."

Chesty Whittaker's smile was strained.

I did that, Canidy realized, *to see what his reaction would be. And he did just what I expected.*

"Why don't we change the subject?" Cynthia said. "And not back to airplanes, if you don't mind."

"Well, I for one would like to hear," Chesty said, "about the Great Cedar Rapids Fire Dick Canidy had, as it were, his hand in."

Fine told the story. He was a good storyteller, and his descriptions of the man whose Studebaker had blown up and the juvenile counselor's disappointment at losing the chance to rehabilitate Fulmar and Canidy had the others laughing boisterously.

"And proving beyond doubt my uncle Max's belief that it's a small world, Eric Fulmar's the reason I'm in Washington," Fine said. "Eric's in Morocco, and that is worrying the studio."

"Why should that worry the studio?" Canidy asked. "Oh, because of his mother?"

Fine nodded. "It would be embarrassing if it became public knowledge that he exists at all, and it would probably kill her at the box office if it came out that he's part German."

"He's not a German, he's an American," Whittaker snorted.

"He may think of himself as an American, but I have to establish that once and for all, and when I do, that opens the next question."

"Which is?" Canidy asked.

"What is the legal position, vis-à-vis the draft, of people with dual citizenship?" Fine said. "And of people like Eric, who are out of the country? Does the law require an expatriate to register for the draft? If so, when? When the law goes into effect? Or when the expatriate returns to the United States?"

"Interesting question," Chesty Whittaker said.

"And then," Canidy said, "there is the question of the draft dodger himself."

Cynthia and Fine both gave him a dirty look.

"Catching him, I mean," Canidy said. "After you ambulance chasers have come to all your solemn legal decisions, there is the question of applying them."

"I can see it now," Jim Whittaker said. "A platoon of Cynthia's Foggy Bottom cronies, in top hats and morning coats, struggling through the sandy wastes . . ."

"With a draft notice in their hands," Canidy ordered.

"And there, on top of the dunes, our hero . . ." Whittaker came in.

"On a white stallion, dressed up like Rudolph Valentino in *The Sheik,* saluting . . ."

Whittaker demonstrated the salute, using the third finger on his left hand in an upward position.

Canidy laughed heartily and went on. "And, with a cry of 'Fuck you! I am the little boy who never existed, you can't draft *me!* Fight your own damned war,' galloping off into the sunset."

"My God, you're disgusting," Cynthia said.

"I think," Jim Whittaker said, "that you're in trouble, Richard."

"I think you *two* owe everyone an apology for your vulgarity," Chesty Whittaker said furiously.

"I'm sorry," Canidy said.

"Well, hell, I'm not," Jim Whittaker said. "And I'm not going to be a hypocrite about it. No harm was intended."

"You don't feel you owe Cynthia an apology, is that what you're saying?" Chesty Whittaker asked, softly and coldly.

"For what?"

"For your language and that obscene gesture."

"This, you mean?" Jim Whittaker asked, making the gesture again. "Cynthia doesn't even know what it means. And Canidy said 'fuck,' not me."

Chesty Whittaker's face whitened.

"Stanley, Cynthia, *I* apologize to you for my nephew and his friend. I can only say that they have obviously had too much to drink."

"I have not yet begun to drink," Whittaker said, "as one sailor or another is supposed to have said."

"Ed," Chesty Whittaker said to Bitter, "can I rely on you to get them home safely?"

"Yes, sir," Bitter said. "And I'm sorry."

"The two of you together are too explosive for your own good," Chesty Whittaker said.

Then he followed Stanley S. Fine and Cynthia Chenowith out of the dining room.

"As Jim's guest, I know I'm not in a position to say this, but I will. The two of you were disgusting," Bitter said.

"Go with the good people, Edwin," Canidy said. "I have all the self-righteousness I can take for one night."

"I told Mr. Whittaker I would take care of you, and I will," Bitter said.

Whittaker and Canidy looked at each other, and then, simultaneously, they both gave Bitter the finger.

"Fuck you, Edwin!" they said in chorus. And laughed.

Bitter walked quickly after the others.

Whittaker caught the sommelier's eye and ordered a bottle of cognac.

"Nothing very elaborate, you understand, my friend and I are just junior officers, but something *decent*."

"I have just the thing, Mr. Whittaker, a very nice, not very well known label, by the people who bottle Grand Marnier."

"That will do nicely," Whittaker said.

When the cognac was delivered, he interrupted the

waiter's ritual pouring by taking the bottle away from him and filling the snifters well over half full.

"I am going to miss you, Richard," he said.

"Me, too," Canidy said.

"Here's to strays and orphans," Whittaker said. "You and me and Fulmar, wherever good ol' Eric may be."

They took a swallow of cognac.

"Aunts and uncles, nephews and nieces," Whittaker said.

"Whatever you said," Canidy said, and they took a second swallow.

"Draft dodgers," Whittaker said.

"Especially good ol' Eric, who is obviously smarter than you or me," Canidy countered.

They drained the snifters with the third toast. Whittaker picked up the bottle and started to pour again.

Not looking at Canidy, and very softly, he said, "I used to wonder how I knew Chesty was bedding her. I never caught them, of course. But I knew."

Canidy looked at him but said nothing.

"You realize, of course, Richard," Whittaker asked, "that I am confiding in you only because I am confident you will get your ass shot off in China?"

Canidy nodded.

"And then I knew how I knew," he said. "Because I love her. And because I love him."

He handed a snifter to Canidy and raised his own.

"Love, Lieutenant Canidy," he said.

"Love, Lieutenant Whittaker," Canidy said.

4
The Plantation
Bibb County, Alabama
June 17, 1941

Ann Chambers had known since she was fourteen that she
had inherited her father's character and his brains and that
her brothers Mark and Charley had gotten from their mother
their charm and their tendency to see things as they wished
they were, rather than as they really were.

They were considered charming and pleasant—and they
were. Ann was considered assertive and aggressive—and
she was. In fact, she had a masculine mind, she thought. She
much preferred the company of men to women. And she
felt she understood men in ways her girlfriends didn't . . .
couldn't; Sarah, for instance, didn't. Sarah had gotten itchy
britches from Ed Bitter the moment she had seen him, and she
had done everything but back up to him like a bitch in heat.

Ann didn't think that was going to get Eddie Bitter to
make a play for Sarah. Eddie was the Boy Scout type, who
would be frightened away if a girl made herself readily
available to him. All Sarah had succeeded in doing was to
make him uncomfortable. As a general rule of thumb, Ann
Chambers believed that the more desirable a man was, the
less responsive he was to feminine wiles.

She had, she admitted, itchy britches for Dick Canidy.
She had been able to face this fact from practically the moment she laid eyes on him. It had been almost immediately
apparent to her that Canidy was cut from the same bolt of
cloth as her father. And she knew that they hadn't made
very much of that particular material.

Even Sue-Ellen had seen this special character, whatever
it was, in Dick Canidy. Ann had seen Sue-Ellen looking at

him, and she wasn't looking at him with the eyes of a
"nice" wife and mother. Ann had heard rumors that Sue-
Ellen was playing around on her husband, and Ann's reaction was that her damned-fool brother should have known
better than to marry a woman who was smarter and stronger
than he was. Ann was reasonably sure that, given the opportunity, Sue-Ellen might very well have made a play for
Dick Canidy.

There had been no opportunity for that, of course. Too
many people around and nowhere to go.

Too many people around had been her problem, too. Canidy would not have responded to staring soulfully at him,
the way Sarah had stared at Ed Bitter, and staring soulfully
was the only card Ann could have played in a house full of
people. If she had given him the goofy looks, Ann was sure
Canidy would have pegged her as a college tease, just a fool
kid.

The way to snag Dick Canidy was to make him come to
her. She thought she had already made the first correct step
in that direction: she had discussed flying with him. And he
had been genuinely surprised to learn that she wasn't cooing
at him like a schoolgirl who simply was thrilled by aviators,
but that she had her private license, two hundred fifty hours,
and had flown the Beech solo cross-country to San Francisco.

When he had time to turn that over in his mind, he would
get the idea that she was something special and come after
her. She would elude him until he was snared. She would
become first his friend, and then give him the sex that all
men were after. What more could he ask for?

Dick Canidy was the man she wanted to marry. The proof
that she made a sound judgment about him was that her
father really liked him. And her father had a favorite saying
when he was with his friends: "The best thing about being

my age, and in my position in life, is that I no longer have to suffer fools.''

Dick Canidy was the first young man she ever saw her father seeking out because he was genuinely interested in what he had to say.

There wasn't much time. She was going to have to move fast, to set her hook in him before he went swimming in distant waters.

Sarah and Charity stayed five days, until June 17, and then Ann and her mother drove them to Montgomery and put them on the train back up north. On the way back to The Plantation, Ann asked her mother if it would be all right if she asked Eddie and Dick Canidy to come for another weekend.

"Well, of course," her mother said. "You liked him, didn't you?"

"I'm going to marry him," Ann said.

"This weekend, or after he comes back from China?" her mother replied dryly.

"I may get unofficially engaged this weekend," Ann said, "but we'll wait until he comes back from China to get married."

"You seem very, very sure of yourself," Jenny Chambers said. "What are you going to do if he has other plans for the weekend?"

"He wouldn't dare!" Ann said.

She called Pensacola Naval Air Station the moment she got back to The Lodge. She asked for Canidy, and when the operator rang the number, another operator came on and said that number was no longer in service. Then she asked for Ed Bitter's number. It was the same number she had been given for Dick Canidy.

"Let me talk to the base public information officer," Ann

said. Her mother walked into the library in time to hear and raised her eyebrows.

"Public information, Journalist Anderson speaking, sir."

"Ann Chambers," she said. "Nashville *Courier-Gazette*."

Jenny Chambers's eyebrows rose even higher and she shook her head.

"What can the Navy do for the *Courier-Gazette*?"

"I'm trying to run down one of two sailors," she said. "Two lieutenants, one of them named Bitter, Edwin, and other one named Canidy, Richard."

"I'm sure we can handle that," he said. "Hang on, please."

He didn't come back on the line. An officer did.

"This is Commander Kersey, Miss Chambers," he said. "I'm afraid we have no officers by those names on the base. May I inquire as to the reason you wanted to locate them?"

"Yeah," Ann Chambers said. "I'm running down a story that they're going to China, and wanted to ask them about it."

There was a pause. "Would you mind telling me where you heard that story, Miss Chambers?" Commander Kersey asked.

"It's all over Washington, Commander," she said. "I'll check it out with the Navy Department."

She hung up and looked at her mother.

"Goddamn it," she said. "They're already gone. Now what the hell am I going to do?" She was furious with herself when she felt the tears well up in her eyes.

5
Rockefeller Center
New York, New York
June 19, 1941

When Bitter and Canidy appeared at the CAMCO office, they were shown to a small, sparsely furnished conference room and given coffee and Danish rolls. A few minutes later, a man in civilian clothing appeared, identified himself as Commander Ommark of the Navy, and opened his leather briefcase.

The briefcase contained the necessary forms and other documentation required for the separation of officers, for the convenience of the government, under honorable conditions from the naval service. Among the documents were checks drawn upon the Treasury of the United States for their pay and allowances through 15 June 1941, including pay for unused accrued leave.

Why they hadn't been given the discharge papers in Washington was not explained, and Canidy decided questioning the bureaucratic mind would be a waste of time.

"Thank you, gentlemen," Commander Ommark said. He shook their hands and wished them good luck.

A secretary came into the conference room a moment after he left, and told them they should return to their hotel and separate their clothing, military and civilian, into that which they would be taking with them, and that which CAMCO would store or send anywhere they designated.

Canidy could see no point in taking blues or whites or any dress uniforms with them, but khakis and aviator-green twill, from which U.S. Navy insignia could easily be removed, would more than likely be of service in the Far East. Ed Bitter asked her about aviator's wings. The secretary said she didn't really know, they could ask when they returned at half past two. She had unassembled corrugated paper boxes and a roll of paper tape for them, and, carrying that, they returned to the Biltmore Hotel, near Grand Central Terminal, and changed into civilian clothing.

Bitter said that he thought that he was going to ship his uniforms to Brandon Chambers to keep for him at The Plantation. They would probably be going to Pensacola anyway, when their year was up.

Canidy asked if Bitter thought Mr. Chambers would mind keeping his Navy uniforms, too. Bitter hesitated before replying, but said finally he was sure his uncle would not mind. Canidy felt Bitter's attitude was cold and strange, as it had been strange for the last week or ten days. Now was the time to bring it to a head.

"You want to tell me what I've done? Or are you planning to sulk from now on?" Canidy asked.

"It's a combination of things," Bitter said after a long pause. "You were disgraceful in Washington."

"I was a little drunk in Washington," Canidy said. "Whittaker and I had a lot to drink."

"You were visibly drunk this morning in Commander Porter's office."

"I won't debate the point," Canidy said. "We didn't go to bed at all. But that's not what's bothering you. And I think we should get whatever it is out in the open."

Bitter looked at him. For a moment, Canidy thought there would be no reply, but then Bitter said, "I know what happened on the boat, Dick."

"What boat?" Canidy asked, confused, and then he understood. "Oh."

"You sonofabitch, that was a filthy thing to do," Bitter said angrily.

"What were you doing, watching?" Canidy asked. Bitter

didn't reply, but it was clearly written on his face that he had indeed been watching.

"You fucking *voyeur,* you!" Canidy said, amused.

Bitter had the most infuriating urge to smile.

"She's my cousin's wife, goddamn it!" he said.

"I didn't rape her," Canidy said.

"She's my cousin's wife," Bitter repeated.

"That's his problem, Eddie," Canidy said. "Not yours."

"You have the morals of an alley cat," Bitter said.

Canidy smiled at him. "Now we both understand that, what next?"

"You *bastard!*" Bitter said, but now he was smiling.

"What the hell did you do?" Canidy asked. "Follow us to the boat?"

"I went down to the river to think," Bitter said. "And saw the light."

"A *gentleman* would not have looked," Canidy said piously.

"Oh, you sonofabitch!" Bitter said. "Jesus Christ, you're impossible."

"Go in the bathroom, Saint Edwin, and get a wad of toilet paper."

"Do what?"

"To moisten the paper tape," Canidy said. "To seal the boxes. Then we can go cash our checks and get a couple of drinks to celebrate our freedom."

"We shouldn't show up there with liquor on our breath," Bitter said.

"We're not in the Navy anymore, Ed," Canidy said.

When they went back to the CAMCO offices in Rockefeller Center at half past two, a civilian, well dressed, well spoken, was waiting for them. His briefcase held their contracts and some other forms. There was, for instance, the question of what to do about their pay. CAMCO was willing

to pay them in American money, or gold, in China, or to
deposit their checks monthly to any bank of their choice in
the United States. If they had no bank, CAMCO would arrange with the Riggs National Bank in Washington for ac-
counts. He would suggest, he said, that they take part, say
$150 or $200, for their pay in China, and have the balance
credited to their bank.

When they had filled out the necessary forms, he gave
them their railroad tickets. They were to share a compart-
ment on the 20th Century Limited to Chicago, departing
Grand Central Station at 5:30 that night, and then were to
have roomettes on the Super Chief out of Chicago. He also
handed them passports. Canidy realized he hadn't even
thought about a passport. He had never been out of the
United States before. But somebody had thought of that detail, someone with influence to get their photographs from
the Navy and have them affixed to passports they had not
applied for.

"When you get to San Francisco," the man told them,
"take a taxi to the Mark Hopkins Hotel and use the house
phone to call Mr. Harry C. Claiborne. If there is some sort
of delay, and you can't make it to the Mark Hopkins by ten
o'clock, go directly to Pier 17. You have passage aboard
the *Jan Suvit,* of the Java-Pacific Line. It sails at midnight
of the day you get to Frisco."

The Super Chief put them in San Francisco at four in the
afternoon four days later. As they made their way through
the station toward the taxi stand, Canidy caught Bitter's arm.

"You know what's going to happen if we go to the Mark
Hopkins?"

Bitter didn't understand the question.

"No, what?"

"You heard what that guy said. The ship sails at midnight. If we go to the hotel now, you know what's going to happen. Someone is going to sit on us, before they lead us by the hand to the taxi that'll take us to the pier.''

''What are you driving at?''

''I don't know if I'm up to six or eight hours of sitting around a hotel room, letting my very active imagination run away with me.''

''Imagination about what?'' Bitter asked.

''Getting killed over there, Eddie. You haven't worried about that?''

''Sure, I have,'' Bitter confessed.

But he was surprised that Canidy was afraid, and even more surprised that he would admit it. Now that he thought about it, it probably explained why Canidy had been drinking so much.

''I've heard a lot about Fisherman's Wharf,'' Canidy said. ''What do you say we go have a look at it?''

It was a plea, Bitter realized.

''What do we do about the hotel?''

''The ship sails at midnight. We go there at eleven,'' Canidy said.

Ed Bitter wanted to do what he had been told to do, go to the hotel. But the prospect of sitting around a hotel room, reading magazines as if waiting for the dentist, now seemed as unpleasant to him as it did to Canidy.

He found a rationalization to go with Canidy: It was unlikely that Canidy would get so drunk that he would forget the time and miss ship. But it was a possibility, especially if he was alone. It was his duty to go with him, to keep him out of trouble.

''What the hell,'' Bitter said finally.

There was gratitude in Canidy's eyes. Bitter was touched by it. He had another thought. Canidy was really his friend. He was damned glad Canidy was going with him to China.

Going alone would have been very difficult, far more frightening.

At 11:15 they took a taxi to the *Jan Suvit,* the steamer that was to carry them to Asia.

6

The steward came to their cabin early in the morning with tea on a tray and told them breakfast would be served in half an hour. Canidy beat Bitter to their shower, and when Bitter came out, he saw that Canidy was wearing khakis, so he took khakis from his suitcase too.

They made their way through the passageways to the dining salon and took a table under a porthole near the door. The porthole was open, but Bitter noticed that the glass had been painted black.

Two large, ruddy men in their forties, wearing ill-fitting business suits, came to the door and stood there uncomfortably. Canidy glanced up at them, then away, and then back again. He knew one of them from Pensacola.

"Sit down with us, why don't you, Chief?" he called out.

The heavier of the two men looked at him, frowning, and then smiled.

"Hey, Mr. Canidy," he said. "I didn't know you'd joined the Chinese Navy." He walked to Canidy, gave him his hand, and sat down.

"Chief, do you remember Mr. Bitter?"

"Yes, sir. How are you, Mr. Bitter?" ex–Chief Petty Officer John B. Dolan said, and gave Bitter his hand. "I don't think you know Chief Finley. He just came off the *Saratoga.*"

They shook hands.

"I don't suppose they have a chief's mess aboard this thing, do they?" the chief said as a white-jacketed steward turned Dolan's coffee cup over and filled it.

"I guess you'll have to put up with this," Canidy said.

"I was a China sailor years ago," Chief Dolan said, "before I signed over to aviation. You can quickly learn to like being waited on like this."

Bitter had by then recognized the chief as a chief aviation machinist's mate who had also been stationed at Pensacola NAS. He was a little embarrassed at not having thought that they would require maintenance and other ground personnel, and that enlisted men as well as officer pilots would have been recruited. He was a little uneasy sitting with enlisted men.

The steward returned with a hand-lettered menu. The variety was impressive, and the food, later, was delicious.

When they had just about finished eating, a man who looked to be in charge rapped his water pitcher with the handle of his knife.

"Gentlemen," he said. "May I have your attention, please?"

There was a shuffling of chairs as people turned around so they could sit facing him.

"My name is Perry Crookshanks," the man said. "And I signed on as a squadron commander. I'm the skipper, in other words. And I have some bad news—which is that this is not a pleasure trip. We'll be at sea for a long time, and all you splendid physical specimens would be piles of blubber with all food and no exercise. So there will be PT every morning for thirty minutes before breakfast, and again at half past two, before you start your drinking. I expect to see everybody there, wearing shorts and a smile."

"Bullshit," Canidy said louder than he intended. The chief chuckled.

"Did you say something?" Crookshanks said angrily.

"I said 'bullshit,'" Canidy replied.

"I'll see you after we've dismissed here," Crookshanks said icily.

Bitter flushed.

"We're going to be flying P40-Bs, as you know," Crookshanks went on. "I was promised dash-ones and other technical material about the aircraft, but it just hasn't shown up."

The dash-one was the pilot's operating manual, a technical manual, for a particular aircraft. For example, TM-1-P40B-1 was the pilot's operating manual for the P40-B. Similarly, TM-1-C47A-1 was the operating manual for the Douglas DC-3, known to the Army as the C-47 and to the Navy as the R4-D.

"Jesus Christ!" someone across the room complained bitterly. "I've never been close to one of the sonsofbitches, and no dash-ones!"

"Fortunately," Crookshanks said, responding to the complaint, "we have several people with us who have flown the aircraft, and what we're going to do is have them tell us about it. We're going to start this program right away. I want you all back here, with notebooks and pencils . . . God, I hope you have notebooks and pencils . . . at 1030. We'll do an hour in the morning and an hour in the afternoon. Any questions?"

There were no questions.

"Dismissed," Mr. Crookshanks said.

Bitter was surprised and angry when Canidy got up and started to leave the dining salon.

"He told you he wanted to see you," he said, grabbing Canidy's arm.

"He knows where to find me," Canidy replied, and, seeing the deep concern on Bitter's face, he added: "I have something in the cabin I think he wants."

"I don't understand you at all," Bitter said.

"I know you don't," Canidy replied, smiling at him.

Perry Crookshanks, white-faced and tight-lipped, showed up at the louvered door of their cabin five minutes later.

"Perhaps you misunderstood me, Mr. Canidy," Perry Crookshanks said. "I asked you to remain behind in the dining salon."

"I understood you," Canidy said. "But I want to clear up a small misunderstanding between us, too."

"What's that?"

"You're no longer a commander in the Navy, and, more important, I'm no longer a junior grade lieutenant. I work for you, maybe, but I'm not commanded by you. There's a big difference."

"You were briefed as to what is expected of you."

"I signed on to fly. That's all. In the air, I'll take military-type orders. On the ground, I won't. That better be very clear between us."

"You'll take orders, or you'll be sent home," Crookshanks said.

"In irons? Come on, Crookshanks." Canidy said. "Get it through your head that neither of us is in the Navy anymore."

"I can't tolerate—and you know I can't—an uncooperative attitude. There has to be discipline."

"Cooperation and discipline are two different things," Canidy said. "Cooperation is why I came to my cabin, knowing that you were certain to come after me like a truant officer."

Canidy unlocked one of his huge tin suitcases and motioned Crookshanks over to it.

"In a spirit of cooperation, you can *borrow* these," he said.

Crookshanks's eyebrows rose. He dipped his hand into the suitcase and came up with a military manual. Bitter looked at it. On the cover in red ink was stamped NOT TO BE REMOVED FROM THE LIBRARY. Right below that was printed TM-1-P40A-1.

"There's one copy of the A-model dash-one and two copies each for the B and C models," Canidy said. "There's also three copies of the tech manual for the Allison 710-33 engine and two for the 710-39. I wasn't able to find out what's in the planes we're going to get. You can have all the duplicates, and you can borrow the single copies whenever Bitter and I aren't reading them."

"Christ knows, we need them," Crookshanks said. "Where'd you get them?"

"I stole them from the Air Corps library at Maxwell Field," Canidy said. "I figured we would need them more than they did."

Crookshanks looked at him for a long moment.

"Interesting, the way you put that," he said. " 'We would need them,' not 'I would need them.' " He paused. "Perhaps you're not entirely the wiseass you act like." He nodded and scooped up the manuals. "Thank you, Canidy."

"You're welcome, Crookshanks," Canidy replied.

Canidy showed up for the first training session in the dining salon. He did not show up for the calisthenics. Bitter went, did what was required of him, and thought that Canidy was a fool. He could have made up for the friction he had caused. The dash-ones and TMs would have gotten him out of that. All he would have had to do was show up and do calisthenics with the others, and all would have been forgiven. Now he was challenging the skipper all over again, and the skipper certainly couldn't let that pass.

But nothing was said to Canidy, and when the others saw that, they stopped going too. By the time the ship sailed into Honolulu, only a half-dozen pilots, including Ed Bitter, and none of the ground crew, regularly met on the deck to keep their bodies in shape.

It was early morning when they sailed into Pearl Harbor. They docked at the Navy wharfs, rather than at Honolulu, even though the *Jan Suvit* was a foreign-flag merchantman. Before they docked, Crookshanks joined Bitter and Canidy on the fantail, where they were watching the Navy Yard tug push them against the pier.

"I have no authority, Canidy," Crookshanks said, "to order you to remain aboard while we're here. But I would like you and the others to remain aboard."

"Loose lips lose ships?" Canidy replied. "Or are you concerned that we'll come back aboard with a dose of the clap?"

"Both," Crookshanks said with a chuckle.

"I don't know about the sex maniac here, Crookshanks," Canidy said, glancing at Bitter. "But I can last another two weeks without getting laid. So I'll stay aboard. I think you're right."

"OK," Crookshanks said. "I'm going ashore. I have to. While I'm there, I'll dishonestly use my old ID card and wipe the commissary out of American steaks."

"*You* had better not come back with the clap," Canidy said.

They were in Pearl Harbor less than twenty-four hours, just time enough to take on fuel, and—from a line of Army trucks—case after heavy case. One of the cases cracked open when the boom operator missed the hold opening, and a stream of brown metal boxes spilled out of the crates and fell into the hold. Each was stamped in yellow: AMMUNI-

TION, BROWNING MACHINE GUN CALIBER .50 IN BELTS FOUR
BALL AND ONE TRACER 125.

They broiled the steaks over coal on the fantail the afternoon they left Pearl Harbor for Manila. Crookshanks had
brought cases of Schlitz beer back aboard with him. He
came to Canidy and handed him one.

"Just so we don't misunderstand each other, Canidy," he
said with a smile. "If you had gone ashore in Honolulu,
you would not have been allowed back on board."

Canidy looked at him a moment, and then he smiled.

"Now you tell me," he said. "*Now!* Ten miles at sea!"

FIVE

The White House
Washington, D.C.
July 11, 1941

"Good morning, Mr. President, Colonel," General George C. Marshall said as he walked into the Oval Office of the White House.

"General," the President said.

"George," the colonel said. The colonel was not being unduly familiar with the senior U.S. Army officer. "Colonel" Henry L. Stimson, as secretary of war, stood in the chain of command between Marshall and the Commander in Chief. But he had been a colonel in World War I, and liked to be reminded of the title.

"I hope you haven't been kept waiting...." Marshall said.

"Not at all," the President said. "Henry just got here." He paused. "Bill Donovan will be here in thirty minutes."

"Oh?"

"I wanted to give the both of you a final look at this," the President said, "before I give the original to him."

He handed each of them a neatly typed sheet of paper.

DESIGNATING A COORDINATOR
OF INFORMATION

By virtue of the authority vested in me as President of the United States and as Commander in Chief of the Army and Navy of the United States, it is ordered as follows:

1. There is hereby established the position of Coordinator of Information, with authority to collect and analyze all information and data which may bear upon national security; to correlate such information and data, and to make such information and data available to the President and to such departments and officials of the Government as the President may determine; and to carry out, when requested by the President, such supplementary activities as may facilitate the securing of information important for national security not now available to the Government.

2. The several departments and agencies of the Government shall make available to the Coordinator of Information all and any such information and data relating to national security as the Coordinator, with the approval of the President, may from time to time request.

3. The Coordinator of Information may appoint such committees, consisting of appropriate representatives of the various departments and agencies of the Government, as he may deem necessary to assist him in the performance of his functions.

4. Nothing in the duties and responsibilities of the Coordinator of Information shall in any way interfere with or impair the duties and respon-

sibilities of the regular military and naval advisers of the President as Commander in Chief of the Army and Navy.

5. Within the limits of such funds as may be allocated to the Coordinator of Information by the President, the Coordinator may employ necessary personnel and make provisions for the necessary supplies, facilities, and services.

6. William J. Donovan is hereby designated as Coordinator of Information.

Franklin D. Roosevelt

"I notice, Mr. President, that it's already signed," General Marshall said.

"Is that the first thing that came into your mind, George?" the President asked.

"Actually, Mr. President," Marshall said, "the first thing that came into my mind was that it sounds as if it was dictated by the British. By that Commander Fleming, say, or by that fellow Stevenson who seems so chummy with Edgar Hoover."

The President smiled broadly, which could mean that he was either genuinely amused or that he was furious.

"What I thought, George," the President said, "when I read it, was that it sounded like me. Or as if it had been written by someone who had studied the carefully ambiguous phrase at Columbia Law."

Marshall and Stimson smiled stiffly. Franklin D. Roosevelt and William J. Donovan had been law-school classmates at Columbia.

"But I also learned there that no contract cannot be improved," the President said. "I agree with both of you that Bill was taking a bit much."

"Sir?"

"In Donovan's original draft, there was a paragraph that went, as I say, a bit far. I knew it would anger you. So I deleted it." The President smiled. "I wouldn't want you to get the idea I was carrying the old-boy network too far."

He handed Stimson a sheet of paper, on which was typed a single paragraph.

4. The Coordinator of Information shall perform these duties and responsibilities, which include those of a military character, under the direction and supervision of the President as Commander in Chief of the Army and Navy of the United States.

Stimson read it and handed it to Marshall without comment.

"Admit it, George," the President said pleasantly, "isn't that what stuck in your craw?"

"If I may speak freely, Mr. President," General Marshall said, "the whole thing sticks in my craw. The military and naval intelligence services are perfectly capable of handling intelligence for the nation. We do not need another bureaucracy—especially one that's openly in bed with the British."

"We've already discussed that," Roosevelt said flatly "I have concluded we need what I have provided for. If this makes you feel any better, I quite seriously considered turning the whole thing over to J. Edgar Hoover, who isn't going to be any more pleased about this than you are. I decided against that because Bill Donovan will do what I tell him, while Edgar sometimes tends to follow his own lights. And

Bill—*Colonel Donovan*—with a few exceptions, gets along with the military and understands its problems.''

"As you say, Mr. President, you have made your decision," General Marshall said.

"If you're not otherwise tied up, General," the President said, "I hope that you will be able to find the time to stay here until Donovan arrives and I make this official. I'd like you to be here for that."

"I am at your orders, Mr. President," General Marshall said.

"Good," the President said, flashing another wide and toothy smile. "The secretary of the Navy, and chief of naval operations, and the director of the FBI seem to be tied up elsewhere. Or so they say."

2
Paris, France
August 12, 1941

Before the Wehrmacht entered Paris fourteen months before, on June 14, 1940, and marched triumphantly around the Arc de Triomphe de l'Étoile and down the Champs-Élysées, Eldon C. Baker had been one of a dozen nicely dressed, softly spoken young men attached to the American embassy as consular officers. Baker had been specifically assigned to the office charged with the issuance and renewal of passports, the issue of visas, and similar administrative tasks.

While it was commonly acknowledged within and without the embassy that many of the consular officers carried on the rolls as agricultural attachés and visa officers spent much of their time gathering intelligence information for transmission to Washington, it was generally believed that Eldon C. Baker was nothing but what he was officially announced to be. Most of his peers thought he was stuffy and more than a little boring.

When the fall of Paris became inevitable, the French government had moved to Vichy, and the neutral embassies, which of course included the United States embassy, had followed it. Few people on the embassy staff had been surprised when Eldon C. Baker was left behind, as officer-in-charge of the deserted embassy building. To them, Eldon C. Baker was the type of man who could be spared for caretaking chores while his brighter associates went about the important business of diplomacy.

Actually, Eldon C. Baker was an intelligence officer. He had been left behind because, to an extraordinary degree, he enjoyed the confidence of his superiors, both in the upper echelons of the embassy hierarchy (where only two people besides the ambassador knew of his intelligence role) and within the State Department's intelligence system itself.

The first time Eldon C. Baker saw Eric Fulmar was in Fouquet's restaurant on the Champs-Élysées. Baker had been taking dinner there with an amiable German counterpart, Frederick Ferdinand "Freddie" Dietz, a junior Foreign Ministry officer assigned to the office of the military governor of Paris.

Fulmar was with two very pretty girls and a dark-skinned young man, an Arab of some kind. Baker's attention had been split between the pretty girls and the Arab, between personal and professional curiosity. At a table across from the one with the two young men and the pretty girls sat three men, drinking coffee. One of them was black, a huge man whose flesh spilled over the collar of his shirt and whose belly pressed against the table. He was Senegalese, Baker decided, and he was certainly not in Fouquet's league socially. Not if the two Frenchmen he sat with were doing what he thought they were doing.

Baker knew one of them by sight, not by name. He was a member of the Sûreté, the French security service, and he was normally assigned to the Colonial Office. All three of them, rather obviously, were assigned to protect the Moroccan, or Algerian, or Tunisian, whatever he was, sitting at the table with the pretty girls and the handsome young man.

"Now, there's a nice pair," Baker said to his dinner partner.

"Which pair?" Freddie Dietz had quipped. "Or, you mean *both* of them."

"Yes."

"The one on the left is the daughter of Generalmajor von Handleman-Bitburg. She's in town with her mother for a short holiday with her father."

"And the other?"

"Don't know. I wish I did."

"Who's the Arab?"

The first word that came to Baker's mind, looking at the Arab, was "arrogant." He was tall, thin, and very well tailored, in a dinner jacket with an old-fashioned high collar. He was sharp-featured, hawk-eyed, and had long-fingered, sensitive hands. When he shook his cuffs, Baker saw heavy jeweled gold cuff links, and both a bracelet and a heavy gold watchband. He had a ring with a stone Baker couldn't identify on the pinkie of his right hand, and there was a large diamond—worth a fortune, Baker thought, presuming it to be real—in a heavy gold setting on what Westerners consider the wedding-ring finger.

As Baker watched, he snapped his fingers impatiently for someone to pour wine, and then a moment later, putting a cigarette to his lips, looked around impatiently for the lackey he obviously expected to provide an instant light.

"I haven't the foggiest, but the fellow is Eric Fulmar."

Eric Fulmar was blond, blue-eyed, lithe and tanned. He

was wearing a dinner jacket, not nearly as well tailored as the Arab's and with simple back studs in a modern, rolled-collar shirt. Baker felt enormous energy coming from this good-looking young man. Not nerves. Not craziness. Power. There was purpose to his gestures and self-assurance he had only rarely met in a kid so young.

"Who's he?"

"Fulmar Elektrische Gesellschaft," Freddie Dietz said. "He was at Marburg with my brother."

Fulmar Elektrische Gesellschaft, FEG, was a medium-sized electrical equipment manufacturing concern in Frankfurt am Main. That explained why the young German, who looked like a recruiting poster for the Waffen-SS, was not in uniform. Baker noticed a tendency on the part of the Germans to excuse the sons of industrialists, particularly those who had early on supported the National Socialists, from military service.

As they left the restaurant, they had passed the other table. Dietz had spoken to Fulmar, and introductions had been made all around. Fulmar introduced the Arab as "His Excellency, Sheikh Sidi Hassan el Ferruch" and the other girl as a Fräulein Somebody.

In their cab on the way to the Left Bank, Freddie Dietz further identified the Arab.

"I recognize him now. He's the son of a Moroccan pasha," he said. "He was at Marburg with my brother and Fulmar."

"What's he doing in Paris?"

"Causing trouble." Dietz laughed.

"How?"

"He's buying racehorses, in direct competition with some very highly placed people. There are, you know, some people who had hoped to take advantage of the . . . shall I say 'depressed market'? . . . to improve their stables. Fulmar's

friend has destroyed many happy dreams. He has annoyed
some very important people, one very important Hungarian
in particular, but mostly Germans. I've also heard he's into
other things—of doubtful legality. But the word is out to
leave him alone. The Foreign Ministry doesn't want trouble
with his father.''

Baker could imagine what these doubtful legal things
were. He had heard some very interesting stories about the
German inability to stop the flow of privately held gold,
Swiss and American currency, investment-quality precious
stones, and fine art out of both occupied and Vichy France.
It had been decreed that gold and foreign currency must be
deposited in banks, where they were to be exchanged for
French francs. The export of jewel stones and fine art was
forbidden except by permit, which was rarely issued.

Short of conducting house-to-house searches of France,
there was no way to make the French turn in their gold and
hard currency for exchange. And many wealthy French, who
hoped one day to leave German-occupied France, were trying every possible means to send their assets, which often
included paintings and objets d'art, out ahead of them.

A highly placed Moroccan who could freely move in and
out of France on some sort of official passport could move
fortunes in his luggage if he was so inclined.

''That being the case,'' Baker said, ''I suppose it's a good
thing we didn't go after the girls.''

''A great pity,'' Freddie Dietz said, ''but it would have
been ill advised.''

Baker found the Moroccan and his American friend fascinating, even more so after he checked his *List of Americans Known to Be Living in German-Occupied France* and
found no Fulmar on it.

Baker dispatched, that same night, a report of the encounter. Item #1 on the report was the most significant item,

he knew: If Generalmajor von Handleman-Bitburg was in Paris with his wife and daughter, it was unlikely his division would be folding its tents to load on trains for movement to the eastern front. Item #2, that it was likely a German-American named Eric Fulmar was successfully smuggling valuables out of occupied France in consort with Sidi Hassan el Ferruch, elder son of the pasha of Ksar es Souk, was not, obviously, of importance. But it was the sort of thing that should be on file somewhere.

The idea of recruiting Fulmar as an agent had, of course, immediately occurred to Baker. He was an American with highly placed German friends and contacts. His friendship with the Moroccan could prove valuable. The problem was that Fulmar would probably not look with favor at any attempt to recruit him. Agents often live shorter lives than other people. And Fulmar did not seem to Baker eager for a short life.

He would, of course, make the attempt to feel Fulmar out, but he was not at all optimistic. And if he went too far, Fulmar was entirely capable of telling his German friends that Baker was more than a caretaker for the empty U.S. embassy.

A few days later—not entirely by chance—he encountered Fulmar at the urinal in the men's room off the bar in the Hôtel Crillon.

"Hello, Fulmar, how are you?" he said, in English. The conversation in Fouquet's restaurant had all been in German.

"All right," Fulmar said. "How're you?"

He looked at Baker uneasily. But the tension almost instantly faded, and a smile as engaging as a Raphael Madonna's spread over his face. Fulmar now had a look so unfeignedly open and warm that Baker dropped his hand on his wallet pocket.

"If I'd known you were American, I would have spoken to you in English in Fouquet's," Baker said.

"It didn't matter," Fulmar said.

"I've been curious about you," Baker said.

"Is that so?" Fulmar said. "I'm thrilled that so many people I don't know well show so much curiosity about me."

"You're not on my list," Baker said.

"What list is that?" Fulmar asked as he washed his hands.

"My list of Americans in occupied France," Baker said.

"I don't live in occupied France," Fulmar said.

"Well, that explains that, doesn't it?" Baker said. He decided to push him a little. "You know, of course, that when your passport comes up for renewal, it'll be stamped 'Not Valid for Travel to Occupied France.' Unless, of course, you have a reason to be here."

"I'll be out of France before my passport expires," Fulmar said.

"What are you doing here?" Baker asked.

"What is this, anyway?" Fulmar asked.

"Nothing. I was just curious. I don't see many Americans in Paris these days."

"I suppose not," Fulmar agreed.

"So you'll let me buy you a drink?"

Fulmar hesitated, then nodded.

They went into the bar and took a table against the wall.

Fulmar knew several of the young German officers and spoke to them in German. There was dialect and slang. Fulmar was perfectly fluent in that language, so fluent that he could obviously be mistaken for a German. His French was impeccable, too.

"I think they're about out of American whiskey," Baker said.

"I drink *fin de l'eau,*" Fulmar said, in English. "I can't stand French beer."

"Bring us a siphon and ice," Baker ordered. "And some cognac."

When they had mixed the drinks, Baker raised his.

"Mud in your eye," he said.

Fulmar chuckled. "I haven't heard that in a while," he said.

"How long have you been over here?" Baker asked.

"I came over for my last two years of high school," Fulmar said. "And then I stayed for college. That makes it eight years."

"You've never been back?"

Fulmar shook his head no. Then he took the cognac bottle, poured the empty coffee cup half full, and added ice and a good spritz from the siphon.

"You say you don't live in France?" Baker asked.

"Are you just making conversation, or is that an official inquiry?"

"Forget I asked," Baker said quickly. "I didn't mean to pry."

"I know curiosity is eating you up, Mr. Baker, but maybe that's your business, so I'll try to satisfy it. I live in Morocco. I have been given a permanent residence permit by the Moroccan government. I would suppose the consulate general in Rabat has all the details."

"I guess my curiosity ran away with me," Baker said, making it an apology. "I didn't mean to offend."

"None was taken," Fulmar said dryly, smiling his open, engaging smile.

"I was told you were German," Baker said with a smile. "That made me curious, too."

"My father is German," Fulmar said, looking directly at Baker. "So far as they're concerned, that makes me a

German. If I was *in* Germany, they'd put me in the army, American passport or no. I don't want to be a German soldier."

"Maybe you should think about going home," Baker said.

"And get drafted into the American army? No, thanks."

"You may have to go home," Baker said. "What if the consulate won't renew your passport?"

"Then I'll become a Moroccan citizen," Fulmar said.

"Can you? Don't you have to be Moslem?"

"How do you know I'm not?" Fulmar asked. "And besides, I have friends there."

"Friends?"

"Um."

"That would be Sidi el Ferruch?" Baker asked, and Fulmar nodded.

"You two are close," Baker said.

"My *God,* you are nosy!" Fulmar said, but he was still smiling. He liked the man, in spite of his nosiness. Baker was smoother and smarter than he looked. "We went to high school together in Switzerland. And then to the university. We're very close. I owe him."

"Indeed?"

"He pointed out to me that I would be a fool to go in either the German or the American army," Fulmar said. "And then put his money where his mouth is by fixing it so I didn't have to. And he is indulging me tonight by taking you to dinner."

"I'm flattered," Baker said. "And surprised."

"You should be," Fulmar said, and chuckled. "It isn't often that you'll have a chance to break bread with a direct descendant of the True Prophet. And besides, it isn't often lately that I've talked to a smart American."

"I'm even more flattered," Baker said. "I'd love to break

bread with a descendant of the True Prophet—and to continue talking with another smart American.'' He paused a moment and then added casually, ''Oh, by the way, when you're not breaking bread with a descendant of the True Prophet, how do you spend your time in Morocco?''

''I try very hard not to wear out my welcome,'' Fulmar said, and laughed. ''There aren't many Europeans who speak Arabic that they trust. Within limits, they trust me.''

Baker nodded, and then Fulmar went on. ''They don't all sleep in tents on the desert, you know, tending camels. They're in business. And just because the French lost the war doesn't mean that the French have stopped trying to screw them.''

''It must be interesting,'' Baker said.

''Sometimes,'' Fulmar said.

When Sidi Hassan el Ferruch appeared at the door of the bar, with his enormous Senegalese bodyguard, N'Jibba, Fulmar and Baker joined him. There was a Delahaye waiting for them at the door of the Crillon, with a Peugeot sedan in line behind it.

The restaurant was small, the lobsters were delightfully fresh, and Sidi el Ferruch told Eldon C. Baker more than he really cared to know about the deplorable state of French racing stables under the German occupation—and absolutely nothing else of interest.

When Baker had undergone his formal training as an intelligence officer, he had been told that the error most often committed by men in the field was their failure to transmit what seemed to be unimportant information because they could see no use for it. Odd facts from various sources often could be put together to form valuable data.

Thus, with that in mind, after he had returned to the Crillon he put together another report on *Fulmar, Eric,* in which he stated that he had come to suspect that there was more to Fulmar than was immediately apparent. In other words, under the cover of his lounge-lizard image sponging on the son of the pasha of Ksar es Souk, he was up to something—something that very likely could be put to use by "our team" when the time came.

3
Hyde Park, New York
August 21, 1941

The President of the United States, Colonel William B. Donovan could tell from the glint in his eyes, was about to be witty. But he was in the process of chewing a cracker smeared with Liederkranz cheese, so the remark had to wait until he finished.

"With Eleanor off spreading the pollen of goodwill," Franklin D. Roosevelt said, "it will not be necessary for us to play bridge before we can move on to the serious drinking. May I suggest we all go in the library?"

There were appreciative chuckles from the three other men at the table. None of Roosevelt's political cronies were present. That and the presence of William B. Donovan and a Navy commander named Douglass convinced J. Edgar Hoover that Roosevelt wanted more from him than the pleasure of his company at dinner.

Roosevelt's valet, a large black man in a white jacket, moved to the President to push his wheelchair.

"I'll do it," Roosevelt said. "And that will be all, thank you. We are now going to tell bawdy stories in private."

He got another appreciative chuckle.

They followed him down a corridor to the library, where decanters of whiskey, a bottle of Rémy Martin cognac, and a silver ice bucket had been laid out on a table so Roosevelt could play the host and make the drinks.

"As your Commander in Chief, I grant you immunity from the regulation which proscribes drinking on duty, Commander Douglass," Roosevelt said.

"The commander is on duty?" Hoover asked.

"Yes," Roosevelt said. "And I really think he needs a little liquid courage before he tells you what he has to say."

"I always thought Edgar was unshockable, like a clergyman," Donovan said.

Hoover ignored that.

"You're ONI*, aren't you, Commander?" he asked.

Hoover took some pride in knowing who was involved in intelligence, and he was not reluctant to let the President, and for that matter Donovan, see again that there was very little that escaped his professional attention.

"No, sir," Commander Douglass said. "I'm now with COI."

Hoover could not conceal his surprise.

Commander Peter Stuart Douglass, USN, was a sandy-haired, freckle-faced, pleasant-looking man of forty-two who had spent his Navy career moving between deep water (his last assignment had been as commanding officer of a destroyer squadron) and intelligence.

"Take a stiff belt, Commander," Roosevelt said. "Give it a moment to warm you, and then get going."

"Yes, sir," Douglass said.

"Let me lay the groundwork," Roosevelt said, changing his mind. "Some months ago, Alex Sachs came to me bearing a letter from Albert Einstein and some other eggheads at that level. They believe it is possible to split the atom."

Hoover looked at Roosevelt, not understanding.

_____

*Office of Naval Intelligence.

"What does that mean, Mr. President?" Hoover asked.

Roosevelt motioned for Douglass to speak.

"It means the potential release of energy from matter at a rate a thousand times that possible from present energy-release methods," Douglass said.

"I don't think I understand that either," Hoover confessed.

"I don't want to insult your intelligence, sir, by—" Douglass said.

"You go right ahead and insult my intelligence, Commander," Hoover said.

"Sir, you understand that explosives really don't explode? An explosion is really a process of combustion? The 'explosive' material burns?"

Hoover nodded.

"If the atom can be split," Douglass said, "it might be possible to extract a thousand times more energy than from combustion."

"A super bomb?" Hoover said.

"Yes, sir," Douglass said.

"We don't know that yet," Roosevelt said. "After my first visit with Commander Douglass, I had Jim Conant for dinner and discussed it with him."

It did not surprise Hoover that Roosevelt had gone to James B. Conant, president of Harvard, for advice. The Roosevelt administration was heavily larded—far too heavily larded, in Hoover's opinion—with members of the Harvard faculty. Roosevelt was a Harvard graduate.

"And what did he say?" Hoover asked.

" 'Yes,' " Roosevelt said, "and 'no.' "

He waited for a laugh that did not come.

"Yes, it is possible," the President said. "No, not now. Maybe fifty, a hundred years from now."

"And you think he's wrong?" Hoover asked.

"I think he underestimates both his own academic community and American industry," Donovan said.

"In other words, *you* think a super bomb like this is possible?" Hoover asked. "It sounds like Buck Rogers in the twenty-fifth century."

"I think so too," the President said. "But I at least believe it's worth the gamble to try and find out. If such a weapon were possible, it would considerably change the odds of our losing a war should war come to us—as I believe it must."

"They've already split the atom," Donovan said. "What they have to do is learn to make it a continuous process, what the scientists call a chain reaction."

"An Italian physicist named Fermi is doing some work at the University of Chicago," Roosevelt said. "He hopes for some positive results by the first of the year."

"Who knows about this?" Hoover said.

He just thought of that, Donovan thought, somewhat unkindly.

"A handful of scientists; the chief of naval intelligence; Bill; Commander Douglass; an Army colonel named Leslie Groves; and now you," Roosevelt said.

"What will be required from the Bureau?" Hoover asked formally.

"Secrecy," Roosevelt said. "Secrecy. Absolute secrecy. This thing, if it works, could decide the war. We have to build a wall of silence around it."

"The FBI can handle it, Mr. President," Hoover said, making it a proclamation.

"I'm sure the FBI, as ever," Roosevelt said solemnly, "will deliver to the country whatever it is asked to deliver."

"It will, Mr. President," Hoover said, equally solemnly.

Donovan suspected the President was playing Hoover for

his, Donovan's, amusement, but there was no question that
Hoover was oblivious to it.

"The FBI will of course have a major and continuing
role in this project," Roosevelt said. "But that will be somewhere down the pike. What I'm concerned about right now,
and the reason I have asked you here, Edgar, is something
that's going to happen almost immediately."

"Yes, sir, Mr. President?" Hoover asked. If he were a
soldier, Donovan thought, Hoover would be standing at attention.

"The British and the Germans have also been working
on splitting the atom," Roosevelt said.

"The Germans?" Hoover asked. Roosevelt nodded.

"Dr. Conant has arranged to send two of his associates,
chaps named Urey and Pegram, to England to see how far
the English have gotten," Roosevelt said. "And to see what
they can find out about the German effort. They'll be leaving very shortly."

"Would it be possible, Mr. President," Hoover asked,
"for me to send a couple of my agents with them?"

"Bill has something like that in mind, Edgar," Roosevelt
said.

" 'Something like that'?" Hoover quoted. "Do I see a
hook in there?"

"Bill thought about sending Commander Douglass. Or to
have Douglass recruit some people from ONI and send
them."

"It's an FBI function, pure and simple," Hoover said,
annoyed.

"You know," Roosevelt said, "I thought you would say
something like that, Edgar."

"It's a statement of fact," Hoover said. "Nothing personal, Bill, you understand."

"Before I say this, Edgar . . . and pout if you like," Roosevelt said, "I want to remind you that you were given the FBI in large measure because of the efforts of Bill Donovan to get it for you."

"Bill knows I'm grateful," Hoover said, not very graciously. "But with all respect to naval intelligence—"

"I'm not finished, Edgar," Roosevelt cut him off. "What I have decided to do, and the operative word is 'decided,' is something entirely different."

He paused there, then put on his smile again.

"You will, of course, recognize this as yet another manifestation of my Solomon-like wisdom," he said.

He got the expected chuckle.

"It occurred to me," the President went on, "that if . . . *when* . . . we find ourselves *in* this war, it will undoubtedly be necessary for us to do certain things of doubtful legality. Things that neither the FBI nor any of the service intelligence agencies would like to be connected with."

"The FBI," Hoover said, "will do whatever is necessary, Mr. President."

"Edgar," the President replied, "under your leadership, the FBI has become the most respected agency in the government. I don't intend to—I will not—see the escutcheon soiled."

OK, Edgar, Donovan thought, *wiggle out of that one if you can.*

"You are very kind, Mr. President, to say that," Hoover said. "However, in the national inter—"

Roosevelt shut him off by raising his hand.

"Edgar," he said with a toothy smile, "I learned a long time ago that if you're going to do something of questionable legality, the first thing you do is find yourself a good lawyer."

Hoover laughed, but it was forced. He took the law seriously, and didn't like jokes made about it.

"So I'm going to give these necessary—but perhaps a little underhanded—missions to Bill, who is the best lawyer I know," Roosevelt said.

"I don't quite understand, Mr. President," Hoover said.

"Among other things you are to do, Edgar," the President said, "is not only to look the other way when you suspect COI is doing something it shouldn't, but . . . and this is very important . . . you are to divert the eyes of other people who may be asking questions."

"Isn't that tantamount to giving COI a license to break the law?" Hoover asked.

"It is giving him license *to do whatever I tell him to do* in any way he can most effectively do it," the President said.

"If this came out, Mr. President, it would be damaging, very damaging, politically," Hoover said. "I respectfully suggest, Mr. President, that the FBI can handle this sort of business, when necessary, better than anyone else."

Donovan was surprised that Hoover was offering the FBI to do the President's illegal bidding. Roosevelt acted as if he didn't hear him.

"I yesterday afternoon sent to the Senate the name of Commander Douglass for promotion to captain," Roosevelt said. "And I instructed the secretary of the Navy to place Captain Douglass on indefinite duty with the Office of the Coordinator of Information. In the absence of Bill, when dealing with COI, you will deal with Douglass.

"I have also instructed the chief of naval intelligence that he is to transfer to COI whatever people Captain Douglass asks for. And I want you, Edgar, to send over six of your best people to Douglass. Your very best people."

"Yes, Mr. President," Hoover said.

The people he will send, Douglass thought, *will be the ones who will spy most effectively on us.*

"From the people so assembled, Captain Douglass will select those who will accompany the scientists to England as their protectors, and to see what other information they can develop."

"I respectfully—" Hoover tried again.

"I told you before, Edgar," the President said, "that this decision is not open for debate."

"Yes, Mr. President," Hoover said. The second most skilled politician in Washington knew when not to argue.

"Is that about it, Bill?" the President asked.

"Just one thing," Donovan said. "Edgar, if we want to arm our people, what would be the most inconspicuous way to do it?"

"Are you asking me if I will see FBI credentials given to your people?" Hoover asked, his face flushing.

"Edgar," the President said, "you missed the point. If Bill asks you for FBI credentials, you will either give him the credentials or explain to me why you can't."

"I don't want FBI credentials," Donovan said. "I want something that won't call attention to our people. The FBI is famous. We want to be anonymous."

"Did you say 'infamous'?" the President asked.

"Deputy U.S. marshal," Hoover said after a moment's thought. "They're armed, and they travel a good deal. How soon will you need them?"

"As soon as you and the Navy send your people," Douglass said.

"I'll take care of it," Hoover said.

"I have heard from the National Institute of Health about you, Bill," the President said.

"The National Institute of Health?"

"You will be thrilled, I'm sure, to hear that you now have offices. In the National Institute of Health."

"The NIH?" Hoover asked, amused.

"I considered St. Elizabeths for a while," the President said, "before settling on NIH. At least it will be close to your place in Georgetown."

"Your kindness overwhelms me, Franklin," Donovan said.

"I wish you'd call me 'Mr. President,' " Roosevelt said.

Donovan's eyebrows went up, but he didn't reply.

"I have another remark I wish to make as President," Roosevelt said. "I consider this atomic-bomb business the most important single thing we're doing. If I have made that point, gentlemen, I think we can finally get down to the drinking part of the evening."

"Yes, Mr. President," Donovan said immediately.

Roosevelt looked at Hoover.

"Mr. President," Hoover said, "the FBI and I are absolutely at your disposal."

"That's very fine of you, Edgar," Roosevelt said. "I expected nothing less."

He really didn't know whether Roosevelt was being sarcastic or not, Donovan thought.

"I think our first little snort," the President said, "should be a toast to the newly promoted Captain Douglass."

4
Rangoon, Burma
16 September 1941

Ed Bitter had presumed the .50-caliber ammunition spilled into the hold at Pearl Harbor had been intended for the American Volunteer Group's aircraft. The P40-B had two .50-caliber Brownings mounted in the nose, and two .30-caliber Brownings in the wings. But when the *Jan Suvit* stopped at Manila, the ammunition had been off-loaded.

After a day and a half in Manila, they steamed back out of the harbor, past the fortress of Corregidor, for Batavia, Indonesia. From Batavia, there was another long leg of the journey, the last, into the Gulf of Martaban, and then twenty-odd miles up the Rangoon River to Rangoon itself. They had been almost ninety days en route from San Francisco.

A representative of the American Volunteer Group, another old birdman in the mold of Chennault, came aboard with the river pilot, and there was a military-type formation in which the 106 Americans aboard the *Jan Suvit* were divided into two groups. One group would consist of most of the pilots, Crookshanks told them, with a few maintenance and administrative personnel, and the other group would consist of the bulk of the maintenance personnel, a few administrative people, and two wingmen, Bitter and Canidy.

Canidy's running warfare with Crookshanks had obviously resulted in his being left behind, as a wiseass, with the other guilty-by-association wiseass, while the rest went off to start their training.

Bitter kept his mouth shut until they were in an ancient Ford taxicab, en route to downtown Rangoon.

"You realize, of course," he said, "that you're the reason I'm doing this with you."

"Oh, that's all right, Eddie," Canidy mocked him. "You can put something extra in my stocking at Christmas."

"The fuckups got left behind, as usual," Ed said. "The trouble is that I'm not fucked up."

"And you're not too bright, either," Canidy said. "The other guys are being loaded on a train for that place with an obscene-sounding name. They're going to be put up in old, and I mean *old,* English Army barracks, and General Chennault is going to read them his book, aloud, until the planes get there."

"And what are we going to be doing?"

"We're going to lie in bed in a hotel, and with just a little bit of luck, not alone, until CAMCO gets the airplanes put together. And then we're going to test-fly them. When they're ready, we'll fly them up to Fongoo—"

"*Toungoo,*" Bitter corrected him. He recognized "Fongoo" as some sort of Italian dialect obscenity.

"Wherever the other dummies are," Canidy went on, "and then come back for more. We're going to have a lot more time in those airplanes than anybody else. I intend to test them very, very carefully."

He was right, Bitter realized.

"How did you pull this off?"

"The chief went to Crookshanks and told him that he happened to know that you and I were damned good test pilots."

"We're not, for God's sake!"

"Nobody I met on the ship was any better," Canidy said reasonably.

5

As they were having breakfast the next morning in the hotel dining room, John B. Dolan came in and sat down with them. There was no fouled anchor insignia pinned to the collar points of his khaki shirt, and there was no brimmed uniform cap perched cockily atop his head, but with those exceptions, he looked no less a chief petty officer of the United States Navy than he had at Pensacola NAS.

Dolan motioned with his finger for a cup of coffee and helped himself to a sugared bun from a basket on the table.

"CAMCO's got a house for use," Dolan said, "with its own mess and laundry. Right now there's only Finley and me and an ex–chief radioman named Lopp. You'd probably be more comfortable there than here. Interested?''

"Fascinated," Canidy said immediately.

Bitter felt uncomfortable sharing quarters with ex–enlisted men, even if they were now, as civilians, technically social equals. Dolan and Canidy immediately made him even more uncomfortable.

"There's more," Dolan said. "They sent me down to the wharves to pick up a car. There's a whole godown full of new Studebaker Commanders. All you have to do, I think, is walk in, sign a chit, and ride out with one the way I did."

"All they can do is tell me to give it back, right?" Canidy said.

"Who owns the cars?" Bitter asked.

"CAMCO," John Dolan replied. "What we need is spare engines and assembly racks, and stuff like that, which we don't have, instead of Studebakers, but what the hell, use what you do have, right? No sense in letting them just sit in the warehouse."

"Isn't the group going to need them?" Bitter asked.

Dolan gave him a patient look.

"The way it is, Mr. Bitter," he said slowly, with more than a little disdain, "is we need all this stuff in China, which is the *other* end of the Burma Road. And we can't get it there, at least right now, you understand?"

"Yes, of course," Bitter said. He was uncomfortable that he had been treated like a fool.

"I'll go change," Canidy said, and got up and walked out of the dining room.

"I guess I'm a little surprised that an old salt like you and Mr. Canidy could be friends," Bitter said.

Dolan gave Bitter a tolerantly contemptuous look.

"Let me put it this way, Mr. Bitter," Dolan said. "There's three kinds of officers. At the bottom are the really dumb ones. That's maybe two percent. Then there's most of them, say ninety-six percent. They do their job, and most of the time they don't cause anybody any trouble. Then there's the last two percent. You learn to spot them, and if you're smart, you really take care of officers like that, because you know that they'll take care of you. Not only when that's easy for them, but when you really need taking care of and it costs them.''

"And you think Mr. Canidy is in the elite two percent?''

"Oh yeah," Dolan said. "I spotted him right away, first time I took a ride with him. I've flown some, Mr. Bitter. I used to be a gold-stripe chief aviation pilot.''

"I didn't know that," Bitter said. The Navy had a small corps of enlisted pilots. The elite of the enlisted pilots were the chief petty officer pilots, and the elite of that elite were the gold-stripe chief aviation pilots. The chevrons of their insignia were embroidered in gold thread.

"I figured if you're not flying, you shouldn't be wearing wings," Dolan said. He was, Bitter realized, letting him off the hook.

"And that's why you recommended Mr. Canidy to be a test pilot?''

"That's part of it," Dolan said. "And at Toungoo, what Chennault's going to do is run everybody through pursuit pilot school, the Army way. Mr. Canidy doesn't need that, especially if it means he has to sleep in some old English barracks knocking bugs off his bunk.''

"You don't think he needs pursuit pilot school?''

"You know the difference between flight training and pursuit pilot training?" Dolan asked.

"Tell me," Bitter said.

"In pursuit pilot school, they unlearn you everything you've been taught so far about what not to do with an airplane, and they try to teach you just how far you can go without dinging it. I think Mr. Canidy's got that down pretty pat already.''

''And you think I have, too?'' Bitter asked. ''I understand you recommended both of us for test pilots.''

Dolan didn't answer for a moment. Then he turned in his chair and looked right into Bitter's eyes.

''There's a couple of things with you,'' Dolan said. ''You went to the Academy, for one thing. For another, Mr. Canidy told me about you losing your engine while you were barrel-rolling. But I guess what's most important is that I know that no matter what some people might think, Mr. Canidy wouldn't have a *genuine* asshole for a buddy.''

For a moment, Bitter was speechless. But finally he managed, ''Well, thank you, Dolan.''

''That's all right, Mr. Bitter,'' the old chief said.

6

The house that CAMCO had acquired for the maintenance people, the communications technicians, and the two pilots was a large Victorian structure in the suburb of Kemmendine. They could see the gold-domed Shwe Dagon Pagoda from the window of their rooms, far away, dominating the skyline.

An hour after they had moved into the house, Canidy stuck his head in Ed Bitter's door, where Bitter was sitting in an armchair rereading the P40-B dash-one.

''You want to take a ride out to the airfield?'' he asked. ''And see what's going on?''

The Studebaker Canidy had signed for at the CAMCO godown had less than a hundred miles on the odometer, and there was still a faint new-car smell—even though the car was chronologically at least a year old and had traveled ten thousand miles to the docks of Rangoon.

Canidy found Mingaladon Air Field without much trouble, and then the CAMCO hangars. In front sat four Curtiss P40-B aircraft. Three of them looked ready to fly, and there was a group of mechanics squatting under the wing of the fourth, peering up into the right wheel well. The right wing of that airplane had been jacked off the ground.

Canidy parked the Studebaker beside the nearest of the aircraft and got out. With Bitter following him, he walked around the airplane, studying it closely, and then he climbed up on the wing root and looked inside the cockpit. A middle-aged man detached himself from the group around the last P40-B and walked over to them.

Canidy jumped off the wing root.

"Canidy?" the middle-aged man asked, and when Canidy nodded, he identified himself as Richard Aldwood, of CAMCO. "Dolan told me about you," he said.

"You're more than just 'of' CAMCO, aren't you?" Canidy asked, shaking the offered hand. "Vice president, right?"

"Yeah, and at the moment in charge of making a studied guess about why that goddamned wheel won't go up," Aldwood said modestly, gesturing at the jacked-up airplane.

"Ed Bitter," Bitter said, and he and Aldwood shook hands.

"How much time do you have in one of these?" Aldwood asked almost idly.

"I read the dash-one real carefully," Canidy said wryly.

"I figured as much," Aldwood said. He looked at Bitter.

"I've never seen one before, sir," Ed Bitter said.

"Well, then, you're both about eight hours behind me," Aldwood said. "And more than a little ahead of me. You're a hell of a lot younger, and Dolan approves of you."

"And he doesn't approve of you?" Canidy replied.

"Not after I told him there's no way I was going to let him fly."

"Why not?" Canidy asked. "I understand he's got a hell of a lot of time."

"Yeah, and some hard hours on his heart, too," Aldwood said. "Why did you think they took him off flight status? I'm surprised the Navy didn't pension him off years ago."

"I suppose," Canidy said, "before we start test-flying these things, somebody's going to have to check us out in them."

"I'll show you around the cockpit," Aldwood said. "And since you've already read the dash-one, that's it, I'm afraid. There's no ground school, unless Claire . . . Chennault . . . is starting one at Toungoo."

"And what if I bend the bird?" Canidy asked.

"Please don't," Aldwood said. "We've already wrecked two, and all we've got and are going to get is an even hundred."

"Are they all here?"

"Sixty-two. God only knows when we'll get the rest. We've been putting them together at the rate of one every day and a half. We hope to get that up to two a day, maybe three," Aldwood said. He climbed onto the wing root and motioned Canidy and Bitter up on the other side.

Aldwood gave them a detailed tour of the aircraft's controls and told them what he knew of its flight peculiarities. He didn't rush through it, but he was finished thirty-five minutes later.

"You want to wait until you've been off the ship another night?" he asked, finally. "Or—?"

"I'm not going to be any better tomorrow," Canidy said.

Ten minutes later, wearing an Army Air Corps leather helmet and goggles, and a Switlick parachute marked PROP-

ERTY USN, Dick Canidy looked out both sides of the cockpit, called "Clear!" and put his hand on the starter switch. It took him a long time to get the engine to even cough, and even when he had it running, it ran roughly and there was a peculiar oily smell he hadn't smelled before. There was also, barely visible in the propeller blast, a faint grayish smoke coming from the engine, obviously not the blue smoke from a too-rich mixture or the nearly black smoke from an oil leak.

It disappeared shortly after the needles moved off their pegs and started to creep up to the strips of green tape indicating the safe operating zones for pressures and temperatures. He then realized what caused the smoke: preserving oil and greases being burned off what was almost a brand-new engine.

Canidy looked at Aldwood, gestured toward the instrument panel, and made an OK sign. Aldwood nodded and gave him a thumbs-up signal.

Canidy put the microphone to his lips. "Mingaladon Tower. CAMCO sixteen by the CAMCO hangars. Taxi and takeoff."

The control-tower operator came back immediately. A crisp British voice gave him the time, the barometer, the altitude, the winds, and cleared him to the active runway as number one to take off. Canidy released the brake and advanced the throttle. Too much. He had more than a thousand horsepower under his hand. The last time he had flown, he had less power, and in a much heavier aircraft. And the last time he had flown, he thought, had been more than three months ago.

Taxiing the P40-B was difficult. The seat was in a full-down position, putting him low in the cockpit. And the P40-B's nose was high, so it was difficult to see out. Because he had to taxi by looking to either side of the taxiway, he immediately saw that controlling the plane on the ground by use of the rudder was a skill he would have to acquire by a lot of practice.

He reached the threshold of the runway and stopped. He ran the engine up, checked the dynamos, moved the stick and the rudder pedals through their movement arcs, and then pulled the goggles down over his eyes. He picked up the microphone.

"Mingaladon Tower, CAMCO sixteen rolling," he said, and then advanced the throttle and turned forward, and moved the fuel-mixture lever to the full-rich indent. The plane began to move. He felt himself pressed back against his parachute. The P40-B lifted off its tailwheel without any action on Canidy's part. The slipstream was screaming past his ears, and he remembered only then that he hadn't slid the canopy forward to close it. To hell with it.

Very carefully, he ruddered the ship to the center of the runway, and waited for the stick to come alive. And then, all of a sudden, it was. He inched back, and the wheels left the ground. Almost immediately, as he reached his hand out for the wheel-retraction control, his right wing dipped and the ship turned right. He corrected, wondering if that had been torque or gyroscopic procession, and knowing—as he felt the sweat of terror soak his khakis—that he would never forget to be ready for that again.

The wheels came up, more slowly than he would have expected, and unevenly, so that he had to correct for the difference in drag until they were both in their wells. He'd been holding the same elevator position, and the angle of climb increased. But the airspeed was holding.

He thought, pleased: *The sonofabitch climbs like a god-damned rocket!*

He took it to three thousand feet before pulling the throttle back to cruise. Then he leveled off, trimmed it up, and flew it for a couple of seconds with his hands and feet off the controls. After that he put it into a gentle climb.

He played, swinging the stick from side to side, using the rudder to make it crab through the air, getting the feel of it, until he had reached five thousand feet. He leveled off there and finally slid the canopy closed. The shrill whistle of the windstream was gone, and what filled the cockpit now was the dull roar of the thousand or so horses turning the three-blade prop in front of him.

A little later he pulled the stick back and climbed until he ran out of power and speed, and it stalled. It really shook when it stalled. He fell straight through it, pushed the stick forward, and waited for life to come back into it. The needle on the airspeed indicator pointed to 300, then 320, then 330, and then came to the red line at 340. He pulled back on the stick, and felt his stomach sink to his knees. There was a moment's sensation of everything turning red, and then that passed, and he was flying level with the needle right on the red line.

''Goddamn!'' he said aloud, absolutely delighted. He took a quick look at the instrument panel to make sure all the needles were where they were supposed to be, and then put the ship first into a loop and when he came out of the loop a barrel roll, and when he still had all the airspeed he needed after that, into an Immelmann turn.

After what he thought was about ten minutes he reluctantly decided that he'd better get it back on the ground. He had been flying visually, keeping himself aware of the position of the gleaming, gold-covered Shwe Dagon Pagoda. If he could see that, he could easily find the field.

He flew to it, put it under his left wingtip at six thousand feet, and made a gentle circle descent to three thousand feet, for the first time looking at the ground with more than idle interest. He saw Rangoon sprawling to the south of the pagoda, and the river, stretching to the Gulf of Martaban. And he saw the thick, lush, deep green jungle.

It was beautiful. Burma was beautiful. The day was beautiful. The P40-B was beautiful. It was, he was sure, one of the best days of his life.

He called the tower and got permission to land.

The sonofabitch came in a lot faster than he thought it would, even with the flaps and wheels down, and he was much farther down the runway than he intended before he felt the bounce and heard the chirp when the wheels touched. And it took longer than he thought it would to get the tailwheel on the ground, too. The sonofabitch wanted to stand on its nose. He would have to remember that, too.

Bitter trotted over to the plane when he taxied it in line beside the others.

"What happened?" Bitter asked, concerned. "We were about to go looking for you."

"I was only gone ten, fifteen minutes," Canidy said.

"You were gone an hour and fifteen minutes," Bitter said.

"That's one hell of an airplane, Eddie," Canidy said.

SIX

Brandon Chambers's secretary put her head into his office in the *Atlanta Courier-Journal* building and held her hand up, palm outward, her signal that what she had to say was important.

"Hold it a minute," Brandon Chambers said to the managing editor of the *Courier-Journal.*

"They just called from the lobby," she said. "Ann's on her way up."

Brandon Chambers made a hmmphing sound. "I wonder what my lovely, impulsive, willful little girl wants now?" he asked. Then he signaled that Ann was to be shown in when she arrived, and resumed his conversation.

Ann Chambers was wearing hose, high heels, a blue polka-dot dress, and a small hat, perched jauntily on her head. The hat had a veil, and beneath it her face was powdered and rouged and her lips were a brilliant scarlet streak.

Brandon Chambers didn't pay all that much attention to what women wore, unless it was uncommonly revealing, but he noticed the way his daughter dressed. She almost never wore anything fancier than a pleated skirt, a loose sweater, and loafers.

"To what do I owe this honor?" he asked pointedly, expecting the worst.

"Can I get you something, Ann?" her father's secretary said.

"I'd love a cup of coffee, Mrs. Gregg," Ann said, "if it wouldn't be too much trouble."

"Is something wrong?" he asked.

"No. Nothing's wrong with me. I was hoping I was going to dazzle you with the way I'm dressed. No comment?"

"It's one hell of an improvement, I'll happily tell you that."

"There was a piece in *College Woman* that said that when women are going for a job interview, they should dress businesslike. I gave a lot of thought to what I'm wearing. I'm here seeking honest employment," she said. "I'll take whatever's offered, no questions asked."

"Is that so?" he said, smiling.

"That's so," she said. "And now that you're dazzled with my businesslike appearance, let's get right on to that. I seek employment on the Memphis *Daily Advocate*. Anything but the women's section."

"How about managing editor?"

"I'm serious, Daddy," she said.

"I was afraid you would be," he said. "What about school?"

"I am bored out of my mind in school," she said. "I'm finished."

"You have three years to go, counting this year."

"I've already withdrawn," she said.

"You can't do that without my permission," he said.

"Can't I?" Ann asked. "What do they do, drag me back in handcuffs?"

"Does your mother know about this?" he asked.

"I suppose she will by late this afternoon."

"And she's going to be both hurt and furious," he said.

"I'm not so sure," Ann said, "and neither are you."

"Was there something specific at Bryn Mawr? Or was it just general boredom?"

She didn't answer the question. She asked one of her own: "Aren't you going to ask why the *Advocate*? Instead of here?"

"OK," he said. "You've been asked."

"Because you spend most of your time here, and that would be awkward for both of us."

"That's 'why not here,' " he said, "not 'why the *Advocate*.' "

"Because the *Advocate* is a medium-size paper where I already have some friends. I've worked there before."

"Just a couple of months," he said.

"I worked there a month last summer," she replied. "And two months after I graduated from St. Margaret's."

"That's three months," he said.

"I'd hate it," she said, rushing on, negotiating, "but I'll even take the women's section. *Temporarily*."

"You've already considered, I suppose, that you're throwing away the chance at a good education?"

"You don't believe that nonsense any more than I do," she said. "College is where women are sent to keep them off the streets until they find a husband."

"I don't believe that either," he said. "And what if I say no, Annie? Then what?"

"Then I don't know," she said. "I do know I'm not going back to Bryn Mawr, or any college, period."

"I'll see what Orrin Fox has to say," he said.

Ann walked to his desk and pushed down on the intercom

TALK switch. "Mrs. Gregg, would you get Mr. Fox of the *Advocate* for Daddy, please?" she said.

When he didn't cancel the call, Ann knew that she had gotten her way. Orrin Fox, the managing editor of the *Advocate,* would probably have given her a job even if her father didn't own the newspaper.

And she was right. Orrin was even willing to start her out city-side, covering hospitals and funerals, which was more than she thought she'd get.

"Thank you, Daddy," she said, beaming, and kissed him.

"Don't look so smug," he said, trying to sound stern— but she couldn't help notice the approval and the pride in his voice. "There's still your mother to consider. She hasn't heard about you quitting college, much less about wanting to go live by yourself in Memphis. I wouldn't think of entering that argument."

"I can handle Mother," Ann Chambers said, "and with a little bit of help from my generous daddy, I can find a nice little apartment. Until the paper pays me enough to support myself."

"I'm serious, Annie," he said. "She's not going to like the idea of you living alone in an apartment in Memphis."

"I won't be living alone," Ann said. "Sarah Child will share an apartment with me."

He didn't know what to make of that.

"And why," he asked finally, "would Sarah Child want to drop out of college and go live with you in Memphis, Tennessee?"

"Because she's pregnant," Ann said. "And not married."

"Christ Jesus!" he boomed. "So the crazy little bitch got herself knocked up!"

"Dad!" Ann cried.

"I didn't think she had it in her."

"Dad!" she screamed. "That's cruel! And it's crude! And it's unfair! And Sarah is my friend. She needs help and she needs me."

"So that's it. *She's* it," he said, angry. "She's why you're quitting school."

"I was ready to quit anyway," Ann said. "But I have to help her. She might as well have no family. Her father's too busy taking care of his bank to take care of her; and her mother's crazy, you know. A certified loony."

"And Sarah can't take care of herself?" He paused to let that sink in. "Or else you may be aware—even as virginal as you are—that these things have now and again been handled successfully with the help of what has come to be called marriage."

"Don't be sarcastic, Daddy." She was crying. So he softened and let up on her.

"I'm sorry, sweetheart; but I'm upset too. I just don't want the kid I love to throw away her education so she can mother a knocked-up little girl. And besides, what about the father?"

"He's in China," she said, holding in her sobs.

"China? Who does little Sarah know in China?" Then he remembered. "Oh my God! My God, do you mean it happened at The Lodge when you were all down there in the spring?" Ann nodded. "Canidy!" he blared. "Christ!"

"Wrong," Ann said. "It was Cousin Eddie."

"Ed? You're kidding."

"It *was* Cousin Eddie, Dad, but if you tell anyone, I'll never forgive you. I gave her my word, and you're the only other person who knows."

Brandon Chambers shook his massive head and exhaled audibly. She was going to win this one, he knew. He might as well accept the inevitability of it. Ann was going to Memphis to take care of the little girl. So that was that.

"And what has Ed got to say?"

"Eddie doesn't know," Ann said. "She won't tell him, and she made me give my word that I wouldn't tell him either."

"Why not?"

"She said because she believes what happened is her fault, not his—"

"It takes two," he flared up, but only halfheartedly.

"But what I think it is is that she's a Jew."

"That wouldn't make a difference to Ed," her father said.

"Wouldn't it?" Ann asked her father. "Would you bet big money on that, Daddy? *What* would Aunt Helen *think*?"

"What are we going to tell your mother?" he asked.

"That Sarah's pregnant, and that's all," Ann said.

2
Berlin, Germany
November 10, 1941

Helmut Maximilian Ernst von Heurten-Mitnitz liked America. He'd graduated from Harvard in 1927 and, in the footsteps of four generations of Heurten-Mitnitz younger sons, had joined the Foreign Service to end up at the German embassy in Washington. Two years later he served as consul general in New Orleans and he remembered that city with particular fondness. He thought often of Kolb's, a German restaurant just off Canal Street, where he was treated with exceptional warmth and good food. And in two Mardi Gras parades, dressed in a fantastic costume, he'd ridden a float and thrown candy and glass beads at the hordes of people jamming the narrow streets of the French Quarter.

On his return to Berlin in 1938, Max discovered that his older brother, Karl-Friedrich, had lent the National Socialist

German Workers' party the prestige of the von Heurten-
Mitnitz name and a great deal of money. Privately both Max
and Karl-Friedrich detested most of the upper-echelon Nazis, but there was no question that the Nazi party had saved
Germany from the fate of Russia. And it was inarguable that
life was better under Nazi rule than it had been before.

But Max did not want to fight the Nazis' wars. He had
his foreign-service exemption, but his brother's loans had
made their family highly visible. Someone was only too
likely to see in him a fine officer with a bright destiny on
the eastern front. He needed some important assignment in
which he could further his career and at the same time remove himself from the doom that would befall him if he
stayed where he was. He needed to get out of Berlin.

Johann Müller was one of the original hundred thousand
members of the National Socialist German Workers' party,
and he was thus entitled to wear the golden party pin. He
had joined the infant Nazi party because he had realized
very early on how useful membership was going to be to a
policeman. Müller never believed for an instant that the
party, or for that matter Adolf Hitler, was the salvation of
Germany. There had been policemen under the Kaiser and
under the Weimar Republic, and there would be policemen
under whatever replaced the Thousand Year Reich.

Müller had been a Kreis Marburg Wachtmann for two
years when he learned that Hermann Göring, as police president of Prussia, was quietly building a secret police force.
Müller applied and was appointed to the Prussian state police as a Kriminalinspektor, grade three. He arrived in Berlin
immediately after Hitler, as boss of what would soon be the
Gestapo, had Göring out and replaced him with the rather
more trustworthy Heinrich Himmler.

Although Himmler immediately retired most of the people Göring had brought in, Müller stayed. He hadn't been with the state police long enough to be corrupted. Besides, a policeman who wore a gold party pin and who had risen from the ranks in rural Hesse was really the sort of man they were looking for. Himmler needed ordinary policemen to handle ordinary crimes.

When the war came, though he remained a policeman, Müller was ordered into uniform. Some of his duties, however, still required ordinary clothes. Without any particular plan, Johann Müller had come to be a specialist in crimes—from embezzlement to currency violations to vice—committed by military officers, senior and influential government employees, and party officials. Müller became the man in Berlin who decided whether or not a case was made. Sometimes he ordered detention or arrest; other times, he merely threatened these—to see what would happen. Other times he decided the charges "had no basis in fact."

And still other times, of course, he kept people under his thumb, either for use as informers, or in positions where they might do him some good, while he made up his mind what to do with them.

His own specialty was the investigation of payoffs and kickbacks, which meant digging up money people had spent considerable time and imagination burying. He was good at it.

He met Helmut von Heurten-Mitnitz when a Swede with a diplomatic passport and a Foreign Ministry official had shown up together in bed at a hotel in Lichtefeld, an incident with implications beyond mere offense against the morality of the state. The liaison officer Müller usually dealt with at the Foreign Ministry had been replaced by von Heurten-Mitnitz. When Müller got to Bendlerstrasse, he was not surprised to find the diplomat looked as elegant as he had sounded on the telephone. He was a tall, sharp-featured, fair-haired East Prussian of about thirty-five. And he was wearing a well-cut British lounge suit that had certainly cost as much as Müller made in a month.

Five minutes with von Heurten-Mitnitz was long enough for Müller to judge that von Heurten-Mitnitz was a far more practical man than his manner and elegant dress implied. At the same time, Max von Heurten-Mitnitz had seen enough of Müller to be convinced that the policeman before him was not the simple Hessian peasant he carefully painted himself to be.

Thereafter (the matter of the Swede and the Foreign Service officer having come to a swift and satisfactory conclusion), von Heurten-Mitnitz possessed an uncanny knowledge of who was paying whom for what secret information. In return, Müller received an unexpected promotion to Sturmbannführer (major, SS-SD) shortly after the invasion of the Low Countries. Their relationship was quite satisfactory.

Max regarded his appointment to Morocco as one of his great diplomatic feats. As Foreign Ministry representative to the Franco-German armistice commission for Morocco, Max would in fact have very little to do with the armistice with France. Rather, the commission (nine senior Foreign Ministry officials and their staff) was the euphemistic title for the official body through which the French protectorate of Morocco was governed. Most important, he'd be in Morocco, and away from Berlin.

His new post would obviously involve certain security and intelligence functions, which in turn would mean dealing with an officer of the Schutzstaffel-Sicherheitsdienst (SS-SD). Since not a few of the SS-SD were very dangerous indeed, Max wanted, as his liaison with the French gendarmerie, an officer with whom he had a degree of mutual understanding. Within the hour he had Müller on the phone.

"Perhaps, Herr Sturmbannführer, if your busy schedule would permit, you could spare me a few minutes of your time?" von Heurten-Mitnitz asked.

"When?"

"Are you free now?" von Heurten-Mitnitz asked.

"I'm tied up now."

"Pity. Are you free for dinner?"

"Yes."

"The Kempinski at seven?"

"I'll be there."

3
The Hotel Kempinski
Berlin, Germany
7:30 P.M., November 10, 1941

Max von Heurten-Mitnitz and Johann Müller had roast loin of boar, oven-roasted potatoes, and a crisp green salad, and they washed it down with Berlinerkindl, the local beer. With boar, there was simply nothing better than a light Pilsner beer.

Von Heurten-Mitnitz told Müller he'd been given a month to settle his affairs before going to Morocco, but thought he could leave a good deal sooner than that. "How much time will you need?" he asked.

"I'll be ready when you are," Müller said.

Unsaid was what they both were a little afraid of: The assignment could be changed so long as they were in Berlin.

"We'll go by air," von Heurten-Mitnitz said.

Müller nodded, caught the waiter's attention, and signaled for another round of Berlinerkindl.

"Is there anything I should do before we go?"

"One small thing," von Heurten-Mitnitz said. "Just before I left the office, I had a call from Richard Schnorr."
He looked at Müller to read in his face whether or not he
knew the name. When he saw that Müller was fully aware
that Richard Schnorr was a highly placed functionary in the
headquarters offices of the National Socialist German Workers' party, he went on. "Does the name Fulmar mean anything to you?"

"The electric company?"

Von Heurten-Mitnitz nodded.

"There is a son, Eric," he said, "who is in Morocco."

"What's he doing in Morocco?"

"He's involved with the son of the pasha of Ksar es Souk,
who is believed to be moving currency and jewels illegally
out of France and Morocco."

"Interesting," Müller said.

"And there are those who believe he is avoiding military
service," von Heurten-Mitnitz said.

"How does he get away with that?" Müller asked.

"He has an American passport."

"Legally?"

"His mother is American. He was born there, and we are
being very careful with the Americans."

"Does he also have a German passport?"

"No."

"Why not?"

"He's a very clever young man," von Heurten-Mitnitz
said, "who realized that accepting a German passport meant
accepting German nationality, and that German nationals
were expected to serve the fatherland in uniform."

"Has he lived here?"

"Oh yes," von Heurten-Mitnitz said, chuckling. "Oh
yes. He spent four years at Philip's University in Marburg
as a candidate for a degree in electrical engineering. He's

perfectly fluent in German; and he is tall, blond, good-looking, and rather resembles the young man on the Waffen-SS recruiting posters.''

Müller chuckled. "I see the problem," he said. "And the solution. Arrest him for the currency violations, bring him to Germany, and put him in uniform."

"It's not so easy as that, unfortunately. No one seems to be able to prove that he *is* smuggling. And if he were arrested, it would be embarrassing to both his father and the party generally."

"Uhhh," Müller grunted in agreement.

"But there's more to the tale," von Heurten-Mitnitz said. "He was in Paris in August with the son of the pasha of Ksar es Souk—*and* traveling on documents issued by the kingdom of Morocco."

"How does he get Moroccan travel papers?"

"Through Sidi Hassan el Ferruch," von Heurten-Mitnitz said.

"That's the son of the pasha?"

Von Heurten-Mitnitz nodded. "They were at school together in Switzerland, and at Philip's University."

"Who's the pasha? Somebody important?"

"There are two factions in Morocco," von Heurten-Mitnitz said. "The king's and the Pasha of Marrakech's. The pasha's loyalty to the king is questionable—"

"How powerful is a pasha?" Müller interrupted him.

"That depends on the pasha," von Heurten-Mitnitz said. "The pasha of Marrakech, Thami el Glaoui, is nearly as powerful as the king. He commands several hundred thousand tribesmen—*armed* tribesmen. Other pashas have only a handful."

"And the smuggler's father?" Müller asked.

"The pasha of Ksar es Souk," von Heurten-Mitnitz explained, "commands nearly as many tribesmen as the pasha of Marrakech. Together, they have roughly as many as the king. And they are close allies.''

"And his son is a smuggler? Why?''

"The amount of money involved boggles the mind,'' von Heurten-Mitnitz said. "In wartime, it seems that people with a lot of money—Americans, South Americans, and we Germans, Müller—are willing to pay extraordinary prices for works of art. So much money is really a matter of state, rather than a mere crime.''

"And you're supposed to stop this, right?'' Müller asked.

"The Americans have an expression,'' Max von Heurten-Mitnitz said, " 'fighting with one hand tied behind you.' But in this case I have both of mine tied behind me. On one hand, I am not to embarrass the party because of Baron Fulmar's son, and on the other, it is possible that the king of Morocco may have to be replaced if he continues to prove uncooperative. If that becomes necessary, it is intended to replace him with the pasha of Marrakech. How cooperative would he be if we threw the son of his ally in jail? Or executed him?''

"Then why don't we just find some other suitable pasha?'' Müller said practically.

"I don't think you understand the Moroccans,'' von Heurten-Mitnitz said. "They'd go berserk. It would be like a holy war.''

"Then you have to let this el Ferruch alone.''

"I have been ordered to stop the flow of gold, currency, precious jewels, and fine art through Morocco,'' von Heurten-Mitnitz said, "by superiors who believe I will be dealing with picturesque characters in bathrobes.''

Müller chuckled again. "And I was so happy when I heard I was escaping from Berlin.''

"The Americans have another interesting saying,'' von

Heurten-Mitnitz said. " 'There's no such thing as a free lunch.' "

Müller thought that over for a moment and then chuckled.

"There's one obvious solution," he said. "We could arrange some accidents."

Von Heurten-Mitnitz did not appear to have heard him.

"There is one other alternative," he said. "One that would possibly not only solve our problems with young Fulmar, but would be of value to the fatherland."

"You mean, turn him into an agent?" Müller asked.

Von Heurten-Mitnitz nodded.

"If we could use him to give us access to the pasha of Ksar es Souk, and through him to the pasha of Marrakech . . ."

"Yes," Müller said thoughtfully.

"I don't think appealing to his patriotism would work," von Heurten-Mitnitz said. "Nor do I think he will frighten easily. We'll have to think of something else."

"It will work out," Müller said confidently. "These situations almost always do, if you work hard enough."

"And don't do anything foolish," von Heurten-Mitnitz added. "Thus it would be helpful if you can get a copy of Fulmar's dossier. Perhaps something of interest happened to him while he was in Marburg."

Müller nodded. "I'd planned to see my family," he said. "This will give me an official reason to go to Marburg. I'll see what I can dig up. But if all else fails, Fulmar will be put on a plane, and you won't know anything about it until you hear he has returned to the fatherland."

"I must ask you not to do anything like that until you have discussed it with me first," von Heurten-Mitnitz said quickly. "Neither of us can afford to be sent home because we have become persona non grata with our Moroccan friends."

4
Casablanca, Morocco
November 28, 1941

There was absolutely no doubt in the minds of the two
agents of the French Sûreté, nor of their adviser, a Sturm-
führer of the SS-Sicherheitsdienst, that if they could stop the
American Cadillac they would find that its occupants possessed nearly three hundred thousand dollars in United
States and half that much in Swiss currency. In addition,
there was a small leather bag stuffed with investment-quality
(that is, heavier in weight than three carats) diamonds and
emeralds and comparable jewels. On the open market these
were worth about as much as the Swiss and American currency combined.

The problem was that the law made no prohibition against
simple possession of foreign currency. Neither was the simple possession of jewels illegal. Such a law would be impossible to enforce.

The other problem for the Sûreté and the Sicherheitsdienst
was that one of the two young men was Sidi Hassan el
Ferruch, the son of the pasha of Ksar es Souk, and the other
young man was an American, Eric Fulmar, traveling on an
American passport. Word had come from the Foreign Ministry on Bendlerstrasse itself that confrontations with American nationals were to be handled with the utmost discretion.
Roughly translated, that meant to avoid touching Americans
unless they'd been caught red-handed.

What the Sûreté and Sicherheitsdienst agents wanted was
to catch the two of them in the act of smuggling the money
and jewels out of the country. If it was not judged wise to
shoot him in the act of escaping, the American could at least
be tried and jailed, *pour encourager les autres,* and Sidi el
Ferruch could become a *much* more valuable chip in the

never-ending game played by the French with his father.

The object, then, was to catch them.

None of the agents believed that tonight would be the night that would happen. For one thing, el Ferruch knew the agents were on their trail, and for another—unless they had guessed very badly—the obvious destination of the two (and el Ferruch's Berber bodyguards, trailing the Cadillac in a Citroën) was a restaurant on the Coastal Highway between Casablanca and El Jadida.

The restaurant, Le Relaise de Pointe-Noire, sat all alone on the rocky Black Point, sixty or more feet above the crashing surf of the Atlantic. There was only one entrance to the restaurant, and there was no way to get from the restaurant down to the beach without passing through that entrance.

The two would never transfer the money or the jewels to someone else at Le Relaise de Pointe-Noire, because that would risk having whoever they gave it to caught with it. Which meant that they intended instead to spend time on one of the *chambres séparées* overlooking the crashing surf, have their dinner, and then pass the evening in the company of firm-breasted and dark-eyed Moroccan ladies of the evening. Le Relaise de Pointe-Noire had the most attractive *poule* to be found in Morocco.

It was raining, which meant that the two policemen who had stationed themselves where they could watch the granite outcropping on which Le Relaise de Pointe-Noire was built were going to become very wet and uncomfortable. There was no way to get a car in there, and it had to be watched, against the off chance that either el Ferruch or the American was foolish enough to try to sneak off down the beach. The third agent would go inside the restaurant to see what he could see.

The man who went inside was the senior Sûreté agent, since the German could not do that without calling undue attention to himself. The Sûreté agent with the longest service elected to stay dry.

He stationed himself at the upstairs bar, in a position that allowed him to keep the corridor leading to the *chambres séparées* under surveillance. He ordered a glass of wine, making careful note of the price in his expense records.

El Ferruch and the American, after an aperitif downstairs, came jauntily up the wide stairs, teasing and joking with one another. They were preceded by the maître d'hôtel, who bowed them into the private dining room. Two of el Ferruch's Berber guards stationed themselves on either side of the door.

The waiters and wine stewards began serving the dinner. Toward the end, two Moroccan women appeared, robed, their faces masked, and entered the *chambre séparée*. The Sûreté man wondered if they were as beautiful as they were said to be, and as skilled in mysterious erotic techniques as legend had it. He knew for a fact that they shaved their crotches. Moroccan men were repelled by pubic hair.

Inside the room, Sidi el Ferruch and the blond American were nearly naked. Meanwhile el Ferruch's huge Senegalese took the women to one side, holding their arms so firmly in his massive hands that they carried dark bruises for weeks. If either of them ever said a word about what they saw in the *chambre séparée,* he warned them, he would slice off their breasts and send them to their families.

Ropes were produced, attached to radiators, and then released out the open windows. There was a rope apiece for each of the men, and one for the small, heavy oilskin package of currency. Once they were in the water, the American would tow the money while the jewels were strapped to the lithe, muscular, practically hairless body of Sidi Hassan el Ferruch. Neither wore any swimming costume.

Fulmar was a better swimmer then el Ferruch, and perfectly capable of handling both the currency and the jewels, but Sidi Hassan el Ferruch insisted on joining him. There was not only greater safety that way, but the boatmen they were meeting would also afterward return to Safi (the village where they made their home) and report that Sheikh Sidi Hassan el Ferruch had swum through the surf at Pointe-Noire. There would be a very nice increase in Sheikh Sidi Hassan el Ferruch's reputation as a result. And in due course other heroic tales and legends. The reward Sidi expected to find as a consequence of tonight's escapades, in other words, had little to do with any increases these would add to his wealth.

Unlike his friend, however, Eric wanted money—and lots of it. But he, too, was grinning like Errol Flynn as the two of them swung down their ropes. Getting the money was necessary, but the adventure of getting it was supreme delight.

But the trick was getting into the water. Dropping into the surf, you ran the risk of being captured by a wave and smashed against the rock. The trick, which they had practiced down the coast, was to lower oneself onto the rock as a wave receded, then immediately dive into the next wave. If that was done properly, there was sufficient force in the dive to carry the diver far enough away from the rock not to be smashed against it.

Coming in was less risky. You just waited until a wave receded, then swam quickly to the rock before another crashed, and scampered up the rope out of the way of the next one.

Beyond the surf, there was only one danger: missing the boats three hundred meters offshore. If there were no boats, Fulmar joked during dinner in Le Relaise de Pointe-Noire, some fisherman's wife walking the beach the next morning would find a surprising gift from Allah.

Twenty minutes after entering the water, Fulmar and then el Ferruch heard the steady slapping of an oar against the water and swam toward the sound. Fulmar was first to find it. He was hauled aboard the black, low-slung, fifteen-foot fisherman's dory and wrapped in blankets before el Ferruch's hand appeared on the rail and he too was hauled in.

It took them almost ten minutes—longer than they expected—before they had stopped shivering and were prepared to reenter the water. Going back was easier, because the lights of Le Relaise de Pointe-Noire were a target, because they would now be carried in by the very strong tides.

An hour after they first entered the water, they were back on the rock, and the fisherman's dory had almost made its rendezvous with its mother ship, a forty-foot single-sailed fishing dhow. The dhow would sail fifteen miles due west into the Atlantic and rendezvous with an Argentine steamer bound for Buenos Aires. The dhow would then cast its nets for the rest of the night and then return to Safi, where the crew would rejoin their friends, laugh and joke and relate the story of how Sheikh Sidi Hassan el Ferruch had swum through the surf at Pointe-Noire and again made fools of the French and the Germans.

When the two naked, shivering men climbed through the windows of the *chambre séparée,* the enormous Senegalese immediately coiled the ropes, and the Moroccan women wrapped them inside blankets. Later the very exciting-looking blond one drank from a bottle of French cognac, then reclined on a chaise longue. One of the women rubbed his legs and back with towels, and then his front. He stopped shivering, sat up, looked down at himself, closed his eyes, and laughed.

She laughed too, and gently—but very cautiously—let her fingers experience his luxurious mat of light golden hair. She was not used to hair so bright.

And he, when not long afterward he began to explore her body with his hands, found her hair to be fuller, richer, and darker than he was used to . . . except where she had carefully made herself baby-smooth.

5
National Institute of Health Building
Washington, D.C.
November 30, 1941

Captain Peter Douglass gave Eldon C. Baker a cup of coffee, poured himself one, then carried it behind his desk.

"I've just been reading your files," he said. "Again."

"I'm a little surprised to hear that," Baker confessed. He wondered how the Navy captain had managed to gain access to his personal records.

"The psychiatrist thinks you have a tendency to indulge your fantasies," Douglass said. He flipped through papers on his desk. "Would you say that's the case, Mr. Baker?"

Now Baker was even more surprised. It was absolutely against regulations for psychiatric evaluation records to be disseminated outside the intelligence division of the State Department, much less casually shipped to some public-relations outfit sharing quarters with the National Institute of Health.

"May I see that?" Baker asked.

"Help yourself," Douglass said.

Baker got out of his chair and walked to Douglass's desk.

"They were more than a little upset when I went over there for these," Douglass said. "And were more than a little reluctant to hand them over."

"You're not supposed to have access to these records," Baker said.

"Nor these either, I daresay," Douglass said. He pushed a stack of manila folders to Baker. They were all stamped SECRET. What they were were his complete files—copies of everything he had transmitted to the State Department since entering his intelligence assignment in France.

"If it's your intention, Captain, to surprise me, you have," he said. "May I ask what's going on around here?"

"What had you heard?" Douglass asked.

"That you were going to handle the national propaganda, should we get in a war," Baker said.

"That, too," Douglass said.

"What is it you want of me?" Baker said.

"Well," Douglass said. "You have a nice speaking voice, and I understand you're perfectly fluent in French and German. Perhaps we could put you to work doing foreign-language broadcasts."

"You're mocking me," Baker said, without anger. "Why?"

"I want to see if the psychiatrist is right," Douglass said. "I'd like to know what your imagination makes of all this."

"Are you serious?"

"Perfectly."

"Anything with enough authority to get my records is some sort of intelligence operation."

"Very good," Douglass said. "But I'm not sure whether that is your imagination at work, or whether Undersecretary Quinn told you that he's heard this is some sort of intelligence operation and suggested you find out as much as you can about it while you're over here."

"Half and half," Baker said. "When Mr. Quinn learned I was coming over, he said something about what he'd heard. But I don't understand how you got the wherewithal to remove my files. That, my unfettered mind suggests, means you have a great deal of authority."

"I report to Colonel William J. Donovan. Donovan answers to the President," Douglass said.

"And what do you want with me?"

"We want you to head up what would be called, in the State Department, the French desk."

Baker just looked at him.

"We're still in the process of starting up," Douglass went on. "The French desk—at least for the near future—includes French North West Africa."

"Why me?"

"Well, for one thing, Robert Murphy thinks very highly of you," Douglass said. "He was furious when he couldn't get you to be one of his control officers."

"I have no idea what you're talking about," Baker said.

Douglass laughed, pleasantly.

"The Weygand-Murphy Accords are only classified secret," he said. "If I can get your dossier and your files, are you really surprised that I know about them?"

"Knowing about something and talking about it are two different things," Baker said.

"We are entitled to know everybody's secrets," Douglass said. "The reverse is not true."

"Forgive me, Captain, isn't that a little melodramatic?"

"Possibly," Douglass said.

"What, exactly, would I be doing on your French desk?"

"Whatever has to be done in what Colonel Donovan decides is the interest of the United States," Douglass said. "Some of the things you may be asked to do might violate the law, and will certainly violate what is commonly thought of as decency and morality. Would that bother you?"

"I'm unable to take you entirely seriously," Baker said.

"Oh, I'd hoped the files would impress you," Douglass said. "They don't?"

"Yes, they do," Baker said after a moment. "But you're throwing this at me awfully quickly."

"Yes, I know," Douglass said. "But don't take that to mean that I am acting impulsively. Before we sent for you, you were gone over very thoroughly. The decision to send for you was made by Colonel Donovan himself."

"What would I be doing?" Baker asked.

Douglass ignored the question. "You're about to be promoted at the State Department," he said. "Which was one of the reasons Mr. Murphy couldn't have you as a control officer. The State Department had high-priority plans for you. Our priority is even higher."

Douglass waited a moment for that to sink in and then went on. "You will, in any case, be given that promotion. If you come over here, State Department records will indicate that you are a special assistant to the undersecretary of state for European affairs. For the time being, at least, you will remain on the State Department payroll. But you will answer to me, not to anyone in the State Department. If I ever find out that you told anyone in the State Department anything that you learn here—and I would, Mr. Baker— you will spend the balance of your government career stamping visas. Do I make that point?"

"We're back to the melodrama," Baker said.

"I'm sorry you feel that way," Douglass said.

"How much time do I have to think this over?" Baker asked.

"Until you leave the room," Douglass said.

"Wouldn't you be likely to think I'm a fool if I jumped into this impulsively?"

"I've read your files; you're no fool. The question before me now is how decisive you are."

"I'll call your bluff," Baker said.

"I'm not bluffing," Douglass said.

"As I understand your offer, I retain my State Department status . . ."

"For the time being. You may be asked to transfer to us later," Douglass confirmed.

"And I am to report to you, as head of a French/French North West African desk that is somehow involved in intelligence?"

"Yes."

"All right," Baker said.

"Would you be offended if I said that I am not surprised? That, in fact, I have already arranged an office for you?" Douglass asked.

Baker thought that over.

"No," he said.

"What is the highest security classification with which you are familiar, aside from Presidential Eyes Only?"

"Secretarial Eyes Only, I suppose," Baker said.

"Until we run you through the administrative process around here, I'm afraid I can't let you take this out of the office," Douglass said. "But I want it running through your head while you're over at State this afternoon cleaning out your desk."

"That quick?"

Douglass ignored the question. "The classification of this—we haven't come up with a satisfactory classification system yet, frankly—is somewhere below Presidential Eyes Only and somewhere above Secretarial Eyes Only. Only those Cabinet members with a need to know have access to it."

He handed Baker a file.

"There's as much information as we have on a man named Louis Albert Grunier in there," Douglass said. "The first thing we have to do is find him, and the second thing we have to do is figure out the best way to get him here without arousing the suspicions of the Germans.''

A quick glance at the first couple of lines showed Baker that Louis Albert Grunier was a French national who was last known to be an employee of Union Minière in the Katanga Province of the Belgian Congo. His present whereabouts were unknown.

''May I ask why this man is valuable?'' Baker asked.

''Grunier knows the location of a certain raw material that is considered of great importance. We think he will be able to help us get our hands on it.''

''You're not going to tell me what kind of material? Or what it is to be used for?'' Baker asked.

''No,'' Captain Douglass said. ''But I'll tell you what I want you to do: indulge your imagination and make guesses. Come in here at nine in the morning and tell me what you've been thinking.''

SEVEN

1
Summer Place
Deal, New Jersey
10:30 A.M., December 7, 1941

Chesley Haywood Whittaker, Sr., had built Summer Place in New Jersey in 1889 because the senior Whittaker did not like Long Island or Connecticut or Rhode Island, where most of his peers had their summer places. He was neither a Vanderbilt nor a Morgan, he said to his wife, just a simple bridge and dam builder; and he could not afford to copy in Newport or Stockbridge a Florentine palace. So she would just have to deal with Deal. The play on words amused him.

The names his wife suggested for the new summer house (twenty-six rooms on three floors, sitting on ten acres that sloped down to the beach of the Atlantic Ocean) also amused him. She proposed Sea View and Sea Breezes and The Breakers and Ocean Crest and Sans Souci (and the English translation, Without Care).

" 'Careless' would be all right, Mitzi," Chesley Haywood Whittaker told his wife. "It would memorialize my foresight in hiring Carlucci."

Antonio Carlucci and Sons, General Contractors, had built the house, graded the dunes, and laid the grass, driveways, and a six-hole putting green for what Chesley Hay-

wood Whittaker, Sr., considered an outrageous ninety-seven
thousand dollars.

Esther Graham "Mitzi" (for no good reason) Whittaker
was alone with the father of her three sons in the privacy
of their bedroom in their brownstone on Murray Hill in New
York City. There were no children or servants within hearing.

"Call it what you damned well please, you ass!" she
flared. "But there had damned well better be a sign up by
next week!"

The house, not quite two miles from the railroad station
in Asbury Park, could not be seen from the road. Mitzi's
sister and brother-in-law had ridden in a hack for two hours
up and down the road before they found it. It was, Mitzi
pointed out to her husband, the only one of more than two
dozen summer places nearby that had neither a gatehouse
nor a sign.

A sign was up when next Mrs. Whittaker went to Deal.
The senior Whittaker had ordered a brick wall six feet high
and eight feet long on the sand beside the road. Mounted
on it was a bronze sign, cast as a rush order and special
favor to Whittaker by the Baldwin Locomotive Works:

SUMMER PLACE
WHITTAKER

"It would have taken six men and God only knows how
much money to take it down, and your father knew it,"
Mitzi Whittaker had often told her sons. It was one of her
favorite stories, and every time that Chesley Haywood Whittaker, Jr., passed the sign he thought of his mother telling
that story.

He remembered the sign when it stood alone on the sand.
Now there was a fence, brick pillars every twenty-five feet,

with pointed steel poles in between. The road had long ago been paved with brick, and Summer Place had become the year-round residence of Chesley Haywood Whittaker, Jr.

After the death of first their father and six months later their mother, Mitchell Graham Whittaker, the older brother, had taken over the brownstone in Manhattan and lived there unmarried (but, it was reliably rumored, seldom without female companionship) until his death.

And the house on Q Street had gone to James Graham Whittaker, the baby brother, who had been killed with Pershing in France four months before his wife delivered their only child. As Chesley Haywood Whittaker often thought, young Jim Whittaker became the only chance the family had to perpetuate its name and fortune. For Chesty and his wife—to their deep regret—were childless.

James's wife, a Martindale girl from Scarsdale, had remarried a couple of years after his death; but she had been extraordinarily kind to Chesty and Mitch about the boy, who had been christened James Mitchell Chesley Whittaker at Saint Bartholomew's on Park Avenue with his uncles and Barbara as his godparents. She had shared the boy with them more than they had any right to expect she would.

Her second husband, a lawyer on Wall Street, was a Yalie by way of Phillips Exeter. Little Jimmy had followed the Whittakers through St. Mark's and Harvard. Every New Year's, they had sort of a delayed Christmas for him at Summer Place, and Jimmy's mother and her husband and their children always gave them the boy for a month in the summer.

It had been planned that when Little Jimmy graduated, they would take him into the firm, but he had instead elected to go into the Army Air Corps and learn to fly. At the time, it had seemed like a good idea. Let him sow a few wild oats before he settled down. But now that Roosevelt had extended his service for a year and he had been sent to the Philippines, it obviously hadn't been such a good idea.

Chesty Whittaker missed Jimmy very much, and so did Barbara, and Chesty was also worried about what the war that seemed imminent would mean for Jimmy. Today he would get some answers. Or thought he would. He was going first to a Giants game, and then to Washington, with his lawyer friend Bill Donovan. Donovan was already doing something very hush-hush for Roosevelt—so hush-hush that the normally cheerful and expansive Donovan changed the subject every time Chesty tried to pry out of him what it was he was doing for Franklin, though it was obviously related to what he and Commander Ian Fleming had been cooking up together last summer.

Donovan, nevertheless, had better access to what the future had in store for him and for Jimmy than Chesty himself did, and Chesty knew that except for those matters covered by secrecy, Donovan would give him straighter answers than he had got from Franklin the night he and Jimmy ate with him at the White House. When he'd asked him for straight answers, Franklin just grinned his enigmatic grin. "If you want to get in the game, Chesty," he said, "you're going to have to join the team."

Chesty Whittaker was damned if short of war he would join Roosevelt's "team." If the man wasn't a socialist, he was the next thing to it.

When he went into the breakfast room to say good-bye to Barbara, she asked him if he had any money. When he looked, he found he didn't, and she shook her head at him, took two hundred dollars in twenties from her purse, and gave it to him.

Barbara was his best friend, he thought, far more than a wife. And whenever she was kind to him, which was often, he was ashamed even more about Cynthia. If Barbara ever found out about that, she would be deeply hurt. Chesty Whittaker would rather lose an arm than hurt her. Mother Nature was a bitch, he thought. If she had caused Barbara to lose interest in the physical side of life, it seemed only fair that she dampen his urges too. And she had not. Cynthia kept him as randy as he had been as a young man.

He left the house by the kitchen door. Chesty squinted against the sunlight. It was so painfully bright as to cause pain. The last damned thing he needed was a headache—or rather *another* headache. For he'd had a few lately. And this sort of surprised him, because he was otherwise in perfect health.

At fifty-three Chesley Haywood Whittaker, Jr., carried only twenty pounds more than the one hundred eighty-two he had carried as a tackle at Harvard. He played golf at least once a week, squash at the New York Athletic Club every Thursday afternoon, and had given up the boat only when he marked his half century of life. He was, his doctor told him, in as good shape as he'd been at twenty-one.

Edward, the chauffeur, had the Packard waiting. He got behind the wheel and pushed the starter button and ground the damned starter gears. You actually could not feel or hear that the Packard engine was running, but that did not keep him from feeling foolish. He put it in gear and moved away.

Chesty saw Barbara wave at him from the breakfast room. He waved back, and he considered again that she probably sensed he had a woman somewhere. But if she knew, she hadn't said anything, or done anything. There had not been so much as a hint or a pointed remark.

He forced that thought from his mind again, and the Packard turned past the sign his father had erected and headed for New York on Route 35, through Perth Amboy and into Elizabeth and then around Newark Airport and over the Pulaski Skyway. He smarted, as he always did, at the thought that he did not build the skyway. His firm had bid on it (all it was, really, was a high, paved railroad bridge; bridges were bridges) and had lost out by a lousy eleven million dollars.

There was a holdup of some sort in the Holland Tunnel—damned Sunday drivers out for a spin. But Edward managed to bring the car up to the box holder's entrance to the Polo Grounds in good time. Chesty told the police to let Edward in after he'd parked the car.

The trouble with charming Irishmen was that they were seldom alone. There were seven people in the box with Bill Donovan. If he was going to have a word with Donovan, it would have to be on the train.

"A little Scotch, Chesty?" Donovan said.

"Is there any brandy?" Chesty asked. He had indigestion, or something. He had the makings of one of those damned headaches—from the fumes in the tunnel, probably. Brandy usually proved more effective for him than aspirin.

"We're getting a little effete in our old age, aren't we?" Donovan kidded.

"I was gassed in the tunnel," Chesty said. "I feel a headache coming."

"I always have some for the ladies," Donovan went on, looking in his bar box. "Oh, here it is. 'For Female Vapors' right on the bottle."

"Go to hell, Bill," Chesty said, taking the bottle.

He drank a shotglassful neat, and then poured another to sip on.

Donovan introduced him to the men he didn't know. A Chicago banker, some relative of Jack Kriendler and Charlie Berns, who ran the "21" Club on Fifty-second Street, a state senator from Oswego (another Republican who, like Bill himself, had been active in Tom Dewey's failed attempt to win the 1940 nomination), and a Boston surgeon. The last, Charley MacArthur, was a writer.

"I want to talk to you seriously later," Donovan said. "There's something I want to ask you to do for me."

"Name it," Chesty said. Tit for tat, he thought.

"On the train," Bill Donovan said.

He could hardly tell Whittaker here that the President wanted Whittaker Construction to gear up with all possible haste for a monumental, multibillion-dollar, highly complex engineering construction project that was concerned with refining a mineral element that had never been refined in quantities larger than a pin could pick up.

The project was now official. As of yesterday, Saturday, December 6, the Office of Scientific Research and Development had been given several million dollars to get things started. And they were still working on building chain reaction at the University of Chicago.

The only thing they were certain of was that if this were going to work, they would need large quantities of an isotope called U 235. Right now in all the world—including what the Germans were known to have—there was .000001 pound of uranium 235.

At one minute after 2:00 P.M., there was an announcement over the public-address system. It was urgent that Colonel William Donovan call Operator 19 in Washington for an emergency message.

"God, it must be nice to be that man's confidant," Chesty said to Donovan as Donovan went looking for a telephone.

"I never voted for him," Donovan said. "It's just that I have this awesome respect for Harvard men."

The door to the box opened again two minutes later, and Donovan beckoned Chesty to come out of the box. He was not smiling, Chesty saw, and he didn't like the look in Donovan's eyes.

"That was John Roosevelt," he said. "The Japanese have bombed Pearl Harbor."

"Jesus Christ!" Chesty said.

"I'm wanted in Washington," Donovan said. "Will you have your chauffeur take me to the station?"

"Certainly," Chesty said.

"Or to La Guardia," Donovan said. "John's trying to find me a seat on the three-fifteen Eastern flight. He's going to call right back."

Chesty Whittaker went back to the box and motioned to Edward. Donovan was called to the telephone as Chesty was telling Edward he was to take Mr. Donovan to Pennsylvania Station, and then come back for him.

When Donovan returned, he said, "It'll be La Guardia."

"They found a seat for you?" Chesty asked.

Donovan's eyebrows went up.

"Young Roosevelt just told me that by the time I get to La Guardia, there will be an Army Air Corps plane waiting for me."

"Ooohooo," Chesty breathed.

"If you still want to go to Washington, Chesty," Donovan said, "come with me."

"How would I get back?"

"I presume that for the immediate future there will be no restrictions on travel," Donovan said. "It will take them time to set something like that up."

Chesty Whittaker made two quick decisions. He would go to Washington. For some reason (and he didn't think it was just Cynthia, but he acknowledged that she was part of his decision) it was important that he go. And there was no car in Washington.

"Edward," he said. "I'm going to Washington with Colonel Donovan. After you drop us at La Guardia, I want you to drive the Packard down there. Take it to the house on Q

Street. If I'm not there, I'll leave word what you're to do next.''

''Is something wrong, Mr. Whittaker?''

Chesty looked at Bill Donovan, who nodded before he replied.

''The Japanese have bombed Pearl Harbor, Hawaii, Edward. It looks as if we're at war.''

2
Rangoon, Burma
0930 Hours 8 December 1941

When Dick Canidy went down to breakfast in the villa in Kemmendine, the houseboy first gave him a cup of coffee and then extended a tray on which sat a small packet of waxed paper tied with a string.

''It came this morning, sair,'' he said.

Canidy nodded, picked up a knife, and cut the string around the package. Inside was mail: a four-inch stack for Ed Bitter, and a half-inch stack for Canidy.

''A couple of eggs, up,'' Canidy said. ''Juice, toast. Is there any ham?''

''No, sair, but small steak.''

''Please,'' Canidy said, and then, handing him Bitter's mail, added: ''This is for Mr. Bitter. Go wake him up with it.''

''Yes, sair.''

Five of Canidy's nine pieces of mail were bills. There were three letters from his father, and one which surprised him. It bore the return address of Ann Chambers, at Bryn Mawr College.

He tore it open and thought, aloud: ''Christ, it took long enough to get here.''

P.O. Box 235
College Station
Bryn Mawr, Pa.
Sept. 4, 1941

Dear Lonely Boy, Far From Home & Loved Ones:

I call you that because a Red Cross Volunteer—a lady
dressed in so splendiferous a uniform I was truly
disappointed to learn she was not a field marshal—told me
that's what guys like you are. She also said that it was
clearly my patriotic duty to become your pen pal.

And she told us (we were in church at the time) that Far
From Home & Loved Ones (I think she had in mind such
remote places as Fort Dix, N.J., and San Diego, Cal., rather
than wherever this finds you, if it ever finds you) there are
Lonely Boys yearning for a demonstration of concern from
Young Ladies At Home while they are off defending All That
We Hold Dear.

By a pleasant coincidence, she just happened to have a
list of addresses of such Lonely, etc., Boys, which she would
be happy to dispense, no more than two to a customer.

While I am as interested as anyone in keeping the
barbarians out of Bryn Mawr, I draw the line at writing
letters to complete strangers. Hence, this. I got the address
from my father, who sends his best regards and asks that
you keep your eye on my idiot cousin.

If you are where you said you were going, and write back,
I can probably win the prize for writing the Lonely Boy
Furthest From Home, etc. I will also get a gold star on my
report card to show my mommy.

I'm also more than a little curious to know if it's true the
ships you will be flying, as Daddy heard (P40-Bs?), are the
ones the English rejected as obsolete. If that's a military
secret, of course, ignore the question.

Take care of yourself, Canidy.

                                        Cordially,
                                        Ann Chambers

Bitter came into the dining room as Canidy was rereading one of his father's letters.

He fixed him with a penetrating stare and kept it up until Bitter finally responded.

"Why are you staring at me?"

"That's what's known as keeping an eye on an idiot cousin," Canidy said, pleased with himself.

He handed Bitter Ann Chambers's letter. He wondered how her father had been able to come up with CAMCO's Rockefeller Center mail-drop address.

Bitter handed the letter back.

"She writes a funny letter," he said. "I got one too. I mean a morale builder. From Ann's friend."

"Which friend?"

"Sarah Child," Bitter said, handing it to him.

"The one with the nice ass," Canidy said. He read the letter.

P.O. Box 135
College Station
Bryn Mawr, Pa.
Sept. 4, 1941

Dear Ed:

I suppose you'll be as surprised to hear from me as I am surprised to be writing. There was a Red Cross program here to get the girls to write to men in the service. I just don't have the courage to write to a complete stranger, and Ann, as usual, came up with a solution that will keep the powers that be off our backs: She's writing Dick Canidy (she got the address from her father) and I'm writing you.

I'm sure that you have absolutely no interest in what's happened since we were at Ann's place, but for lack of anything else to write about, I spent most of the summer in New York, except for two weeks, when we went to

Mackinac Island, where there is an enormous old hotel and
no automobiles. It was kind of nice, probably just the way it
was in the 1890s.

Charity came in and said that what we're doing is no fair.
She was going to write one or the other of you, but we told
her that would be unfair to you, that you had more
important things to do with your time than solve what must
seem like a silly problem for us.

It was very nice meeting you and Dick Canidy in
Alabama, and I hope this finds both of you happy and in
good health. If you do have a spare moment sometime, it
would be nice to get a postcard. Or do they have postcards
in China?

> Sincerely,
> Sarah Child

"Holy shit!" Bitter exclaimed excitedly. Canidy looked
at him. Bitter was pointing to an enormous insect crawling
across an ancient copy of the *Times of India* on the table
beside Canidy. "Kill the fucking thing!" Bitter said.

"My God, you're learning to swear and everything,"
Canidy chuckled. "*You* kill it. I'm willing to talk things over
with it."

"Fuck you," Ed Bitter said. He dumped the insect on the
floor by turning the newspaper over and then stamped on
the bug.

Canidy handed Sarah Child's letter back to him.

"Clever," he said. "Not as clever as Ann's, but clever."

"Are you going to reply?" Bitter asked.

"Sure," Canidy said. "Why not?"

"She's a little young for you, isn't she? Not quite your
style?"

The reference was obviously to what had happened between Canidy and Sue-Ellen.

"I hadn't planned to send her dirty pictures, Eddie," Canidy replied. "Just help her get her gold star to show her mommy."

Ex–Chief Radioman Edgar Lopp rushed into the dining room.

"The Japs just bombed Battleship Row at Pearl Harbor."

"Oh shit!" Canidy said.

"Oh my God!" Bitter said.

Lopp turned on the Hallicrafter's communications receiver they had "borrowed" from the CAMCO warehouse, and they listened for bulletins all over the dial.

At eleven o'clock, a messenger delivered a radio message from Toungoo:

AIRCRAFT OF THE AVG WILL NOT REPEAT NOT PARTICIPATE IN ANY REPEAT ANY OPERATION WITHOUT THE SPECIFIC AUTHORIZATION OF THE UNDERSIGNED. CHENNAULT.

Since Canidy and Bitter were the only AVG aviators in Rangoon, the message was obviously intended for them. Bitter was powerfully disappointed. He took the Japanese attack as a personal affront, and wanted to rush out to Mingaladon Field, jump into a P40-B, roar into the sky, and take revenge on whatever treacherous Japanese aircraft happened to be conveniently there.

Canidy, on the other hand, felt something closer to fear. The Japanese had not attacked Pearl Harbor foolishly. They had imagined, and now had proved, that they could get away with it. And if, as the radio reported, they had destroyed most of the Pacific Fleet, things were going to be very bad for the United States and its allies in the Pacific.

As a practical matter, Canidy decided the smart thing to do was try to get in touch with Crookshanks at Toungoo.

Incredibly, the telephone call went through immediately.

"This is Canidy, Commander," he said. "For your information, there are two we can bring up there right now, if you think that's best."

"Are they in revetments?" Crookshanks asked.

"Yes, sir," Canidy said. "I'd say they're safe from anything but a direct hit."

"I think the thing to do is let them sit right there until things settle down a little. You got the general's TWX?"

"Yes, sir. Just now."

"Our priority, obviously, is to get the aircraft to China," Crookshanks said. "Unless you hear to the contrary, ferry them up here first thing in the morning."

"Yes, sir," Canidy said.

"My, aren't we courteous this morning?" Crookshanks said dryly, and hung up.

"What did he say?" Bitter asked after Canidy had hung up.

"Tomorrow morning, we take the two that are flyable up to Toungoo."

"And what are we supposed to do today?"

"We've been invited to tiffin," Canidy said. "At Wing Commander Hepple's house. With a little bit of luck, that redheaded Scottish lassie will be there. Maybe she'll have a friend for you."

"For God's sake, we're at war," Bitter said.

"*Whatever,* old chap, has that to do with tiffin?" Canidy replied in a British accent. "Stiff upper lip! Cheerio! Pip-pip and all that!"

"You go ahead if you want to," Bitter said. "I'm going to stick by the radio."

"Suit yourself," Canidy said. "When the Japs start climbing over the rose garden wall, give me a yell, and I'll come help repel them."

When Canidy came down from his room at half past three, Bitter was sitting in the front seat of the Studebaker. Canidy said nothing about his change of mind. It did seem a little incongruous that with the Pacific Fleet on the bottom of Pearl Harbor, he was going out to get laid.

3
Gravelly Point Airport
Washington, D.C.
4:45 P.M., December 7, 1941

The Douglass C-47 airplane waiting for Colonel William Donovan at La Guardia Field was painted the dull olive green of the Army Air Corps. It also bore the Army Air Corps insignia, a red circle in a white star, and it was flown by men in Air Corps uniforms. But when Donovan and Chesley Haywood Whittaker got inside, the interior was civilian. There was even a brochure in a pouch on the back of the seat in front of Chesty Whittaker. In it was a picture of Captain Eddie Rickenbacker welcoming travelers aboard a flagship of Eastern Airlines' Great Silver Fleet.

There was no stewardess, but ten minutes after they broke ground and the white beaches of the Atlantic Coast of New Jersey sped by under the left wing, a young officer with pilot's wings on his tunic came out of the cockpit with a thermos of coffee and two china mugs and told them they should be on the ground in about ninety minutes.

"I see the airplane was just drafted," Donovan said as he took the coffee.

"Yes, sir." The young officer chuckled. "We just took it away from Eastern. Tomorrow . . . we're adding insult to injury by making them do the work . . . they were going to strip the interior. I don't know what will happen now."

"I think we can safely presume that they'll go ahead and strip it," Donovan said. "The military cannot stand creature comforts."

"If you gentlemen need anything, just come forward," the young pilot said. "I better go help steer."

When he had gone, Chesty Whittaker asked the question on his mind:

"Are they going to requisition all civilian airplanes?"

"They're going to requisition what they need right away," Donovan replied, "and then replace them as soon as they can from production. Don Douglas's purchase order is going to make him rich: 'Make as many airplanes as you can as quick as you can, on cost plus ten percent.' "

"It couldn't happen to a nicer fellow," Chesty Whittaker said.

"Speaking of requisitioning, Chesty," Donovan said. "How attached are you to the house on Q Street?"

"I don't think I'm going to like this," Chesty said.

"I'm going to need a place like that," Donovan said.

"I thought you had an apartment in the Hotel Washington," Whittaker said, "as well as the place in Georgetown."

"I don't mean me, personally," Donovan said carefully. "The organization I'm setting up is going to need a place where I can bring people together, put them up overnight— or for a couple of weeks, maybe—a place where they won't be seen or attract attention. A place, bluntly, to hide people, where they can be protected. A place with a wall around it; a place with a good kitchen and half a dozen bedrooms. A place just like Jimmy's house on Q Street, Chesty."

"What, exactly, Bill, are you up to?" Whittaker asked, then quoted, " 'A place to hide people'?"

"I can't tell you, exactly, Chesty, what I'm doing," Donovan replied.

"No, I suppose not," Whittaker said after a moment.

"Jimmy, obviously, won't be using the Q Street house for a while," he went on. "If the government really has a need for it, Bill, of course you can have it."

"I'll have somebody get in touch," Donovan said. "Work out the details. I'll fix it, of course, so that there will always . . . or almost always . . . be a room for you and Barbara."

"How good of you," Chesty said dryly. "There's one thing, Bill. Someone lives in the garage apartment."

"He'll have to move, I'm afraid," Donovan said.

"It's a she," Chesty said.

"Oh?" Donovan asked, smiling. "How much are you paying her?"

"It's Tom Chenowith's daughter, you foulmouthed Irishman," Chesty said.

"Cynthia?" Donovan asked. "I thought she was at Harvard."

"She's through law school and working for the State Department."

"Christ, we're getting old," Donovan said.

"She wants to be a foreign service officer," Chesty said. "The old-boy network is fighting tooth and claw, of course. But they couldn't keep her from a job as a lawyer. She was on the *Law Review*. A very determined young woman. She'll wind up, I wouldn't be surprised, as Secretary of State."

"We can work out something about her, I'm sure," Donovan said. "Which brings us to you."

"What does that mean?"

"I'd like for you to come work with me, Chesty," Donovan said.

"Doing what?"

"What do you know about intelligence?"

"Spying, finding out troop movements, order of battle,

and that sort of thing, I guess. Other than that, absolutely nothing.''

''There's more to intelligence than spying and military intelligence,'' Donovan said. ''I think of what we're doing as *strategic* intelligence.''

''Bill, I really don't know what you're talking about,'' Chesty Whittaker confessed.

''Military intelligence is concerned with things of interest to the military. Navy intelligence concerns itself with the enemy's naval capabilities. The Army is interested in the capabilities and weaknesses of the enemy ground and air forces. Strategic intelligence is concerned with the enemy's overall intentions and capabilities.''

''Wouldn't that be, for lack of a better term, 'diplomatic' intelligence?''

''State Department intelligence should deal with diplomatic intelligence,'' Donovan said. ''Strategic intelligence is the whole picture. Do you understand?''

''I don't really know,'' Chesty Whittaker confessed.

''*My* function, Chesty,'' Donovan said, and then stopped. ''Christ, that was a regal 'my,' wasn't it? You know, I sort of like that thought. Anyway, the function of the organization I'm setting up . . . and it's still in the formative stage . . . is to have a group of really knowledgeable people sift through all the intelligence gathered. I want them to see what this stuff means vis-à-vis the total conduct of the war without having to get caught up in the individual needs of the armed forces and the State Department. To boil it down in other words, for Roosevelt. Franklin does not want an Army or Navy picture, he wants a total picture of what's going on in the world. He wants to know what's likely to happen, who's doing it, why they're doing it, and what we should do in return.''

''Oh,'' Whittaker said.

"And the reverse," Donovan said.

"I don't understand."

"When a strategic decision has been made, we need to be able to decide how it can best be accomplished—economically, quickly, considering available assets and the overall requirements for those assets. Who gets the shipping tonnage, for example, to what part of the world."

"OK," Whittaker said, understanding.

"And finally, Chesty, we're going to be responsible for dirty tricks. If we can buy some German general, we're going to buy him."

"Espionage, you mean."

"Including espionage. There's more to it than that."

"Where are you going to get the people to do that sort of thing?"

"From all over. The people who are now looking at the big picture are known, somewhat irreverently, as the Twelve Disciples. Actually, so far there are only ten. I'd like you to be the eleventh."

"I'm flattered, Bill," Whittaker said.

"You'll work your ass off, and I'll pay you a dollar a year," Donovan said.

"Did your 'Twelve Disciples' know what was going to happen this morning?" Chesty Whittaker asked.

Donovan ignored the question.

"I asked you a question, Bill," Chesty said.

"A question you should know I couldn't answer," Donovan said. It was a rebuke.

"I don't know what good I would be," Whittaker said. "I don't know anything about this sort of thing."

"You have been traveling all over the world since you were a boy," Donovan said. "You know a wide assortment of people, including a number of our enemies. Let me be the judge of the rest."

"Obviously," Chesty said, "the war will require a mind-boggling amount of heavy construction. That's really my field, Bill. I build railroads and bridges. Wouldn't I be more valuable doing that?"

"No," Donovan said simply. "You will be of greater value working for me. There are a lot of people who can put up a bridge. What I need from you is your brains and your fund of knowledge."

Chesley Haywood Whittaker was both flattered and excited. He was going to have an opportunity to meaningfully participate in the war they had just entered. He looked at Donovan.

"What kind of knowledge?" he asked.

"Just off the top of your head, Chesty, if I came to you and said it was necessary for the government to build an enormous plant, and do so rather secretly—"

"What kind of a plant? Making what?"

"I can't tell you that," Donovan said. "Say a complicated chemical process."

"Poison gas?"

"Something like that," Donovan said. "Something that should not be built, say, any closer than a hundred miles to a population center."

"Chemical processing takes enormous amounts of power," Whittaker said. "So it would be best to put it near a source of hydroelectric power. That means, I would say, off the top of my head, either Alabama or Tennessee, because of the TVA's electric-generating capability—or maybe Washington State."

"That kind of knowledge, Chesty," Donovan said, smiling.

"Will I have to call you sir?"

"And stand to attention." Donovan put out his hand.

"Are you serious about this plant, or plants?" Whittaker asked.

"Just as soon as you can, do me up a one- or two-page briefing paper," Donovan said. "This is a very high priority, Chesty."

"That much poison gas? Are we in that much trouble?"

"Yes, we're in that much trouble. Maybe it isn't poison gas. Think of complicated chemical processes. Don't limit your thoughts to poison gas."

"All right," Whittaker said. "I'll have it for you tomorrow."

"The less help you have, the better," Donovan said.

"Meaning the less people who know?"

"Yes," Donovan said.

Whittaker nodded his understanding.

"Bill," he asked, "what's going to happen to Jimmy? He's in the Philippines."

Donovan's face grew serious. He thought about his reply before he offered it.

"There are two schools of thought," he said. "One believes it is in the best interests of the United States to try to defend our territory and our interests in the Far East. The other believes that we should deal with the Germans before we knock out the Japanese. I think we are going to follow the second choice."

"At the expense of the first, you mean?"

"There's neither the men nor the matériel for both at once," Donovan said.

"We're going to lose the Philippines?"

"What's Jimmy flying?" Donovan replied, ignoring the question.

"Pursuit planes," Chesty said. "P40s. What else, considering Jimmy?"

"Then he'll be in the thick of it," Donovan said. "The

basic defense strategy for the Philippines is to destroy the Japanese invasion fleet from the air. They just sent a flock of Flying Fortresses over there . . . you know, those four-engine Boeings?''

''Jimmy's flying a pursuit plane.''

''The Japanese will try to destroy our bombers on the ground. Defending them will be the job of the pursuit pilots.''

''And will they be able to?''

''If they try hard enough, and if they don't run out of planes,'' Donovan said. ''There's a convoy, accompanied by the cruiser *Pensacola,* en route to Manila now. There's several shiploads of fighter planes in it.''

''What are you telling me, Bill?'' Chesty asked.

''That Jimmy will be in the thick of it,'' Donovan repeated. ''You wanted the truth.''

The conversation ended there, because there was simply nothing else to say.

The C-47 made a wide descending sweep over the District itself. The Capitol Building was on the left, and the White House on the right. They were so low he could see the flags flying. It was a peaceful scene, and he wondered for a moment if Washington, like London, would be bombed. Was he perhaps having a last look at a Washington that had not been bombed since the English themselves did it in 1814?

They descended over the Tidal Basin and the Jefferson Memorial and the bridges over the Potomac. And then approach lights to the runways of the Gravelly Point airport appeared, and a moment later the wheels chirped as the plane touched down.

They taxied off the runway and stopped. A black Cadillac limousine drove up beside them, and the young pilot who had given them the coffee came out of the cockpit.

''Your ground transportation is here, gentlemen,'' he said.

"Thank you for flying Eastern Air Corps Airlines."

"I prefer the coffee passers in skirts," Donovan said.

The young pilot chuckled and went to open the door.

Whittaker noticed that the pilot had shut down only the right engine. And as soon as they were inside the limousine, he restarted the other one.

There were guards, soldiers in helmets and uniforms, on both ends of the Fourteenth Street Bridge across the Potomac, and more on Fourteenth Street. And on Fifteenth, Chesty saw still more soldiers guarding the Bureau of Printing and Engraving, the Department of Agriculture, the Post Office, the Treasury Department. And marines were stationed at twenty-yard intervals outside the White House fence.

A lieutenant colonel in a helmet came up to the limousine when it stopped at the gate in the White House fence.

"I'm Colonel William Donovan," Donovan said, rolling down the window. "I'm expected. Mr. Whittaker is with me."

The officer carefully consulted a typewritten list clamped to a clipboard.

"May I have your identification, please?" he asked. Donovan extended a plastic-covered card. The officer examined it and handed it back. "Thank you, sir," he said.

"I haven't had time to get Mr. Whittaker identification," Donovan said. "I'll vouch for him."

"I'm sorry, sir," the officer said. "The only personnel I am permitted to pass inside are those on the list. Mr. Whittaker is not on the list."

"I told you he's with me," Donovan said. The officer started shaking his head. "Not only is he my deputy," Donovan went on, "but he's a friend of the President."

"What you're going to have to do, sir," the officer said, "is drive over to the old Army-Navy-State Building. You can arrange to have this gentleman passed through there. Ask for Colonel Retter.''

''Bill,'' Chesty Whittaker said, ''I'll just catch a cab and go over to the house. I'd just be in the way, anyway.''

''The President needs all the friends he can get today,'' Donovan said. ''He would be glad to see you.''

''Tell him, Bill, please, that I'm ready to join his damned team,'' Whittaker said. ''If he wants to see me, call the Q Street house.'' He started to open the door.

Donovan stopped him. ''You take the car,'' he said. ''I'll walk up the drive.''

He got out of the car.

''Colonel,'' he said, ''your devotion to duty is commendable.''

Chesty could not tell if his friend was being sarcastic or not.

The officer made a gesture to a White House policeman, who stepped out onto Pennsylvania and stopped the traffic so the limousine could back out of the drive.

Chesty gave directions to the chauffeur, and five minutes later was at the house on Q Street.

He let himself into the house and put his suitcase at the foot of the stairs leading to the upper floors. Then he checked the thermostat. It was set at sixty. He moved it to seventy-two and a moment later heard the oil burner kick on.

He then walked down the corridor to the butler's pantry and through it to the kitchen. He unlocked the kitchen door, went down the shallow flight of stairs, and crossed the brick-paved drive to the garage.

All three doors of the garage were closed, and he could see no lights in the apartment over the garage. It was possible, he thought, deeply disappointed, that Cynthia wasn't home.

He climbed the stairs and pushed the doorbell button. There was a chime from inside, and a moment later he heard movement.

And the door opened.

Cynthia Chenowith smiled with genuine pleasure when she saw him.

"I didn't know you were coming," she said.

"Wild horses, that sort of thing," he said.

She was in a robe, and her hair was wrapped in a towel. There was a stray wet lock on her forehead. Her skin glowed.

"I just got out of the shower," she said.

"No!" he said mockingly.

"Wiseass," she said, laughing, and kissed him quickly, then beckoned him inside. He noticed she had not dried her left buttock, and the robe was glued to it.

He followed her into the living room. She started to make him a drink, but he stopped her.

"I think cognac," he said.

She looked at him curiously.

"I've been on the edge of a vicious headache all day," he said. "The cognac seems to help."

She found a snifter, filled it generously with Courvoisier, and handed it to him. "Drink this while I get dressed," she said.

She saw the look on his face.

"At least let me dry my hair," she said.

He smiled.

"You are impatient!" she said. "I'm glad."

She went into her bedroom. He took a swallow of the cognac and followed her into the bedroom. She was sitting at a vanity, vigorously drying her hair with a towel. She smiled at his reflection in the mirror. He sat down on the bed.

"You didn't go to the game? Or they called it off? What I mean is that you're earlier than usual."

"I was with Bill Donovan," he said. "The President sent an airplane for him. He gave me a ride."

"How nice," Cynthia said.

"He wants me to work for him," Chesty said.

She turned to look at him.

"Are you?" she asked, and he nodded. "They really hate Colonel Donovan at the State Department," she said. "He's trying to take over the whole intelligence setup."

"If he hasn't taken over yet," Chesty said, "he will. He wants me to be one of what they call the Twelve Disciples."

"Oh, then they hate you, too," she said. "Will that bother you?"

"With one notable exception, I have never cared what diplomats think of me."

"And I'm not even a diplomat," she said. "More on the order of an uppity female."

"Jimmy," he said. "I'm worried about him."

"Oh my God, I didn't even think about him!"

"You should have," he said. "When he gets back, Barbara intends to pair you off with him. If he gets back."

"He'll get back," Cynthia said. "The pairing off is something else, of course."

"Jimmy has excellent taste in women," Chesty said. "He would really appreciate you."

"Are you trying to send me some sort of message?"

"Every time I see how young and beautiful you are," Chesty said, "it takes me some time to adjust to our situation."

"Every time I see how handsome and distinguished you are," she said, "it takes me some time to believe how lucky I am."

"Having a dead-end affair with a man old enough to be

your father can hardly be called lucky," he said. "Odd, maybe. Interesting."

"Not satisfying?" she asked. "I'm satisfied."

"I feel guilty," he said. "Your father was my friend."

"Don't start that again," she said.

"I love you," he said.

"That you can say," she said. "And I love you."

She turned away again and brushed her hair while he propped himself against the headboard, sipped his cognac, and watched her. On top of the headache he had some kind of damned indigestion again. He tried to belch and could not.

She finished brushing her hair, walked to the side of the bed, and looked down at him. Then she shrugged out of the robe.

"My God, how beautiful you are!" he said.

He started to get off the bed. She pushed him back.

"Let me undress you," she said. "It makes you horny when I undress you, and I like it when you're horny."

"Before you're so nice to me, I had better tell you that you're going to be evicted."

"I don't understand that," she said as she untied his shoes and pulled them off.

"Donovan wants this house for cloak-and-dagger purposes," he said. "I told him he could have it."

"Well, he gets me with it," she said. "Did you tell him that?"

"Certainly," he said. "I said, 'Bill, our old pal Tom's daughter isn't just living in the garage apartment, she's my mistress.' "

"I don't like that word," she said. "It suggests I'm doing it for money."

"No offense, my darling," he said.

"I'm your lover," she said. "I don't know why you re-fuse to accept that."

"Possibly because I am afraid there is an element of grat-itude in our relationship."

"Who seduced who?" she asked.

"I wish I really knew," he said.

"I don't know whether to cry or throw something at you," she said.

They looked at each other for a moment, and then he shrugged.

"Will you ask if I can keep the apartment?" she asked.

"Or I'll get you a better place," he said.

"If I can't stay here, *I'll* get another place," she said. "Maybe that will shut you up once and for all about this. I want you in my bed because you're you, not because you're paying the rent."

She had his zipper open. His erect organ sprang out. "Will you look at that!" Cynthia said.

"You're lewd and shameless," he said, pushing her away, getting to his feet.

"And doesn't that make you happy?" she asked.

She walked around to the other side of the bed, slipped under the covers, and watched him finish undressing.

When he was done, she threw the covers off herself and held out her arms to him. In a moment he had entered the incredible warm soft wetness of her. At the same moment, tragically, his body had had enough.

He cried out, and the goddamned headache he had been trying to avoid all day finally struck him—with a vengeance. He'd never known pain so sudden and so sharp.

And then he was dead.

"Chesty? Chesty, what's the matter?" she asked.

She worked her way out from under him and sat up. Then with all her energy she rolled him over on his back. His eyes stared at her, but she instantly knew he did not see her.

"Oh, Chesty!" she said, putting her balled fists to her mouth. As she had been taught to do, she felt the artery in his neck for a pulse. There was none.

After a few minutes, Cynthia pulled her robe on, and with infinite tenderness, as tears ran down her cheeks, she pulled Chesty's eyelids shut.

4
The White House
Washington, D.C.
7:05 P.M., December 7, 1941

Captain Peter Stuart Douglass, USN, was in the White House because he had become de facto deputy director of the Office of the Coordinator of Information. It hadn't been planned that way. The original notion was that he would be assigned to Donovan because it would take him (and the fission-bomb project) out from under ONI and put it under Donovan, who had the ear of the President.

But in the beginning of the fission project, there really hadn't been much to do beyond sending the people to England to see what could be learned of English and German efforts and to wait for the results of the experiments being conducted at the University of Chicago.

So he had started doing one thing and another for Donovan, and later it had seemed perfectly logical for him to assume duty as acting deputy director of COI until Donovan could find the proper man for the slot.

Then, the week before, the President had decided to place the entire fission project under a group of academics headed by Dr. J. B. Conant, of Harvard. This had the logical cover of a scientific program being run by the Office of Scientific Research and Development.

The change had taken place as of December 6, 1941, and Douglass had not moved over to OSRD.

"Pete, you're not a physicist, and I need you more than they do," Donovan had said, with irrefutable logic.

"Colonel, I'd like to go back to the Navy."

"Come on, Pete, I need you more than the Navy," Donovan said. "I can't do without you, and you know it."

"I'd hoped for a command, Colonel," Douglass said.

"Think that through, Pete," Donovan said. "If you went back to the Navy, it would be to ONI. They're not going to give you a sea command. You're too valuable as an intelligence officer. And you would be of more value here than you would be in the Navy."

Donovan was of course right. And what that meant was that after a lifetime of preparing for war at sea, Captain Peter Douglass was going to spend the war behind a desk. His friends and peers would be on the bridges of ships while he stayed in Washington. And the price he was going to pay for working for Donovan, he clearly understood, was that he could never make admiral.

When the telephone call came for Donovan, Douglass took it. And then he quietly opened the door to the Oval Office and stepped inside. The office was heavy with cigarette smoke, and although there had been a steady stream of stewards passing in and out, doing their best to keep it shipshape, the place was a mess. Sandwich remnants and empty coffee cups on every flat surface but the President's desk itself. That was covered with sheets of paper and a large map.

Douglass found Colonel Donovan sitting beside General Marshall on a couch against the wall. The President had rolled his wheelchair close to the other two. They were all facing each other, deep in conversation.

It was almost a minute before Donovan sensed Douglass's presence and looked up at him. And when he did, it was with only partly hidden annoyance in his eyes.

"What is it, Pete?" Donovan asked.

"I've got a Miss Chenowith on the line," Douglass said. "She's calling for Mr. Chesley Whittaker, and says it's important."

"See what she wants," Donovan said impatiently.

"She insists on talking to you, sir," Douglass said.

"Try again," Donovan said, and returned his attention to the President.

"Did he say that Chesty Whittaker was on the phone?" the President asked.

"Chesty's in Washington. He rode up with me from New York. I've asked him to work with me."

"And he accepted?" the President asked. "He probably hopes you're leading a palace coup."

"He said to tell you he's ready to join the team," Donovan said.

The President laughed.

"As in 'of jackasses'?" he quipped.

Captain Douglass returned.

"Miss Chenowith said to tell you it's an emergency," Douglass said.

"Take the call, Bill," the President ordered. "Chesty wouldn't have her call under these circumstances unless he thought it was necessary."

Donovan looked around for a phone. Douglass handed him the base of one, but kept the handset. "Miss Chenowith, here's Colonel Donovan," he said, and then handed the instrument to Donovan.

"Hello, Cynthia," Donovan said. "Put Chesty on."

"I can't do that, I'm afraid," Cynthia Chenowith said.

"What is this, Cynthia?"

"Chesty's dead, Mr. Donovan," she said. "And unless I have some help, right away, there's going to be a mess."

"Did I understand you correctly?"

"I said he was dead. Is that what you mean?"

"Where are you?"

"At the house on Q Street," she said.

"I'm going to send my deputy, Captain Douglass, right over, Cynthia," Donovan said. "He'll take care of the matter."

"It would be better if you came yourself," she said.

"Captain Douglass will leave immediately," Donovan said. "You're there, I presume?"

"Yes."

"He'll leave immediately," Donovan said sharply, and hung up. He reached for a notepad and scrawled the address.

"Go over there, Peter, please," he ordered. "See a Miss Chenowith. Do whatever has to be done."

"Yes, sir," Captain Douglass said.

"Cynthia Chenowith? Is that Tom's daughter?" the President asked.

"Yes," Donovan said. "She's a lawyer in the State Department. Chesty rents her his garage apartment."

"Is something wrong?"

"She said that Chesty is dead, Mr. President," Donovan said.

EIGHT

I

Captain Douglass left the White House through a basement exit and went to the visitors' parking lot. He had a gray Navy Plymouth, which a young sailor normally drove, but today he found behind the wheel a long-service boatswain's mate first class who'd responded to the attack on Pearl Harbor by leaving his sickbed in the Washington Navy Yard Dispensary and reporting for duty. The young driver was now guarding the perimeter of the Navy Yard.

Douglass found the old sailor huddled in his peacoat in the front seat of the Plymouth.

"What are you doing here? Why didn't you wait inside with the other drivers?"

"With all respect, sir. I don't mind filling in in a pinch, but I won't *consort* with them candy-asses."

Douglass, hiding a smile, handed him the slip of paper with the address Donovan had written on it.

"Can you find this?" Douglass asked. "It's somewhere near Dupont Circle."

"Sure," the sailor replied.

Soon Douglass found himself standing outside a ten-foot brick wall, pushing a doorbell.

Then a faint noise caught his attention, and he looked in the direction of the sound. Eighty feet away a young woman appeared on the sidewalk. She had a kerchief over her head and was wearing a trench coat.

"Miss Chenowith?" Douglass called.

"I think you'd better bring the car inside," Cynthia Chenowith said.

Douglass signaled the boatswain's mate to move the car, and he walked down the sidewalk toward the young woman. She looked a little pale—not entirely, because she was wearing makeup. She was shaken. But she also looked in control of herself.

"I'm Peter Douglass, Miss Chenowith," he said. He offered his hand. She neither replied nor took the hand, but she gave him a little smile.

She waited until the Plymouth had passed inside the gate, then motioned him through. There was a switch inside the wall. She pressed it, and electric motors closed the double gate.

Then she walked down the brick drive to the garage. She had, Peter Douglass noticed, a graceful carriage, a firm step. She was both attractive and self-assured.

She stopped at the door to an outside stairway to the floor above the garage.

"What about your driver?" she asked. "Can he be trusted to keep his mouth shut?"

Douglass hadn't even considered that. He didn't even know the boatswain's mate's name.

"Is there any reason he has to know about the problem?" Douglass asked. She nodded. "In that case, he can be trusted." He was a Regular Navy boatswain's mate. He would do what he was told.

Cynthia Chenowith nodded again and started up the stairs.

Douglass signaled to the boatswain's mate to come along, and he got out of the Plymouth and adjusted his white hat in the prescribed cocky position over his eyes.

She led them through what was obviously her apartment and opened a door, standing to one side so that Douglass could go inside.

It was her bedroom, obviously. And on the bed was a body under a sheet.

"Mr. Whittaker?" Douglass asked.

She nodded.

"I'm sorry," he said.

The boatswain's mate, muttering, "Coming through," pushed past Douglass, went to the bed, and pulled the sheet off Chesley Haywood Whittaker's head and torso. Whittaker was naked.

The boatswain's mate put his hand on the artery of Whittaker's neck, then placed his hand flat on his chest.

"He's been dead maybe an hour," he announced matter-of-factly.

"I think you'd better tell me what happened, Miss Chenowith," Captain Douglass said, turning to look at her.

She flushed, but she met his eyes.

"We were in bed," she said. "He made a cry, and went limp."

The man on the bed was old enough to be the girl's father.

"A stroke, probably," the boatswain's mate said professionally. "If it's a heart attack, they generally . . . wet the bed. With a stroke, they're dead right away and nothing works."

Douglass looked at him.

"I was a China sailor," the boatswain's mate said. "We didn't have a medic for a while on the *Panay,* and I had to fill in."

"For obvious reasons," Cynthia Chenowith said, "it must not come out where and how he died."

Cynthia Chenowith was having some difficulty maintaining control, but she was far from hysteria.

"Where'd he live?" the boatswain's mate asked.

"New Jersey," Cynthia replied automatically.

"Well, we can't take him home, can we?" the boatswain's mate said.

"And here," Cynthia said. "And of course he lives here, too."

"Here, or do you mean the house?" the boatswain's mate pursued.

"The house," Cynthia said.

"Is there anybody over there?" the boatswain's mate asked.

Cynthia shook her head. "No," she said. "And he can't be found here. Mrs. Whittaker can't find out that he died in my bed."

"Then what we do is carry him over there and put him in his bathroom. Then we figure out who found him and call the cops," the boatswain's mate said.

There were two ways to handle the situation, Douglass realized. The legal way, which was to telephone the police and hope the circumstances of his death could be kept private. Or to violate the law (which might well be a felony) and do what the boatswain's mate suggested. Donovan had told him to handle the matter, and that did not mean getting the police and the press involved. Donovan had told Douglass that he planned to bring Whittaker into COI.

"What we will say," Douglass said, "is that I was sent by Colonel Donovan to pick him up. When there was no answer at the house, I saw lights here, and asked you, Miss Chenowith, to let me into the house—you have a key?— and we found him there."

"If he didn't answer the bell," she said, "you would be standing on the sidewalk. You couldn't see light here."

He thought that over.

"I was leaving," she said, "and found you ringing the bell?"

She thinks under pressure, he thought with admiration. A very tough-minded young woman.

"The first thing we had better do," Douglass said, "is move the body. Next we'd better run through what we're going to say happened."

"I was thinking," Cynthia Chenowith said, "that we have to appear completely natural. A suspicious policeman could cause us trouble."

"If you'll carry his clothes, miss," the boatswain's mate said, "I'll move him."

"I don't know your name," Douglass said to the boatswain's mate.

"Ellis, Captain, Edward B.," the boatswain's mate said.

"I want you to understand, Ellis, that if it comes down to it, I will accept full responsibility for what we're doing here today."

"I understand that, Captain," Ellis said.

"There are good reasons for doing what we're doing," Douglass said.

"Yes, sir." Ellis chuckled. "I understand that, too."

"I don't mean only with regard to Miss Chenowith—"

Ellis interrupted him. "I don't need any explanations, Captain. And I know how to keep my mouth shut."

"I'm in your debt," Douglass said.

"Since you brought that up, Captain," Ellis said, "I may need a character reference. The candy-ass at the dispensary told me that if I left, he'd have me before a court-martial."

"When you're not at the dispensary, what do you do at the Navy Yard?"

"Work in the arms room," Ellis said. "They don't like China sailors over there, and they don't know what to do with us when we come home."

"Are you married?"

"China sailors don't get married," Ellis said simply.

"Would you like to come to work for me?"

"Yes, sir, I would like that."

"You don't know what I do," Douglass said.

"Whatever it is, it looks more interesting than checking out forty-fives to the duty officers and master-at-arms," Ellis said.

Then he jerked the sheet off Whittaker's body, bent over the bed, and hoisted it onto his shoulders.

Douglass glanced at Cynthia Chenowith. She was looking at the body, biting her lower lip.

"Anytime you're ready, miss," Ellis said.

He carried Whittaker's body down the stairs and across the driveway to the house. Upstairs, he arranged the body against the tile wall of the shower in the master bedroom.

Cynthia Chenowith put Whittaker's clothing over an armchair, and his underwear in a hamper.

Then they left the house as they had entered it, through the kitchen. Cynthia opened the gate for them, and Ellis drove the Plymouth through, made a twelve-block circle through back streets, and returned.

He stopped in front of the small gate, and Captain Douglass got out and rang the bell. A moment later, the driveway gates opened, and Cynthia Chenowith's La Salle convertible drove through. She pulled up on the wrong side of the street, nose to nose with the Navy Plymouth, and then unlocked the gate for Captain Douglass with her key.

Five minutes later, sirens screaming, a police car and an ambulance arrived.

By then, Cynthia Chenowith had telephoned Summer Place and gently broken the news to Barbara Whittaker.

2
The White House
Washington, D.C.
9:25 P.M., December 7, 1941

After he left the President, Colonel William Donovan found
Captain Peter Douglass in the staff cafeteria drinking coffee
with boatswain's mate Ellis.

Both stood up when he approached the table.

"Colonel," Douglass said, "this is Boatswain Ellis. I've
learned he can be counted on in a pinch, and I've told him
I'm going to have him reassigned to us."

Donovan gave Ellis a quick but penetrating look. It had
obviously been necessary to bring this enlisted man into
whatever was going on. Douglass would have done that only
if he found it necessary, and then only if he believed Ellis
could be trusted. Donovan put out his hand.

"Welcome aboard," he said.

"Thank you, sir," Ellis said.

"You can tell me what's happened on the way to the
office," Donovan said. "You have a Navy car?"

"Yes, sir," Ellis said.

Donovan led the way out of the cafeteria to the parking
lot.

"I don't know where to go, sir," Ellis said after he'd
gotten behind the wheel.

"The office is at Twenty-fifth and E, the National Institute of Health," Donovan said. "But what happened in the
house on Q Street?"

"Mr. Whittaker died of a stroke," Douglass said, "in the
bedroom of the garage apartment."

"What was he doing in the garage apartment?" Donovan
asked curiously.

"The police believe that when I went to pick him up to

bring him to the White House, I rang the bell in the gate in the wall. There was no response. But Miss Chenowith, who was leaving to have dinner with friends, stopped and asked if she could help. I told her why I was there, and she let me into the house. We found Mr. Whittaker in his shower. He had apparently suffered a stroke an hour before, shortly after you called to tell him when I would pick him up.''

Donovan thought that over for a moment. The story was credible. It was unlikely that anyone would challenge it.

"What shape is she in?" Donovan asked. "The girl, I mean?"

"Miss Chenowith telephoned Mrs. Whittaker and broke the news to her," Douglass said. "And then made the arrangements for the funeral director to pick up Mr. Whittaker's body from the morgue. I took it upon myself to ask Dr. Grubb to go to the morgue, examine the body, and sign the death certificate.''

"And he did?"

"Ellis took him there, and then home. Dr. Grubb felt there was no need for an autopsy; the cause of death was obvious to him.''

"Does Dr. Grubb know where the body was found?" Donovan asked.

"He knows we found the body in Mr. Whittaker's shower," Douglass said.

"Then the one weak link in this is Cynthia Chenowith?" Donovan asked.

"She's no weak link, Colonel," Ellis volunteered. "That's one tough little lady."

"Take us to the house on Q Street," Donovan ordered. "She's there?"

"Yes, sir," Douglass said. "She thought there might be something else you might want her to do."

When they passed through the gate in the wall, Chesley

Haywood Whittaker's Packard was parked on the brick drive. Donovan found Edward, the chauffeur, with Cynthia Chenowith in the kitchen of the main house. She had made something to eat, and then given him several drinks. Edward had been close to Chesty Whittaker, and there were signs that he had wept.

"Edward," Donovan asked, "how is the Packard fixed for gas?"

"I'll see if I can find a station open," Edward said, obviously welcoming the chance to make himself useful.

"I think that would be a good idea," Donovan said. "Thank you."

Edward found his chauffeur's cap and went out the kitchen door.

Donovan saw that Cynthia Chenowith was still calm, although her face remained pale and there was a strange look in her eyes.

"The thing to do, Cynthia, is to decide how we're going to handle this," Donovan said, "before I call Barbara."

She looked at him and met his eyes and nodded.

"I think the thing to do is send Chesty home as soon as we can. The way to do it is see if we can get a hearse somewhere tonight."

"Or a panel truck from Hertz," Ellis said. "Getting a hearse might be difficult this time of night. People would wonder why we couldn't wait until tomorrow, or send the body on the train."

"Baker has a station wagon," Douglass said. "Will a casket fit in a station wagon?"

"What kind of a station wagon, Captain?" Ellis asked.

"Ford," Douglass said. "Four-door. A '41."

"You'll probably have to run the seat all the way forward," Ellis said with certainty. "But it'll take a casket."

Donovan believed him. It was extraordinary that Ellis had

such obscure knowledge at his fingertips, but he was not surprised.

"The question is," Donovan said, "whether we want to bring Baker in on this."

"I think it might be a good idea," Douglass said. "I'm not very experienced in such matters. Baker might be able to see if we've made any mistakes."

"The duty officer should know where he is."

Douglass called the office. Baker was there.

"Are you driving your station wagon?" Douglass asked. "Good. I would like to borrow it," Douglass said. "Could you drop what you're doing and come right away?"

He gave the address and hung up.

"He'll be right here," he said.

"What's he doing in the office?" Donovan asked.

"I guess he feels that he should be doing something besides sitting in his apartment listening to the radio," Douglass said.

"Presuming," Donovan said, getting back to the problem at hand, "that we can find a casket that fits in Baker's station wagon, we'll have Edward drive the body to New Jersey."

"I'll go with him," Cynthia Chenowith said.

"You think that's necessary?" Donovan asked after a moment.

"Mr. Whittaker," she said levelly, "was very good to me. It's the least I can do. I want to. I can probably be helpful."

Donovan nodded.

"Get on the phone, Pete," he said. "Arrange with the funeral home for a casket. Tell them we'll pick it up in an hour."

Eldon C. Baker arrived a few minutes later. He did not seem very surprised to find Colonel Donovan, a sailor, and an attractive young woman in the kitchen of a mansion; and he asked no questions.

"We have something of a problem here," Douglass said.

"What were you doing at the office?" Donovan asked somewhat abruptly.

"I had hoped to see either you or Captain Douglass, Colonel," Baker said. "There has been an interesting development in the Moroccan business."

Donovan didn't reply to that.

"I didn't mean to interrupt, Pete," he said.

"As I was saying," Douglass began, "we have a difficult situation here, and need your help. Specifically, we need to use your station wagon for a couple of days."

"Certainly," Baker said.

Douglass told Baker the story the police had been told. He had the feeling from looks Baker directed at Cynthia Chenowith that Baker knew he was being lied to, but Baker asked no questions.

"Whatever I can do to help, of course," he said when Douglass had finished. "When can we pick up the body?"

"I'll do that," Donovan said, "in forty-five minutes."

"Then, sir, may I get into the Moroccan matter?"

"You think it's important?" Donovan said.

"Yes, sir," Baker said. "I do."

"Cynthia," Donovan said, "I'm afraid this is rather confidential. Could I ask you to leave us alone for a few minutes?"

"Why don't you go in the library?" Cynthia asked. "It'd be more comfortable in there."

"You'll be all right?" Donovan asked.

"Yes," she said simply.

"All right," Donovan said, and led the way into the library.

"OK, Baker," Donovan said. "What's so important?"

"I don't know how deeply Captain Douglass has gone into this with you," Baker began.

"Not at all," Douglass said. "So you'll have to start at the beginning."

"This came into my hand about one-thirty this afternoon," Baker said, handing Donovan a sheet of yellow Teletype paper, so blurry that Donovan thought it must be fifth or sixth carbon.

URGENT
FROM US CONSULATE GENERAL RABAT MOROCCO
FOR G2 WAR DEPARTMENT WASHINGTON DC
COPY TO DEPARTMENT OF STATE WASHINGTON DC
6:50 PM DECEMBER 6 1941
PASHA OF KSAR ES SOUK ASSASSINATED 2:30 PM 6
DEC BY UNKNOWN PARTIES STOP SIDI EL FERRUCH
BELIEVED ALIVE STOP J. ROBERT BERRY MAJOR

Donovan read it, shook his head, and handed it to Douglass.

"Who the hell is the pasha of Ksar es Souk?" Donovan asked tiredly. "And why is it classified secret? The pasha knows he's dead, and so do the people who shot him." He gave Baker a look of impatience. "I have no idea what any of this is all about."

"I have been working under certain constrictions," Baker said. "Starting with Captain Douglass's inability to tell me why we are interested in Louis Albert Grunier."

"Who the hell is he?" Donovan asked.

"He's a mining engineer," Douglass furnished, "who worked in the Union Minière mines in Katanga Province of the Belgian Congo before the war."

"OK," Donovan said. Now he had an idea what was going on. "You've found him?"

"When the war started, he tried to return to France," Baker said, "and got as far as Casablanca. He was not permitted to return to France. The French need engineers in the Atlas Mountain phosphate mines. Phosphates, of course, are essential to the manufacture of various kinds of explosives and gunpowder."

"Good work," Donovan said.

"I have also found out that it is unlikely he would willingly help us," Baker said. "Not only does he still hope to return to his family in France, but there is the additional possibility of reprisals against them if he does not walk the straight and narrow. With that in mind, I have gone into the area of bringing him here involuntarily."

He had captured Donovan's attention.

"And?" Donovan asked.

"Captain Douglass made it quite clear that there is an extraordinary requirement for secrecy in this matter," Baker said. "Inasmuch as I don't know the reason for that, this makes matters difficult."

"Baker, you just don't have the need to know," Donovan said.

Baker nodded.

"How do you propose to get Grunier out of Morocco without the help of the consul general?" Donovan asked. "I really hate to use him, or any of those control officers, but if necessary . . ."

"There is a way, I think, to do this without Robert Murphy. He'd have to be told, of course, but neither he nor the control officers would be directly involved."

"Let's hear it," Donovan said.

"I've discussed it with Captain Douglass, who I'm afraid thinks I have let my imagination run away with me."

"Let's hear it," Donovan repeated impatiently.

"There is an interesting young American in Morocco, a fellow named Eric Fulmar," Baker said.

"Some friends of mine, as it happens, are friends of young Mr. Fulmar," Donovan said. "What's he doing now?"

"Making a good deal of money as a smuggler."

"From what I know of him, that's not surprising. Is he working with the locals?"

"With the son of the late pasha of Ksar es Souk," Baker said. "He and the son, known as Sidi el Ferruch, were in school in Germany together—Fulmar's father is German, as you may know. El Ferruch runs a very efficient intelligence operation for the pasha of Marrakech."

"Your idea is to have Eric Fulmar smuggle Grunier out of the country."

"Yes, sir," Baker said. "He and the Moroccan."

"You think they would?"

"There is a chance they would, if we paid them enough," Baker said.

"How much is enough?"

"A great deal. I proposed an amount that shocked Captain Douglass."

"What was that figure?" Donovan asked.

"One hundred thousand dollars," Baker said.

"That's an awful lot of money," Donovan said. "Try offering him fifty."

"You think this idea has merit, Colonel?" Douglass asked, genuinely surprised.

"If it fails, they would believe that Grunier went to a smuggler. Not to the United States government," Donovan said.

"Or that he was involved with Sidi Hassan el Ferruch," Baker said.

"Yes," Donovan said thoughtfully. He nodded at Baker. "Go ahead with this. Come with something definite."

"I have more, sir," Baker said.

"Something to do with the assassination?"

"And the fact that we are now at war. The possibility exists that France will enter the war on the side of Germany. If that happens, we could just about forget Grunier. And for that matter whatever is so vital in the Congo."

Donovan realized, astonished, that he had forgotten that there was now a war on.

"Fulmar could not participate in any operation to remove Grunier from Morocco without the permission of Sidi Hassan el Ferruch," Baker said. "And then I think we have to consider the possibility the Germans are also likely to go looking for Grunier."

"Why would they do that?" Douglass asked innocently.

"To put him to work in the mines at Joachimsthal in Saxony," Baker said.

"Why would they want to do that?" Donovan asked.

"Because that is the only other source of uraninite, the other being in Katanga in the Belgian Congo," Baker said.

There was no response from either Donovan or Baker for a moment, and then Donovan chuckled.

"Douglass has been worried about your unfettered imagination, Baker. I see he has cause. Why do you think we or the Germans are so interested in a . . . what did you say, uranium? . . . mining engineer?"

"I said 'uraninite,' which is the source of uranium. All I know is that it is radioactive—it actually glows in the dark. I don't know yet why we want it, but I rather doubt we're going to make a lot of luminescent watch faces."

"OK," Donovan said, "you really are dangerous, Baker. This whole thing has something to do with uranium."

"That will help," Baker said. "But to get back on the

track. I believe that if we're going to do anything about Grunier, we're going to have to do it as soon as possible.''

"OK, go on.''

"I had the FBI do a check on Fulmar,'' Baker said. "It seems his mother is the actress Monica Carlisle.''

"As it happens, I know about Fulmar's mother, too. Are you suggesting she would be helpful?''

"No, I don't think she would,'' Baker said. If he was surprised that Donovan knew the name Fulmar, or that he was the son of Monica Carlisle, it did not register on his face.

"The worst possible scenario,'' Baker said, "is that I approach Fulmar after he has decided he is at bottom a German and he turns me over to the SS.''

"You think he'd do that?''

"I think we have to consider the possibility,'' Baker said.

"Go on,'' Donovan said.

"I think Fulmar could turn me over to the Germans and get a good night's sleep the same night,'' Baker said. "But he does have a couple of American friends, whom he's very close to. I don't think he'd turn them in.''

"Who are they? How do you know?''

"I talked to the father of one of them,'' Baker said, "the Reverend Dr. Canidy, headmaster of St. Paul's School in Cedar Rapids, Iowa.''

"You're talking about Dick Canidy and Jimmy Whittaker,'' Donovan said.

Now genuine surprise registered on Baker's face.

"Is somebody else working on this?'' he blurted, and then answered his own question. "I don't know why I didn't think about that. Is there some reason we can't compare notes?''

"Nobody else is working on this,'' Donovan said. "The

fact is that this house belongs to Jim Whittaker. It is his uncle who died here tonight.''

"Jesus Christ!" Baker said. "I just didn't make the connection. All I've found out so far about Whittaker is that he's in the Air Corps. I expect to find out tomorrow where he is.''

"He's in the Philippines," Donovan said. "So you can forget about him. And you can forget about Canidy, too. He's off in China with the Flying Tigers.''

Baker was silent for a moment.

"Is there some reason I can't think of why I couldn't recruit Canidy?" he asked.

"How would you get over there to recruit him?" Douglass asked.

"That would be a question of travel priority," Baker replied. "I don't think any priority would get me into the Philippines right now. But China is something else.''

"You think Canidy is that important?''

"I think he's important in that he might keep Fulmar from turning us in," Baker said. "At least that. He might even be able to blow on what small ember of patriotism may be left in Fulmar.''

"You don't like Fulmar, do you?" Donovan asked.

"No," Baker said, "I don't.''

"When would you like to leave?" Donovan asked.

"As soon as I can," Baker said.

"Go pack," Donovan said. "By this time tomorrow, I should be able to have your travel priority arranged.''

3

Ellis drove Donovan to the morgue, where he was given the paperwork involved in certifying Chesty Whittaker's death.

Cynthia Chenowith and Douglass stayed at the house, where they taped brown kraft paper over the side windows of Baker's station wagon.

When Donovan and Ellis returned, Chesty's Packard was put into one of the garages. Then Donovan called Barbara Whittaker at Summer Place. After he expressed his condolences, he told her how they had worked things out. Barbara knew a funeral parlor in Asbury Park. She would telephone and tell them Edward was coming.

"Cynthia Chenowith will be with him," Donovan said.

"Oh?" Barbara asked, and Donovan thought he heard a catch in her voice. "Is she up to that?"

"She says she is," Donovan said.

"Well, tell her I'll have a room waiting for her," Barbara said.

"Is there anything else I can do for you tonight?" Donovan asked.

"Yes," she said, surprising him. "There is. I tried to get in touch with Jimmy. I couldn't. Is there some way you could get word to him?"

"I'll take care of it, if you'll give me an address."

She gave it to him and thanked him; then, without saying good-bye, she hung up.

They drove to the funeral home. The casket fit as Ellis said it would in Baker's station wagon. Cynthia Chenowith got in beside Edward, and they drove off.

While the others went to take care of the body, Ellis drove Donovan and Douglass to their homes. Donovan owned a town house in Georgetown, and Douglass had a small apartment nearby.

Donovan, exhausted, fell into bed without even taking his ritual shower. But as he mashed the pillow beneath him, he remembered that he had told Barbara he would do what he could to get word to Jimmy Whittaker that Chesty was dead.

The international operator told him that they weren't accepting calls for the Philippines. And both Western Union and Mackay told him that while they would accept messages, they would not guarantee delivery. The military had priority, and all the circuits were tied up with official business.

He put the handset in the cradle and started to turn off the light. Then he thought of something he had to do right then.

He dialed a number from memory. A woman's voice answered.

"This is Bill Donovan. Is he still up?" Donovan said.

"Yes, Bill?" the familiar voice came on the line a moment later.

"Mr. President, if you hadn't ordered me to report on this, I wouldn't bother you. We've sent Chesty Whittaker's body to New Jersey," Donovan said.

"I'll telephone Barbara in the morning," the President said. "But you'll have to represent me at the funeral, Bill."

"Yes, Mr. President."

"And I'll see you in the morning. Thank you for calling."

"Good night, Mr. President."

The President of the United States had a personal, kind thought when he hung up the telephone. Poor Chesty had never had any children. But he had looked upon Jimmy as his son, and Jimmy would have to be told. Communication with the Philippines was difficult.

He summoned one of his military aides. "If there's a moment's free time on the lines to the Philippines, I would like to ask General MacArthur to pass the word to Lieutenant James Whittaker that his uncle Chesty has passed away. I'm sure he'll know where he is."

"Yes, Mr. President," the aide said. "I'll take care of it."

An hour later a radio message went out from Washington:

PRIORITY
THE WHITE HOUSE WASHINGTON
0005 HOURS 8 DEC 41
HEADQUARTERS US FORCES PHILIPPINES
PERSONAL FOR GENERAL MACARTHUR
DIRECTION OF THE PRESIDENT STOP LOCATE
AND RELAY 2D LT JAMES M. C. WHITTAKER
US ARMY AIRCORPS CONDOLENCES OF PRESI-
DENT RE CHESLEY HAYWOOD WHITTAKER DE-
CEASED WASH DC OF STROKE 7 DEC 1941
STOP LEWIS MAJOR GEN USA

4
Memphis, Tennessee
8:30 P.M., December 7, 1941

Ann Chambers had been in the city room of the Memphis *Daily Advocate* when the bells had rung on the AP and the INS, and finally the UP Teletype machines, announcing the arrival of a flash. She was covering the hospitals with the "good" funerals (as opposed to routine obituaries, the province of a feisty old lady). When the bells rang, she was working on a feature story about questionable business practices of certain funeral directors.

The instant he was told of the Pearl Harbor story, Orrin

Fox, the editor of the *Daily Advocate,* decided to put on an extra. Since the *Advocate* was a morning paper, which normally went to bed at two in the morning, he had to move the deadline forward to six that night, which he thought would give him and his staff time both to get out the news the paper would normally print eight hours early and to assemble the facts about the Japanese attack from the wires.

Ann's greedy funeral directors' story went into a drawer as she and everybody else worked frantically to put together the paper. It was half past eight when Ann went home to the four-room suite she shared with Sarah in the Peabody Hotel.

Ann found Sarah sitting on the windowsill, looking in the general direction of the Mississippi River, tears running unashamedly down her cheeks. Her pregnancy was now obvious: she was in her sixth month.

"Well," Ann said, "I finally got a byline on page one. It took a war to do it."

She handed Sarah a copy of the *Advocate,* the ink still slick, and pointed out a box on the front page: "Last-Minute War News From Our Wire Services. Compiled by Ann Chambers, *Daily Advocate* staff writer."

"Ed could be dead right now, you know that?" Sarah said.

"Oh, I don't think so," Ann replied. "They attacked Hawaii, not Burma."

"I've been listening to the radio," Sarah said, turning to Ann to argue with her. "There's fighting all over, over there."

Ann shrugged.

"I want a father for my baby!" Sarah said, close to tears.

Tears weren't going to help anything, Ann thought. A fight would be better.

"Then maybe you should have written and told him," she said sarcastically.

"I couldn't do that," Sarah said illogically, but rising to the bait.

"And when he comes back? Do you plan to tell him then?"

"*If* he comes back, you mean," Sarah said.

"He'll be back," Ann said, hoping she sounded more convincing than she felt. She had spent the day reading the wire-service yellows: the Japanese had struck all over the Orient. She hadn't seen any specific story about an attack on Rangoon, but that didn't mean anything. And if the Japanese had struck Rangoon, Ed and Dick would have been in it. They were fighter pilots. Fighter pilots, by definition, fought.

God, Ann prayed silently, *protect those two bastards.*

"It's not really fair, is it?" Sarah asked.

"You should have thought about that before you took your pants off," Ann said, and immediately regretted it.

"Ann!" Sarah replied, shocked and hurt.

"I'm sorry," Ann said. "I'm really sorry." Sarah looked at her, Ann thought, like a kicked dog.

"I had an interesting thought today," Ann said. Sarah didn't seem at all interested in her interesting thought. "I thought that you were one up on me."

"What's that supposed to mean?"

"If mine doesn't come back, I don't have anything."

"What do you mean, 'yours'?"

"I thought you'd figured that out," Ann said. "Did you really think I've been writing him as my 'patriotic duty'? The only reason he didn't get in *my* pants is because he didn't ask."

"Ann," Sarah said, disapproving but unable to keep from smiling. "You're outrageous."

"I really wish he had," Ann said. "I almost—but not quite—wish I was in your condition."

"Oh, Ann!"

"Well, knowing those two, we have nothing to worry about," Ann said. "Unless you want to worry about them being picked off by some exotic foreign female, while we sit here and wait."

"I thought," Sarah said, ignoring Ann's last remark, "that you'd . . . never done it."

"I never have," Ann said. "That's what I meant when I decided you were one up on me."

"Thanks a lot," Sarah said.

"If you knew then what you know now, would you have?" Ann asked.

Sarah thought that over a moment.

"Yes," she said.

"See what I mean?" Ann said. "Pity you can't drink," she said. "I could use some company."

She picked up the telephone and told the bell captain to send up a quart of bourbon.

"I worked it out," Sarah said. "At this moment, it's half past nine tomorrow morning in Rangoon. If he's still alive, he's already had his breakfast."

5
Rangoon, Burma
0930 Hours 9 December 1941

If there had been any tea at Wing Commander Hepple's house, six blocks away, Bitter hadn't seen it. But there had been a good deal of gin and whiskey, and even a bottle of bourbon. A redheaded Scottish woman had also been there.

She was private secretary to a Briton high in the colonial bureaucracy, and she and Stephanie Walker, the woman with whom she shared an apartment, found the newly arrived young American fliers a welcome addition to the British officers and civil servants.

Stephanie Walker was small and pale, and in some ways reminded Ed Bitter of Sarah Child. It was, Ed Bitter told himself when he woke up in Stephanie Walker's bed, partly that, plus the excitement of the war starting, plus all the liquor they had put away at Wing Commander Hepple's tea, that had brought him to her bed.

Stephanie Walker was married to an RAF fighter pilot "temporarily, for eight damned months" posted to Singapore, but by the time Ed learned that, they were already in the apartment.

He got out of bed and found Canidy naked and entwined with the redhead in another bedroom. Then he walked on tiptoe to the bed and shook Canidy's arm. The obvious thing to do was get out of the apartment as quietly and quickly as possible.

Canidy was hungover, he announced quite unnecessarily, and before he did anything he wanted a good breakfast and a lot of coffee. There was no sense in rushing off to get it, since they had been invited to eat right here.

Breakfast was actually rather pleasant, and Stephanie Walker was neither as coarse nor as crude as he thought he would find her when he was sober.

He would, he thought, telephone her in a day or two.

Then he thought, *Good Christ, I'm getting as amoral as Canidy.*

When they stopped by the CAMCO house to change clothing, there was another radio message for them, taped to Canidy's mirror:

CANIDY BITTER RELIEVED RANGOON STOP RE-
PORT ME WITH FERRY GEAR STOP CROOK-
SHANKS

There was a penciled note on the bottom of the Teletype
paper: *I've got a truck going up there this afternoon. Your
gear would probably make it OK on it. Dolan.*

"Shit," Canidy said. "I knew this was too good to last."

They packed their clothing, then drove out to Mingaladon
Air Base.

Canidy, without making any kind of preflight examination
of aircraft, climbed into the cockpit and put his helmet on.
Bitter was at first surprised that he was taking chances like
that, then angry that he was probably still drunk and didn't
know what he was doing. But finally he was angry with
himself when he realized what Canidy was actually doing.

It was folklore among pilots that the best cure for a hang-
over was oxygen. Since Bitter had never flown hungover,
he had had no chance to test the theory. But that was clearly
what Canidy was doing.

Two minutes later, Canidy climbed out of the plane and
handed Bitter the mask and the oxygen bottle.

"It's leaking," Canidy announced blandly. "You might
as well use the rest. I'll go check the weather and get another
bottle."

Ed Bitter was very surprised at how good the cool oxygen
felt in his nasal passages, and how quickly it seemed to blow
the cobwebs away.

When Canidy returned from Operations, he had two .45
Colt Model 1911A1 pistols.

"This should make you happy, Admiral Farragut," he
said. "We are now officially armed to make war." And then

he had a second thought. "Speaking of which," he said, "don't push the red button. They've put ammo aboard."

Five minutes later, they lifted off. The hip-holstered automatic got in the way, and Bitter resolved to get an aviator's shoulder holster just as soon as he could. But having the pistol was comforting. Even more comforting was to be in control of an armed fighter plane. This is what he had been trained for, at the Naval Academy and at Pensacola. He was indeed going in harm's way in the defense of his country, even though he was an employee of the Chinese government in a uniform without insignia.

There were no other aircraft in the bright blue skies between Rangoon and Toungoo.

NINE

Donovan found Barbara Whittaker in the breakfast room.

"I'm afraid I'm going to have to be going, Barbara," he said. "We're driving and . . ."

"I'm glad you could come," she said. "It was a nice funeral, I thought. Just his friends, really."

"The President wanted to come," Donovan said.

"He telephoned just a few minutes ago," she said. "After what Chesty called him, and to his face, I thought it was a nice thing to do."

"Franklin forgives those of us who don't agree with him. He's convinced we're just not capable of understanding his noble motives," Donovan said.

"I wonder if Jimmy knows yet," she said.

"We're trying," Donovan said. "Communications to the Philippines are a problem."

"Franklin said he was trying to help," Barbara said.

"Oh?"

"He said he had sent word to General MacArthur to find Jimmy and tell him," she said.

"Then by now, Barbara, I would think Jimmy knows. But

it will be as difficult for him to get back word from there as it is to reach him.''

"I was thinking before," she said calmly, "that if anything should happen to Jimmy over there, the Whittaker name would die with him. I would really hate to see that happen."

"I'm sure Jimmy will be all right," Donovan said with a conviction he did not feel.

"Something like this does strange things to you," Barbara said.

"Of course it does," he said comfortingly.

"I was just thinking," she said, "that it would have been nice if Chesty had made her pregnant."

"I beg your pardon?" Donovan said, astonished.

"Her," Barbara Whittaker said, nodding out the window.

Donovan looked. Cynthia Chenowith was on the beach, her head wrapped in a kerchief, her hands jammed in the pockets of her trench coat.

Barbara Whittaker smiled at Donovan.

"Don't be so naive, Bill," she said. "If you took a young mistress, don't you think Ruth would know?"

She smiled at his discomfiture.

"When I saw her out there," Barbara went on, "I felt sorry for her. After Chesty, what's left for her? And then I had another thought. I wanted so much for him to have a child. If there was a child, it wouldn't quite be the end of everything."

"There's something I would like to ask you," Donovan said, wondering if he was asking now because he desperately wanted to change the subject.

"Oh?"

"I talked with Chesty about this on our way to Washington," he said, "and he was willing to let me have the house on Q Street."

"I thought you had a place in Georgetown," she said.

"We do," he said. "I meant for . . . what I'm doing."

"What are you doing?" she asked.

"I'm Coordinator of Information," he said.

"Whatever you're doing, Bill, it has nothing to do with information," she said. "If I shouldn't have asked, forgive me."

"Information in the intelligence sense," he said.

"Oh," she said. "I thought you were trying to make me believe you were some kind of press agent."

"That, too." He chuckled. "I've got Bob Sherwood handling that. But, as I told Chesty, I need a house in Washington near the office—we're Twenty-fifth and E—a place where I could put people up, have dinners, that sort of thing. Chesty was willing to let me have the house. I want to know if that's all right with you."

"It's really Jimmy's, you know. It was his father's. But there's no reason you can't have it. Whatever happens to Jimmy, I don't think he'd ever want to live in that old house. And he'll get this one, of course. I have no idea what it's worth. And I can't legally sell it."

"I was thinking of leasing it."

"If Chesty said you can have it, Bill, of course you can have it."

"I am being paid a dollar a year," he said. "How does that strike you as annual rent?"

"I don't like it at all," she said. "It seems as if Franklin, aided and abetted by his friend Wild Bill Donovan, is finally succeeding in taking advantage of the Whittakers."

"I'll get an idea of what a fair rent would be and see if I can't find the money."

"No," she said. "You misunderstand me. I don't like it, but if Chesty would have rented it to you for a dollar a year, Jimmy would want me to do the same."

"Pressing the bargain," he said. "We talked about furnished."

"I don't want anything in that house," she said bitterly. "Nothing. I don't ever want to think about it again."

"I'll see if there's anything of Chesty's," Donovan said. "And—"

"Nothing," Barbara Whittaker said. "*Nothing,* Bill. Understand?"

"Yes," he said.

She leaned up and kissed him on the cheek. "Thank you for coming," she said.

"If there's anything I can do, Barbara . . ."

"Keep Jimmy alive," she said. "By fair means or foul. If you want to do something for Chesty or for me, do that."

"I don't know what I could do."

"Think of something," she said.

She turned and looked out the window at Cynthia Chenowith again.

"What's she or her mother going to do for money now that Chesty's gone?" she asked.

"Chesty told me," Donovan said, "that he set up some sort of trust for her mother when Tom died. I don't think he was giving the girl money."

"I didn't mean to suggest that he was . . . keeping her . . . in the usual sense," she said. "I don't think either of them was like that. If he didn't make some provision for her in his will . . ."

"I don't think he would do that," Donovan said, "because of you."

"Then I will have to do it," she said. "Chesty always met his obligations. Does her mother know about her and Chesty?"

"I didn't know about them," Donovan said. "And I was very close to Chesty."

"Good," she said. "I like Doris, and it would be painful for her if she learned about them."

"There is no reason she ever should," Donovan said.

"You know what's really funny?" Barbara asked bitterly. "I've always had the thought in the back of my mind that I would match Jimmy up with her."

He patted her shoulder and walked away.

"Bill," she called after him. "I don't want her ever to know that I know."

Donovan met her eyes and nodded his head.

Then he found his overcoat and hat, put them on, walked down the wide front steps of Summer Place and down the brick walk to the beach.

"It's time for us to go," he said.

"I'll say my good-byes to Mrs. Whittaker," Cynthia said. "My stuff is already in the station wagon."

He hadn't considered that possibility and was embarrassed. Barbara obviously would have preferred not to speak to Cynthia Chenowith again. But he could not suggest to Cynthia that it would be best if she left Summer Place without saying good-bye. Cynthia was both bright and sensitive. She would know that meant Barbara knew.

"All right," he said.

Cynthia walked briskly toward the house. Donovan walked slowly after her, so that he could see both of them in the breakfast room.

They kissed and embraced.

Then Cynthia came out of the front door again and walked with Donovan down the veranda to Douglass's station wagon.

"May I drive?" Cynthia asked.

"Certainly," Donovan said. "I'll spell you if you get tired."

Forty-five minutes later, as they drove through the New

Jersey Pine Barrens toward Philadelphia, out of the blue Cynthia said, "She knows about Chesty and me."

"Yes," Donovan said.

"I'm really sorry," Cynthia said. "I don't think I could be so much of a lady, under the circumstances."

"Barbara is a fine lady," Donovan agreed.

"I'm not sorry," Cynthia said. "I'm sorry she knew, but I'm not sorry."

"We're taking over the house on Q Street," Donovan said after a long pause.

"Chesty told me," she said. "How much time do I have to get out?"

"Perhaps that wouldn't be necessary," Donovan said.

"I don't understand," Cynthia said.

"I'd like you to stay to work for me. For openers, whatever your civil service grade is now, I'll raise it two numbers."

"I don't think you're suggesting you want to take Chesty's place," she said after a moment. Then she made it a challenge: "Are you, Colonel?"

"No," he said, laughing. "As Barbara said, Ruth would suspect."

"Then why the offer? I'm a lawyer, Colonel Donovan," Cynthia said.

"The most difficult personnel problems we have, doing what we're doing—"

"What is it, exactly, that you are doing?" she interrupted. "I've been wondering about that for a long time."

He didn't reply immediately, and Cynthia correctly suspected he was very carefully, lawyerlike, framing his answer. She was suddenly aware that she was fencing with one of the best legal minds in the country.

"Franklin Roosevelt has asked me to organize and operate an intelligence organization which will control all the other intelligence agencies during the war," he said.

"And where would I fit in?" she asked.

"I don't know," he confessed. "Which brings us back to what I was saying about our most difficult personnel problem."

"Which is?"

"Recruiting people who can function under pressure," Donovan said. "There is no way to prejudge that. Forgive me if this sounds insensitive, Cynthia, but you have just demonstrated how well you function under pressure."

"The . . . circumstances . . . of Chesty's death?"

"A very awkward situation," he agreed, nodding his head, "that you handled as skillfully, as—forgive me—ruthlessly as you considered necessary."

"Is that a compliment?"

"*And* a statement of fact," he said.

"That brings us back to my question. Where would I fit in?"

"I don't know. For the moment, I would want you to take over the house on Q Street. Starting immediately, we're going to have to think about security precautions, communications . . ."

"About which I know nothing," she said. "It sounds like you want a housekeeper."

"You didn't really think I was going to ask you to go to Berlin and make eyes at Adolf Hitler, did you?"

That annoyed her.

"I have a responsible job at the State Department," she said. "And I have been led to believe that I can be commissioned into the WAC."

That, in turn, annoyed Donovan.

"If you went in the Women's Army Corps," he said, "you would spend the war as a clerk in uniform. If you stay at the State Department, you will spend the war performing legal functions that your superiors feel are unimportant enough to be handled by a woman. If you complain, you will be told that is the sacrifice you must make for the war effort. Your naiveté surprises me, frankly.''

She successfully fought down the urge to express the rage she felt. They rode along in silence for five minutes.

''I want you on board,'' Donovan said, finally breaking the silence, ''as an asset in place, someone I can put to real work as soon as the need arises. In the meantime, I want you to take over the house on Q Street. I have to have absolute faith in the ability, common sense, and even ruthlessness of whoever is running it for me. If you consider that beneath your dignity, there is no point in continuing this discussion. Please forget it ever took place.''

She didn't reply at first, but a moment later said, ''Chesty's Packard, the convertible, is in the garage. And he has personal things. Should I load it all up and send it to Summer Place?''

''No,'' he said. ''Barbara told me she wants nothing from the house on Q Street, and unless she changes her mind, I'm going to leave it that way.''

''I'll pack his personal things and put them in the attic,'' she said. ''And I'll run the Packard every couple of days. If it's all right, I'll move into the house.''

She had accepted his offer.

He looked at her, and they laughed together. Later they stopped in Philadelphia for a late supper, boiled lobsters at Bookbinder's, and then drove on to Washington.

2
Iba, Luzon
Commonwealth of the Philippines
1205 Hours 9 December 1941

As the sixteen P40-E aircraft returning from a fruitless patrol over the South China Sea approached Iba, a single dirt runway auxiliary field in the hills forty miles from their regular base at Clark Field, Second Lieutenant James M. C. Whittaker went on the horn.

"Delicious Leader, Delicious Blue Five."

"Go ahead, Blue Five." There was a tone of impatience in the squadron leader's voice, even over the clipped tones of the radio.

"My fuel warning lights are on," Whittaker said. "Request permission to land as soon as possible."

There was no reply for a moment, and then:

"Delicious Blue Five, you are cleared to land as number three. I'll want to see you on the ground."

"Blue Five leaving the formation at this time," Whittaker replied. He dropped the nose and pointed the P40-E toward the tail of the second plane making its approach.

"I want to see you on the ground, Whittaker," the squadron commander said. "Acknowledge."

"You want to see me on the ground, acknowledged," Whittaker said.

Whittaker knew his squadron leader did not like him, and most of the reasons why he didn't. The squadron commander was a Regular, and he was a reservist who had not troubled to conceal his annoyance at having been kept on active duty. He had not displayed what the squadron commander believed was the proper team spirit, and, probably just as important, he hadn't seen any point in trying to hide the fact that he had an independent income.

Instead of spending his spare time with his peers at Clark, he had rented an apartment in the Hotel Manila, to which he would drive in his brand-new yellow Chrysler New Yorker convertible. He spent his time there playing polo with wealthy Americans, Filipinos, and officers of the 26th Cavalry. His photograph appeared regularly on the society pages of the *Manila Times*.

Whittaker touched down and taxied directly toward one of the three fuel trucks. He was sure that the first thing the squadron commander was going to do when he got on the ground was ask the fuel guy how much Whittaker had taken. The commander didn't trust people he didn't like, and he didn't like Whittaker. Therefore he believed that Whittaker's fuel warning lights had not been glowing, and that Whittaker had simply wanted to refuel immediately, rather than wait his turn, which would have been just about last.

Fuck him. He would find out that Whittaker had been running on the fumes.

There were no hangars in Iba auxiliary field, just a radio shack, which doubled as the control tower. There were several field tents, a canvas fly–covered mess and kitchen area, three olive-drab fuel trucks, two vans, two jeeps, a staff car, and Second Lieutenant Whittaker's new yellow convertible.

The Chrysler was another bone of contention between Whittaker and his squadron commander. Once they had moved to Iba, the Old Man had forbidden his officers to return to Clark Field for any purpose, including picking up their personal vehicles. Jim Whittaker felt that he had obeyed the order. He had not returned to Clark. He had called Manila and ordered his Filipino houseboy to go from his suite in the Manila Hotel out to Clark and drive the Chrysler to Iba.

"You're a guardhouse lawyer, Whittaker," the Old Man had told him when the Chrysler appeared. "You know I meant no cars up here. I don't like guardhouse lawyers.''

''We don't have enough transportation, Captain,'' Whittaker replied. ''The car is at the disposal of the squadron.''

Under the circumstances, the Chrysler had remained. For one thing, Whittaker's Filipino boy had taken off, and there was no other way to get the car back where it belonged. For another, Whittaker was right: they needed transportation. But so far as the Old Man was concerned, it was another example of Whittaker's near insubordination whenever he could interpret an order to his own satisfaction.

After Whittaker had been refueled and was taxiing to his parking space, and seven of the squadron's sixteen aircraft touched down and were lined up to refuel, the Japanese began their attack. When the first Japanese plane appeared, Whittaker knew he had two choices. He could go to the threshold of the runway and wait until the last of the out-of-fuel P40-Es had landed before he tried to take off, or he could take a chance of getting safely into the air by simply forcing his way into the landing pattern.

He pushed on the left rudder pedal and advanced the throttle as he turned onto the runway. During his takeoff roll, he test-fired his guns.

It was later learned from observers on the ground that there had been fifty-odd Mitsubishi dive-bombers and about as many Zeroes, possibly as many as fifty-six. In the air at the time, things were much too confused for anyone to count with any degree of accuracy.

The engagement didn't last long. The carrier-based Japanese were operating at the far end of their operational radius, and when they had done what they had come to do, they headed home.

Whittaker made two passes over Iba. The runways were blocked with furiously burning P40s, shot down as they tried to land, and others, who had landed before the attack began, and been destroyed by bombs and machine-gun fire. The Japanese had gotten all three fuel trucks.

Whittaker saw the Old Man, standing and watching his aircraft burn. Hands on hips, he looked up as Whittaker flew over, but he made no signal of any kind.

Whittaker turned the nose of the P40-E toward Clark Field, forty miles away. There was no way he could land at Iba, and with the fuel trucks gone, no reason to.

3
Marrakech, Morocco
December 9, 1941

Two days after the burial of the pasha of Ksar es Souk, Thami el Glaoui, a man in his late sixties, wearing his customary white robes, climbed into his Delahaye convertible sedan and went to the mosque to pray that Allah had taken the pasha of Ksar es Souk into heaven.

When he had finished praying, he dismissed his bodyguards with a curt wave of his hand and walked slowly and alone through the cool arches of the mosque, circling and circling again the fountain and pool.

This was always comforting when he was troubled and confused. The mosque had been there for several hundred years before the French had come, and would be there several hundred years after the French were gone. Thinking about that helped him put things into perspective. And often it reminded him of the quatrain of Haji Abdu Yezdi: "Cease, atom of a moment's span, to hold thyself an all in all. The world is old, and thou art young."

He missed Hassan el Moulay, the late pasha of Ksar es Souk, both personally and in the discharge of the duties Allah the All-Wise had placed on him.

Personally, they had been close friends. And Hassan had been an especially valuable chamberlain, whose intelligence network was beyond price.

As he walked slowly through the mosque, his face hidden under the hood of his burnoose, Thami el Glaoui recalled that Hassan el Moulay had made first report on Helmut von Heurten-Mitnitz and Sturmbannführer Johann Müller not long after their arrival. These two were most likely the people responsible for his friend's assassination.

The report had given their ranks and titles—minister in the case of von Heurten-Mitnitz (which, el Moulay had told el Glaoui, gave him equal footing in diplomatic protocol with the consuls general of the governments accredited to the French colonial authority and the kingdom of Morocco) and security adviser in the case of Müller. It gave the locations and telephone numbers of their quarters, and the make and license numbers of the automobiles assigned for their use. Within days, their dossiers contained information about their alcohol, drug, and sexual proclivities. Hassan el Moulay had also discovered, among other things, that it was von Heurten-Mitnitz's intention to stop the flow of jewels and currency from France through Morocco.

The intelligence apparatus set up by the pasha of Ksar es Souk had been extraordinarily capable. Thami el Glaoui wondered if Allah the All-Wise had chosen to strike the pasha of Ksar es Souk down because the pasha had grown too sure of himself.

There were several questions connected with his death. The first and most important of these was whether Hassan himself had been the intended victim, or were the assassins actually after Sidi Hassan el Ferruch? Thami el Glaoui was inclined to believe the latter.

If the assassins were sent by the king of Morocco or by the Germans they would have been after the son, not the

father. The son was the smuggler. Killing him would have
stopped that immediately and simultaneously warned the father that these activities were known.

The answers would come sooner or later, Thami el Glaoui
decided. But for now what would happen was in the hands
of Allah.

Since the pashas of Ksar es Souk had been hereditary
chamberlains to the pashas of Marrakech for three hundred
years, and since Sidi Hassan el Ferruch had become pasha
of Ksar es Souk on the death of his father, Sidi now assumed
the same responsibility for intelligence his father had carried. The apparatus was still in place, and the files his father
had built over so many years would now be his.

Only Allah knew if he would use them as well as his
father had. El Glaoui had sought an answer in the Koran
and in prayer, and had concluded as he walked around the
reflecting pool that if Allah did not intend for Sidi Hassan
el Ferruch to serve him as loyally and well as his father had,
it would be better to find this out now.

Thami el Glaoui was so far pleased with Sidi Hassan el
Ferruch. For instance, after Sidi returned from "buying
horses" in France, el Glaoui politely suggested that it was
time for him to marry and produce children. And, since the
Germans were growing suspicious of his travels, he'd suggested that the boy stay out of the public eye as much as
possible.

Sidi went that day into the desert to Ksar es Souk and
took two Berber wives, both of whom were now pregnant.
And then, so far as el Glaoui knew, el Ferruch had not left
Ksar es Souk until the day he buried his father.

Immediately afterward el Glaoui once again ordered Sidi
back to the palace at Ksar es Souk, with instructions that he
was not to leave without his permission. El Ferruch had not
been pleased with the order; but el Glaoui had no reason to

suspect that he would not do what he was told to do.

Thami el Glaoui was therefore surprised the day after he had walked in the mosque when one of his guards came into his chamber escorting one of Sidi el Ferruch's Berbers. The Berber had come by motorcycle from the palace at Ksar es Souk carrying a message.

"Noble Father, my lord begs forgiveness for disturbing you, and prays that you will forgive him for seeking audience on such short notice. He is presently en route, and if you cannot find the time for him, I will meet him on the road and so inform him, and he will return to Ksar es Souk to await your pleasure."

Thami el Glaoui sat for a full minute before replying. "Please let the pasha of Ksar es Souk know that I will be honored to offer him what hospitality is at my disposal. And that I pray to Allah the All-Merciful for his safe journey."

El Ferruch obviously had something important on his mind.

Sidi el Ferruch arrived in a three-car convoy. In front there was a 1940 Ford convertible coupe, full of heavily armed Berbers, their faces masked. The pasha of Ksar es Souk himself rode in the backseat of a 1939 Buick Limited open touring car; following that was another 1939 Buick Limited, this one a closed sedan, also full of masked and armed Berbers.

Thami el Glaoui, gazing down through a screen, was surprised that el Ferruch did not—as the pasha expected him to—scurry quickly up the stairs into the villa. Instead, he walked to the Ford convertible coupe. And then Thami el Glaoui saw why. El Ferruch had elected to ride in the convertible, dressed as one of his Berbers. If there had been assassin's bullets they would have been directed at the man impersonating him.

El Ferruch quickly put on the headdress with the golden

cords of his rank and then walked quickly into the villa through a knot of his Berbers, all of whom were armed with American Thompson .45-caliber machine pistols.

Thami el Glaoui pushed himself to his feet and walked toward the narrow private flight of stairs leading to the reception room downstairs.

Three minutes later the gaunt old man in white faced the tall, hawklike el Ferruch in the blue robes of a Berber. They kissed, and then walked hand in hand to sit on the red leather hassocks on either side of a round brass table five feet in diameter.

"Allah the All-Merciful has answered my prayers for your safe journey," the pasha said as tea and jellied orange slices were put before them.

"Thank you, noble Father," el Ferruch said, "for receiving me."

The pasha slipped an orange slice into his mouth and looked at el Ferruch, his eyebrows raised in question, waiting to hear what el Ferruch wanted.

"I have come about my guest, Eric Fulmar," el Ferruch said.

"The infidel under your roof," Thami el Glaoui said, "concerned your father."

"When my father was killed, noble Father, Eric Fulmar was in Casablanca, meeting with the master of a ship owned by an Argentine with whom we were in school."

"You trust him to negotiate for you?"

"He suggested the arrangement. In addition, he can move with greater ease than I."

"And you trust him?" el Glaoui pursued.

"Yes," el Ferruch said simply.

Thami el Glaoui nodded.

"My friend was in the Hôtel Moulay Hassan, protected

by my men. After my father was killed, they moved him to my apartment in the Hôtel d'Anfa.''

"Before or after the transaction was completed?" el Glaoui asked practically.

"After, noble Father."

"You are sure your profits are safe?" el Glaoui asked.

"They are now deposited in the National City Bank of New York in Argentina. Later they will be transferred to New York."

"And now that the Americans are drawn into the war?" El Ferruch did not respond to the question.

"My friend is in danger," he said.

"Because of the business with the Argentine?"

"So far as the Germans are concerned, my friend should be in the German Army. He is an embarrassment to his father in Germany," el Ferruch said. "His father is a German nobleman, a baron, and he is close to the Nazis."

"And if his father is a German, so he should be," Thami el Glaoui decided. "Is he a man or not?"

"In every way. He has taken the risks of our trade. My tribesmen respect him. And he enjoys women. But in the end, he thinks of himself as an American. And now that the Americans are in the war, he wishes to go to the American consulate in Rabat and put himself under their protection until he can be sent to America."

"And you are asking me to let him go to the American consulate?" Thami el Glaoui asked.

"I am asking your advice, noble Father," el Ferruch said. "Fulmar has been approached three times by von Heurten-Mitnitz, who has suggested to him that there is a way for him to avoid induction into the German Army."

"By informing on us?"

"Yes," el Ferruch said.

"And he told you this?"

"Yes," el Ferruch said. "He is very loyal to me."

Thami el Glaoui inclined his head. Whether in agreement or skepticism el Ferruch was not sure.

"Ahmed Mohammed has learned that the German secret police officer, Müller, intends to return Fulmar to Germany by force. Even though Fulmar has not refused their offer, and pretends that he is still considering it, the Germans now believe that he will never become a reliable agent for them."

"Then why hasn't Müller done it? Is Ahmed Mohammed sure of his information?"

"Ahmed Mohammed is always sure of his information," el Ferruch said. "The Germans are reluctant to enter the Hôtel d'Anfa to take him. However, Germans are waiting outside the hotel grounds. The Sûreté and Deuxième Bureau will look the other way."

"The Germans are 'reluctant' to enter the hotel because he is protected by your men, is that what you mean?"

"No," el Ferruch said. "Because it would cause trouble with the American consulate."

"Why doesn't he telephone his consulate and ask for their protection?"

"He has tried that," el Ferruch said. "No lines were available. I saw to that."

Thami el Glaoui looked at him in genuine admiration.

"I would rather he did not contact the American consulate," el Ferruch continued. "I want to take him to Ksar es Souk."

"I am old and don't think clearly. It is hard to see where you are heading."

"In the future, as the Americans come more and more into the war, we will need someone to inform us about American attitudes and intentions—and perhaps to use as a go-between."

"I've become interested, my son," Thami el Glaoui said

after he let that sink in a moment, "that the Filipinos have elected to fight beside the Americans against the Japanese."

"I don't quite follow," el Ferruch said.

"They do so for one of two reasons," el Glaoui said. "Because they prefer the devil they know. Or because they believe the Americans' claim that they will grant them independence. What I am saying is that the French profess to be willing to grant us independence, and I don't believe them. Why do you suppose the Filipinos believe the Americans?"

"Perhaps because they are telling the truth," el Ferruch said.

"An interesting thought," el Glaoui said.

"The Americans also gave back Cuba to the Cubans," el Ferruch said.

"If they now possessed Morocco, would they give it back to us?" el Glaoui asked rhetorically.

El Ferruch raised both hands, palms up, an elaborate gesture meaning, "Who could tell?"

"You have a plan to get your guest past the Germans?"

"I have, but plans go wrong sometimes," El Ferruch said.

"You are asking me if this is worth an armed confrontation between your men and the Germans—and possibly the Sûreté and the Deuxième Bureau?"

"And for your permission to take him to Ksar es Souk," el Ferruch said.

"What makes you think he will want to go to Ksar es Souk?"

"I'll tell him that I will protect him from the Germans only if he doesn't attempt to go to the Americans."

"Will he believe this?"

"Yes, noble Father, I think he will. And he will give me his word of honor to accept the conditions."

Thami el Glaoui met his eyes, but el Ferruch could not

read his expression. Then he signaled for more tea, and
poured it when it came with great care and formality.

"Have you considered that your heart and not your head
may be speaking?"

"That is why I come to ask for your wisdom."

"I must look carefully to see what is immediately evident
to younger men."

The pasha sipped thoughtfully on his small cup for a long
time.

"The answer is always in the Koran," he said finally.
"At the risk of arrogance, I sense what the Lord of Lords
would have me do. If taking your friend within the walls of
Ksar es Souk is the way you believe you may best serve
Allah and me, my son," the pasha said, "then you must do
that.

"You are in the hands of Allah," he concluded. "I will
pray for you."

4
Casablanca, Morocco
December 10, 1941

When the three-car caravan left Marrakech, there was no
way to avoid the attention of the Sûreté, and it was not
difficult for the Sûreté to guess its destination. Thus when
the three cars reached the outskirts of Casablanca very early
in the afternoon, a Citroën sedan was parked beside the Atlantic Ocean road.

It followed them to the Hôtel d'Anfa near Casablanca,
but stopped outside the gate. One of the French Deuxième
Bureau agents from the Citroën followed el Ferruch and his
entourage of blue-robed Berbers up to the rooftop restaurant

of the hotel. He had a glass of wine while el Ferruch ate a leisurely luncheon.

At half past three, Sidi el Ferruch nodded his head at one of his men. He had seen Eric Fulmar coming off the hotel tennis courts five stories below. Najib Hammi went to the men's room, and a moment later appeared to sneak out, thereby attracting the attention of the alert agent from the Deuxième Bureau, who immediately began a pursuit that would lead him up and down stairwells, into the basement, through the garden, around the walls, and ultimately, fifteen minutes later, back up to the roof garden, where he had been instructed to sit down and finish his crème caramel.

The moment Najib Hammi and the man from the Deuxième Bureau entered the stairwell, Sidi el Ferruch boarded the elevator and descended to the fourth floor of the hotel, where he kept a six-room apartment.

Sweat-soaked from his tennis, Eric Fulmar was leaning on his dresser, pulling a sock off his foot.

"I wondered when you were going to show up," he said.

"I'm sorry about your father, Ferruch."

"We Arabs say, 'It is the will of God,' " el Ferruch said.

"Who did it?"

"I don't know *who* did it," el Ferruch said. "But I know who ordered it done."

"Who?"

"Your German friends," el Ferruch said. "I have also found out they were after me, and not my father."

"I'm not surprised." He laughed. "But tell me why anyway."

"Why do you think?" el Ferruch said. "If they killed me, it would have put you and me out of business, and it would have made it much easier for them to get you back to Germany."

"Shit, if that goddamned ship had waited until December

eighth to sail, I would be in the middle of the Atlantic by now.''

"What would you do in Argentina?'' el Ferruch asked.

"Probably the same thing I do here.'' Fulmar chuckled. "Play tennis, and try to get laid.''

"For someone about to be hauled off to Germany, you're remarkably cheerful,'' el Ferruch said.

"I've been trying to get through to the American consulate,'' Eric said, turning more serious. "The Rabat lines keep going out, but sooner or later they're going to make a mistake, and I'm going to yell like hell at whoever answers the consulate phone. In the meantime, I'm safe.'' He saw the look on el Ferruch's face, and added: "Aren't I?''

"No,'' el Ferruch said simply. "Ahmed Mohammed has learned that the Germans' patience is exhausted. They're going to come for you probably tonight, and the Sûreté and Deuxième Bureau are going to look the other way.''

"And?'' Fulmar said.

"I saw the pasha of Marrakech this morning,'' el Ferruch said. "About you.''

"And?'' Eric repeated.

"Somewhat reluctantly, he gave me permission to take you to Ksar es Souk.'' He added, significantly, "Provided I can *get* you to Ksar es Souk.''

"You needed his permission?'' Fulmar asked. El Ferruch nodded. "What the hell would I do at Ksar es Souk?''

"I don't know, since there's no tennis court and no women,'' el Ferruch said. "None that you could go after, in any event.''

"Why don't you get on the telephone, call the consulate, say you're me, and have them send somebody to get me?''

"Because I have been told not to,'' el Ferruch said.

"By the pasha?'' Eric asked. El Ferruch nodded. "Why not?''

"I went to ask his permission to take you to Rabat," el Ferruch said. "He doesn't think you should leave Morocco right now. The reason the telephone lines are out for you is that Thami el Glaoui doesn't want you talking to your consulate."

"Why, that miserable, crazy sonofabitch!" Fulmar fumed.

"Don't say that out loud, Eric," el Ferruch said coldly.

"What does he want from me?"

"I told you, he doesn't want you to leave Morocco right now."

"Well, fuck him!"

"You have two choices: You can go back to Germany—I can't stop you from walking out of here. Or you can give me your word you will not try to contact the Americans, and return to Ksar es Souk with me."

"Give *you* my *word*?"

"That presumes, of course, that I can get you past the thugs from the Sicherheitsdienst."

"Give *you* my word?" Fulmar repeated. "Whose side are you on?"

"This is the real world, Eric; won't you ever learn that?" el Ferruch said. "And in the final analysis, I am on my own side. I went as far as I can, asking Thami el Glaoui to help you."

"I made the crazy old bastard a lot of money," Eric said petulantly.

"You made yourself what you think is a lot of money in the process. What you made for el Glaoui is less than what watering his golf course costs in a month."

Fulmar glowered at him.

"You're an ass sometimes, Eric," el Ferruch said nastily. "An ungrateful ass!"

They locked eyes for a long moment; then Fulmar shrugged, giving in.

"The one thing I don't want is the German Army," he said. "How are you going to get me out of here? In addition to the Sicherheitsdienst people, there is also a pair from the Deuxième Bureau out there sitting in a Citroën just outside the gate."

"Before we go any further, do I have your word?"

"OK, Christ. Sure." He held three fingers extended at the level of his shoulder. "Boy Scout's honor," he said. "How's that, you prick?"

Sidi el Ferruch slapped his face as hard as he could.

"Don't forget again where you are, and what you are, and who I am," el Ferruch said.

Fulmar balled his fists, and for a moment el Ferruch thought he was going to punch him. But in the end, Fulmar relaxed his fingers.

"OK," he said, his voice strained. "I give you my word of honor. Before I try to get in touch with any Americans, I'll tell you first. Is that good enough?"

"Don't expect to impose on the friendship between us," el Ferruch said.

"Oh, don't worry about that," Fulmar said sarcastically. "Just tell me how you're going to get me out of here."

"The Germans are not paying any attention to the natives, and the Deuxième Bureau will not interfere with me unless I give them cause," el Ferruch said. "So the trick is not to give them cause."

Five minutes later, Sidi el Ferruch, accompanied by one of his Berber guards, whose lower face was masked in the Berber tradition, rode the elevator down to the lobby, where Najib Hammi was waiting along with four other Berbers. They walked across the lobby and went outside and entered the automobiles in which they had arrived.

There was a Sicherheitsdienst agent in the lobby, but he paid little more than perfunctory attention to the small group of natives who came out of the elevator, chattering like gossiping women.

Across the street from the Hôtel d'Anfa, one of the Deuxième Bureau agents pointed his finger at them as he counted them like sheep. He was satisfied. Seven had gone into the hotel, and seven had come out.

In twenty minutes they were out of Casablanca on the Atlantic coast road to El Jadida. There they turned onto the road which would take them—via the Tizi-n-Tichka pass—through the mountains. The road was narrow, unpaved, and there were no barriers. The French Foreign Legion had built it using only picks and shovels.

The trip to the palace of the pasha of Ksar es Souk took them all night.

5
Kunming, China
18 December 1941

When the P40-Bs and the First and Second Squadrons of the American Volunteer Group began to land at Kunming, Wingmen Canidy and Bitter were waiting for them. They had been there three days. Canidy and Bitter had been officer- and deputy-officer-in-charge of moving the ground element from Toungoo to Kunming.

The ground element of the American Volunteer Group had made the first leg—about 350 miles—of the trip to China aboard a special train, made up of thirty-three flatcars, a dining car, and three first-class passenger cars.

"Army bodied" (canvas-roofed flatbed) Studebaker and International two-ton trucks (some olive drab with Chinese

Army insignia, some with the CAMCO legend on their doors, and some unmarked), all loaded to capacity, were chained to the flatcars. So were two aircraft-fueling trucks, a fire truck, half a dozen Chevrolet pickup trucks, four jeeps, and three Studebaker Commander sedans, one of them Canidy's.

The train passed through Mandalay shortly after midnight, and arrived at Lashio, the eastern terminus of the Burma Road, as dawn was breaking.

While the Americans of the AVG group ate breakfast in the dining car, the vehicles were unloaded from the flatcars and inspected by a team of American mechanics. Six of the trucks and one of the pickups were judged unfit to make the trip. They would follow with subsequent convoys.

As Canidy was being given instructions for the road trip, the CAMCO Twin Beech D18S appeared in the sky, and thirty minutes later John B. Dolan, carrying two canvas suitcases, walked up to Canidy's Studebaker and asked if he had room for a hitchhiker.

Once the convoy set out it averaged 20 mph over the Burma Road, and it took them forty-four hours to drive its 681 miles. This included a ten-hour overnight stop. The road was too narrow and too dangerous to drive in the dark.

At more than a dozen places along the road, they had seen human chains of Chinese manhandling cargoes of trucks, which had gone over the edge back up the steep mountainsides. And there had been three large black gashes burned in the thick vegetation where fuel trucks had exploded and burned.

In the Studebaker, Dolan volunteered to explain how the American Volunteer Group would have to function now that the United States was in the war.

They were supposed to have one hundred pilots. They had eighty. There were supposed to be about three hundred people in the support element. There were just over one hundred thirty. And there would be no more "volunteers" released from the Army and the Navy and Marine Corps to "work for CAMCO."

Of the one hundred P40-Bs shipped from Buffalo, seventy-five remained. Ten were simply missing, probably riding the Orient in the hold of some freighter, or on the bottom of the sea in ships sunk by the Japanese. Twelve had been wrecked beyond repair in training. Of the seventy-five aircraft now in AVG hands, twenty were grounded, more than likely permanently, because of missing parts.

When they reached Kunming, very early in the morning, smoke had been still rising from the fires started by the Japanese bombing attack the previous day. The Japanese tactic was to bomb the city with incendiaries. They knew that fires were going to cause more physical and psychological damage than high explosives.

Kunming's only defenses against the aerial attack were a half-dozen batteries of 20-mm antiaircraft cannon, which the Japanese could easily fly around, and some .50-caliber water-cooled machine guns protecting the air base against strafing attacks. Since it was unnecessary for the Japanese to descend into range of the .50s, the machine guns were seldom fired.

But the Kunming air base itself was far better militarily than anyone expected. There were solid revetments for the planes, and piles of stones and sandbags protected the maintenance buildings against anything but a direct hit. The runways were long and smooth. And because they were made of crushed stone, a bomb striking a runway would knock it out only until the hole could be filled with more crushed stone.

It was literally hand-built. Thousands of people had spent

long days, using only the most rudimentary hand tools, to build it.

For the AVG itself, something like a U.S. military base had been established. There was a BOQ (called a hostel), with showers, dayrooms, a bar, and a library. There was a baseball field and tennis courts, a small medical facility, and even a pistol range.

Dolan, Canidy, Bitter, and the others were not the first Americans at Kunming. They had been preceded by people from CAMCO and by more old China hands from Chennault's staff.

Since Canidy and Bitter had not been assigned to one of the three squadrons as the other pilots had, and since all the rooms in the hostel had been reserved for the squadrons, Canidy and Bitter moved in with Dolan and the support personnel, as they had in Rangoon.

The operation of the airfield was under a Chinese major general, Huang Jen Lin, an enormous man who—Canidy and Bitter were promptly and significantly informed—was a devout Christian. General Huang spoke fluent English and seemed quite competent. After meeting Huang, Canidy and Bitter were immediately issued brand-new U.S. Army Air Corps horsehide flight jackets. On the back of these had been hand-painted a sort of signboard. At its top a legend in Chinese announced that the wearer was an American who had come to China to fight the Japanese, and that it was the duty of every Chinese to give him whatever assistance he required.

The food in the mess was astonishing. Not only was it very good, but it was American. The Chinese chef had learned his trade as number-one kitchen boy aboard a U.S. Navy gunboat on the Yangtze River patrol. And there was something else in the mess Canidy found delightful: Chinese girls from the American Missionary College. They had been enlisted for service as interpreters. They were quite lovely, adored American food, spoke excellent English, and one of them, a slight, delicate, graceful girl, was receptive to Canidy's invitation to come to his room and see what they could pick up on the Hallicrafter's shortwave radio.

Sensing that Ed Bitter really disapproved of what he had in mind, Canidy spent a moment with him before he left with the girl.

"What's the matter with you now?"

"Nothing."

"Because they're Chinese? Amazing thing about Chinese girls," Canidy said, "they get better-looking by the minute."

"You don't think you're taking advantage of her?" Bitter asked. "That doesn't bother you? For Christ's sake, she's from a *missionary* school. She doesn't know what you want from her."

"What I'm doing, Eddie," Canidy said patiently, "is getting laid." Then, grasping Bitter by the arm, he theatrically proclaimed, "Live today, Edwin, for tomorrow you may wish you were dead! Into the valley of death fly the noble ninety-five."

Bitter was not amused.

A few minutes later, Canidy had learned that General Huang's thoroughness in providing for the needs of the Americans went so far as providing interpreters with supplies of foil-wrapped U.S. Navy–issue condoms.

6

Early in the morning of December 20, Canidy was awakened before dawn by a shy and giggling interpreter who shielded her eyes from the interpreter in his bed and sweetly singsonged that "Meester Crooooookshanks" would be happy if "Meeester Can-Eye-Die" would join him immediately at breakfast.

Ham and eggs, pancakes, strawberry preserves, and good black coffee were already on the table when Crookshanks waved him into a chair. There was another pilot wearing an Air Corps green shirt and trousers, with a piece of white parachute silk tied as a foulard around his neck. There were wings, similar to Air Corps wings, with the flaming sun of China where the federal shield usually went. It was the first time Canidy had seen such insignia.

"You know Doug Douglass, of course?" Crookshanks said.

"Sure," Canidy said. Doug Douglass was short, crew-cutted, and young-looking. The first time Canidy had seen him had been on the ship on the way over. He had thought then that Douglass looked more like a Boy Scout than an officer and pilot. He had subsequently learned that Douglass was a West Pointer, one of those rare "natural" pilots. Douglass also shared (as much as could be expected of a West Pointer) much of Canidy's amused scorn for Crookshank's attempts to "shape up" the Flying Tigers.

Canidy wondered if Douglass's irreverence for proper behavior and the "wrong attitude" had earned him a place on Crookshank's shit list.

"What I'm going to do, Canidy," Crookshanks said, "is send up early-morning patrols of two aircraft, to watch the area the Japanese usually come through."

Canidy nodded.

"There's the ground spotter network, of course," Crookshanks continued, "but we don't really know yet whether that really works. And we don't really know how well our air-to-ground communications are going to function. That's what we hope to find out from you two."

"When do we go?" Douglass asked.

"First light, about fifteen minutes."

"OK," Canidy said. "Why me?"

"Because you're a pretty good navigator," Crookshanks said. "I want a pretty accurate position report, to compare with the ground spotter network's report."

"OK," Canidy said.

"Any other questions?"

"You plan to have me doing this regularly?"

"For the time being. You and Bitter can alternate. I plan to have an afternoon patrol, too. And we'll rotate the pilots from the squadron who will fly with you."

"I don't like to fly pool airplanes," Canidy said.

"The only aircraft we have are assigned to squadrons. You'll have to fly what's available."

"I don't care *which* one," Canidy said. "I would just like the *same* one, time after time."

"I don't see how I can arrange that," Crookshanks said. He waited until Canidy nodded, and then went on. "Now, the way this will work this morning is that you will fly patrol until we send you a report of incoming aircraft from the ground spotters. You will then confirm sighting. When you have their location, you will so report by radio. We're not sure about our communications, so while you're reporting by radio, Doug will hightail it back here with the same information. You will remain in sight of the Japanese formation."

"OK," Canidy said. "And what if we sight a formation before we get it from the ground spotters?"

"Same thing. Fix the location, course, altitude, and so on, radio it, and send Doug back here immediately."

"OK," Canidy said. "Am I supposed to attack the formation?"

Crookshanks met his eyes. "Use your own judgment," he said softly.

Canidy nodded. Then he drained his coffee.

"I'll see you on the flight line in ten minutes, Doug," he said.

"If I'm late," Douglass replied, "you just go on without me."

Canidy smiled at him. At least he wouldn't be going out for the first time with some damned hero, eager to do battle with the Dirty Jap.

They found a Japanese formation before they were advised of its presence by ground spotters relaying the information through Kunming.

They were on oxygen at fifteen thousand feet. Six thousand feet below, flying directly toward them between two cloud formations, were a dozen Japanese airplanes, too far away to be typed, flying in two uneven Vs.

Canidy waggled his wings, and at the same time turned to look at Doug Douglass, who was flying two hundred feet off his right wingtip. Douglass was also waggling his wings and pointing ahead. Canidy nodded and held up his chart for Douglass to see. Canidy marked the location on his chart and went on the air long enough to transmit, once, the coordinates. Just the coordinates, not the altitude or direction or airspeed. He had no way to judge those. Doug Douglass would have to estimate their altitude, airspeed, and direction and report them as well as he could. It was possible that the Japanese would have their radios tuned to the same frequency they were using.

Douglass bent his head over his lap, obviously marking down the coordinates Canidy had given him; then he raised his head and shook it exaggeratedly: *OK.*

Canidy made a motion with his right hand: *Go.*

Douglass nodded and peeled off to his right, toward Kunming.

Now that Douglass was gone with the information, it was safe to try to send it by radio.

"Kunming," Canidy said to his microphone. "Dawn patrol leader. Twelve Japanese single-engine aircraft at nine thousand feet, course one hundred seventy-five degrees."

He waited a moment, redialed the transmitter frequency, and repeated the message. There was no reply to either call.

He turned the P40-B slowly, in a wide arc, maintaining his altitude. When he completed the 180-degree turn, the Japanese were now almost directly below him. He lowered his left wing and looked down at them, then straightened the wings and made a long, flat 360-degree turn. When it was completed, the Japanese aircraft were some distance ahead of him.

As he flew along, his hands inside his gloves were sweating, and he felt the chill when the sweat on his forehead encountered the cold air of fifteen thousand feet.

"Shit," he said, and he pushed the stick forward and tested his guns. The two .50s on the nose ahead of him spit fire. He could not see the .30s in the wing.

The gunsights on the P40-B consisted of crosshairs on a foot-high pedestal mounted on the fuselage in front of the canopy, and a foot-high pedestal eighteen inches in front of that. He lined the sights up on the last aircraft in the Japanese formation, the third aircraft in the right of the V.

He could identify the aircraft now. The facts he had learned about the Mitsubishi B5M in Rangoon came to him:

1000-horsepower 14-cylinder radial engine.

Crew of three.

1700-pound bomb load.

One flexibly mounted 7.7-mm machine gun facing aft.

Two 7.7-mm machine guns in the leading edge of each wing.

Maximum speed 325 mph. Cruising speed 200 mph.

The Japanese observer-gunner had spotted him and frantically charged his machine gun, a Japanese copy of the Browning.

Canidy held him a second or two in the crosshairs of his gunsight, then raised his nose so that the crosshairs were now pointing twenty yards ahead of the Mitsubishi. He pushed down with his thumb on the machine-gun button.

The .50s, he realized, were off. The stream of their tracers was to the right of the Mitsubishi. But the stream of tracers from the .30 in his left wing stitched the fuselage from just forward of the vertical stabilizer. He saw the Plexiglas of the long, narrow canopy shatter. He held his position as long as he dared; then he pushed the nose farther down, diving first under the Japanese aircraft and then banking steeply for the nearest cloud cover.

As soon as the gray of the cloud surrounded the P40-B, Canidy put the aircraft into a steep, climbing turn, welcoming the feeling of invisibility the cloud gave him.

When the cloud began to break up at its tops he realized that he was ready to return to the fight, prepared now to compensate for the off-to-the-right firing cone of the .50 calibers. And he knew how to fight.

He would dive to pick up speed and then come up under the rear aircraft of the rear wing. That would severely limit the ability of the Japanese machine gunners to fire on him. He could fire on at least one aircraft before making a dive turn away from him. He doubted that they would try to pursue him. He was faster.

There were only three planes in the rear V now. The aircraft he had first attacked had left the formation. He looked for it but couldn't find it. He changed his original plan and came up instead under the forward V, attacking the last plane in the right arm of the V, then the aircraft ahead of it.

He was still in position under the second aircraft when the .50s in the nose stopped, and a moment later the .30s in the wings. He was out of ammunition. He began a steep, diving turn to the left, looking frantically over his shoulders. In the fraction of a second he had it in sight, he thought he saw flickers of fire in the Mitsubishi's engine nacelle, but he concluded that he was probably looking at its exhaust.

He straightened out and headed back to Kunming, dropping as he flew. Five minutes out of the airfield, he saw ten P40-Bs, flying in pairs, climbing out in the direction of the Japanese.

When he called the tower for permission to land, the radio worked perfectly.

One of the eager warriors of the Second Squadron, to whom the plane Canidy was flying was normally assigned, was waiting for Canidy when he taxied up to the revetment. He had his helmet on and his pistol, and Canidy realized that he had forgotten to wear his. The pilot obviously intended to race off after the others just as soon as his ship was fueled and rearmed. He was to be disappointed. There were four bullet holes in the aircraft fuselage, and two in the right wing. There had been no indication of any kind of damage to the controls or the engine, but John Dolan firmly announced that the plane wasn't going anywhere until they had a close look at it.

The eager warrior, denied the joy of combat, furiously pulled his helmet off and threw it on the ground, smashing the right lens of his goggles.

Shaking his head, Canidy started walking toward the mess. Crookshanks appeared in what had been Canidy's

Studebaker. He had been relieved of it as soon as they'd reached Kunming.

Canidy opened the door and got in beside him.

"I made two radio calls," Canidy said, handing Crookshanks the chart. "There was no response to either. I marked where they were when we spotted them."

"You spotted them?" Crookshanks asked innocently.

"Douglass spotted them," Canidy corrected himself. "When I waggled my wings, he was already signaling me."

"Did you attack?"

"Yeah."

"And?"

"Having thirties *and* fifties is a pretty stupid idea, you know that?" Canidy said. "You don't open fire until you're within thirty range, which means giving away the safety factor the extra range of the fifties gives you."

"What would you suggest?"

"I'd rather have all fifties."

"Impossible."

"Then two fifties with more ammo. Fair over the thirty barrel openings in the wing."

"There's no more room for fifty ammo in the nose."

"Then I'd still get rid of the thirties," Canidy said. "I like the idea of being able to shoot at people beyond the range they can return it."

"As a matter of fact, Canidy," Crookshanks said, "there is hardly any distance in the maximum range between them. Not enough to make any real difference."

"The dispersal is different," Canidy argued. "At two hundred yards, the thirties scatter all over."

"So do the fifties."

"Not as bad as the thirties," Canidy continued to argue. "Because the fifty-caliber projectile is heavier and more stable. And a fifty hit is like three hits, or four, with a thirty."

"I will take your suggestion under advisement, Mr. Canidy," Crookshanks said. "But getting back to my original question, what happened when you attacked?"

"If you mean, did I shoot anything down, I don't think so."

"But you did attack. And when did you break off engagement?"

"When I ran out of ammunition," Canidy said.

Crookshanks dropped him at the hostel. Canidy went to the club. There was no one there. They were all, he realized, in the air, or else over at the radio shack, vicariously getting their thrills by listening to the radio chatter.

The bartender, a Chinese Christian from the Missionary College, appeared.

"I would like a glass of Scotch," Canidy said. "A double double."

"So early, sair?"

"Just the booze, please," Canidy said. "No moral judgments."

He took a stiff swallow, and a moment later another. Then he mixed water with what was left and started to sit down at a table to read an old copy of *Life* magazine.

And then, very suddenly, he was sick to his stomach. He barely made it to the john before he threw up everything he'd eaten for breakfast.

He looked at his watch. It was quarter to ten.

7

Crookshanks sent for Canidy at half past seven that night. He slid a leather box, three inches by eight, across his desk to him. It was open. It held a medal of some kind.

"What's that?"

"That's the Order of the Cloud Banner," Crookshanks said. "Which I was given a couple of weeks ago to present to the first pilot who scored a victory."

"They got one, did they?"

"We got six of the eight," Crookshanks said.

"That makes me feel pretty inept," Canidy said. "Is that why you called me in here, to point that out?"

"I called you in here to give you the medal," Crookshanks said. "I didn't think you'd want a parade."

"One of mine went down?" Canidy said, genuinely surprised. Crookshanks nodded. "Well, I'll be damned!" Canidy said. "Are you sure?"

"We're sure," Crookshanks said. "It was witnessed from the ground. We have pieces from all of them."

"*All* of them?" Canidy asked. "Oh, you mean the other five."

"Yeah. Your five and the other one."

Canidy looked at him to make sure he had heard right.

"You are surprised, aren't you?" Crookshanks asked.

"I didn't stick around a second longer than I had to," Canidy said. "Yeah, I'm surprised."

"You think it was luck?"

"Sure it was luck," Canidy said. "What else?"

"It's going to cost you," Crookshanks said.

"How?"

"I want you to talk to the others so maybe they'll get lucky too."

"I'd probably get as many laughs as Groucho Marx."

"It was an order, Canidy, not a suggestion," Crookshanks said.

"In that case, yes, sir, Commander Crookshanks, sir."

"Because you are such a paragon of cheerful, willing obedience, Mr. Canidy, I have decided to give you a little reward of my own."

"I'd like my own ship."

"That's what I had in mind," Crookshanks said.

"Thank you," Canidy said.

"There's a hook there too, I'm afraid."

"Which is?"

"Martin Farmington didn't get back today," Crookshanks said.

"I didn't know him."

"He was a flight leader in the First Squadron," Crookshanks said. "I want you to take his place." When Canidy did not reply, Crookshanks said, "It's another seventy-five dollars a month."

"OK," Canidy said.

Martin Farmington returned early the next morning to Kunming on the back of a farmer's cart, in time to be a hero at breakfast. He had crash-landed his plane, demolishing it, but aside from a couple of bruises and a cut on his arm from a sharp piece of canopy Plexiglas, he was unharmed.

Canidy was readying his plane for flight when Crookshanks came out to the line.

"You're not going," he announced. "Can Bitter handle it?"

"Sure. But why not me?" Canidy asked.

"Because there was a TWX from Chennault. He's flying in here with some big shot. They want to talk to you."

"He's not going to make a production about that medal, is he?" Canidy asked.

"All I know," Crookshanks said, "is what the TWX said. And what it said is 'Ground Canidy until further notice.' "

TEN

Dick Canidy watched Brigadier General Claire Chennault walk across the tarmac from his Twin-Beech to where he and Commander Crookshanks stood waiting.

Chennault was wearing a horsehide leather jacket, a leather brimmed cap, from which the crown stiffener had been removed, and sunglasses. He also had a .45 hanging low, like a cowboy's six-shooter, on his hip; and his feet were in half-Wellington boots. It was the pursuit pilot's uniform, and Chennault was entitled. He had, literally, written the book. A thousand Army Air Corps, Marine, and Navy fighter pilots—including Ensign Richard Canidy—had been trained according to the theories Chennault had laid down in *Pursuit Aviation.* Before the war was over, tens of thousands of fighter pilots would be so trained. Chennault was the acknowledged expert.

But Chennault has never shot down an airplane, Canidy thought. *I have. If Crookshanks's spotters are to be believed, I have shot down five of them. I am therefore an ace. Since we have been in the war only two weeks, it is entirely possible that I am the only ace so far.*

From everything he had heard, the fighter force in the Philippines and the Hawaiian Islands had been wiped out on the ground.

He wondered what Chennault wanted with him, and for the first time he considered it might very well have something to do with yesterday's actions. God knows, he thought, the American public needs some good news. That an American had shot down five Japanese on his first sortie was good news. It was therefore possible that he was about to be shown off.

This theory seemed to be confirmed when he saw the briefcase-carrying civilian with Chennault. The man was American; he was clearly not one of the AVG civilians, and he was just as clearly not a soldier in civilian clothing. He looked to Canidy like a bureaucrat. A little overweight, pale, and more than a little self-important.

Crookshanks saluted when Chennault came close, and Canidy followed his example.

"Good morning, General," Crookshanks said. "This is Wingman Canidy."

Chennault offered Canidy his hand.

"Canidy is one I recruited myself," he said. "How are you, Canidy? How does it feel to be our first ace?"

"I'm not entirely sure the Chinese know how to count, General," Canidy said.

"They know how to count." Chennault chuckled. "Damned well done, son."

"Thank you, sir," Canidy said.

"This is Mr. Baker," Chennault said. "Commander Crookshanks and Wingman Canidy."

They shook hands.

"We need someplace to talk in private," Chennault said.

"Would my office be all right, General?" Crookshanks asked.

"If we can run everybody out and have some coffee," Chennault said.

"Of course, sir," Crookshanks said.

As they walked toward the building which housed Crookshanks's office, Canidy noticed, amused, that Crookshanks did the little dance military inferiors did to stay in step with their superiors.

As soon as coffee and sweet rolls were served, Baker got down to business.

"What is said here," he announced, "is not to leave this room. I want you both to understand that."

"Yes, sir," Crookshanks said. Canidy nodded.

Baker opened his briefcase, took an envelope from it, and handed it to Crookshanks.

"General Chennault has seen that," Baker said to Crookshanks while Crookshanks was reading.

Whatever it was, Canidy thought, was impressing the hell out of Crookshanks. His eyes actually widened. When he was finished, he looked at Baker, who gestured with his hands to give it to Canidy.

It wasn't long, but it was certainly impressive:

THE WHITE HOUSE
WASHINGTON, D.C.

December 8, 1941

Mr. Eldon C. Baker is engaged in a confidential mission of the highest priority at my personal direction. United States military and civilian agencies are directed to provide whatever support he requests. Military and civilian agencies of the Allied Powers are requested to do so.

Franklin D. Roosevelt

Canidy looked at Baker.

"Has this something to do with me?" he asked.

"I came here from Washington to see you, Mr. Canidy," Baker said.

"My immediate reaction," Canidy said, "is that you've got the wrong man. *This* Canidy is a former Navy lieutenant junior grade, now flying for General Chennault."

"I know who you are, Mr. Canidy," Baker said. "You were acquainted with Mr. Chesley Whittaker, I believe?"

"Yes," Canidy said.

"I'm sorry to have to tell you Mr. Whittaker is dead," Baker said. "He suffered a stroke on December seventh."

"You didn't come to China to tell me that."

"I told you that to show that I know who you are," Baker said. "I came to China to recruit you for an important mission."

"What kind of a mission?"

"I can't get into that just yet," Baker said.

"That's wonderful!" Canidy said, rolling his eyes.

"It comes with the standard caveat," Baker said. "It is a mission considered of great importance to the war effort, and it entails a high degree of risk."

"But you won't tell me what?" Canidy asked.

"For Christ's sake, Canidy," Crookshanks snapped. "That letter is from the President!"

"I saw," Canidy snapped back. He looked at Baker. "A flying job?"

"I'm not at liberty to say," Baker said.

"I can't imagine what else it could be," Canidy thought aloud. Then he added: "I'm under a year's contract to the AVG. I don't suppose that matters?"

"What you would be doing is considered of greater importance," Baker said.

"Would I come back here?"

"That hasn't been determined," Baker said. "Most probably, you would not."

"Jesus," Canidy said, exasperated. "You understand that the only skill I can bring to this war is flying single-engine airplanes?"

Baker nodded.

"Unless you're willing to tell me more, my answer is no," Canidy said.

"Canidy," Chennault said, "Roosevelt would not have sent Mr. Baker here unless this was damned important."

"Colonel Donovan told me to expect that Canidy would be difficult," Baker said, smiling.

That surprised Canidy. He knew that Donovan was engaged in hush-hush work for the President. Baker was, therefore, sending him a message. He looked quickly at Chennault and Crookshanks. Their faces showed no sign that they knew Donovan.

"How is the colonel?" Canidy asked dryly.

"He sends his best regards," Baker said. "He hopes to have dinner with you soon."

Canidy doubted that. But he understood he was being told that if he went along with Baker, he would be going to the States.

"That would be nice," Canidy said, dryly sarcastic.

What the hell is the matter with me? Canidy thought. *All the questions of rushing to the bulwarks to defend the flag aside, my option is either to remain here, where I'll likely be shot and killed, or to go along with whatever this guy has up his sleeve. The odds are that it will probably be less dangerous than what I'm doing now. Donovan probably needs a pilot, and I'm a pilot. It may be as simple as that.*

What's wrong with that theory is that the President would

not send a high-level bureaucrat halfway around the world to recruit an airplane driver.

"Can you tell me what my status would be?" Canidy asked.

"Oh, you mean who's going to pay you?" Baker asked. "You would be a civilian employee of the U.S. government. There would be at least as much money as you're making now. Including bonuses I understand you earned yesterday."

Oh, what the fuck!

"All right," Canidy said. "What the hell, why not?"

Baker nodded.

"When does all this happen?" Canidy asked.

"You'll go back with General Chennault and me," Baker said. "Which raises the question of how we explain your departure around here."

"What difference does that make? Let them ask Crookshanks if they're curious."

"The situation is such that we can't let you tell your friends what you're doing," Baker said. "That means I have to come up with some sort of credible explanation why you suddenly vanished the day after you became an ace and got a medal."

"The Cloud Banner is not common knowledge," Crookshanks said. "The only person who knows about it is Canidy's wingman, Douglass."

"That would be Douglas Douglass?" Baker said, brightening.

"Yes," Crookshanks said, surprised that Baker had that information.

"The word you will spread about my visit is that I came to see Douglass," Baker said. "To bring him a package from his father. Why isn't Canidy's medal common knowledge?"

"That was Douglass's suggestion," Crookshanks said. "I was going to make Canidy a flight commander, and planned to combine that announcement with the story of his kills and the medal."

Baker nodded.

He's thinking profound thoughts, Canidy thought; *you can almost smell the wood burning.*

"I have a somewhat unpleasant suggestion," Baker said a moment later. "I think it necessary for Canidy to leave China in disgrace. People are less apt to talk about cowards than heroes. Thus we'll have to alter the past a little. The word will therefore be spread that Canidy turned tail yesterday and fled, and that you consequently relieved him and sent him home."

"A hero's life is a short one," Canidy said.

"I don't think Douglass would go along with that," Crookshanks said stiffly.

"I also have a letter with me from Douglass's father," Baker said. "It asks him to do whatever I ask."

"His father's a Navy commander, isn't he?" Chennault asked.

"Captain," Baker said.

"And he's involved with you?" Canidy asked.

Baker ignored the question. "If we did this," he said thoughtfully, "it would obviate the necessity of Canidy saying anything at all to anyone. He would simply walk out there on the airplane and be gone. Afterward, Douglass could reluctantly say that he didn't know what happened. I think he could manage that."

"Is this really necessary?" Chennault asked.

Baker ignored him, too.

"It's up to you, Canidy," Baker said. "I am open to other suggestions."

It was a moment before Canidy replied.

"I don't much give a damn what people think of me," he said.

"Mr. Crookshanks," Baker said, "would you send someone for Douglass, please?"

2
Ksar es Souk, Morocco
December 22, 1941

Eric Fulmar, el Ferruch was surprised to see, was not at all unhappy at the palace at Ksar es Souk. He had expected him to almost immediately grow bored with life in the middle of the desert and to promptly start wheedling to be taken to Rabat and put safely into the hands of American diplomatic personnel.

He had to be watched around the clock, of course, in case it should enter his mind to take his chances and make for Rabat on his own. That would involve stealing a car, as well as breaking his word, and el Ferruch thought that was unlikely. But he was a prudent man, and it was not difficult to have Eric watched by the Berbers, discreetly, "for his own protection."

Since they had not been able to walk out of the Hôtel d'Anfa carrying suitcases, the only Western clothing Eric had with him was what he had worn under his burnoose. Once in the palace at Ksar es Souk, he had no choice but to dress in Moroccan clothing, and from the third day, not by intention, he had grown a beard. With his modern American safety razor in Casablanca with his clothing, he had borrowed el Ferruch's English straight razor. One slice in his cheek was enough to encourage him to let his beard grow.

But before long his golden-blond beard pleased him, so he didn't shave it off when his things finally arrived from Casablanca. And because that amused him too, he continued to wear Moroccan clothing.

They rose early in the morning, when it was still quite cool, mounted horses, and hunted (quail, with shotguns and dogs, and peccary—a type of wild pig—with machine pistols borrowed from the guards) until the sun sent the temperature up. Then they returned to the palace and spent the rest of the day deep inside, where the thick stone-and-mud walls kept the temperature comfortable.

One afternoon Fulmar came across a book by T. E. Lawrence in the small collection of European-language books el Ferruch had inherited from his father. There was a faded photo of Lawrence at the front wearing Arab garb and sitting cockily astride a horse.

"You will henceforth refer to me as Lawrence the Second," Fulmar said, showing the book to el Ferruch, "and treat me with the appropriate respect."

"When the Turks caught Lawrence," el Ferruch said, "they buggered him."

"You're kidding," Fulmar said, disgusted.

"No," el Ferruch said. "And he finally killed himself riding a motorcycle drunk."

"Forget I brought it up." Fulmar laughed.

El Ferruch thought—but did not say—that astride a stallion, in flowing robes and burnoose, carrying a machine pistol and bandoliers of ammunition, Eric looked more capable of taking on the Turkish Army than Lawrence, who had been a small, slight, sickly faggot.

In his role as pasha of Ksar es Souk, each afternoon el Ferruch had to receive his subjects in the main hall of the palace. He sat on cushions and drank (and offered) tea while hearing his Berbers' complaints and giving (or denying) his permission for marriages and business transactions. After these audiences were over he evaluated with Ahmed Mohammed the information that had come into their possession, then dispatched a daily synopsis to Thami el Glaoui in Marrakech.

While el Ferruch was engaged in what Fulmar called, sarcastically but not inaccurately, the discharge of his King Solomon duties, Fulmar himself, trailed by Berbers awed by his ability to handle (dead) electric mains that (live) knocked them down, practiced the profession he'd learned in Germany and went around the palace doing what he could to improve what he called the Edison Model #1 electrical system.

To do so required copper wire, transformers, switches, and other electrical devices. The Berbers were of course willing—even delighted—to acquire the necessary supplies by stealing them from the French and Germans. But after they kept bringing back the wrong equipment, and several of them were knocked unconscious grabbing the wrong wire, Fulmar asked permission to go along with them on their nightly forays.

At first el Ferruch wanted to say no. But then he realized that Fulmar was speaking fluent Arabic, and that while he was no Berber, still, in his blue robes and blond beard and deeply tanned skin, he could not be told from one.

"Theft only, Eric," el Ferruch said. "And that discreetly. No sabotage. No suggestion that what you are stealing is being used for its intended purpose. Let them think that the wire is being stolen to be melted down for the copper."

Fulmar nodded.

"If, however, it should be necessary at some later time to sabotage the electrical or telephone systems, I would be very interested to know the best way to do that.''

"I'll make the drawings," Fulmar said. "No problem at
all. And I can tap into their telephone lines, if you'd like.
Or their telegraph and teletypewriter lines. You'd need a
Teletype machine if I tapped those lines, or a telegraph
printer. But we can listen to their telephone calls very easily.''

"They couldn't tell?''

"I was educated at Marburg," Fulmar said. "Remember?
Right about now I was scheduled to be Herr Doktor von
Fulmar, Elektroingenieur.''

Sidi el Ferruch rode with Fulmar on several middle-of-
the-night wire and transformer raids, and proved to his own
satisfaction that Fulmar could do what he promised.

As a reward, he satisfied Fulmar's curiosity about his
wives, whom Fulmar had never seen. He took them to the
wives' wing of the palace, and from behind a screened window he let Fulmar have a quick look at them without their
veils. They were sitting together, sewing.

"And they're both pregnant?'' Fulmar asked.

El Ferruch nodded.

"And that's how they're going to spend the rest of their
lives, that's it? That's all they get out of it?''

"That's all they expect from it," el Ferruch said.

"Just when I think I'm beginning to understand things,''
Fulmar said, "I realize I don't understand anything.''

"The Koran says that is the beginning of wisdom.''

3
Washington, D.C.
December 31, 1941

It took Canidy and Baker nine days to travel from Kunming,
China, to Washington, D.C. And they had hardly been out

of each other's sight from the moment they had left Kunming. Even so, Canidy knew no more about what he was expected to do when they walked through Union Station in Washington than he had when he left Kunming. Baker knew how to keep his mouth shut. Nor did he give any hint that their final destination was Jimmy Whittaker's house on Q Street until their cab pulled up to the door in the brick wall.

"Under happier circumstances . . ." Canidy said.

He wondered what had happened to Jimmy. He'd heard that the Air Corps in the Philippines had been wiped out in the first few days after Pearl Harbor, and they'd handed the pilots rifles and told them they were now in the infantry.

The poor bastard.

Canidy recalled their last meeting together in Washington, when they had gotten drunk and Jimmy had told him that he was in love with Cynthia Chenowith—even though she was screwing his uncle.

When he climbed out of the cab after Baker, he saw that there were two policeman types sitting in a black Chevrolet parked at the curb. A third policeman in plainclothes walked up to them.

Baker took a leather folder from his jacket, opened it, and showed it to the cop. He examined Baker's face with a pencil flashlight.

"We didn't know when you were coming," the cop said.

"We just got here," Baker said.

The cop held the gate open for them to pass through.

Canidy wondered idly what had become of Cynthia now that Chesty Whittaker was dead and the house obviously under the control of Colonel Donovan. Obviously, she would no longer be living in the garage apartment.

A silver-haired black man Canidy did not recognize opened the door, greeted Baker by name, then led the way to the library.

"If you'll just wait here, gentlemen, someone will be with you in a minute."

The furnishings were unchanged, so Canidy decided it would be worth chancing that whiskey would still be kept where it formerly had been. He opened the antique credenza. And when Baker saw what he was doing, his eyes went up, but he said nothing. There was whiskey and several bottles of soda inside.

"Scotch and soda?" Canidy asked.

Baker nodded. Canidy made the drinks, then sat down in one of the leather-upholstered chairs by the fireplace.

Cynthia Chenowith came into the room a few minutes later. She was wearing a house robe, and sleep was in her eyes.

"Hello, Canidy," she said. "Welcome home. I see you found the whiskey."

"Hello, Cynthia," Canidy said. "How are you?"

He was really surprised to see her.

She gave him her hand. It was soft and warm, and her breasts moved unrestrained under the housecoat. She was a very good-looking female. It would be nice to get her out of that housecoat.

Jimmy has told me he loves her, he realized. *Only a prick would try to jump his best friend's lady love. Ergo, that makes me a genuine prick.*

He glanced at Baker and saw on his face that he, too, admired Cynthia Chenowith's unrestrained bosom and other physical charms.

"You don't seem very surprised to see me," she said.

"Nothing much surprises me anymore," Canidy said.

"We didn't know when you were coming," Cynthia said to Baker. "The last we heard was that you were in Lisbon."

"We?" Canidy asked. "Are you involved in whatever this is?"

"Mrs. Whittaker has turned the house over to the colonel for the duration," Cynthia said.

"That wasn't what I asked," Canidy said.

"I know it wasn't," she said. She looked at Baker. "Well, I expect you're tired. He's here. You can go home."

"Yeah, Eldon," Canidy said. "Take a walk. The lady and I want to be alone."

Neither Cynthia nor Baker seemed amused.

"Is the captain going to be available in the morning?" Baker asked.

"After nine," Cynthia said.

"I'll be here then," Baker said. "Is there a car?"

"Yes. You need a ride?"

"Please," he said.

"I think the driver's in the kitchen," Cynthia said.

"Then I will head for home," Baker said. "Good night, Canidy. Good night, Cynthia."

"Good night, good night," Canidy said cheerfully. "Finally parting with you, Eldon, is such sweet sorrow."

"He's yours, Cynthia," Baker said, ignoring him.

"Entirely," Canidy said. "Heart and soul."

"Oh, shut up, Dick," she said, but didn't quite manage to suppress a smile.

"I was sorry to hear about Mr. Whittaker," Canidy said after he was sure Baker was out of hearing.

"It was a stroke. The day the war started."

"I know how much he meant to you," Canidy said.

"What do you mean by that?" she asked.

"Just the way it sounded," he said. "Has there been any word about Jimmy?"

"Not a word," she said. "Except a letter he wrote to his aunt a week or so before the war started."

She seemed genuinely concerned.

"What's going on around here?" Canidy asked.

"I suppose you'll have the chance to ask about that tomorrow," she said.

"And what's your role in all this?"

"Can I get you something?" she asked, ignoring the question. "Something to eat?"

"I ate a sandwich on the train," he said. "I asked, what's your role in all this?"

"I knew you were probably going to be difficult," she said. "Can't it wait until morning, Dick?"

"And if I said no, you would say 'It'll have to,' right?"

"Yes." She grinned. "Now, is there anything I can get you? Or can I take you to your room?"

"Is there a phone in my room?"

"Why?"

"I want to call my father," he said.

"You're not supposed to do that," she said. Then she saw the look on his face and quickly went on. "You're under certain restrictions here, Dick. They'll be explained to you in detail in the morning. Until they are, you aren't supposed to use the telephone or mail letters. . . ."

"For Christ's sake!" Canidy fumed. "That's absurd!"

"That's the way it is," she said. "I'm sorry."

He started toward the library door. "Nice to have seen you again, Cynthia," he said.

"And you're restricted to the property," she said. "You can't leave."

He stopped. "Those cops, you mean?"

"Dick, I can get you an outside line to call your father," she said. "Provided you don't tell him you're here. Just to say hello, that's all. And I'll have to listen. If you say anything you shouldn't, I'll cut you off."

He looked at her, then turned and came closer to her.

"All I want to do is let him know I'm in the States," he said. "Can I do that?"

"Sure," she said. "Give me a minute to place the call; then pick up the extension in here. You have the number?"

"Sure."

"OK, wait sixty seconds, then pick up," she said, and walked out of the library.

When he picked up the telephone, his father was on the line.

He told him he was back in the United States and safe. But he had no idea when he could get a leave to come home.

"The FBI has been to see me," his father said. "They were asking all sorts of questions about you and Eric Fulmar. Do you have any idea what that was all about?"

"No, Dad," Canidy said. "Maybe they think he's a spy in Morocco."

"I assured them that there was no question of his patriotism or character," the Reverend Dr. Canidy said.

After Dick said good-bye to his father, Cynthia reappeared at the library door.

"Come on," she said. "I'll show you to your room."

He followed her upstairs.

At the door to a room across from the master bedroom, she touched his arm.

"Dick, I'm really glad you came through China in one piece," she said. And then she surprised him by quickly kissing him on the cheek. "Good night," she said. "Happy New Year."

The kiss meant two things: She liked him. And she was not going to screw him. He had been kissed that way before.

4
Washington, D.C.
January 1, 1942

A hand stabbing his shoulder woke Canidy and a ruddy-faced chief boatswain's mate stood over him, a cup of coffee in his hand.

"Good morning, Mr. Canidy," he said. "I'm Chief Ellis. I figured you could use this. As soon as you can make it, they're waiting for you."

"Thank you," Canidy said. He looked at his watch. It was nine o'clock. "Who's 'they'?"

"The captain, Mr. Baker, Miss Chenowith," Ellis said.

"You're a long way from the briny deep, Chief," Canidy said.

"Yeah." Ellis smiled. "Ain't we?"

Five minutes later, Canidy followed Ellis into the dining room. Cynthia Chenowith was in a sweater and skirt that reminded him painfully of her platonic kiss. Doug Douglass's father was in uniform, and Baker wore a business suit.

"Welcome home," Douglass said, shaking Canidy's hand with a strong grip. "I'm Captain Peter Douglass."

"How do you do?" Canidy said.

Douglass pushed a box across the table to him.

"That's yours," he said. "You left it behind. Doug sent it to me."

Canidy opened the box. It was his Order of the Cloud Banner.

"I'm sorry that had to go the way it did," Douglass said. "But Baker was right. It kept a lot of questions from being asked. Anyhow"—he looked at Canidy—"I thought you might want to send that to your father."

A thin black woman appeared and laid ham and eggs in front of Canidy.

"I took the liberty of ordering for you," Douglass said. "We've already eaten."

"Fine," Canidy said.

"Can you eat and read?" Douglass said. "It would save time."

"Yes, sir."

"Give him Hansen's report, Ellis," Douglass ordered.

Hansen's report came in a manila folder, stamped SECRET. Canidy opened it and found several sheets of paper.

SECRET

INTERNAL MEMORANDUM

DATE: 16 DECEMBER 1941
FROM: P. D. HANSEN
TO: E. C. BAKER
SUBJ: FULMAR, ERIC

THE FOLLOWING ADDITIONAL INFORMATION HAS BEEN DEVELOPED CONCERNING SUBJECT FULMAR. (SOURCE INDICATED.)

(1) (FROM POSTAL INSPECTION SERVICE):
SUBJECT HAS BEEN IN REGULAR CORRESPONDENCE WITH REV. GEORGE CRATER CANIDY, D.D., HEADMASTER ST. PAUL'S SCHOOL, CEDAR RAPIDS, IOWA.

(2) (FROM FBI):
1. REV. CANIDY HIGHLY RESPECTED CLERGYMAN/EDUCATOR (EPISCOPALIAN) WITH NO KNOWN AXIS SYMPATHIES.

2. FBI INTERVIEW WITH REV. CANIDY PRODUCED THE FOLLOWING:

   (a) SUBJECT SPENT SIX (6) YEARS AS BOARDING STUDENT AT ST. PAUL'S SCHOOL, AND HIS CLOSE PERSONAL RELATIONSHIP WITH REV. CANIDY DATES FROM THAT PERIOD.

(b) REV. CANIDY BELIEVES IT IMPOSSIBLE THAT
SUBJECT COULD BE GERMAN SYMPATHIZER.

(c) REV. CANIDY STATES THAT SUBJECT'S CLOS-
EST FRIEND WAS CANIDY'S SON, RICHARD CANIDY
(SEE ONI INFORMATION FOLLOWING) WHO WAS AT ST.
PAUL'S SCHOOL WITH SUBJECT AND LATER WITH
SUBJECT AT ST. MARK'S SCHOOL, SOUTHBORO, MASS.
(3) (FROM FBI):

3. FBI INTERVIEW WITH VARIOUS FACULTY MEMBERS,
ST. MARK'S SCHOOL, PRODUCED THE FOLLOWING:

(a) SUBJECT ATTENDED ST. MARK'S SCHOOL FOR
TWO YEARS. SUBJECT WAS ORDINARY STUDENT, WITH
NO OUTSTANDING ACADEMIC OR DISCIPLINARY PROB-
LEMS.

(b) SUBJECT WAS WITHDRAWN FROM SCHOOL INTO
CUSTODY OF STANLEY S. FINE (SEE FBI INFORMATION
FOLLOWING). SUBJECT'S ACADEMIC RECORDS WERE
SUBSEQUENTLY REQUESTED BY AND FURNISHED TO DIE
SCHULE AM ROSENBERG, IN SWITZERLAND.

(c) SUBJECT'S CLOSEST FRIENDS AT SCHOOL WERE
RICHARD CANIDY AND JAMES M. C. WHITTAKER.
(SEE WD G-2 INFORMATION FOLLOWING.)

4. SUBJECT'S MOTHER, MOTION-PICTURE ACTRESS
MONICA CARLISLE (B. MARY ELIZABETH CHER-
NICK), REFUSED FBI INTERVIEW ON ADVICE OF COUN-
SEL.

5. FBI INTERVIEW WITH STANLEY S. FINE, VICE-
PRESIDENT, LEGAL CONTINENTAL STUDIOS, PRODUCED
THE FOLLOWING:

(a) FINE IS HIGHLY REGARDED ATTORNEY AND BUSI-
NESS EXECUTIVE WITH KNOWN ANTI-GERMAN SYMPA-
THIES.

(b) FINE STATED THAT FOR BUSINESS CONSIDERA-
TIONS, CARLISLE/CHERNICK DID NOT WISH THE EX-
ISTENCE OF A SON KNOWN PUBLICLY. FINE STATED HE
HAD HANDLED BOARDING SCHOOL AND SUMMER CAMP
AND OTHER ARRANGEMENTS DESIGNED TO KEEP SUB-

JECT OUT OF PUBLIC NOTICE UNTIL 1933, WHEN, OVER
HIS OBJECTIONS, CARLISLE/CHERNICK AGREED TO
HAVE SUBJECT EDUCATED AT HIS FATHER'S EXPENSE
IN SWITZERLAND.

(c) FINE STATED HE BELIEVES CARLISLE/CHER-
NICK HAS HAD NO CONTACT WITH SUBJECT SUBSE-
QUENT TO APPROXIMATELY 1937. FINE MAINTAINED
SOCIAL CONTACT WITH SUBJECT UNTIL 1940.

(4) (FROM OFFICE OF NAVAL INTELLIGENCE):
RICHARD CANIDY COMMISSIONED ENSIGN USNR ON
GRADUATION (A.E.) FROM MASS. INSTITUTE OF TECH-
NOLOGY 1938. DESIGNATED NAVAL AVIATOR, PENSA-
COLA, FLA., MAR. 1939. ASSIGNED NAS PENSACOLA
PRIMARILY AS INSTRUCTOR PILOT. PROMOTED LIEUTEN-
ANT (JG) JUNE 1940. CANIDY HON. DISCH. (CONVE-
NIENCE OF GOVT.) JUNE 1941 TO ACCEPT ONE-YEAR
EMPLOYMENT CONTRACT WITH AMERICAN VOLUNTEER
GROUP, CHINA. CANIDY BELIEVED TO BE IN KUNMING,
CHINA.

(5) (FROM G-2, WAR DEPARTMENT):
JAMES M. C. WHITTAKER COMMISSIONED SECOND
LIEUTENANT ARTILLERY ON GRADUATION (B.A.) FROM
HARVARD COLLEGE 1938. TRANSFERRED ARMY AIR
CORPS. DESIGNATED PILOT RANDOLPH FIELD, TEXAS,
1940. TRANSFERRED USAAC IN PHILIPPINE COMMON-
WEALTH. PRESENT WHEREABOUTS UNKNOWN. WHITTA-
KER'S RECORDS INDICATE CONSIDERABLE POLITICAL
INFLUENCE. KNOWN TO BE SOCIALLY ACQUAINTED WITH
THE PRESIDENT.

(6) (FROM TREASURY DEPARTMENT):
(a) SUBJECT CAME TO TREASURY DEPARTMENT AT-
TENTION FOLLOWING REPORT BY FIRST NATIONAL CITY
BANK OF NEW YORK THAT SUBJECT TRANSFERRED
TO SMALL, DORMANT ACCOUNT AMOUNT OF $21,545
FROM FIRST NATIONAL CITY BANK BRANCH IN BUENOS
AIRES, ARGENTINA. SIX (6) SUBSEQUENT TRANSFERS
FROM FNCB BUENOS AIRES, TOTALING

$111,405, HAVE BEEN MADE, THE MOST RECENT NO-
VEMBER 12, 1941.

(b) PRIOR TO DEC. 12, 1941, WHEN UNLICENSED
FOREIGN TRANSFER OF U.S. DOLLAR FUNDS WAS PRO-
SCRIBED BY PRESIDENTIAL ORDER, SUBJECT DREW
NINE (9) TIMES UPON THESE FUNDS AT THE FNCB
BRANCH IN CASABLANCA, MOROCCO, FOR A TOTAL OF
$6,500.

(c) IRS RECORDS SHOW SUBJECT HAS NEVER FILED
PERSONAL INCOME TAX RETURNS.

(d) IF SUBJECT CLAIMS GERMAN CITIZENSHIP, HIS
FNCB ACCOUNT IS SUBJECT TO IMPOUNDMENT UNDER
THE ENEMY ALIEN PROPERTY ACT, AS AMENDED. IF
SUBJECT CLAIMS AMERICAN CITIZENSHIP, HE IS IN VI-
OLATION OF THE IRS CODE, AND THE FNCB ACCOUNT
LIABLE TO SEIZURE FOR NONPAYMENT OF APPLICABLE
TAXES, PLUS PENALTY.

(7) PSYCHOLOGICAL PROFILE (HOMER HUNGERFORD,
M.D., CHIEF OF PSYCHIATRIC SERVICES, GEORGETOWN
MEDICAL CENTER [AND OTHER]):

"BASED ON THE INFORMATION MADE AVAILABLE IT IS
NOT OF COURSE POSSIBLE TO PREPARE A THOROUGH
EVALUATION, MUCH LESS A PROFILE, BUT SEVERAL
THINGS SEEM PROBABLE, AND WHAT FOLLOWS IS THE
CONSENSUS OF THOSE CONSULTED.

PATIENT WOULD INESCAPABLY HAVE EXPERIENCED
REJECTION AS THE RESULT OF HIS FATHERLESS CHILD-
HOOD, AND THESE FEELINGS WOULD HAVE BEEN EXAC-
ERBATED BY THE EXTRAORDINARY REJECTION
BEHAVIOR OF PATIENT'S MOTHER. PATIENT HAS AP-
PARENTLY TRANSFERRED (JUDGING BY LETTERS SEEK-
ING APPROVAL) PARENTAL FEELINGS TO THE REV. DR.
CANIDY, AND PATIENT STILL APPARENTLY FEELS A
STRONG SIBLING BOND WITH CANIDY AND WHITTA-
KER. (IN OTHER WORDS, HAVING BEEN DEPRIVED OF A
FAMILY, PATIENT HAS FORMED HIS OWN FROM THOSE
PERSONS WHO HAVE BEEN CLOSE TO HIM.)

PATIENT, WHOSE ACADEMIC RECORDS INDICATE HIGH INTELLIGENCE, HAS NECESSARILY DEVELOPED SELF-RELIANCE TO AN UNUSUAL DEGREE. THIS WOULD LIKELY MANIFEST ITSELF THROUGH DISTRUST OF THOSE WHO HAVE NOT PROVEN THEIR TRUSTWORTHINESS; A HIGH LEVEL OF DETERMINATION; A RELUCTANCE TO SEEK, OR HEED, ADVICE FROM OTHERS; AND A LACK OF CONCERN FOR THE APPROVAL OR DISAPPROVAL OF HIS PEER GROUP.

PATIENT IS PROBABLY VERY STABLE, ANY INSTABILITY HAVING BEEN RESOLVED IN PATIENT'S FORMATIVE (IMMEDIATE PRE- AND POSTPUBERTY) PERIOD. IT IS IMPORTANT TO NOTE HERE THAT THIS STABILITY WILL PROBABLY TEND TO MAKE PATIENT IMMUNE TO MOST NORMAL SOCIAL PRESSURES, AND DISRESPECTFUL OF NORMAL AUTHORITY FIGURES. PATIENT'S PSYCHOLOGICAL MAKEUP IS PROBABLY FIRMLY ESTABLISHED, AND PROBABLY RELATIVELY IMMUNE TO CHANGE. IF, HOWEVER, THERE WERE TO BE A FURTHER PROFOUND EMOTIONAL TRAUMA (FOR EXAMPLE, IF ONE OF HIS "FAMILY" BETRAYED HIM), THERE WOULD PROBABLY BE SOME PSYCHOLOGICAL DIFFICULTY."

(8) COMMENTS:

INASMUCH AS SUBJECT HAS BEEN ABROAD FOR SO LONG AND UNDER THE CIRCUMSTANCES DESCRIBED HEREIN, IT IS BELIEVED LIKELY THAT HE WILL CONTINUE TO REFUSE OVERTURES FROM OFFICIAL REPRESENTATIVES OF THE U.S. GOVERNMENT.

TWO (CANIDY, RICHARD; WHITTAKER, JAMES M.C.) OF THE THREE INDIVIDUALS WHO MIGHT BE ABLE TO APPEAL TO HIM ON PERSONAL GROUNDS ARE OBVIOUSLY UNAVAILABLE. FINE IS NOT CONNECTED WITH THE GOVERNMENT.

SHOULD IT BE DECIDED ADVANTAGEOUS TO ESTABLISH A WORKING RELATIONSHIP WITH SUBJECT, HIS FNCB FUNDS MAY PROVE USEFUL. THEY ARE MOST LIKELY SUBJECT'S PROCEEDS FROM HIS ACTIVITIES IN MOVING

CASH AND NEGOTIABLES, IN CONCERN WITH HIS FRIEND
SIDI EL FERRUCH (A MOROCCAN NOBLEMAN), FROM
OCCUPIED FRANCE, AND ARE HIS ONLY ASSETS.
INASMUCH AS THE DEATH PENALTY HAS BEEN PRE-
SCRIBED FOR ILLEGAL TRANSFERS OF MONIES AND VALU-
ABLES, AND INASMUCH AS SUBJECT WAS SO ENGAGED
WITH SIDI EL FERRUCH, IT CAN THEREFORE BE LOGI-
CALLY PRESUMED THAT SUBJECT ENJOYS TRUST AND
CONFIDENCE OF EL FERRUCH, AND WOULD HAVE A
CORRESPONDING DEGREE OF INFLUENCE WITH HIM.

                                            HANSEN
                SECRET

"If I thought I could get an answer," Canidy said, "I'd
ask, why all the interest in Eric Fulmar?"

Douglass didn't reply directly. "Fulmar is so important
that a radio over General Marshall's signature was sent to
the Philippines ordering Lieutenant Whittaker home at the
first opportunity. There has been no reply."

"Meaning what? That he's dead?" Canidy asked.

"That he can't be located, or that Douglas MacArthur is
once again expressing his contempt for George Marshall—
or for the President," Douglass said. "The point is that
you're the only person we have we feel can deal with Fulmar."

"Deal with him how?"

Again, Douglass avoided a direct response. "Baker tells
me that in China he put it to you that we're asking you to
volunteer for a mission of great importance to the war effort
and that the mission involves a considerable risk. If you
don't mind, I'd like to put the same question to you now,
Canidy."

"Baker wouldn't tell me what this mission is all about,"
Canidy said. "Will you?"

"The question you were asked," Douglass said, "is whether or not you are willing to go into it under the conditions outlined."

"What are my options?" Canidy said. "What if I say no?"

"Yes or no, Canidy."

He's acting like a character in a bad spy movie, Canidy thought. *In every dangerous-mission thriller I have ever seen, there was a scene where the commanding officer gave the hero one last chance to change his mind: "Are you sure you want to go through with this?" The hero always wanted to go through with it. That doesn't mean I will have to go through with it. I know how to say, "I quit."*

"OK," Canidy said.

"All right," Captain Douglass said. "Thank you. But you mentioned options a moment ago. I think I should tell you that if you had declined the offer, you would have been sent to some very secure psychiatric institution for examination. That examination would take a very long time. In the Civil War, Lincoln suspended the rules of habeas corpus. President Roosevelt isn't going to do that. The attorney general has told him that under existing law, persons suspected of being non compos mentis don't fall under the rule of habeas corpus. They are being *examined,* not incarcerated."

Canidy and Douglass locked eyes for a long moment.

"Canidy," Douglass said, "if I could tell you what's behind all this, that threat would not have been necessary. But I can't tell you, and it was."

He's dead serious, Canidy thought. *Maybe truth really is stranger than fiction.*

"Yes, sir," he said.

"There is a Frenchman now in Morocco," Douglass began, "whom we absolutely have to bring to the United States. It is critically important that when we bring him out, the Germans will not connect his disappearance with us. Otherwise they would doubtless realize *why* we want him. What we desperately hope they will believe is that he escaped by his own means to join General de Gaulle in London.''

''And you want Fulmar to smuggle him out,'' Canidy said. ''And think I can talk him into it.''

''Not exactly,'' Douglass said. ''Not him alone. For reasons we can't get into, we want Sidi Hassan el Ferruch involved as well.''

''Why?''

''We have other plans for him later,'' Douglass said. ''The best possible scenario is that you meet Fulmar, he greets you as a beloved friend, and he instantly agrees to persuade el Ferruch to help you. Mr. Baker does not believe that. He thinks the worst possible scenario is more probable. In that Fulmar would denounce you to the Germans.''

''Why do you think he would do that?''

''Despite your father's character reference, it is Baker's belief that Eric Fulmar's loyalties are solely to Eric Fulmar.''

''I've seen him since you have, Dick,'' Baker said. ''You have to keep in mind that he was educated in Germany and is in many ways German. When I first met him, he was having dinner in Fouquet's restaurant in Paris with the daughter of a German major general. His father is a member of the Nazi party.''

''He's an American,'' Canidy said loyally.

''We're taking what solace we can from his skillful avoidance of German military service,'' Baker said. ''It's not much. You saw that psychological profile.''

''It also said he thinks of me as a brother,'' Canidy said.

''Furthermore,'' Douglass said, ''el Ferruch is an unknown quantity. We have to go on the presumption that el

Ferruch is even more likely to turn you over to the Germans.''

"There are several other scenarios," Baker said. "One is that we establish contact with Fulmar, he tells us he wants nothing to do with us at all, no matter what the price, but, because you are old friends, he won't turn you over to the Germans."

"Pleasant thought," Canidy said. "So where is good old Eric?"

"We found out a few days ago," Douglass said, "that he's in the palace at Ksar es Souk in the middle of the desert. Which gives us the opening for one of the happy scenarios."

"What's that?"

"We get you to Ksar es Souk," Baker said. "We offer Fulmar and el Ferruch a lot of money to grab the Frenchman—and Fulmar a way out of Morocco."

" 'Grab' the Frenchman?" Canidy asked.

"That's another little problem," Baker said. "Our information is that the Frenchman desperately desires to return to his family. Thus he works for Vichy and the Germans in the hope they'll give him permission to return to France. Likewise, because he's concerned about reprisals against his family in France, it's extremely unlikely that he will leave Morocco voluntarily."

"You mean, we kidnap him," Canidy said. Baker nodded. "Then what happens to his family?"

Baker shrugged.

"Jesus!" Canidy said, repelled by what he took to be unconcern.

"Which is another reason we need the cooperation of el Ferruch," Douglass said.

Canidy looked at him, eyes flaring.

"It's not that we don't care about that sort of thing," Douglass said.

"Of course not," Canidy said. "But whatever you need this guy for is more important, right?"

"Yes, it is," Douglass said.

"How do you propose to get this man and Fulmar out of Morocco—presuming that 'happy scenario' comes true?" Canidy asked.

Baker looked at Douglass for permission to reply. Douglass shook his head no.

"We don't think you should know that yet," Douglass said.

"How am I supposed to see Fulmar? Or, for that matter, enter Morocco?" Canidy asked.

"That at least is fairly simple," Baker said. "We're going to send you to the consulate in Rabat as a foreign service officer. Cynthia will arrange for you to be issued a diplomatic passport, and we'll run you through a quick program to show you how to behave, that sort of thing."

"She wouldn't tell me last night," Canidy said, "how she fits in this."

Cynthia looked at Douglass for permission. This time he gave it.

"You'll be an agent in this operation," Cynthia said. "Every agent has a handler. I'm your handler."

"How are you going to 'handle' me?" Canidy asked.

"Take care of your pay, your travel, your training, your briefings, your last will and testament, do whatever I can to get you where you're going as quickly as possible. In other words, be responsible for you."

"You're too young to be my mother," Canidy said. "And too pretty."

"I know, Dick, I know," Cynthia said. "But I'll just have to do."

"Actually, I could do a lot worse," Canidy said, meaning it. "Meanwhile"—he switched his attention to Baker—"where are you going to be while I'm running around in the desert looking for Fulmar?"

"Mr. Baker is leaving tomorrow for Rabat," Douglass said. "He will be there when you arrive. As soon as we can make it through the bureaucratic niceties and your briefings, you'll go to Rabat."

"Via Lisbon and Vichy," Baker said. "An ordinary junior foreign service officer would spend a week being briefed at the embassy in Vichy before moving on to a consulate general assignment. If you didn't do that there would be questions. You do understand, don't you, that since Morocco is still a French protectorate, our consulate general there reports to our ambassador to France."

"No," Canidy said.

"We'll get into that in the briefings, Dick," Cynthia said. "There's a lot of material we have to give you."

"Chief Ellis will stick with you through all of this," Douglass said. "I'm sure you'll find him helpful. He's an old sailor."

"He makes a pretty good guard, doesn't he?" Canidy asked.

Douglass met his eyes.

"Yes," he said. "That too."

5
Kunming, China
18 January 1942

The sixteen B5M Mitsubishis the ground spotters reported en route to Kunming turned out to be, when Ed Bitter and

his wingman found them, eight B5Ms and eight K1-27 Nakajima fighters.

"What the hell are they?" Bitter's wingman asked.

"Nakajima K1-27s," Bitter reported excitedly. "Get the
hell back to Kunming."

It was the AVG's first encounter with the K1-27s. They
had been told that their P40-Bs were superior in several
important ways, but that was theory. He was about to test
that theory.

Bitter waited until his wingman was nearly out of sight
before he pushed the nose down to attack formation. He
wondered if that was prudent. It was insane for one man to
attack a formation of sixteen aircraft, eight of them fighters.

He got a B5M on his first pass. He had put several .50-
caliber tracers into the fuel tanks in the left wing, and the
tanks had blown up. He just had time to consider, as he
pulled away from the formation in a steep dive, that it was
his third kill, when he looked over his shoulder. There were
three K1-27s on his tail.

He had no trouble pulling away from two of them in the
obviously faster P40-B, but the third, obviously a first-class
pilot, kept turning inside Bitter's turns, and once when Bitter
looked over his shoulder he was chilled by little red bursts
coming from the Jap's wing guns.

He put the P40-B into a steep dive, dropping from seven
thousand feet almost to the ground. When he saw the Nakajima was still on his tail, farther back than he expected,
he knew that he could get away with what he planned. He
pulled back on his stick, feeling the g forces force his body
down in the seat. The world turned red and then nearly black
as the blood drained from his head, and he prayed he
wouldn't black out.

He remained conscious enough to feel the life of the stick,
and when his vision cleared, he was through the loop and

the Nakajima was ahead of him, falling out of a loop he had tried to make inside Bitter's, which he now realized he could not complete in time. He went through the fall and tried to dive to safety.

Bitter caught up with him, got on his tail, and opened fire. He saw the .50 tracers pass the Nakajima, and reminded himself that for every tracer there were four armor-piercing ball projectiles. He was certainly getting his fire in the Nakajima, but there was no sign of it. The guns stopped, first the .50s and then the .30s. He was now, except for speed, defenseless. He looked over his shoulder. The other two Japanese fighters, the ones he had lost, were now diving on him. He banked sharply to the left. In the last second he had the first Nakajima in sight; it burst into a ball of orange flame and disappeared.

He headed for Kunming, the P40-B's throttle lever past the takeoff indent, as far as it would go, into full emergency military power. The Nakajimas on his tail fell farther and farther behind, and finally, convinced they had chased him off, broke off and started back to the bombers they had been sent to protect.

He had, he realized, shot down his third and fourth enemy aircraft, one of them a fighter. But then he had a follow-on, an unpleasant thought. As soon as it worked its way through the Japanese command structure that the Nakajima K1-27s were no match for the Curtiss P40-Bs of the American Volunteer Group, the Japanese high command would send in something better. The destruction of the AVG was at least as important as the bombing of China. They would send the best aircraft they had to win that battle. The AVG was already playing its ace, and there was no hole card.

He realized he was far more frightened of that prospect than he had been when the K1-27 was on his tail.

Ed Bitter got drunk that night and, for the first time, took an interpreter to his quarters.

Right after Canidy had been sent home in disgrace, Doug Douglass had been given command of the squadron. Douglass had not, however, moved into the suite of rooms that were now his by right of command, but stayed where he was. Bitter realized when he saw the light under Douglass's door that he had not changed his nightly habits. Since assuming command, he had rarely gone to the bar, and when he did, hadn't taken liquor. Nor did he drink in his room.

It was therefore meet, right, and just, Ed Bitter decided, to annoy the sober sonofabitch. Bitter staggered into Douglass's room with the girl under his arm.

Douglass was alone in his bed, writing on a clipboard propped against his knees.

"Why, Romeo, Romeo," Douglass mocked him when he saw the giggling interpreter. "Wherefore goeth thou, Romeo?"

"If I can get a straight answer out of you," Bitter said, carefully pronouncing each syllable, "I would like a straight answer to a straight question."

He realized that he couldn't think of a question, but that didn't seem to be important.

"Both of your kills were confirmed," Douglass said. "That makes four, right?"

"That's not what I'm talking about," Bitter said. He was just sober enough to see that Douglass was smiling at his condition, which annoyed him. "I said, I wanted to ask you a straight question . . ."

"Generally speaking," Douglass said, smiling, "the best technique for beginners is if the lady gets on her back and spreads her—"

"Goddamn you, I'm serious."

"Ask away," Douglass replied. He laid down the clipboard he had been holding. Bitter saw that he was writing a letter.

"Why did Canidy turn yellow?" Bitter asked.

He was surprised to hear those words.

"I thought we had agreed not to talk about him," Douglass said.

"I want to know why, goddamn it!"

"I don't know, Ed," Douglass said.

"You were with him, goddamn it!"

"What brought this up all of a sudden?" Douglass asked.

"Because I was scared out there today."

"You're afraid it might get the best of you?"

"Yeah, maybe," Bitter said.

"Well, you're not alone," Douglass said. "If that makes you feel any better."

"Is that what happened? It got the better of Canidy?"

"I don't know, Eddie," Douglass said. "Probably."

"But he was my friend," Bitter said.

"For what it's worth," Douglass said, "he's still my friend."

"He's a fucking coward, goddamn it!" Bitter said righteously, and then quickly walked out of Douglass's room.

As he walked down the corridor, he realized he was crying. The Chinese girl looked at him, half concerned, half frightened.

ELEVEN

1
**The Consulate General
of the United States
Rabat, Morocco
February 20, 1942**

In the briefing he had received from Cynthia Chenowith in
Washington, and later in Vichy at the hands of a mousy,
schoolteacherish foreign service officer in the U.S. embassy,
Canidy learned about the Alice in Wonderland diplomatic
situation in France and in the French protectorate in Morocco.

Though the United States was at war with Germany, neither the United States nor Germany was now at war with
France. That country, following the signing of the armistice
agreement with the Germans at Compiègne, was legally neutral. Consequently, the United States maintained an embassy
at the French seat of government at Vichy and consulates
and consulates general throughout the French colonial em-
pire. The embassy in Paris stood empty, because that part
of France was occupied by the Germans.

Vichy, a small town whose prewar fame was solely due
to the mineral water bottled there, was now the capital of
"unoccupied" France. In Vichy, and cities such as Rabat,

where there were embassies and consulates general, American diplomats daily encountered their German, Japanese, and Italian enemies on the street and at cocktail parties and dinners. Each side generally pretended the other was invisible.

In 1942 the French, as a general rule of thumb, were far more impressed with the Germans who had so soundly defeated them than they were with the Americans and their allies, who seemed then far from likely to do to the Germans what the Germans had done to the French. The only organized resistance to the new Franco-German relationship was a tall, rather ungainly, but nonetheless regal French brigadier general, Charles de Gaulle, who had escaped to London just before France capitulated. There, solely on his own authority, he had proclaimed himself leader of the Free French. The Free French consisted of the handful of French military who had managed to make it to England.

Canidy was told that no one in Morocco paid very much attention to the Free French or Brigadier General Charles de Gaulle. It was indeed believed that his activities in England made things awkward for his brother officers who had obeyed their orders—the orders of Marshal Pétain himself— to accept defeat and cooperate in implementing the new relationship with Germany.

In Morocco, the training officer in Vichy told him, French neutrality was of necessity tilted toward Berlin, but the French were a civilized people, and their attitude toward the Americans in Morocco was always correct and sometimes even friendly.

Canidy traveled by train from Vichy to Marseilles, and then by ship—brilliantly floodlit at night to show the French tricolor painted on its sides—from Marseilles to Casablanca. His diplomatic passport quickly passed him and his luggage through customs control, and the consulate general had sent a Ford to meet the ship.

At the consulate proper, he was met by an assistant consul, who welcomed him warmly and marched him around introducing him as the newest member of the team.

Later he was introduced to Eldon C. Baker, the vice consul for visas and passports. Baker acted as if he had never seen Canidy before.

"I believe," the assistant consul told Eldon Baker, "that Mr. Dale has spoken to you about Mr. Canidy?" Mr. Dale was the deputy consul general.

"Oh yes, indeed," Baker said, with no enthusiasm whatever, "Mr. Dale asked me to offer to let Mr. Canidy share my apartment . . . *temporarily,*" he added significantly. "Naturally, I'm happy to do that."

Canidy accepted.

"And I suppose you'll need a ride, too, won't you, until you can get a car?"

"Yes, I'm afraid I will," Canidy said.

"Meet me here at five o'clock," Baker said with a limp handshake.

The apartment was downtown, not far from the royal palace.

"Everybody else in the building is in communications," Baker said when he'd closed the door after them. "Which means that people are used to seeing people coming and going in the middle of the night.

"So far as I can find out," Baker said, "Fulmar is still in Ksar es Souk. The information came via the military attaché, Major Berry. Since, however, Major Berry is an ass, that doesn't mean it's reliable. Still, I think we have to go with what we've got, and what we've got is that Fulmar's at Ksar es Souk."

"How far is that from here?" Canidy asked.

"They didn't brief you?" Baker asked, annoyed.

"I know where it is on the map," Canidy said. "But not how to get there, or how long it will take."

Baker took a *Guide Michelin* road map from a desk drawer and spread it out on the desk.

"It's been said that the only thing the French have done right is the *Guide Michelin,*" Baker said. He pointed. "Here we are, and there's Ksar es Souk. Do you read French?"

Canidy shook his head.

"What that says," Baker said, pointing to an explanation of symbols box, "is that the road from Ouarzazate to Ksar es Souk is 'dirt, single lane, unpassable after rain.' "

"Great. Does it rain in the desert? I have visions of sand dunes."

"This is just arid soil. No sand dunes. They're farther south. And, yes, every once in a while it rains in this desert."

"Where is this Frenchman we're looking for?" Canidy asked, looking up from the map.

Baker hesitated just a moment before replying.

"Here," he said. "Between Benahmed and Oued-Zem. He works in the phosphate mines. His name is Grunier. Louis Albert Grunier."

Baker went in the drawer again and came out with half a dozen snapshots. They showed a not very good-looking man in round spectacles. Though only about thirty, he was already balding.

"These were taken a little over two years ago," Baker said, "in the Belgian Congo. By now, he's lost some more hair, and he's a little thinner."

"What was he doing in the Belgian Congo?"

"He's a mining engineer," Baker said.

"And we want to know what he's doing, is that it?"

"You don't need to know why we want him."

"OK." Canidy shrugged theatrically. "I'm not at all curious."

"That's the *right* attitude, Dick," Baker said, with the barest hint of a smile.

"So what am I supposed to do besides be agreeable and smile at my long-lost friend?"

Baker caught Canidy's eyes. "Rather a lot more than that." Canidy raised his brow. "There are a few more pieces to what we're up to in Morocco than you've learned yet. First, you already know that we have to act with a bit more subtlety here than Americans are used to. We're not—shall we say?—totally welcome. On top of that you know that it is crucial for us to conceal from the French and the Germans our connection with the sudden disappearance of Monsieur Grunier. Which is why we need to approach Sidi el Ferruch. He has the facilities to do for us what we can't do for ourselves. On top of that, I don't want to *need* to trust him with the knowledge of the value Grunier has to us. That knowledge is a tempting and quite salable morsel. Next, we have another piece of knowledge which, on the surface, is even more tempting and salable. This morsel we intend to entrust to el Ferruch."

"What is that?"

"The commander of the French naval base at Casablanca is an ancient, salty, irascible vice admiral d'escadre, whose name is Jean-Phillip de Verbey. Some people say he's daffy. De Verbey has sent delicate feelers to us hinting that he would be willing 'temporarily' to leave his command in order to join the Free French in their battle against *les Boches*. These feelers reached Robert Murphy and then me. Neither of us failed to notice that de Verbey outranks Brigadier General de Gaulle and that thus he and not de Gaulle would by rights—according to protocol—assume command of Free

French forces. De Gaulle is not popular in London and Washington. . . . Is this making sense?''

"A little. What you're saying, I gather, is that in Morocco and France de Verbey is a big fish and Grunier is a little fish. But that as far as you're concerned, you need Grunier more. Still, de Verbey is a lever against de Gaulle.''

"Right.''

"So, in other words, de Verbey can be used as a smoke screen.''

"Doubly right. You're catching on. We'll take de Verbey aboard the submarine with the maximum publicity that secrecy allows, and we'll also find room in the sub for poor Monsieur Grunier, who is an agent of ours who has had the bad luck to be compromised. Luckily for him, we have gone to the trouble of providing the sub for the admiral.''

"Fucking devious. Why?''

"Well, to keep the devious and very bright pasha of Ksar es Souk off the scent. And also, to do the same for the French and the Germans, should they get wind of what we're doing. And so we'll approach el Ferruch with a request that we'd love for him to transport the admiral in great secrecy to our submarine, which will be waiting a few miles west of Safi. We'll haggle about how much his cooperation is worth. And we'll agree to a figure in the neighborhood of a hundred thousand dollars.''

"And Grunier?''

"That's where you and your vagrant friend Eric come in. While el Ferruch is taking care of the admiral, you and Fulmar will snatch Grunier.''

"Delightful.''

"I thought you'd be pleased.''

"What's in it for Eric?''

"He can go home and he can keep his money,'' Baker said, smiling. It was not a smile that made Canidy comfortable. "And there's one more piece to this business that you should know about," Baker went on. "Monsieur Grunier would much prefer to go home to his wife and kids than help us with the war effort. And he—rightly—fears that they are at risk if he does not play ball with the Germans. As a consequence, we are going to have to help him out with his family."

"OK, so when do we start?"

"Tomorrow."

2

The blue 1941 Ford four-door Baker took from the consulate motor pool the next day carried two extra tires and wheels, four five-gallon cans of gasoline, a five-gallon can of water, and a crate of canned food.

"That survival equipment isn't really necessary?" Canidy asked.

"It may be," Baker said, with one of his rare smiles. "I've been here before. My experience is that when Michelin says 'dirt, single-lane road' it's a euphemism for 'rocky camel trail.' I wouldn't be at all surprised if we need the tires and wheels. I hope we don't need the food and water."

A few miles outside Marrakech, the road narrowed, and a mile later the paving disappeared as they began to climb the Atlantic slope of the Atlas Mountains. The road was steep, twisting, and before long one lane; and there were long delays waiting for Marrakech-bound trucks, some battered buses, and a very few automobiles to pass.

It was half past four when they reached Tizi-n-Tichka pass. From there they went downhill in low. It was dark when they reached Ouarzazate, where they would turn off the "highway" onto the "unpaved dirt road" to Ksar es Souk.

They put up in the Hôtel des Chasseurs, drank two bottles of surprisingly good Moroccan burgundy with a roast lamb dinner, and then went to their simply furnished but clean and comfortable rooms.

They left Ouarzazate early the next morning, and reached Ksar es Souk shortly after two in the afternoon. The palace was larger than Canidy thought it would be, an enormous structure of what looked like adobe. The whole thing, built of dried mud and narrow flat stones upon a rocky outcropping, looked medieval, a castle out of the Crusades.

As they drove near, masked horsemen appeared and rode with them as the Ford bucked and lurched over the rocks in the road.

"Berbers," Baker said. "They're Caucasian—white. There's a theory that they're descended from the Crusaders. Notice anything unusual about them?"

"Those are Thompson machine guns and Browning automatic rifles. You'd expect swords and flintlocks."

"That's not what I meant," Baker said. "What I mean is that we're surrounded. We couldn't turn back now if we wanted to."

Canidy turned and looked. There were now more than thirty horsemen, all armed, all masked, all riding on fine-looking horses, and none more than twenty feet behind them.

When they reached the palace, they found a village built around the outer wall. Through a small gate and then a larger one, Canidy saw that there was another wall.

A few horsemen who had come out to meet them rode through the large gate, but the majority just milled around the Ford when they stopped. Baker made up his mind, put the car in gear again, and drove through the gate.

Once inside, Canidy saw that they were in a dry moat, and the wall he had seen was the wall of the palace, rising five or six stories above them.

One of the horsemen dismounted, walked to the car, and spoke to them in French.

Baker, offering his diplomatic passport, asked for an audience with the pasha of Ksar es Souk.

The Berber pretended utter incomprehension.

The standoff went on until a new group of eight horsemen walked their animals through the gate into the dry moat. Two of them wore golden cords on their burnooses, identifying them as noblemen. The noblemen carried shotguns, but the other six were armed with Thompson submachine guns and rifles.

"Who are you, and what do you want?" one of the two men with gold-corded burnooses asked from under his mask.

"My name is Baker," Baker said. "I'm an American consular officer. May I ask who you are?"

"What are you doing here?" the tall, bright-eyed Moroccan asked. Baker recognized the voice of the pasha of Ksar es Souk.

"I was looking for the pasha of Ksar es Souk," Baker said. "I'd hoped to have a word with him."

"Yes? Perhaps."

"If I'm not mistaken, I believe I have the honor of addressing the pasha. Your Excellency and I shared a delightful meal in Paris not long ago."

"How could I forget, Mr. Baker?" Sidi el Ferruch said, removing his mask. His face, though, remained masklike. "You were just passing through the neighborhood, I gather, and on an impulse decided to drop by?" he said with unmoving eyes.

Baker grinned. "Not exactly. As I said, I'd be quite

pleased to have a word with you. And''—he paused a moment—''with your friend Eric Fulmar.''

''There is no one here of that name,'' the noble said.

In Arabic, the other noble said, ''I know the other one. I grew up with him. His name is Dick Canidy.''

Canidy recognized both his own name and the voice.

''Get off that horse, Eric,'' he said. ''Before you fall off.''

Fulmar pulled the cloth mask free of his face. He was smiling warmly.

''Canidy, what the *hell* are you doing here?''

Then he dismounted gracefully and ran toward Canidy, arms extended, and wrapped his arms around him.

3

There was no question that Sidi Hassan el Ferruch would invite the two Americans to stay. He took seriously the teaching of the Koran about treating well the friend of a friend. And besides, he was mightily intrigued by this strange American way of catching his attention. Not wishing, however, for matters to move swiftly, he allowed Canidy and Fulmar only the briefest of greetings, then hustled Eric off to his room, where he would presumably bathe and change. After that he ordered a servant to show Baker and Canidy to guest rooms where they could presumably do the same.

A meal would be served in the garden in two hours, he announced. And wine would be made available before and during the meal to those who were not of the faith . . . and to those inclined to wink at certain less than divinely inspired teachings of the Holy Koran, he added, with a hint of laughter in his voice.

• • •

Canidy was not surprised when Eric Fulmar came to his room a half hour later, bearing a bottle of wine. What did surprise him was the intensity of his own emotions at seeing Fulmar again. It was some time before he was able to remind himself that he was here on business.

"The scenery aside, don't you get lonely here?" Canidy asked.

"No," Fulmar said, quickly, defensively.

"Well, I suppose the smuggling does keep you busy," Canidy said.

Fulmar's eyes went cold.

"You know about that, do you?"

Canidy nodded. "Someday the Germans will stop it."

"So?"

"Then what?"

"You have something in mind." It was not a question. "What's your offer, Dick?" he asked, his voice hardening.

"We need you."

"So?"

"So when Baker makes his offer, get all you can. His offer will include getting you out of here, home, I mean. Plus fixing things for you with the Internal Revenue Service."

"And what do I have to do to get your man Baker to be so nice to me?" Fulmar asked, matter-of-factly.

"There's no free lunch, did I ever tell you that?"

"Thanks a lot, pal."

"Baker will tell you."

"I'm sure he will."

They sat down for lunch in the shade of some kind of flowering tree that Canidy did not recognize. Servants carried in sizzling chunks of skewered lamb, peppers, and onions. These were drawn off the skewers and laid over beds of steaming rice. There were also plates of tomatoes and mixed fruits and baskets filled with breads. The wine was Château Figeac.

El Ferruch having sent word ahead, the Americans were already seated when the pasha of Ksar es Souk arrived. He was wearing an elaborately embroidered caftan, and he was accompanied by his huge black bodyguard. A powerful man, Canidy thought to himself as he studied his host. Obviously ruthless. And *my* age?

After the pasha had addressed each of his guests, Baker handed him a small package.

"I hope Your Excellency will honor us by accepting our gift," Baker said.

"Of course, thank you," el Ferruch said, stretching out his hand for the package. He said something in Arabic, and the large black man walked quickly out of the room.

He opened the package. It contained a wristwatch.

"Lovely," he said, with no enthusiasm.

Baker raised his hand a little as though to call a halt to el Ferruch's misperception.

"Your Excellency certainly will recognize that as an airman's chronometer," Baker said. "But perhaps Your Excellency might be interested to note that it is of American manufacture."

That caught el Ferruch's attention, and he looked at the watch more closely.

"It is the very first to come from the factory," Baker said. "Your Excellency will see that it is serial number one."

"Extraordinary," el Ferruch said, still without enthusiasm. "I suppose you've made several of these for all the wog chiefs you want to buy."

"We have ordered two hundred thousand," Baker said,

pressing on, "for our aircrews. The first was presented by the manufacturer to President Roosevelt."

"Two hundred thousand?" el Ferruch asked. "But this is number one?"

"President Roosevelt said that since it was unlikely he will be flying one of our airplanes, he thought Your Excellency might find some use for it."

"I am overwhelmed by President Roosevelt's generosity," el Ferruch said dryly. But he *was* impressed. "When you leave, I will ask you to take a small gift from me to President Roosevelt."

"I would be honored, Your Excellency."

Soon the enormous black man returned, carrying two objects wrapped in silk and tied with cord. He gave them to el Ferruch, who leaned forward again and handed them to Canidy and Baker.

"Please be good enough to accept a small gift of my own," he said.

Inside the silk wrappings were curved-blade daggers. The hilts of the daggers and their scabbards were of carved silver chased with gold.

"I am really overwhelmed, Your Excellency," Baker said.

"Thank you," Canidy said.

"And now," el Ferruch said, "may I suggest we eat? Later we can discuss the reason for your visit."

"Well, then?" Sidi Hassan el Ferruch asked, gazing at Eldon Baker. The dishes had been removed, and except for the fruit, so also was the food. El Ferruch's long, thin fingers lightly brushed a glass of port that had been old before he was born.

Baker smiled, cocked an eyebrow, and said nothing. He

wants to find out what el Ferruch knows, Canidy thought, before he begins to commit himself.

"Well, then," the pasha repeated. This time it was not a question. "Let's get to the point. You're not a visa clerk, Baker. You are some sort of intelligence agent.

"And Mr. Canidy, according to Eric, was until quite lately in China flying for the American Volunteer Group there. Somehow or other he is now here, which leads me to suspect that the two of you are birds from the same nest. Beyond that, I'm led to believe that Mr. Canidy's long-standing friendship with Eric had some influence on the decision to pull him out of China and send him to Morocco."

"Go on."

"Next, I don't see myself as more than peripherally useful to you . . . unless of course you plan an invasion of North Africa?" He glanced quickly at Baker, but there was no visible reaction. "And Eric is a nice boy." Fulmar screwed up his mouth. "But I don't see any possible use you could make of him. Morocco, in other words, is *only* Morocco, Mr. Baker. So tell me what you have on your mind."

"Your Excellency's sources are reliable." Baker said. "I hope the French and Germans aren't using the same ones."

"Not if I can help it," el Ferruch said, laughing. "But I'd be surprised," he said more soberly, "if they don't know that the two of you have come to see me. They will then draw conclusions."

"I'm sure they will," Baker agreed.

"That potentially compromises me."

"But, Your Excellency," Baker said with a subtle but significant edge in his voice, "you're already compromised . . . *potentially.* You and Eric are smugglers. Either the French *and* the Germans consider you above the law or else you have managed to outwit the French and Germans. Whichever your talent is, it makes you the kind of man we want to work with . . . not to mention, of course, all your other valuable talents.''

''I don't know whether to thank you,'' said el Ferruch, ''or sell you to the Germans.''

''If I were in your shoes, I don't know what I would do either. But why don't we get down to serious business?''

''You want me to help with an invasion of North Africa?''

''No, nothing so vast, I'm sorry to say. As far as I know, we have no plans to invade North Africa. Rumor has it, in fact, that we might go into Dakar and push up that way.''

''I don't believe that.''

''I'm sure you know your own mind. Meanwhile, a high-ranking French officer wishes to join his brothers who have thrown in their lot with the Allies in their fight against the Nazis. We'd like to help him do that. So we are providing a submarine to transport him to safety.''

''One of the French officers?'' el Ferruch meditated aloud. ''Which one? Bethouard?'' He looked at Baker. ''General Bethouard?''

''I'm sorry, Your Excellency, I can't give you an answer at this time.''

''Do you expect me to help you?'' el Ferruch said, annoyed.

''Well, yes, of course,'' Baker said. ''But may I continue?''

The pasha of Ksar es Souk waved his hand in imperious assent.

It was a gesture a barbarian chieftain would make, Canidy observed. But this man was no barbarian chieftain. Most of the time he was as smooth as Talleyrand. Thus, it was likely that by his act he would tip Baker a little off balance.

''As you know, our relations with the French are delicate,'' Baker said, in no way ruffled. Canidy realized more than ever why he had been chosen for this job. "If the French discover that we have given aid to a man they perceive as a deserter and traitor, our relationship with France would certainly deteriorate."

"But if I help him," el Ferruch said, "my relationship with France would *not* deteriorate?"

"If the French discover you have given aid to him, sure. But, as I said, you are a man of many gifts and talents."

"And if I help you—in return . . . ?" His voice trailed off.

"I'm sure you have needs."

"Not really, Mr. Baker. My major needs are taken care of. And I have few minor needs. Though naturally I'm not completely satisfied. A week alone with Greta Garbo would be pleasant. Or, more practically, I imagine your country has the resources to irrigate the desert you can see from your bedroom windows."

Baker paused reflectively. "Well, Your Excellency," he said, "you could probably irrigate a good piece of it for $100,000."

"Done," Sidi el Ferruch said.

"There is one other thing," Baker said. He pulled out of his pocket the photo of Grunier. "I need a double for this man. It doesn't have to be an exact twin. Just a rough approximation." He gave height, weight, hair, and skin color. "And if the double should vanish, he should not be missed."

"What's this all about?"

"We have an agent—someone who matters to us—who appears to have been compromised. He's helped us considerably, and we don't want to take chances with his life, especially now that there is a submarine available for the French officer."

"You won't tell me who he is?"

"No. He *is* French, and he works in a strategic industry."

"What is that?"

"The phosphate mines."

"I see. And?"

"He has a family in France. If it were to become known that he had defected to us, reprisals would be taken against them. But if he were to be, say, robbed and murdered by hoodlums and, as it were, left in a gutter, no harm would come to the family."

Jesus Christ! Canidy thought. Eldon Baker, charming diplomat, was simply going to have some guy off the street done away with! Shocked in spite of himself, Canidy said nothing.

"Of course, and then?" el Ferruch asked.

"There is one other man who must absolutely be on that submarine."

"Who is that?"

"Eric Fulmar."

"I don't see why. I like him, and we're useful to each other. . . . We have talents in common." He smiled, and reflected a moment, then went on. "And what possible use is he to you? One more soldier in uniform doesn't make a difference, does he?"

"No, we don't need him for that. We want him for several other reasons: He's half German, knows Germany like a native, knows Morocco, and can pass for an Arab. He's also *very* well connected in the United States. These together make him uniquely valuable."

"To me as well."

"I can well understand that."

"Go on."

"In conclusion, I would like Eric and Dick Canidy to effect a rendezvous with our agent, while you transport the

French officer to Safi. Eric, Dick, and the agent will meet you there and proceed to the submarine.''

El Ferruch took a long look at Fulmar. ''Eric,'' he said at last, ''do you want to go?''

''I think, my friend,'' Fulmar said with unusual seriousness for him, ''that I'm less immune to the German infection than you are. I better go.''

''All right,'' el Ferruch said. ''Then let's return to the question of recompense. Make me a better offer.''

''One hundred thousand dollars strikes me as quite handsome,'' Baker said.

''Mr. Baker, I think you should understand that for me the issue now is not money. There's much more money for me in French gold and paintings. The issue is dignity—what the Chinese call face. I'll have to take your proposals to Thami el Glaoui for approval. My approach must be dignified.''

''How dignified?''

''More than one hundred thousand dollars.''

''OK, one hundred ten thousand dollars.''

''All right, I agree. But this could take time,'' he said, raising himself from his cross-legged sitting position. ''Perhaps a week or two. Meanwhile, all of us need to relax. What do you have in mind to do next?''

''Canidy and I will return to the consulate in Rabat tomorrow. We'll wait there for your word.''

''Very good,'' el Ferruch said. ''By the way, Mr. Baker, do you play chess?''

''Why, yes, Your Excellency, in fact I do.''

''I thought so. Eric, Mr. Canidy,'' he said, looking at them, ''I imagine you'd like to spend time together. Come, Mr. Baker, we'll play chess.''

4
Headquarters, U.S. Armed Forces, Far East
Corregidor
Commonwealth of the Philippines
23 February 1942

The Signal Message Center received the message (PRIORITY
FROM CHIEF OF STAFF PERSONAL ATTENTION COMMANDING
GENERAL US ARMY FORCES FAR EAST) in two parts, radio
reception having been interrupted when a shard of Japanese
artillery fire sliced through the long copper wire antenna
mounted on the hill over Malinta Tunnel. When it was re-
strung, and USAFFE reported itself back on the air, the balance of the message was retransmitted, decoded, and sent
by messenger to General Douglas MacArthur.

By direction of the President, General Douglas MacArthur was to proceed at the earliest possible time to Mindanao
Island, where he would determine the feasibility of the
lengthy defense of that island in the event it became possible
to defend successfully the Bataan Peninsula and Corregidor.
After no more than seven days on Mindanao, General Mac-
Arthur would proceed by means of his own choosing to
Brisbane, Australia, where he would assume command of
all U.S. military forces in the western Pacific. He was authorized to designate whichever general officer he considered best qualified to assume command of U.S. Forces in
the Philippine Islands.

MacArthur was being ordered out of the Philippines at a
time when his troops in Bataan were singing, with ever-
increasing bitterness:

"We are the battling bastards of Bataan,
No mama, no papa, no Uncle Sam;
No aunts, no uncles, no cousins, no nieces;

*No pills, no planes, no artillery pieces;
And nobody gives a damn.''*

His forces were being whipped, not because of a lack of valor, and certainly not because of a lack of highly skilled leadership, but because they had been left high and dry, without resupply worth mentioning of food, personnel, medicine, aircraft, or munitions. As constitutional Commander in Chief of the Armed Forces of the United States, the President bore the ultimate responsibility for the decision not to resupply the Philippines.

And now Franklin Roosevelt was ordering him out, ordering him to desert his men just when they needed him most.

MacArthur's face whitened when he read the cable, and he sharply demanded that his aide-de-camp, Lieutenant Colonel Sidney Huff, locate Mrs. MacArthur. That told Huff that whatever the cable said was really bad news. MacArthur always turned to his wife when he was deeply emotional. She could often temper his responses, and he seemed to understand that was often desirable.

Huff told him a minute later that she was in one of the laterals off Malinta Tunnel. MacArthur headed in that direction, with Colonel Richard K. Sutherland on his heels.

Forty-five minutes later, Huff was directed to call a staff conference.

When the officers were assembled, MacArthur read them the direction of the President's radio message.

He had made his decision, he announced. In all of his commissioned service, he had never disobeyed an order. As an officer, he never would. But never in his military service had he deserted comrades in arms, and as a man he could not do so now. He intended to resign from the officer corps of the United States Army, go by boat to Bataan, and enlist

as a private in the ranks. The officers would be advised
when this change in status would take effect.

He then went to his desk, a standard GI folding desk
exactly like that issued captains commanding companies in
the field. There, in longhand, he wrote out his resignation.

The question arose as to who should receive his resignation. By regulation, resignations were addressed to the
senior commander. General Douglas MacArthur was the
senior commander in the Philippines, and in the entire U.S.
Army subordinate only to General George Catlett Marshall
(whom MacArthur had once officially described as unwor-
thy of promotion beyond colonel). Now Marshall was a
four-star general, the Chief of Staff, and sitting at the right
hand of Franklin Delano Roosevelt.

There was no question in MacArthur's mind that Marshall
was behind the cable, compliance with which would force
him to violate everything he had held sacred since he had
taken the oath of allegiance at West Point.

Sutherland suggested that he think the whole matter over
overnight, and in his required acknowledgment of the Roosevelt cable be careful to say nothing that indicated his
plans.

A radio message was sent acknowledging the order, but
asking permission to pick his own time to leave. General
MacArthur said his "departure from the Philippines, even
to assume command of 'relief forces' in Australia, had delicate morale overtones, that had to be carefully weighed."

Marshall, not Roosevelt, replied almost immediately to
the first radio message. Since "maintaining the Luzon defense was imperative," General MacArthur was permitted
to choose his own time, and means, of going to Australia.

The resignation was put in a drawer.

5
Near Ksar es Souk, Morocco
February 23, 1942

Dick Canidy drove the first leg of the trip back to Rabat—in silence. He was tired and hungover after a very late night with Eric Fulmar. And Eldon Baker was more than glad to oblige him in his wish for quiet, for Baker had spent almost as much time playing cutthroat chess with Sidi Hassan el Ferruch and, inevitably, negotiating the details of their agreement. But by the time they reached the foothills of the Atlas Mountains, Baker sensed that Canidy had emerged from his fog.

"So," Baker said, "did you have an exciting time?"

"Splendid. And you?"

"Satisfactory. How is your friend Eric taking all this?"

"I actually think he's looking forward to the change."

"Hmmm. I believe he's going to do us a lot of good. And what do you think about the pasha of Ksar es Souk?"

"He's a man with a promising future."

Baker laughed. "I know what you mean. A few like him in their royal family and the English would before long find themselves without a Parliament."

Canidy laughed, agreeing.

"And are you satisfied," Baker went on, "with your part in our Grunier plans?"

Canidy looked hard at him. "It all seems very nasty and cold-blooded," he said. "Or does murdering a stranger in cold blood matter to you spies?"

"Grunier is *that* important to the war," Baker said quietly. "You know it's hard, Dick, after growing up and taking seriously all that Mom, Dad, pastors, and teachers taught me about being a good boy, to have to choose not to be a good boy. I expect that there's an especially unpleasant room in hell waiting for people like me . . . and for you, Dick. I'm certain you have the gift. And I expect you and I will have a lot of time to chat when we meet in that room.''

"Some gift," Canidy groaned. "So what do I do next?''

"We wait. I have a lot of books. I get a lot of reading done waiting.''

6
Café des Deux Sabots
Rabat, Morocco
February 23, 1942

Müller will always be recognizably a cop, Max von Heurten-Mitnitz reflected as the headwaiter led Müller to the table. Like a priest, naked on a beach where everyone would recognize him for what he was.

"How are you?'' von Heurten-Mitnitz said, rising just enough to show proper regard for a friend in Müller's station. "Are you well?''

"I'm late," Müller said, "but with excuses.''

"I'm aware you are late,'' von Heurten-Mitnitz said. He was already into his main course, which was a more than passable Moroccan imitation of bouillabaisse. "Whose bed were you under? Or do you have a better excuse?''

"Better," Müller said, laughing. "Two *minor* American consular officers drove to the pasha of Ksar es Souk's palace yesterday. They have returned to Rabat today. My guess is that the two *minor* consular officers were not paying a social call on Sidi el Ferruch.''

"Who were the officers?''

"One was a man named Baker. For a time he was a *minor* American official who watched over their embassy after we liberated Paris from the French. The other is named Canidy.

He seems enough of a nobody that we have no file on him in Morocco. The two of them are obviously intelligence agents.''

"The Pope is Catholic," von Heurten-Mitnitz agreed. "So what did they tell el Ferruch?"

"I don't know."

"And they are now back in Rabat?"

"Yes."

"Put surveillance on them. *Real* surveillance, not Sécurité surveillance."

"That's already done."

"Good. And what about el Ferruch?"

"I don't know."

"You don't know what he's doing? Or you don't know where he is?"

"Neither."

"Shit," von Heurten-Mitnitz said, "the elusive Pimpernel."

"What's that?"

"The hero of a very bad novel that was turned into a very good film with Leslie Howard. The Pimpernel was a British nobleman who saved a number of his French colleagues from the Revolutionary guillotine. None of the French officials could ever figure out who he was, what he was up to, or where he'd turn up next. By rights, Müller, Sidi Hassan el Ferruch ought to be one of the more visible people in Morocco. Find him and keep an eye on him. Let him go about his enterprises, but *find out* what those are."

"It will be done."

"And what about young Herr Fulmar?"

"Still in Ksar es Souk."

"That's as good as a jail. But if he leaves, attend to him like a mother—without letting him become aware of your attentions."

"Yes, sir."

TWELVE

On 6 March, there had been another radio message from
Chief of Staff George Marshall to Douglas MacArthur. It
was not an order, MacArthur judged, but a gloved reminder:
"The situation in Australia indicates desirability of your
early arrival there."

MacArthur offered no comment on the cable to his staff,
nor did anyone bring up the subject of his handwritten resignation, still in his desk.

Today, there had come a third radio message, priority
URGENT, on the subject, and this time it was an order. General MacArthur was informed that he, "by direction of the
President," was expected to depart Corregidor no later than
15 March, to arrive in Australia no later than 18 March.

General MacArthur then replied to someone (no one later
remembered who) softly, in bitter resignation, that an order
was an order, and that he would have to obey. He would,
he said, probably leave on the submarine *Permit*, which was
en route to Corregidor.

Later that day, someone told him that the *Permit*'s arrival was by no means assured, and that even if it came, it would probably not arrive in time for MacArthur to comply with his latest orders.

MacArthur then issued two orders to Huff. First he told him to contact Navy Lieutenant Johnny Buckley and have him consider their chances of getting through the Japanese blockade in Buckley's remaining patrol torpedo boats, then tied up in battered condition at a fishing wharf in Sisiman Bay, on the Bataan Peninsula.

The second order was to locate Lieutenant James M. C. Whittaker of the Army Air Corps and, if he was still alive, order him to Corregidor.

2
Near Abucay, Bataan
1330 Hours 10 March 1942

First Lieutenant James M. C. Whittaker, United States Army Air Corps (Detailed Cavalry), late of the 414th Pursuit Squadron (disbanded 10 December 1941) and late of the 26th Cavalry (which had been dismounted and for all practical purposes disbanded 16 January 1941), was wearing pink cavalry officer's breeches and knee-high riding boots. Most of his uniforms had been destroyed when BOQ at Clark Field had been bombed out on 9 December. The cavalryman's breeches and boots had been in the apartment in Manila.

On 12 December 1941 he had managed to get to the apartment en route to Clark Field, where he had been handed a message informing him that Chesty Haywood Whittaker, Jr., had died of a stroke. While still terribly

shaken by that, his turn came to appear before a hastily
convened board of officers.

"The situation, gentlemen," an Air Corps major told
thirty-three young Air Corps officers, fliers and nonfliers,
"is that we have a surplus of Air Corps officers and a crit-
ical shortage of ground force officers. You have been selected for detail to ground duty. The board will determine
where your past experience will permit you to best fit in."

His appearance before the board, four field-grade officers
of the combat arms and the Signal Corps, had been brief.

As Whittaker was still in the process of saluting, a cavalry
officer smiled and turned to the others.

"We'll take this one," he said. "How are you, Jim?"

Two weeks after the cavalry major, a fellow polo player
in happier times, had welcomed Whittaker into the "gentleman's branch of service," he was killed by mortar fire on
the Bataan Peninsula. And just two weeks after that, an even
more informal board of officers, convened to reassign what
was left (not much) of the officer corps of the 26th Cavalry,
had assigned Lieutenant Whittaker to the Philippine Scouts.

That assignment hadn't lasted long either. Lieutenant
Whittaker, who had let it be known that he had had summer
jobs in construction, where he had learned to handle explosives, became commanding officer of the 105th Philippine
Army Explosive Ordnance Disposal Detachment. The unit
consisted of two Americans, himself and a Regular Army
staff sergeant, George Withers, and eight Philippine Scouts,
one second lieutenant, one master sergeant, and six technical
sergeants. Lieutenant Whittaker had unit promotion authority to technical sergeant, and he had promoted all of the
Scouts, none of whom had previously held rank above cor-
poral.

Lieutenant Whittaker's tall riding boots were highly polished. They formed an interesting contrast to the rest of his

uniform: a peasant's wide-brimmed straw hat, a short-sleeved white (nonuniform) polo shirt, and a Colt Model 1917 .45 revolver (manufactured for the last war) stuck in the waistband of his breeches.

For a number of reasons, Lieutenant Whittaker was highly thought of by his subordinates. For one thing, they were all eating well. Lieutenant Whittaker carried with him a strongbox containing gold coins. One of his missions when assigned to the 26th Cavalry was to visit a rural branch bank and relieve it of its gold before the bank fell to the Japanese. When he returned with the coins, the officer who had sent him was dead, and he decided that he could put the gold to better use keeping his troops fed than it would serve in a box sent to Corregidor.

The natives on Bataan did not trust paper money. But they would sell rice, eggs, chickens, and pigs for gold, and Lieutenant Whittaker had kept first his Filipino troopers of the 26th Cavalry and now his Boom Boom Boys well fed with the coins from the bank. The gold had also purchased transport, when other units had none, and gasoline. The Boom Boom Boys had two pickup trucks and one fenderless 1937 Ford convertible. Some of the fuel came from dwindling Army stocks (because getting Explosive Ordnance Disposal people where they were needed enjoyed a high priority), but most of it Whittaker bought from the natives.

He was regarded highly even by Staff Sergeant George Withers, who did not ordinarily have much respect for officers who were not West Pointers with fifteen years' service. Staff Sergeant Withers was a highly skilled Explosive Ordnance Disposal expert, and Whittaker readily acknowledged Withers's superior technical skill when it came down to taking the fuse from an unexploded 105 or 155 shell.

But the 105th EOD Det spent most of its time blowing things up, and Lieutenant Whittaker—who had learned the art at sixteen from a man who had blown a railroad tunnel through the Rocky Mountains—was the most skilled son-ofabitch Withers had ever seen with any kind of explosives. He took down bridges, closed tunnels, ruptured dams, and laid trees across roads with a skill that could only be called artistry. And when he was not blowing something up, he was leaving lethal traps for the advancing Japanese.

The one thing Luzon Force had in abundance was field artillery ammunition. There weren't, in fact, enough cannon and howitzers to fire all they had, although the cannon were seldom silent. Whittaker had decided that the less of this abundance that fell into the hands of the Japanese, the better. Thus bagged powder charges for the larger cannon were converted into demolition material, and the smaller, integral ammunition converted to mines.

Only lately had the advance of the Japanese been so re-lentless against weakening Philippine-American forces that it had been necessary to blow ammo dumps that couldn't be moved in place.

Whittaker's reaction to their inevitable defeat was to look forward to blowing up the last three ammo dumps on the Bataan Peninsula. He made elaborate plans to do this the moment the first Japanese stepped inside the fence.

"It will look like Mount Vesuvius," he promised.

Most Americans in Luzon Force based their hopes of sur-vival on making it to Corregidor when the Japanese finally occupied the Bataan Peninsula. Whittaker had other plans. He had found an ancient thirty-four-foot boat, a bit damaged by small-arms fire, sitting with decks nearly awash on the bottom of a small harbor near Mariveles. But her engine was intact, and her tanks were full, and there was extra fuel in fifty-five-gallon barrels in her hold. When the time came, her pumps would work. Whittaker had scuttled her, and he intended to refloat her, make for one of the other islands, and take his men with him.

The major contributing factor to the high morale of the 105th Explosive Ordnance Disposal Detachment was their faith in their commanding officer's ability to get them off Bataan. The rest of the Battling Bastards were doomed, and everybody knew it, but there was hope for them.

The officer who came looking for Lieutenant Whittaker had both a jeep and relatively clean clothes, although he was as gaunt from the three-eighths rations, no malaria pills, and overwork as anybody else on Bataan. The jeep and clean clothes identified him as a staff officer, probably from as far back as United States Armed Forces, Far East (USAFFE), at the tip of the peninsula.

He carried with him the astonishing information that Lieutenant Whittaker had been ordered to Corregidor, there to report to General MacArthur personally.

"Go back to him and say you couldn't find me," Whittaker said. "I don't intend to get stuck on the Rock."

"It's an order, Lieutenant," the captain said. "No one's giving you a choice."

"I've got all kinds of choices, Captain," Jim Whittaker said. "I'm only a temporary soldier."

"You're wearing an officer's uniform," the captain said. "You took an oath."

"Good Christ, under these circumstances, aren't oaths and the rest of the trappings of officers and gentlemen pretty useless?" Whittaker snapped. "Jesus, the President of the United States gave his word to MacArthur that we would be reinforced and resupplied. With the Commander in Chief lying through his teeth, don't talk to me about an officer's honor."

"Under these circumstances, Lieutenant," the captain said after a moment, "I would say that an officer's honor is more important than ever. I won't try to force you to go with me, but I will not go back and say I couldn't find you. It took gasoline to come up here.''

Whittaker said something in quick, fluent Spanish, and one of his technical sergeants went to the pickup truck and returned with a gallon tin can of gasoline.

''You can have another five gallons if you're really low,'' Whittaker said.

''Hoarding gas, too? You're a real credit to the officers corps, Whittaker,'' the captain said. But he pulled the cushion off the passenger seat so the offered gas could be put into his tank.

''Withers,'' Whittaker said, making up his mind. ''If I'm not back in twenty-four hours, go to Mindanao.''

''What about Mount Vesuvius?'' Withers asked.

''Fuck it, let someone else do it. Go to Mindanao.''

''You're counseling this man to desert?'' the captain said.

''Fuck you, Captain,'' Whittaker said. ''Mind your own business.'' He took the Colt .45 revolver from his belt and extended it, butt first, to Withers.

''You better keep it, Lieutenant,'' George Withers said. ''You never know.''

Whittaker put it back in his belt.

''I hope to come back,'' he said.

''No, you don't,'' Withers said. He put out his hand.

Whittaker had another thought. He had the only watch. He took it off and handed it to Withers. It was the Hamilton he had received in Cambridge from Chesty Whittaker on his graduation.

''I hope I can give this back to you sometime,'' Withers said, and then he surprised Whittaker by tossing him a very snappy parade-ground salute.

''Good luck, Lieutenant,'' he said.

The captain was surprised to see tears in the eyes of the

Filipinos when they shook Whittaker's hand. They saluted as they drove away.

Between Abucay and Mariveles, what the captain had heard kept gnawing at him.

"You don't really think your sergeant is going to make it to Mindanao, do you?"

"They're going to give it a good try," Whittaker said.

"They'd need a boat," the captain said. "Where would they get a boat?" And then, when it became obvious Whittaker wasn't going to reply, he went on: "You sonofabitch, you've *got* a boat, don't you?"

Whittaker looked at him but said nothing.

"Where?"

"So you can go requisition it?" Jim Whittaker asked. "I told those men if they would stick with me to the end, I'd do what I could to get them out of here."

"I don't want to surrender," the captain said. "The Japanese have the Bushido notion that soldiers are supposed to die, not surrender. Surrender is disgraceful; those who surrender are treated accordingly."

"You're going to be ordered to surrender," Whittaker said. "How are you going to reconcile disobeying an order like that with your officer's code of honor?"

"Not easily," the captain said, "but I am not going to surrender."

"I realize how absurd this sounds," Whittaker said, "but if I tell you where the boat is, will you give me your word of honor you won't try to stop them?"

"What I was thinking of doing was going back up there and telling them you told me to take over," the captain said. "My colonel will let me go, if I give him half an excuse."

"If you knew where the boat was, Withers would believe you. Otherwise, he wouldn't," Whittaker said.

"Are you going to tell me?" the captain said.

"Let me think about it," Whittaker said.

There were half a dozen pleasure cruisers tied up at Mariveles. Two of them were still capable of making the run between Mariveles and the island fortress of Corregidor.

As he waited to board a thirty-two-foot ChrisCraft whose interior had been stripped to the hull ribs by a fire, Whittaker turned to the captain.

"I want those guys to try for Mindanao," he said. "Withers believes that Corregidor can hold out until help comes. I don't think help's coming. Corregidor's going to fall, and everybody on it is going to be captured. If I tell you where the boat is, will you try for Mindanao?"

The captain nodded. Whittaker asked the captain for his name, and then wrote a note to Withers. The captain read it. It said that he was going to help them get to Mindanao.

"It doesn't say where the boat is," the captain said.

"I don't want you to suffer a relapse of officer's honor," Whittaker said. "When it's time to go, Sergeant Withers will show you where the boat is."

The captain met his eyes.

"Thank you," he said. "Good luck on the Rock."

"If you see a large flash and hear a large bang, that'll be me," Whittaker said. "I think I made the mistake of letting the brass know that I'm very good at blowing ammo dumps."

"Is that why they sent for you?"

"Either that or MacArthur wants me to take over," Whittaker said.

The other passengers, nurses, some of them weeping because they had been ordered to leave their patients, some of them simply looking dazed, arrived in the back of a truck and were put aboard the gutted ChrisCraft.

A sailor ordered Whittaker aboard.

Whittaker and the captain looked at each other and

shrugged shoulders; then Whittaker jumped into the ChrisCraft. He put his hand out to steady himself. Whatever it was that he put his hand on moved. He looked at it. It was a very clever stainless-steel device in which yachtsmen could put their glasses so that Scotch on the rocks—or whatever they were drinking—would not splash on the carpet and leave a stain.

They were strafed twice by Japanese aircraft between Mariveles and Corregidor, but the sailor was good at his job. He knew the exact moment when to spin the wheel and throw the engines in reverse, so that the stream of machine-gun fire went over their heads.

3
Malinta Tunnel
Fortress Corregidor
1550 Hours 11 March 1942

"Get rid of that hat," Lieutenant Colonel Sidney Huff said to First Lieutenant Jim Whittaker.

Whittaker did as he was ordered, laying the Filipino peasant's straw hat on the concrete floor of the lateral of Malinta Tunnel.

Huff went into a tiny cubicle off the lateral and then came immediately out.

"General MacArthur will see you now, Lieutenant," he said, gesturing for Whittaker to come.

MacArthur was sitting behind a GI table. Except for a telephone and IN and OUT boxes, his famous gold-embroidered cap was the only thing on the desk.

"Lieutenant Whittaker reporting as ordered, sir," Whittaker said, and saluted.

"I understand you were strafed on your way here," Mac-Arthur said.

"Yes, sir."

"But you came through all right," MacArthur said.

"Yes, sir."

"I was acquainted with your uncle," MacArthur said. "In happier times, we played bridge. I was distressed to learn of his passing."

"Thank you, sir."

"He would have been proud of you," MacArthur said. "Colonel Huff has made inquiries for me. Yours was the only fighter craft to rise and challenge the enemy at Iba, as I understand it."

"I took off, sir, because I knew that I would have no chance at all on the ground," Whittaker said.

"I have also been informed that you downed three of the enemy before you were yourself shot down. Is that the case?"

"I wasn't shot down, General," Whittaker said. "When the Japanese, who were out of fuel, broke off engagement, Iba's runways were blocked. I couldn't land there, so I made for Clark. I was machine-gunned as I made my approach to land."

MacArthur obviously did not want to pursue that subject. "But you did down three of the enemy?" he asked.

"Yes, sir."

"And your subsequent performance of duty, I have been informed, with the 26th Cavalry and with the Philippine Scouts, has been exemplary."

Whittaker did not reply until MacArthur made it plain with his expression that he expected one. Then he said, "Thank you, sir."

"Deserving of formal recognition," MacArthur said. "I am therefore about to award you the Distinguished Flying

Cross for your service as an aviator, and the Silver Star for your gallant service on Bataan. And you are promoted, effective today, to captain. I will pin the decorations on you, but you'll have to give them back. Our supply of the medals, like everything else, has been exhausted. Colonel Huff has found a captain's insignia for you somewhere.''

MacArthur got up and walked around the little table and pinned the two medals to the pocket of Jim Whittaker's white civilian shirt. Then, with some difficulty, he unpinned Whittaker's silver lieutenant's bar and replaced it with the twin silver bars of a captain.

MacArthur stepped back and then shook Whittaker's hand with both of his.

''Congratulations, Captain,'' he said. ''It is a great honor to command courageous men such as yourself.''

Whittaker was at once embarrassed, pleased, and confused. He was made uncomfortable by the flattery, but pleased (although a corner of his mind said ''So what?'') to be a captain. And confused because it looked as if he had been ordered to Corregidor on some sort of whim by MacArthur.

War is insane, Whittaker reasoned. *Therefore, I should not be surprised that I have been sent for to be given medals I can't keep, and a meaningless promotion.*

''I believe, Captain, you are acquainted with the Commander in Chief?'' MacArthur asked.

''Yes, sir,'' Whittaker said.

''Sufficiently close to the President that he considered it his obligation to use military communications to direct me to inform you of your uncle's unfortunate demise,'' MacArthur said.

He's pissed about that, Jim Whittaker thought. *But certainly, he can't blame me for it.*

''I have received other communications from our Com-

mander in Chief, Captain Whittaker, via the Chief of Staff,
General Marshall. I have been ordered to leave Corregidor,
the Philippine Islands, to assume command of United States
forces in Australia. My wife, Colonel Sutherland, Colonel
Huff, and others have put it to me that I cannot, as I would
prefer to do, resign my commission and go into the ranks;
that I have to obey that order.

"At sunset tonight, we are leaving Corregidor aboard PT
boats. You are going with us, Captain. On our arrival in
Australia, you will be sent home, carrying a letter from me
to our Commander in Chief, which you are ordered to deliver to him personally. As I recall, Mr. Roosevelt is a gra-
cious man, and it is my hope, considering his affection for
your late uncle, that he will give you a few minutes of his
time. I wouldn't be surprised if he had you to dinner. If that
should take place, I feel sure that you will be able to make
him *really* aware of our situation here. Perhaps you will
even be able to make the Commander in Chief aware of
how difficult it has been for me to obey his order to desert
my command."

Out of the corner of his eye, Jim Whittaker could see
Lieutenant Colonel Huff and read on his face that Huff had
not known about this until just now.

"Perhaps you will be good enough, Captain, to assist in
loading the boats," MacArthur said.

"Sir," Whittaker said, "I would prefer to go back to
Bataan."

"So would I, Captain," MacArthur said. "You are dismissed."

4
The Golf Course
Palace of the Pasha of Marrakech
Marrakech, Morocco
March 12, 1942

Thami el Glaoui's eighth hole was a long, dogleg par five. A stroke—at least—could be saved by cutting across the dogleg, but that risked entanglement in a tall stand of trees beyond which was a cleverly placed pond. The pasha of Marrakech always played his eighth hole conservatively. The pasha of Ksar es Souk, on the other hand, when he was playing with Thami, always tried a shot across the trees. More often than not, this aggressiveness worked for him. But the pasha of Marrakech's more conservative play usually was victorious over the full eighteen holes. His final score would be five or six over par. On his good days, however, Sidi el Ferruch played under par. Today he was having a good day. He birdied the eighth while Thami doubled-bogied. Having chosen a five iron when he should have used a seven, he overshot the green.

For a moment, this made him especially grumpy, because he knew he had only himself to blame. But his spirits improved after he made the ninth green—a nice little par three—in one. Since the pasha of Ksar es Souk also made it on, they walked to the green together.

"Have the Americans revealed yet the name of the French officer?" Thami el Glaoui asked about halfway down the fairway.

"No," said Sidi el Ferruch, "and in fact if I were them I would not reveal it until I had to."

"Yes, I understand."

"But I have tracked down the identity of the other man they plan to take away on their submarine."

"Good."

"His name is Grunier, and he is a mining engineer. I also found something else interesting about him: He is no American agent."

"Oh?"

"So I naturally asked myself why they want him—and badly enough to spirit him away by submarine."

"And you found?"

"Little, I'm sorry to say," el Ferruch said. "He has only recently come to Morocco. Before that he was in Katanga for a number of years. Since in Katanga there are no minerals the Americans need they can't obtain elsewhere, I'm puzzled about why the Americans want him. They have thousands of mining engineers, so it's not for his profession. He must therefore know about something either here or in Katanga that they want."

"Why don't you question him?"

"I'd like to, but unhappily that's not prudent. If I had him detained, the Sécurité or the Gestapo—which means both in the end—would hear about it. And this would, as a minimum, displease our American friends, who, I'm convinced, prefer to keep the man obscure. And a casual conversation with him would bring the same result, since he would run to the Sécurité the instant the conversation was over."

"Then leave him to the Americans."

"Yes, honored Father, I think that's best," Sidi el Ferruch said. "Although," he continued, "in light of my knowledge, we might be able to obtain more money for Grunier."

"No," Thami el Glaoui said. "The Americans will invade North Africa this year, I'm sure of it. We are the back door to Europe. When that happens, they will need you and me. But before that happens, I don't want to be close to

them—in their pocket, as they say. Deal with them now,
but stay distant.''

''Yes, dear Father, I will.'' The old man was quite right,
Sidi knew. ''So then we don't need them waiting?''

''Move. We've held them off long enough.''

''Good.''

''And their submarine?''

''It will take two or three days for them to bring their
submarine in.''

''Then send Mr. Baker his message.''

That evening, as Eldon Baker walked from his apartment to
the café where he usually took his supper, a Berber boy,
backing out of a doorway with a huge basket of oranges in
his arms, stumbled against him. They both collapsed onto
the walk in a tangle of limbs and oranges. After they were
up and straightened out, there was a piece of paper in
Baker's jacket pocket that had not been there before. On the
paper one word was written in curling, Arabic script: *Hejira*.

Later, in the café, Baker walked into the toilet, set fire to
the paper with his Ronson, and flushed the ashes away.

5
Rabat, Morocco
March 13, 1942

Diego García Albéniz was a Catalan who had fought against
Franco in the civil war and who had escaped to French Africa soon after the fall of Madrid. He was also a pretty good
physician, who—understandably—knew more than a thing
or two about battlefield wounds. This skill had made him
useful now and again to both the current and the former
pashas of Ksar es Souk. It was, however, not Sidi el Ferruch

who needed Dr. Albéniz today. It was Richard Canidy.

Since the doctor's office was only half a mile from the American consulate in Rabat, and even though it was raining buckets in Rabat, Canidy decided to walk, his reason being that this was the only way he could be sure not to lose the Sécurité agent who was this day's tail. ("I thought they were supposed to use a team," Canidy had said with deeply wounded vanity to Eldon Baker soon after the Sécurité first started to keep an eye on them. "You're not worth a team," Baker had replied, rubbing it in.)

So, in raincoat, hat, scarf, and galoshes, Canidy trudged the half mile to Dr. Albéniz, happy at least that the Frenchman following him was getting soaked too.

The doctor's office was on the second floor, which was reached by a stairway up the outside of the building. At the top of the stairs, Canidy glanced around to make sure his tail was still around. He was. He'd found a modicum of protection in a doorway down the block.

Suffer! Canidy thought, then knocked.

Even though he had fought against the fascists, Dr. Albéniz was an aristocrat. For a Spaniard he was tall, and his dark hair was combed straight back. With him was the American deputy consul, William Dale. Dale was there solely because he was roughly the same height and build as Canidy. And he had been waiting an hour for Canidy's arrival with an impatience born of the diplomat's distaste for doing the work of spies.

Dale acknowledged Canidy's arrival by tearing away the brown paper wrapping from a bundle he had brought with him, as though silence made his own sin in consorting with Baker and his gang merely a venial one. He handed the bundle over to Canidy and took from him his soaked gear. The bundle contained clothing until recently worn by one of Ferruch's Berbers. Canidy changed into it while Dale put on the rain gear.

"I'll be going now," he said to the doctor, pointedly ignoring Canidy.

"I'd wait, sir, if I were you, for at least another fifteen minutes. The theory is that I'm seeing the doctor professionally."

"As indeed you are," said Dr. Albéniz, with a little smile.

Dale shrugged in defeat and took a seat, while the doctor went to a cabinet and took from it a syringe and needle. He screwed the needle into its socket, then pointed out to Canidy the markings on the side of the syringe.

"I'm going to give you a sedative that will keep someone blissfully unconscious for perhaps three or four hours," Dr. Albéniz said in very good but heavily accented English. "Fill the syringe to about three hundred cc's"—he pointed—"here."

"OK."

"You know to squirt a little out before you inject?"

Canidy nodded.

"Good." Albéniz walked over to a cabinet, unlocked it, and removed a small box. "Yes, good," he said, examining it. He then found a case for the syringe and the sedative in his doctor's bag. He placed all this equipment inside the case and handed it over to Canidy.

"Can I expect these back?" Dr. Albéniz asked.

"I hope so," Canidy said.

"Please try," the doctor said. "Medical shipments have been haphazard."

"I'll do my best," Canidy said. Personally, he was doubtful that he'd be able to return the doctor's gear to him.

"Thank you. Please follow me, then." The doctor led Canidy down an inside stairway and out a door that issued into a back alley. In the alley stood a tiny *deux chevaux*

Citroën van, its engine put-putting. The doctor opened the rear door, and Candidy crawled inside.

"Hi, Dick," said Eric Fulmar. "How the fuck are you?"

6
Oued-Zem, Morocco
March 13, 1942

It was close to ten in the evening by the time that Louis Albert Grunier reached his cottage in the mining compound near Oued-Zem. Grunier had gotten into the habit of spending his evenings at a café in town, where two or three unexpectedly sweet girls worked. For a couple of francs the girls would dance, and for a few more they'd take a customer upstairs. Grunier neither danced nor went upstairs, but he paid the girls for their time just the same, and he also sweetened their time with vermouth or Pernod.

When Grunier switched on the light inside his cottage, he saw that the inside was a shambles. And there was—*mon Dieu!*—a dead man on the floor. Two Berbers—no, two Europeans in Berber dress, he corrected himself—had been waiting in the dark for him, drinking his best brandy.

Grunier didn't speak when he saw them, nor did he do what he really wanted to do, which was to go back outside as fast as he could. One of the men held a very large and nasty-looking Thompson submachine gun aimed more or less at him.

"Bon soir, Monsieur Grunier," said the one with the Thompson. "We've been waiting several hours for you."

"This is an outrage," Grunier managed.

"You'll be astonished to hear this," Eric Fulmar said, "but we've come to save you."

"Who is this man?" said Grunier, ignoring that and

pointing to the apparent corpse on the floor. "And why have you killed him?"

"He's not dead ... yet," said Eric. "But he will be shortly; and I imagine that event will please you, because the Sûreté and the Germans will believe the dead man is you, which is going to keep your wife and kids safe. Because you see, Monsieur Grunier, we are going to take you to America in a submarine."

For a few seconds Grunier seemed unable to breathe. Then he sat down and waved his hand around as though making conversational gestures. But no words came out of his mouth.

Finally he spoke. "You are mad," he said.

"Probably," said Eric Fulmar. "Meanwhile, we need to take you to the submarine. And, I'm sorry to say, we need you unconscious for that."

"This is outrageous!" Grunier said.

"Absolutely," said Eric Fulmar, "but please cooperate"—he waved the gun menacingly—"and take your pants down."

The other man, who was in fact Richard Canidy, removed the syringe and the anesthetic from their box, plunged the needle into the rubber top, and drew a full five hundred cc's from the bottle. "The doc said three hundred cc's," he said in English, "but I think we can do better than that."

"Just don't kill him," Fulmar said, hoping that Grunier didn't know English. He didn't. He just stared blankly ahead and dropped his trousers so that Canidy could plunge the needle into the fleshiest part of his thigh.

In seconds, Louis Albert Grunier was unconscious.

Next, Canidy flipped the light off, then on, then off; and he and Fulmar carried the unconscious Frenchman out to the van.

The driver passed them on their way out. He was headed inside, and he was carrying a ten-liter can of gasoline.

7
Safi, Morocco
March 14, 1942

Fulmar, Canidy, and Grunier spent the next day in the hold of a Moroccan fishing boat anchored in the harbor at Safi waiting for the arrival of Admiral de Verbey. It took a little time, unhappily, for them to become as malodorous as their surroundings. A bottle of Black & White that Eric had thought to bring along made the two of them a bit more comfortable. Nothing mattered to the Frenchman.

Toward evening, Canidy and Fulmar heard a commotion and decided to poke their heads up to take a look. Two large trucks had just pulled up on the quay, one a flatbed evidently loaded with sacks of cement. The truck behind it was a cement mixer.

One of the drivers climbed up onto the rear of the cement mixer and did something to the funnel at the back that caused it to swing away from the hole at the top of the tank. The tank now looked like a reclining volcano—from which a moment later erupted a little old man.

"The admiral, I guess," said Canidy.

"Probably," Eric agreed.

The old man was helped into a rowboat in which four Moroccan fishermen were already waiting. The trucks rumbled away, and the fishermen rowed out to the boat where Eric and Dick were hiding. Moments later Vice Admiral d'Escadre Jean-Phillipe de Verbey was seated in the hold next to Lieutenant Richard Canidy sharing the now much-diminished bottle of Black & White. His rescuers had taken

him through two roadblocks (word was out that he was escaping, but who'd think to look in the tank of a cement
mixer truck?); and he was now very excited and voluble—
too excited to pay much attention to his unconscious coun-
tryman.

Soon after the admiral's arrival, the crew hoisted the fishing boat's sail, and twenty minutes after that the boat's rolling motion told those in the hold that they were beyond the
harbor. De Verbey talked nonstop the whole time, telling
again and again the story of his escape—at least as far as
Canidy could make out. Fulmar wasn't bothering to trans-
late, and it didn't seem to matter to the admiral that no one
was listening to him.

Later, one of the fishermen swung down into the hold and
motioned for them to come out on deck. Out in the distance
was a dark shape on the water. Then, without warning, there
was a brilliant flash of light.

"Jesus!" Canidy said.

A voice hailed them across the water. "Stand by to take
aboard a rubber-boat party." The voice was American.

A couple of fishermen went down into the hold and
hauled Grunier out. He was now semiconscious, but not yet
up to walking.

The sail rattled down its single mast; and a moment later
there was the sound of oars splashing. Another flash of light
came, and then the sound of an oar banging against the hull
of the fishing boat.

"Ahoy, on board," a voice called. "Lieutenant Edward
Pringer, USN."

"Lieutenant Richard Canidy," Canidy called back,
"USNR."

A moment later a man with a blackened face, wearing a
dark sweater and trousers, hauled himself over the side.

"Right on the goddamned button," he said, giving Canidy his hand. "Position and time."

"I'm damned glad to see you, Lieutenant," Canidy said.

"Those our passengers?"

"Yeah," Canidy said.

"OK. We can put a line on each of them and lower them over the side."

That took several minutes.

"So long," Lieutenant Pringer said after the two were safely aboard. "And good luck!"

"What the hell do you mean by that?" Canidy said. "We're going with you."

"I'm afraid not," Pringer said.

"Listen to me," Canidy said. "Didn't you hear what I said? I'm Lieutenant Richard Canidy."

"Then you'll understand about orders," Lieutenant Pringer said. "I have mine. And mine were rather specific."

"What orders?"

"My orders say that personnel accompanying passengers are not to be taken aboard the sub."

"I don't believe that!" Canidy said.

"The use of force is authorized," Lieutenant Pringer said. "I hope you won't make that necessary, Lieutenant."

"We're armed," Fulmar flared. "We ought to blow your fucking little boat out of the water!"

"That wouldn't get you onto the submarine," Lieutenant Pringer said.

"I'm going to kill that sonofabitch," Canidy said.

"I'm really sorry," Lieutenant Pringer said. "And now I'm going to get in the boat."

"That miserable, treacherous sonofabitch!" Canidy fumed.

"I'll say it again," Pringer said. "Good luck!"

Fulmar chuckled. "How do you know I won't shoot you anyway?" he asked.

"I don't," Pringer said. "I hope you won't."

He went over the side and was gone.

"I didn't trust that sonofabitch Baker the first time I saw him," Fulmar said. "In Paris, I didn't trust him. But I'm surprised he fucked you, too, Dick."

"What happens now?" Canidy said.

"Well, I think I can get you to Rabat," Fulmar said, his anger quickly dying. "Baker may hope you get caught by the Germans, but I don't, and I don't want to give him the satisfaction."

"What are you going to do?"

"Back to Ksar es Souk, where I will hope this doesn't make Thami el Glaoui turn me over to the Germans."

"You seem pretty goddamned calm about this," Canidy said.

"I'm half German, half American, and half Moroccan, Dick. Cross out the German half. And all this proves I can forget the American half, too. So I've now become a full-blooded Moroccan."

8
Rabat, Morocco
March 15, 1942

Just before eleven the next day, a truck backed up to the kitchen door of the United States consulate general in Rabat. The canvas flap opened wide enough for Canidy to jump down from the bed, and then the truck drove quickly off.

Canidy stormed past a surprised cook into the dining room, then into the consulate proper. He headed for the of-

fice of the consul general. Robert Murphy did not seem to
be surprised to see him.

"I'm very sorry about this, Canidy," Murphy said.

"What the hell is going on?" Canidy demanded furiously.

"It was necessary for you to stay here," Murphy said,
"because it was even more necessary that Fulmar do the
same."

"And why was that another of those little things that unimportant people like me can't be told about?" Canidy
fumed.

"*Why* is because we're going to invade North Africa,"
Murphy said matter-of-factly. "And soon. And we need Fulmar and el Ferruch to help us in that. We hope that we can
enlist Thami el Glaoui's Berbers on our side. And your
friend is going to be just as useful to Sidi el Ferruch as he
is to us—as a kind of go-between. Sidi wanted him to stay
and he wanted to stay. So he stayed. If you had been told
this was planned, things would have gotten terribly messed
up."

"We promised him . . . *I* promised him . . . we'd get him
out of Morocco," Canidy said. "Right now, he thinks we're
lying sonsofbitches. What makes you think he'd help us
again?"

Murphy shrugged. "That's one of those bridges to be
crossed when we get to it. Grunier and the admiral had the
highest priority. Once we got them to the sub, the priority
shifted to the invasion. As I said, you weren't told before-
hand because it was better that you didn't know."

A marine appeared with doughnuts and coffee.

"I thought you could use a little something to eat," Murphy said.

"May I ask you a question?" Canidy asked.

"What happens now?"

"No," Canidy said. "How come you told me about the invasion? Isn't that secret?"

"Top secret, actually," Murphy said. "Around here I decide who has the need to know. I decided that it was in the best interests of the U.S. government that you should know. Eldon Baker is too valuable to us for you to break his neck."

Canidy chuckled. "That thought did cross my mind," he said.

"That would have been inefficient," Murphy said. "One very good intelligence officer dead and another one in jail for murder. We don't have that many good intelligence officers."

"That sounds like soft soap," Canidy said.

"You did very well," Murphy said. "Better than some thought you would. Thus, I agree with Eldon. You seem to have a talent for the clandestine, Canidy."

I'll be goddamned. I am flattered. I am as pleased as a little boy with a gold star to take home to Mommy.

"What does happen to me now?"

Murphy reached for a Teletype message.

"Before I give you this, listen carefully," he said. "It's not true. It's designed for the French and Germans to read."

STATEWASH 26 FEB 42
FOR CONSULGEN RABAT MOROCCO
PASS TO RICHARD CANIDY AT EARLIEST OP-
PORTUNITY QUOTE REV DR GEORGE CRATER
CANIDY IN STABLE BUT SERIOUS CONDITION
CEDAR RAPIDS IOWA GENERAL HOSPITAL FOL-
LOWING HEART ATTACK END QUOTE STOP CA-
BLE CONSTITUTES AUTHORITY CONSULGEN

RABAT TO PLACE FSO CANIDY ON EMERGENCY
LEAVE IF DUTY LOAD PERMITS AND TO AR-
RANGE TRANSPORTATION TO US STOP JOHN G
GLOVER DEPUTY UNDERSECRETARY OF STATE
FOR PERSONNEL END

Canidy wondered if this was yet another weird idea of
Eldon C. Baker's.

"You'll leave by air tomorrow," Murphy said.

"OK, I guess," Canidy said. "If you're going to be
fucked, you might as well enjoy it."

9
Café des Deux Sabots
Rabat, Morocco
March 17, 1942

Jean-François, Max von Heurten-Mitnitz's regular waiter,
hovered expectantly over his table. "Your orders, mes-
sieurs?" he asked.

"Please, use your imagination, Jean-François," said von
Heurten-Mitnitz. "Anything but lamb."

"And I'll have the same," said Müller.

"And so," von Heurten-Mitnitz said after Jean-François's
departure, "the little admiral has flown away."

"I'm afraid so," Müller agreed.

"As have your two *minor* American consular officials."

"Ah yes, I'm afraid so."

"And Sidi el Ferruch and his friend Fulmar have now
returned to Ksar es Souk from their recent vanishings. I

imagine there is absolutely no connection among all these occurrences?''

"None whatever," Müller said, smiling. "But I wonder why Fulmar stayed behind. We can safely arrest him now."

"Interesting, isn't it? I would have left . . . though I suppose he believes he'll be safe enough with el Ferruch. And indeed he probably *is* safe with el Ferruch—at least as long as the French are the only resources available to us."

"So then what do we do?"

"The loss of the admiral will have to be punished, lest you and I are given Russia as a reward. Round up a substantial number of suspects and throw the book at them. Is there any other business? It would be pleasant for a change to enjoy my meal."

"Not much. A French mining engineer was robbed and burned to death after the criminals set fire to the house."

"Too bad for him. But I expect that the French can take care of it."

"Exactly my thought."

10
Washington, D.C.
March 17, 1942

During the two days of his trip home Canidy did a lot of thinking. The result of this was the conclusion that he had nothing to complain about. He was home from China—alive—and he was now home from Morocco—alive. He wasn't even especially worried about Eric Fulmar. Fulmar seemed perfectly capable of taking care of himself.

He now only had to quit his present employment. Once the pleasure he had taken from Murphy's compliments had passed, he had realized that all of those had been soft soap.

He had done nothing extraordinary, nothing that suggested he would make a good spy. Almost the reverse was true. He didn't know what a spy was supposed to do, much less how to do it. He had no business being a spy. And since he was not a fool, he was not going to be one.

That was very simple. All he had to do was say "I quit." He had done what he had been asked to do. He didn't think they would really lock him up in the funny farm without reason, and he would give them no reason. He didn't know any secrets (except that they were going to invade North Africa, and that was not much of a secret).

With a little bit of luck, he could go to work as an aeronautical engineer. With a little more luck, he could get an exemption from the draft. He would not have to stick his neck out again.

Everything had come out in the wash.

Chief Ellis was waiting for him at the airport in Washington.

"I'm not sure if I'm glad to see you or not," Canidy said as they shook hands. "What do you want?"

"Well, the captain wants to see you," Ellis said. "And I was told to pick you up."

"I don't suppose by any chance that Mr. Baker is there?"

"No, he's not."

"Pity," Canidy said. "The sooner I kick his ass, the sooner I can put this whole unpleasant business behind me."

"The captain said you would probably still be pissed at Mr. Baker," Ellis said.

"Understatement of the year," Canidy said. "Do I have to go to the house on Q Street?"

"No. But unless you want to sleep on a bench in Union Station, it would be a good idea. There's *no* hotel rooms in Washington."

"In that case, Q Street," Canidy said.

"Anyway, your clothes are there," Ellis said. "They flew 'em back one day last week."

"My clothes came by plane, but not the same one as I did," Canidy said.

"What the hell, the food was good, wasn't it?"

"Yes, come to think of it, it was."

"You got to learn to relax, Mr. Canidy," Ellis said.

"Oh, I'm going to," Canidy said. "From now on."

Cynthia Chenowith met him at the door of the house.

"Welcome home," she said.

"Thank you," he said. "If you really mean that, you will have dinner with me tonight."

"You plan to drink yours, obviously," she said.

The telephone rang. She answered it, then handed it to him.

"Hello?"

"Bill Donovan, Dick," the familiar voice said. "Welcome home. Well done."

Oh shit.

"Thank you, sir."

"We've got you on an eleven o'clock plane tomorrow to Chicago, with a connection to Cedar Rapids," Donovan said. "We thought you would like to see your father for a couple of days."

"Thank you, sir."

"Least we can do," Donovan said.

What's the matter with me? What is there about this man? Why can't I say, "Stick your airplane ticket up your ass, I quit"?

"I'm grateful," Canidy said.

"We'll talk when you get back," Donovan said.

"I'll look forward to it, sir," Canidy said.

"So will I," Donovan said. "Please give my regards to your father."

There was a click. Canidy took the telephone from his ear and stared at it.

He looked up at Cynthia.

"I didn't get an answer about dinner," he said.

"Dick, I really shouldn't. I have work up to here," she said, lifting her arm above her shoulder.

"Well," he said, "we must all make our little sacrifices for the war effort, mustn't we? Yours is to have dinner with me."

NOW AVAILABLE IN HARDCOVER

JACK HIGGINS

FLIGHT
OF EAGLES

PUTNAM